ONE
IN A
MILLION

ONE
IN A
MILLION

JANET
DAILEY

KENSINGTON
PUBLISHING CORP.

www.kensingtonbooks.com

KENSINGTON BOOKS are published by

Kensington Publishing Corp.
119 West 40th Street
New York, NY 10018

All Kensington titles, imprints, and distributed lines are available at special quantity discounts for bulk purchases for sales promotion, premiums, fund-raising, educational, or institutional use.

Special book excerpts or customized printings can also be created to fit specific needs. For details, write or phone the office of the Kensington Special Sales Manager: Attn. Special Sales Department. Kensington Publishing Corp., 119 West 40th Street, New York, NY 10018. Phone: 1-800-221-2647.

The K with book logo Reg. U.S. Pat. & TM. Off.

Library of Congress Card Catalogue Number: 2023944263

ISBN: 978-1-4967-4480-7
First Kensington Hardcover Edition: February 2024

ISBN: 978-1-4967-4486-9 (ebook)

10 9 8 7 6 5 4 3 2 1

Printed in the United States of America

ACKNOWLEDGMENTS

This novel could not have been written without the friendship and contributions of my fellow writer Elizabeth Lane.

Chapter One

Summer had arrived early. It was barely the end of May, but the season already promised to be a scorcher. The Texas plains sizzled under a blazing sky. Heat waves shimmered above the scrubby yellow landscape. A rattlesnake, coiled in the shadow of a mesquite, stirred, then slithered into the deeper cool of an empty badger hole.

Mirages swam like water over the narrow asphalt road that branched off Highway 277 and led to the Culhane Ranch and Stables. But Lila Culhane knew better than to be fooled by these, or by mirages of a different sort, like the illusion of a solid marriage.

Lila had paid the investigator she'd hired and tucked the damning evidence into her purse. The only remaining question was when and how to use it. Did she want to keep Frank? Did she want to punish him? Or maybe both?

The AC was blasting air from the vents of Lila's white Porsche 911 Carrera, but the silk blouse she wore still clung like glue to her skin. When she reached up to brush back a lock of tastefully streaked blond hair, she could smell her own sweat. She stank like an oil rig worker.

At thirty-eight, she was no longer the teen queen who'd won the Miss Idaho pageant nor the Vegas showgirl who'd lured a rich Texas rancher away from his middle-aged wife. But she still looked good. She'd kept her figure and taken care of her skin. She'd given him everything he wanted in bed; and for the past eleven years of their marriage, she'd been one hundred percent faithful to the bastard.

She'd even shared his passion for horses—at first, as a way to catch his attention, then later as a genuine enthusiast. Either way, she'd given Frank no cause to be sneaking around.

Lila's hands tightened around the steering wheel. Frank deserved the worst punishment she could give him. But first she had to take care of her own needs.

Too bad about that prenup she'd been forced to sign. Without it, she could hire a lawyer and take him to the cleaners, just as his first wife had done. But no such luck. If she were to divorce Frank, she'd probably end up living in a two-room flat and driving a ten-year-old Chevy.

In the distance, through the blur of heat waves, she could see the stately white house and the vast horse complex—the covered arena, the stable with its fifty-four stalls and attached treatment facility, the breeding shed, the round pen for breaking horses, and the well-watered paddocks where spring colts frolicked under the watchful eyes of their dams. The distant pastures were dotted with black Angus cattle, an important cash source that enabled Frank to focus on his real passion, working with the champion quarter horses he bred, raised, and showed in reining and cutting competitions.

Even before they were married, Lila had understood that the horses were Frank's first love. For eleven years she'd settled for second place in his heart, learning to understand the sport and cheering him on at every reining event. But now everything had changed.

Lila ran a hand over the back of her neck. Her palm came away slicked with moisture. *Damnation*, but she hated this infernal heat—almost as much as she hated Frank.

What she craved now was a dip in the pool behind the house, followed by an ice-cold mojito under the shade of the pergola. But that wasn't likely to happen. Not as long as Frank's daughter, Jasmine, was staying in the house awaiting a call from her phantom Hollywood agent.

Jasmine had made the pool and patio her own little kingdom. She might tolerate a visit from her father or her brother, Darrin. But when Lila was around, Jasmine radiated pure, seething hostility. The great house was her castle. As Frank Culhane's daughter, she was its princess; and her stepmother was the wicked queen.

Lila sighed as she swung the car off the road and up the long driveway, bordered with drooping magnolias. Frank and his daughter had always been close. If Jasmine knew about Frank's affair, she was probably cheering him on.

Back in her upstairs bedroom, Lila gazed out the window that overlooked the pool. Visible from below the roof of the pergola, she could see a pair of suntanned legs and manicured feet adorned with electric blue toenails. The princess had staked out her territory. And a swim wasn't worth the price of dealing with her sidelong glares and verbal jabs.

Lila still craved the mojito. But she would drink it in her private office, after a shower. Seated at her desk, she would rake over Frank's betrayal, until she'd worked up enough rage to do what had to be done.

The covered arena stood thirty yards back from the rear of the house, with the attached stable beyond. Jasmine had angled the lounge chair to give her the best view of the cowboys doing chores and riding her father's blooded performance quarter horses. Here on the ranch, with nowhere to go and not much to do, it was the best live entertainment to be had.

Not that she was complaining. Most of the cowboys were either kids or old hands, but some of the men were handsome enough to stir her interest. Jasmine took pleasure in devouring them with her eyes—and if they caught her watching, what was the harm? They enjoyed the game as much as she did.

In the past, she might have done more than watch. At thirty, she was wiser and more discreet than in her younger years. Still, now and then, a man would show up who was hot enough to dampen her panties—like that tall, dark-headed trainer who'd hired on since the last time she was here.

Jasmine had done her homework. Roper McKenna was the firstborn son of the scab-knuckled family who'd bought the small ranch fifteen miles from the Culhane property. In the two years since their move from a Colorado cow town, the McKennas had remained outsiders, ignored by their wealthy Texas neighbors. They drove old cars and trucks, bought their clothes at Walmart, and were never invited to barbecues or joined for neighborly chats.

The McKennas were all right. They just weren't what you'd call quality folk. It was almost as if they were invisible—except for the one thing that set them apart.

The four younger McKenna siblings—three brothers and a sister—had taken the national PRCA rodeo scene by storm, winning every event from barrel racing to bull riding. They'd even appeared on the cover of *Sports Illustrated*.

According to an article Jasmine had Googled, Roper's bronc riding career had ended years ago with a spectacular wreck at the National Finals Rodeo in Vegas. Sidelined for months, he'd taken a job at a stable, exercising high-strung show horses. That was when he'd discovered a natural gift—a way of fostering trust between horse and rider that produced winners in the arena and brought in prize money for wealthy owners like Frank Culhane.

Jasmine shifted in her chair, shading her eyes to get a better view of the cowboy who'd caught her fancy. She knew that Roper was good at his job—otherwise her daddy wouldn't have hired him to train his precious horses. But truth be told, Jasmine wouldn't have cared if Roper couldn't swing his leg over a horse's rump. The man was so hot that she could feel the sizzle all the way across the yard.

This afternoon, Roper was riding Frank's retired champion American quarter horse, One in a Million. Over the years, the big bay roan had competed in showing and cutting events for prize winnings of over a million dollars. But his real value to the ranch lay in his prowess as a stud. Since his retirement from the show arena, the winnings of his colts and fillies and their offspring had totaled more than four million dollars. A straw of his frozen semen sold for more than a thousand, his IVF embryos with eggs from a champion mare went for several times that. His fee for a live breeding was listed in the EquiStat Stallion Registry at $10,000, although live breeding was rarely performed here at the ranch. If Roper had his way, the dangerous practice would cease entirely.

At the age of thirteen, One in a Million could still perform the strenuous spins, patterns, and sliding stops that had made him a champion. But the demands of the arena were judged too risky for his aging body. He was given a special diet and exercised every day to keep him healthy and fit for the breeding shed.

A smile curved Jasmine's lips as Roper loped the stallion

around the arena. The horse still had his elegant moves. The speed it took to win might have tapered off. But the man was a master, putting the great horse through his paces with subtle moves of his hands, knees, and feet. She wouldn't mind getting a closer look. But the timing was wrong today. There were too many people around. Roper would be tired and wanting to finish his work. And today, after a hard swim in the pool, she was a stringy-haired, red-eyed mess.

Roper usually arrived at work early in the morning. That would be the best time for her to take a stroll and bump into him—purely by chance, of course.

She laughed, imagining the surprise on his handsome face. She'd tried more than once to catch his eye. So far, he'd seemed unaware of her. But Jasmine knew her way around men, and she knew how to get herself noticed. She looked forward to the challenge.

It was a long-standing custom for the Culhane family to eat dinner together every Friday night. The tradition had started two generations ago when a giant oak tree on the ranch was felled by lightning. Frank's grandfather, Elias Culhane, had declared the strike an act of God, sliced a long, diagonal section of the trunk and had it made into a table for the family dining room. It had been Elias—a preacher's son—who'd given orders that hereafter, his descendants should sit down at the table and share a weekly meal in peace, harmony, and love.

Nobody crossed Elias, not even decades after his death. But over the years, peace, harmony, and love had become a joke. And the table had become more of a Friday night battleground.

Wearing a yellow sundress, with her fiery hair twisted into a high bun, Jasmine surveyed her family around the table. Not a bad-looking bunch. But in other respects . . .

"Hey, sis, what have you heard from that fancy agent of yours?" Darrin, her brother, was seated across from her. "Is Ron Howard still begging you to come and star in his big movie?"

Butthead. Always was, always would be. And as usual, he knew right where to jab. "I'm still weighing my options," she said. "How's that Supreme Court nomination coming? Any word from the president?"

"Good one, sis." Darrin was four years older than Jasmine. Redheaded like his sister and their mother, he kept an office in the house he rented in the nearby town of Willow Bend, but the ranch had always been his home, just as his destiny had long since been carved out as the Culhane family lawyer.

"Actually, Jasmine, your brother has a point." Simone, Darrin's petite blond bride, was from Dallas oil money via finishing school. "Get real, honey. You're never going to make it as a movie star. Find yourself a job—or better yet, find a man who'll take care of you and give you some babies to raise. You're not getting any younger."

Jasmine caught the amorous glance that passed between the newlyweds. *Heavenly days, was Simone already pregnant?*

Anxious to change the subject, Jasmine spoke to her father, who sat at the head of the table.

"Daddy, have you chosen your horse for the Run for a Million?"

Frank Culhane speared a second slice of prime rib, taking his time to answer. He was a strikingly handsome man— his body fit, his hair thick and streaked with silver. A respected trainer and champion rider, he was still winning cash prizes at reining events. This past March, at the Cactus Classic in Scottsdale, he had qualified to be one of sixteen top riders in the biggest reining event of the year—the

Run for a Million, to take place later that summer at South Point Arena in Las Vegas.

"It's too soon to decide," he said. "The Run for a Million won't happen until mid-August. There's plenty of time."

"Come on, I know you, Dad," Jasmine teased. "Give me a hint. Is it Million Dollar Baby?"

He shrugged. "Can't say. You know the drill. I'll be taking three horses to the competition, two of them as backup. I probably won't make my final decision until the night of the competition. Meanwhile, I'll be riding in two other events. That should help narrow down the choice."

Yes, Jasmine knew the drill. She'd grown up in stables and arenas where both her parents were competing for prize money. Not all Jasmine's memories were happy. Sometimes the tension between her parents would get so heavy that she could almost taste it in the air. Maybe that was why, although she was a capable rider, she'd never wanted to compete.

In reining events, each rider chose the horse to show. And there were rules. A horse could be shown by its owner, a family member, or an employee. A trainer without a suitable horse could lease one from an owner or ride a client's horse. Prize money would be split between the owner, the rider, and usually the runners-up.

"When are you going to retire, Dad?" Darrin asked. "You'll be the oldest rider in this year's competition. Isn't it time you stepped back and let the next generation take over?"

"Some of your trainers are good enough to win," Jasmine said. "Look at Roper. When he rides, it's as if he creates a mind link with the horses. Put him on a winner and he could make some serious money for the ranch. When are you going to give him a chance?"

Frank chuckled. "After I win the Run for a Million, I'll think about it. But don't talk to me about retiring. I'd rather die in the saddle than in a rocking chair or, heaven forbid, in some blasted hospital bed. Give me my horses and the thrill of competing for a prize. For me, that's heaven."

"I understand, Dad. But you're not as young as you used to be. We want you to take care of yourself."

Jasmine did understand, although she knew better than to speak the truth. Frank enjoyed being the center of attention. He didn't want anybody stealing his thunder in the arena—especially a younger employee who was probably a better rider than his boss. And Frank wouldn't be too keen on sharing the prize money either, or having his best trainer quit for a better offer.

One person at the table hadn't spoken. Lila sat at Frank's left, toying with the food on her plate. She was a stunning woman, tall and elegant, her stylishly streaked hair tied back with a silk scarf. Usually she held her own in the weekly dinner table conversations. But tonight she appeared troubled.

Whatever was wrong, the bitch deserved it, Jasmine told herself. She had hated her stepmother from the moment she'd set foot in the great house and started redecorating. At first, Lila had tried to make friends with her husband's daughter. But there could be no forgiveness for the woman who'd destroyed her parents' marriage. After the first few months, Lila had abandoned her overtures and settled for cold civility.

The tension had eased when Jasmine left for L.A. to pursue acting and modeling work. But when she came home between gigs, it was as if she'd never been away.

Frank finished his pecan pie and stirred in his chair. "I'm going down to check on that mare who's about to foal," he said, turning to Lila. "If she's in labor, I'll stay with her, so don't wait up for me."

"Fine." The word was spoken with no change in Lila's expression. "Try not to wake me when you come in."

"I won't. I know my girl needs her beauty sleep." He pushed his chair away from the table and stood. " 'Night, all. If I'm not here in the morning, don't come looking for me. I'll just be with the mare or having coffee with the boys."

"Do you want some company, Dad?" Jasmine asked. But Frank had left the room. In the kitchen, she heard him say a few words to the cook. Then the back door opened and closed as he headed outside. Never mind, Jasmine told herself as she excused herself and left the table. It was early, but she could read or watch TV for a while, then get a good night's sleep. Tomorrow morning, if she managed to catch up with Roper McKenna, things could get interesting.

As she washed her face and brushed her teeth, Simone's words echoed in her memory.

You're never going to make it as a movie star . . . Find a man who'll take care of you. You're not getting any younger.

Jasmine tried to shrug off the comment. Simone always seemed to be putting other people down. But what if she was right? Not about the man, of course. Jasmine's marriage, at twenty, had been an eleven-month nightmare that had included an early miscarriage. She wasn't in a hurry to try again, if ever. But the part about never making it as an actress had stung. True, she hadn't been offered even a small movie part in more than six months. Even TV commercials, once her bread and butter, had dwindled to two or three a year. The agent call that never seemed to come had become a family joke.

She couldn't live here and be Daddy's baby doll forever. Maybe it was time she put on her big-girl panties and looked for other options.

But not tomorrow. Tomorrow, what she needed was a distraction—a tall, dark, and gorgeous distraction.

At 5:00 on Saturday morning, Roper pulled his battered Ford pickup into the Culhane Stables employee lot. After swigging the last of his coffee, he put the mug into the cup holder and climbed out of the truck to start the workday.

At any given time, there were between fifty and sixty horses on the Culhane Ranch. They belonged to Frank or to clients who paid to have their horses trained and boarded here. Some of the brood mares were pregnant or nursing foals. The other horses were required to be ridden every day.

The quarter horses currently in competition were usually trained by Frank. The rest of them—about forty animals, including the senior stallion, One in a Million—were Roper's job. He decided which ones should be passed down to the assistant trainers. The rest were trained by Roper himself. By the time he'd exercised them all and put them through the turns, patterns, and slide stops of a reining display, the sun would be low in the sky.

Roper whistled an off-key tune as he strode toward the stable. The first rays of morning were painting the sky above the distant hills. Birds trilled from the pastures. A Mexican eagle flashed white-tipped wings as it swooped down on a rabbit in the yellow grass.

Roper liked his job, for now at least. Frank was a decent boss, and the pay was good. But he missed the clients and horses he'd left behind in Colorado, and he missed the freedom to compete. Frank had hired him on condition that he focus strictly on training and forget about entering contests. Roper had needed a good job close to home. Even more urgently, he'd needed an introduction to the big-money events. For now, he'd accepted the limitation. But he knew that he was good enough to hold his own in reining and cutting. Next year, he vowed, he'd be out there proving it. All he needed was knowing the right people and having the right horse.

As he entered the stable by the front door, Roper decided to start the day with a sharp dun mare at the far end. He would work his way forward, saving One in a Million for last. Riding the seasoned older stallion would be a relaxing way to end the day.

As usual, he was the first one here. By the time he'd wrapped the mare's legs and saddled her, the stable hands and grooms had shown up—youngsters willing to shovel manure, haul feed, and rub down horses for their chance at a dream. They were local kids who lived in town, unlike the cowboys who tended cattle and slept in the bunkhouse.

Roper left the stall door open for the cleaner and rode the mare out of the barn into the spacious training arena. The dun mare was a client's horse, three years old and in the early stages of training. Roper warmed her up, then started on circle patterns. She was smart, her hooves steady on the deep layer of sand, loam, and sawdust.

By now the sun was coming up. Giving the mare a pat and a moment's rest, Roper found himself gazing toward the rear of the Culhane mansion. The patio was empty, sunlight sparkling on the surface of the pool. There was no sign of Frank's glamorous daughter yet, but then, it was early.

He was aware that she watched him, but they'd never spoken. He didn't even know her first name—but that didn't matter because if they were to meet, he would address her as Miss Culhane, and he would keep his hands off her. If ever there was a shortcut to professional suicide, it was fooling around with the boss's daughter—or worse, his wife.

Enjoy your day, Miss Culhane, he thought. *You may be beautiful and sexy as hell, but I've been burned before, and it's not going to happen again.*

With that, he put the mare through one more pattern and rode her back inside, where the grooms waited to hose her down and put her away. His next horse was waiting, saddled, wrapped, and ready.

Dressed in jeans, boots, and a white shirt open to the third button, Jasmine strode down the corridor that separated the facing rows of stalls. The activity at the far end gave her hope that her timing was good. With luck, when Roper finished his ride, she'd be there to meet him. They wouldn't be alone. That couldn't be helped. But she had her story—and as the boss's daughter, she could expect him to be agreeable.

As he rode in from the arena and swung off a filly, she stepped forward. Only then did he appear to notice her.

"Miss Culhane." He tipped his hat. His eyes were dark gray, like clouds before a storm. His voice was cold to the point of indifference. "Is there something I can do for you?"

She gave him her most winning smile. "I know you're working, so I won't take much of your time. I'm just hoping you might be willing to do me a favor."

"That depends. You've got five minutes to tell me about it. But no promises. I'm on the clock."

"I understand." She nodded, tilting her face at what she knew to be a flattering angle. "I promise to be on the clock, too. Cross my heart." Her fingertip traced an *X* across her chest, its path meant to draw his gaze downward to the hollow between her breasts.

"I'm listening," he said. "Go on."

"I've enjoyed riding in the past," she said. "I wouldn't mind trying it again. But it's been a few years, and I've forgotten most of what I used to know. I could use your help in choosing a horse, and riding it—it shouldn't take long, and you'd be paid extra for your time, of course. Come by tonight, after work, and we can talk about it—maybe over dinner. There's a nice steak house in Willow Bend. What do you say?"

She'd at least expected some interest. But his expression was as icy as ever. "Miss Culhane, I work for your father. You should take this up with him, not me. If he wants me to help you, as part of my job, fine. If not, you'll have to find another way. Now, if you'll excuse me, I've got horses to exercise."

Turning away, he mounted the waiting stallion and headed back toward the arena.

The three grooms—two boys and a girl—had unsaddled the filly and were leading her to the wash station. The grooms had pretended to ignore the conversation, but they'd probably heard every word. Jasmine's face burned with humiliation.

Fine, she told herself. If Roper expected her to ask her father, that was just what she would do. Frank usually said yes to whatever she wanted. Soon she would have Roper McKenna at her beck and call. And he would learn to like it.

She hadn't seen her father this morning. But he couldn't be far. He'd mentioned sitting up with a mare in labor or sharing breakfast coffee with some of the cowboys. Finding him should be easy enough.

Taking her time, she walked back along the double row of stalls. The last stall on her right belonged to Frank's prized stud horse, One in a Million.

As she came closer, she noticed that the stall gate had been left open a few inches. Maybe Frank had stopped by to spend a few minutes with his old friend. That should put him in an agreeable mood.

"Dad?" Her voice echoed strangely in the space below the rafters. From over the top of the stall gate, she could see the stallion. Usually the calmest of horses, the big bay roan was snorting, tossing his head, and showing the whites of his eyes. She couldn't see her father anywhere, but something was upsetting One in a Million—and he was telling her the only way he could.

Her hand felt cold as she slid the gate farther open and stepped into the stall. At first, she could see only shadows. Then her foot bumped something solid. Looking down, she gasped.

Her father lay sprawled facedown in the straw.

He wasn't moving.

CHAPTER TWO

Jasmine's scream echoed down the corridor, startling a pair of doves from their nest on an overhead beam. Dropping to her knees in the straw, she huddled over her father's motionless body, her arms clutching her ribs. This couldn't be happening. Not to her father. Not to her life.

Do something!

Summoning her strength, she forced herself to move. But even as she fumbled for a pulse, she sensed that she'd found him too late. His skin was cool, his flesh rigid. He was dressed in the clothes he'd worn at dinner last night. There was no visible mark or blood on him; and nothing appeared to be missing, not even the wallet in his hip pocket.

Numb with shock, she stared down at the man who'd always been there for her. She had idolized her father, but now her emotions were frozen. No fear, no grief, not even tears. It was as if she were seeing herself in a movie where, at any moment, the lights would come on, and she would get up and walk out of the theater.

A snort from the stallion roused her. She could hear voices and the sound of running feet.

The gate swung outward. The stallion whinnied and

lunged as Roper burst into the stall with two grooms behind him. Seeing the body, he stopped as if he'd hit a wall. But he swiftly recovered and took charge.

"Get the horse out of here," he ordered. "Put him somewhere calm and safe. And have somebody call nine-one-one."

The stallion had backed into a corner, his rump slamming the boards. His front hooves flailed. The husky grooms rushed to get him under control. Gripping his halter on either side, they soothed him until he was calm enough to be clipped onto a lead.

"Try not to handle him any more than you have to," Roper warned. "The police will want to check him for evidence. You don't want to leave anything of yours behind."

As the horse was led away, Roper dropped to a crouch next to Jasmine. He felt his boss's neck for a pulse. His jaw tightened. "I'm sorry, Miss Culhane," he said.

"You sound like a character from *Law and Order*." Jasmine took refuge in mindless chatter. She could feel herself crumbling around the edges. She kept talking, as if words could hold her together. "I was on one of their shows. I played the murder victim. I looked spectacular laid out on a slab." Tears were welling. She blinked them back. She probably sounded like an idiot, but she'd be damned if she was going to cry in front of this man.

"Tell me what happened?" he said.

"Nothing you can't figure out for yourself. The gate was partway open. I thought my father might be with the stallion, so I stepped inside, and I found Dad like this. I could tell right away that he was—wasn't alive." She swallowed hard, took a breath, and kept talking. "I heard what you said about the police. That horse loved my dad. He would never have hurt him."

"I agree with you about the stallion," Roper said. "But the crime scene unit will want to go over him before they can rule out that possibility." He frowned, a notch deepening between his dark eyebrows. "Did your father have heart trouble?"

"Not that he ever mentioned. But it's possible. Dad isn't—wasn't—" She stumbled over the words. "He wasn't a young man. And look—no blood, no sign of injury. It had to be a heart attack, or maybe a stroke."

"We won't know any more until he's been gone over for evidence, but for the family's sake, I hope you're right," Roper said. "Meanwhile, somebody will need to break the news to your mother. Can you manage that?"

"*She's not my mother!*" Rage washed over Jasmine's grief. "My mother lives in Austin. That floozy who broke up their marriage is my stepmother. And no, I don't think I should be the one to tell her. I wouldn't know what to say. The police can do it."

"She should be prepared before the police get here."

"Then *you* can damned well tell her yourself. I'll phone my brother and our real mother. But right now, Lila is all yours."

She pushed to her feet and fled, leaving Roper standing in the stall. He'd sensed the tremor in her voice and the tears that hovered on the edge of the breaking point. But Miss Culhane would be all right, he told himself. She impressed him as a strong woman. She just needed time to deal with her loss.

She'd left him with a difficult job—but under the circumstances, he had little choice except to do as she demanded and give Frank's wife—now his widow—the news.

He took time to check with the stable hands and make sure the police were on their way. The training sessions were to be put on hold until the crime scene—if that's what it was—had been cleared. One in a Million had been moved to an unoccupied stall with hay and water. The stallion was calmer now, but still plunging and rolling his eyes. Maybe later, he could safely be let loose in the paddock to run off his anxiety.

Until today, Frank would have made that decision. But Frank was gone. That reality was still sinking in. Roper didn't know who'd be running the ranch in the days ahead—only that it wouldn't be up to him.

As he walked the cobbled path to the house, he tried to piece together what he would say to Lila Culhane. He'd been briefly introduced to her when he'd taken the job; and he'd seen her from a distance, driving her car or going in and out of the house. But he couldn't say he knew the woman or anything about her, except for what he'd just been told—that she was a floozy who'd allegedly broken up Frank's first marriage.

He could see her now, as he neared the house. She was on the patio, seated at a table a few yards back from the pool, wearing sunglasses and a silky blouse. A coffee mug sat next to an open book on the table.

The patio was surrounded by a low, wrought-iron fence with a gate. As Roper released the latch, she raised her head.

"If you're looking for my husband, Mr. McKenna, he isn't here. He said something last night about a mare in labor. That was the last I saw of him." Her voice was as sensual as a warm breath in his ear. But Roper detected an undercurrent of tension—almost as if she already suspected the reason he'd come. As he approached, she slipped off her sunglasses. Her coppery eyes gazed directly at him.

"You look uneasy, Mr. McKenna," she said. "Has something happened? Sit down. I'll order more coffee if you'd like." She was calm—almost too calm.

"No coffee, thanks." He took the nearest chair. Leaning back, he studied her across the table. She was a beautiful, confident woman. He didn't look forward to delivering his blow and watching her fall apart.

"It wasn't your husband I came to find," he said. "It was you. I'm afraid I have bad news, Mrs. Culhane. You'll need to prepare yourself."

"Has something happened to Frank?" She paused, as if sensing the answer in his silence. "I had a feeling. Don't bother to cushion it. Just tell me."

Beneath her calm manner, Roper caught a glint of steel. "Yes, it's Frank," he said. "Your stepdaughter found him this morning, lying in the stallion's stall. There was no pulse. It appeared he'd been deceased for several hours."

"I see." She reached out and closed the open book on the table, as if she were closing a chapter on her life. "How do you think it happened?" she asked.

"I don't know. There was no visible injury, no sign of a struggle. The police are on their way. They'll want to talk to you, of course."

"Of course, they will. Isn't it always the spouse they question first?" She stood, replacing her sunglasses. "I suppose I should take a look at Frank before they get here."

"I was going to suggest that. But you shouldn't go alone. I'll walk you to the stable."

He offered his arm as they passed through the gate and set off down the path. She ignored the gesture, striding beside him. She was tall—about five-nine, he estimated—with a dancer's long legs.

"How's the stallion?" she asked.

"Spooked. But the grooms moved him out of the stall. He'll need some time to calm down."

"And how's Jasmine? You said she was the one who found Frank."

"I'd say she's in shock. But she seemed to be handling it. The last I saw of her, she was headed out to call her mother and brother."

"The gathering of the clan." Her husky voice dripped cynicism. "Ah, here we are. If you'll show me to the scene."

The stable door stood open. The stallion's usual stall, its gate closed, was first on the left. From the far end of the stable came the faint sounds of cleaning. But the usual flow of conversation was missing.

Frank's wife—now his widow—took a step toward the gate, then hesitated.

"There's no reason to see him if you don't want to," Roper said.

"I must see him," she said. "There'll be major decisions to make in the days ahead. Before I can do what has to be done, I need to face reality. My husband is dead. That changes a lot of things."

Head high, she crossed the distance to the stall and slid open the gate, revealing Frank's body in the straw. Roper stood back and watched, expecting her to break down. But she made no sound and no move to touch her husband, not even when a buzzing horsefly landed on Frank's neck and began biting into his flesh.

Turning away, she sighed and closed the gate behind her. "I'm going back to the house now," she said. "No need for you to go with me—I'll be fine. Send the police up when they're ready."

Roper stood in the open doorway of the stable and watched her stride back to the house. He had just witnessed a stunning performance. But what kind of performance was it? Was the woman in shock? Did she care so little for her husband that she couldn't pretend to grieve his loss? Or was she, as Jasmine might have implied, a scheming manipulator, already making plans to use her power as Frank's widow?

The question hung unanswered in his thoughts as he stepped outside to see two police vehicles coming along the drive. He knew what to expect. The county troopers in the cruiser would talk to the family and any witnesses. The crime lab people in the white van would process the scene, including the stallion. Frank's body would be bagged and taken to the morgue for an autopsy to determine the cause of death and whether any foul play had been involved.

As the vehicles rolled up to the house, Roper realized that no one else was in sight. Lila had disappeared indoors, and there was no sign of Jasmine or her brother. Unless someone in the family showed up, it would be his job to greet the responders and show them to the body.

Two uniformed troopers stepped out of the black-and-white car. The bigger, older man had a weary look about him, as if he'd seen more than he ever wanted to see again. The younger officer, who looked like a rookie, was as lean and eager as a half-grown coonhound.

They made their introductions while the crime lab team unloaded their gear. "Were you the one who found the body, Mr. McKenna?" the older man asked.

"His daughter found him first. I got there right after."

"And you're sure he was dead? Has anybody touched the body?"

"Only to feel for a pulse. Mr. Culhane's prize stallion

was in the stall. We had to move the horse for everyone's safety."

"The lab team will want to inspect the horse. Will that be a problem?"

"It shouldn't be, as long as I can be there to manage him."

"That'll be fine. Let's have a look at the deceased first."

Frank's body lay unmoved and unchanged, except for the flies that droned around his head. The two officers nodded, spoke a few words, and moved away to make room for the lab team.

Wearing masks, gloves, boot covers, and disposable coveralls, the technicians worked with cool efficiency, taking photos, bagging samples of hair and nail clippings, and stirring through the straw. One man broke away from the group and approached Roper. "I hear there was a horse with the body."

"That's right. The horse might be nervous. If you're ready to process him, I'll go with you."

"I'll come, too." The young officer looked pale. Roper, too, was glad for a reason to be leaving the scene before the body was turned over. He had respected Frank Culhane. He had no desire to see the look on the man's face as he died.

Who—or what—had been last to see that face? Roper wondered as he walked to the stallion's temporary stall. But the question was premature. So far, there was no proof that Frank had died of anything but natural causes.

"What a gorgeous horse!" the young trooper exclaimed as he stepped into the stall. "I'll bet he's worth a pile of money!"

"You might say that, but he's never been bought or sold." Roper held the stallion's halter while the technician combed his haircoat and dropped the combings into a plastic evidence bag. "One in a Million was born on this ranch thirteen years ago. He's never left except to compete for prizes."

"So how much would you say he's worth?"

Roper lifted the stallion's left rear hoof and held it steady while the technician, who'd clearly done this before, scraped the bottom and bagged the scrapings before going onto the next hoof. The well-trained horse was accustomed to having his hooves cleaned, trimmed, and shod. He snorted but made no move to resist.

"How much is he worth?" the lawman persisted.

"He's past his prime," Roper said. "But discounting that, maybe half a million. His winnings and stud fees have paid for a lot of improvements on this ranch. And he's sired some real moneymakers. With performance horses, that's the bottom line—earnings and bloodlines."

"Bloodlines? I'm a city boy. Can you explain that?"

Roper steadied the stallion's foreleg. "One in a Million is retired except for breeding. Our top competition earner now is a mare named Million Dollar Baby. This stallion was her sire. One of her colts, Gunnin for Millions, was a top futurity winner last fall."

"So how does a prize-winning mare like that manage to have babies? Does she get to take, like, you know, maternity leave?"

"It's generally done using IVF and a surrogate mare. Sometimes the foal's pedigree will list both mothers."

"Sheesh!" The young trooper shook his head. "It's like science fiction! Don't the mares and stallions ever just get together and . . . like, you know, do it the natural way?"

"Maybe you'd better ask a horse." Roper gave the stallion a pat as the technician finished his job and stowed the samples he'd taken. "Let's go—we've all got work to do."

As Roper followed the two men out of the stall and closed the gate, he heard the sound of raised voices from the entrance to the stable. Roper sighed as he recognized the loudest one. He'd been wondering who'd be in charge now that Frank was gone. The answer should've been an easy guess.

Maybe now, at least, he could get back to working the horses.

The voices grew louder. Now he could see Darrin, Frank's son, blocking the way as two of the crime lab staff attempted to carry a body bag on a stretcher outside to the van. Jasmine stood behind him. Seeing Roper, she ran to him.

"Do something, Roper! These people are taking Dad away. They're going to lay him out on a table and c-cut him open! I've seen it on TV—it's horrible." Her voice shook. Tears welled in her eyes. Time to step back, Roper told himself. Way back.

"There's nothing I can do, Miss Culhane." Roper eased her away from him. "The police have the right to investigate your father's death. Since he died with no evident cause, that requires an autopsy. Your brother's a lawyer. He should know that. So should you."

In his gray designer suit, Darrin Culhane looked as if he'd stepped out of an ad from *GQ*. Only the sweat beads glistening on his forehead betrayed his anxiety.

He'd been raging at the older officer. Now he turned on Roper. "McKenna, did you give these people permission to come on the property and take my father's body?"

"I didn't realize the police needed my permission." Roper kept his tone reasonable. Darrin could be a pompous ass, but this time, he'd just lost his father. He deserved some slack.

"You didn't ask to see a warrant?" Darrin demanded.

"I saw no reason to interfere with police officers doing their duty. But now that you're here, you can deal with them yourself. I've got horses to exercise—including the ones your father was training. So if you'll excuse me, I'll leave you and get back to work."

Jasmine had latched onto Roper's arm again. Loosening her grip, Roper turned to walk away. Darrin's voice brought him up short.

"I'll tell you when you can leave, McKenna," Darrin snapped. "Right now, I've got more to say to you."

"I'm listening." Roper recognized a power play when he saw one. But he wasn't in the mood for games. All he really wanted was to get back to the horses.

"Before today, you worked for my father," Darrin said. "As long as the clients were happy, he let you call the shots. But there's a new boss in town, and he doesn't like your attitude. Starting now, you're under orders to show me some respect. That means you're not to take so much as a piss without my say-so. If that doesn't suit you, you can pile your gear in your truck and get your ass off my property. Do you understand?"

Roper counted silently to ten. "I understand."

"Wrong answer." Darrin's voice dripped sarcasm. "Try this. 'I understand, *Mr. Culhane.*' Now, repeat that after me, and you can go back to work."

Roper felt the rage seething inside him. This job had its advantages, and he was fond of the horses in his care. But Darrin Culhane had just crossed the line.

"I understand, Mr. Culhane," he said. "And now it's your turn to understand something. Your father was fair with me. We respected each other. But I won't work for a boss who thinks he can treat his employees like livestock. I quit."

He unhooked the ring of ranch keys from his belt loop and tossed it into the dust at Darrin's feet. "One more thing," he said. "As long as you're running this ranch, there's a stable full of horses behind you, waiting to be fed, groomed, and exercised. You might not give a damn about them, but it's paying clients that keep this stable running—and there's a bunch of working kids who won't know what to do unless you tell them. So I suggest you pick up those keys and take some responsibility—or find somebody who can."

Since Roper kept his gear in his truck, there was no need to take anything from the stable. With anger surging in his veins, he forced himself to walk calmly out to the parking lot, unlock his truck, and climb into the cab, where he released his breath in a torrent of profanity.

Starting the engine and punching the AC, he headed past the row of luxury stock trailers emblazoned with the Culhane logo. For a trainer with his reputation, finding another job wouldn't be a problem. But until today, he'd been happy at the Culhane Stables. The operation wasn't gigantic, like the nearby Four Sixes, but the facility was state-of-the-art, the help dedicated, and the horses top quality. Frank had been a decent boss, not a friendly sort, but passionate about horses, just as Roper was. The two men had understood and trusted each other.

Damned shame, Frank gone like that, and neither of his kids fit to run the place. A spoiled, man-hungry actress and a country lawyer in eight-hundred-dollar shoes, neither of them with a lick of interest in the horses except as a way to make money. What's going to become of this place?

But that was no longer his problem. Roper opened the

ranch gate with a click of the remote control, drove through, and closed it behind him. As an afterthought, he stopped, got out of the cab, and flung the small device back over the gate, onto the driveway. With luck, it would be crushed to pieces by the next vehicle coming through.

The sun was a blinding glare through the truck's windshield. It was barely midmorning, but the air was already like a furnace. He would go home, cut himself a slab of his mother's chocolate cake, and wash it down with ice-cold milk. Then he'd do some work around the home place, maybe mend a broken gate or two, while he weighed his options. The younger McKenna siblings, Stetson, Rowdy, Chance, and Cheyenne, were competing at a big weekend rodeo in Fort Worth. They wouldn't be home until late Sunday night or Monday. At least that should give him some peace and quiet to think.

The McKenna Ranch was about fifteen miles from the Culhane spread. The family had bought the land two years ago at a good price because the previous owners were in foreclosure. The sprawling frame house had needed a new roof and a fresh coat of paint, but the McKennas had agreed that even in its run-down condition, it was better than their old place in Colorado.

The most urgent repairs had been made, but the family's rodeo needs had to come first—new stalls for Cheyenne's barrel-racing mares, as well as the horses that Rowdy and Chance used in team-roping, and a few spare animals for general work. The ranch operation had needed a new horse trailer, a round pen for exercise and training, repairs to the barn, and fields of hay and grass to be plowed and planted. A couple of bucking bulls and a small herd of calves and steers were kept around to give the young rodeo stars plenty of practice. These, too, needed food, water, shelter, and care.

In the off-season everybody pitched in to help with the work. But when Cheyenne and the boys were out on the circuit, most of the responsibility fell to Roper.

He parked in the front yard, gathered up the cooler with his lunch, and strode into the house. His mother and step-father were in the kitchen, Rachel icing a chocolate sheet cake and Kirby in his wheelchair, drinking coffee at the table.

Rachel, her face worn by time, childbearing, sorrow, and hard work, had married twice. Roper was the son of her first husband, a truck driver who'd died in a crash so long ago that Roper barely remembered him. A few years later she'd married Kirby, a small-time rodeo rider who'd sired the rest of the McKenna brood before a two-thousand-pound bull had crushed his lower back. The injury had left him unable to walk and in constant pain, which he dulled with alcohol. Kirby was never really drunk—but then again, he never seemed to be quite sober.

Rachel McKenna had never had it easy, but she'd been raised to believe in the sanctity of the family. She'd stuck by her husband, raised God-fearing children, and provided the strength that held all their lives together.

Without being asked, she cut two generous squares of cake and scooped them onto saucers, which she set on the table. "Well, Roper, what are you doing home so early?" she asked. "Maybe you can tell us while you're eating your cake."

Roper filled a glass with cold milk and pulled out a chair.

"You don't look very cheerful." Kirby dribbled a few drops of Jack Daniel's into his coffee, which his wife pretended not to notice. "What happened? Did you get fired or something?"

Roper glanced down at his plate. For a drinker, his step-father could be surprisingly sharp. "I didn't get fired," he said. "Frank died. When Darrin tried to push me around, I quit."

"Frank died?" Rachel stared at him. "My word, what happened?"

"His daughter found him lying dead in a stall. Somebody called the police. We'll know more after the autopsy," Roper answered before remembering that he was no longer a Culhane employee. Unless the autopsy results were in the paper or on TV, he might never know how Frank had died.

Kirby added more whiskey to his coffee mug. "Well, however old Frank met his end, the bastard got what he deserved."

Roper raised an eyebrow. "It's odd you should say that. Frank was always fair with me. I'm sorry he's gone."

Kirby snorted. "You wouldn't say that if you knew what I know."

"Does that mean you're about to tell me?" Roper asked.

Kirby took a sip from his mug. "Well, I suppose you've got a right to know . . ."

"Stop it, Kirby!" Rachel turned to face her husband, her eyes blazing. "We agreed that we wouldn't talk about it. So keep your word and keep your mouth shut."

Roper glanced from one parent to the other. "Dad, you said I had the right to know. So, what's it to be? Are you going to leave me hanging?"

Kirby sighed and shook his head. "Your mother's right. Frank's dead. The sooner he's buried and forgotten, the better."

Roper finished his cake, shoved back his chair, and stood. He might be smart to put the matter aside. But his parents were hiding something dark about a man he'd respected in life. How could they expect him to live the rest of his days without knowing what it was? It just didn't seem right.

He planted himself in the doorway. "This isn't fair," he said. "You brought it up, Dad. You owe me the truth."

In the silence that hung in the kitchen, the ceiling fan rotated lazily above the table. Kirby and Rachel exchanged glances. At last Rachel spoke.

"It's not our place to tell you, Roper," she said. "If you want to know the truth, ask your sister."

CHAPTER THREE

Roper strode outside, collected his tools from the shed, and started mounting the new gate for the round pen. As he measured, drilled, and pounded, his thoughts clashed like dueling aircraft in a World War I-era movie.

Had he done the right thing, leaving his parents in the kitchen without another word? Or should he have stood his ground, refusing to leave without hearing the truth?

Had anything really happened between Cheyenne and Frank, who was old enough to have been her father? If true, would the full story give him any satisfaction? Would telling it give his sister any peace?

Let it go, Roper told himself. Frank was dead. Cheyenne was twenty years old, and her personal life was nobody's business but her own. He might share the same house with his sister, but they existed in different worlds.

Not that Roper had planned things that way. He'd adored his baby sister the first time he held her. But time and circumstance had kept them from becoming close.

Roper had been a Colorado ranch kid when Cheyenne was born. She'd been a two-year-old hellion when he'd left home to go on the rodeo circuit. While she was learning to rope her first calf, he was in rehab, recovering from a crushing wreck with a saddle bronc named Hellboy. In more recent years, Roper had discovered a passion for reining and was moving up through the ranks as a trainer, while Cheyenne was bringing home the rodeo buckles, first as a junior rank competitor, then joining her three brothers on the national stage. The boys' skill and grit had made them champions. Cheyenne's charisma had made them celebrities.

Two years ago, with a mountain winter looming, the McKennas had decided to sell their property and move to Texas. The warmer location would allow the young riders year-round training and easier access to the big-city rodeo venues.

Things were falling into place. A neighbor had made an offer on their ranch, and the family had put down earnest money on the property they'd found in Texas. They were packing to move when everything fell apart. The buyer for their Colorado ranch had declared bankruptcy, leaving them with no way to close the loan on their new Texas home.

But all was not lost. With the help of a near-miracle—involving a late balloon payment to the bank, Rachel's prayers, and Roper's offer to stay in Colorado until the ranch could be sold, the McKennas had finally made their move and become Texans.

For Roper, the delay had meant nine months of cold, storms, and loneliness, broken only by training sessions for his clients and their horses. But his sacrifice had been worth it. Once more, the family was together again in a good place, doing what they loved best.

And fitting somewhere into the picture was the alleged encounter between Cheyenne and Frank. Maybe it had happened during Roper's solitary vigil in Colorado. Or maybe it hadn't happened at all.

Let it go, he told himself again. And for a while, he almost did.

By the time he got the gate properly hung and balanced, the sun was riding the peak of the sky. Rachel had driven into Willow Bend for groceries, taking her husband along in his wheelchair. Roper was relieved to have them gone. He wasn't in the mood to have Kirby asking him how Frank died or dropping hints about a scandal with Cheyenne.

For lunch, he made do with the sandwiches he'd planned to eat at work that day. Strange how everything could change in the blink of an eye. He'd left for the Culhane Ranch at dawn, expecting an ordinary day. But he could never have imagined the turns the morning would take.

After the round pen was completed, he spent the afternoon in the unfinished stable, mounting the sliding gate kits and adding vital parts to each stall—the handles, the latches, the anchoring bolts, the hitch rings, and the floor mats. Every finished stall meant another horse that could be raised, trained, and shown in the coming years—more horses and better horses—maybe even champion studs like One in a Million.

Losing himself in his work, he barely raised his head until it was too dark to see outside. Rachel and Kirby had returned home earlier, loaded with groceries. The aroma of sloppy joes with homemade barbecue sauce simmered on the twilight breeze.

Sore from the long day, he gathered up the tools and the extra parts and packed them away in the shed. His hip twinged from the day of lifting and bending as he walked toward the house. On the porch, the aging cattle dog pricked his ears, wagged his tail, and trotted off to investigate a sound in the brush.

Rachel was setting a basket of warmed buns on the table along with the sauce and a bowl of potato salad. Roper washed his hands and sat down at the table. His mother's cooking was frugal, but it was always good. A warning glance passed from her eyes to his. He understood. The issue of Cheyenne was not to be discussed. For now, small talk would be limited to the ranch and the weather.

They were finishing the meal with butterscotch ice cream when the phone rang. Rachel jumped up to answer it. She spoke a few words, then paused, frowned, and nodded before passing the receiver to Roper. "You might want to take this in the other room," she said.

His raised eyebrow asked a silent question, but she didn't answer. Maybe it was the police. They'd be wanting more answers about Frank's death. It would only be a matter of time before they found his name on their list.

Roper's parents were watching him. He carried the phone into the living room before he answered.

"This is Roper McKenna."

"Mr. McKenna . . ." The female voice was as seductive as a blues song in a smoky bar. "This is Lila Culhane."

Startled, Roper swallowed the tightness in his throat. "Can I do something for you, Mrs. Culhane?"

"It's Lila. You and I need to talk. Tonight." Her voice had taken on a businesslike tone. "How soon can you meet me?"

He was intrigued—who wouldn't be? But he was also suspicious. Why would Frank's widow be calling him—a man she scarcely knew—mere hours after her husband's death? Was he being set up?

"Are you aware that I no longer work for the Culhane Ranch, Lila? I quit this morning. That means I no longer take orders from your family or from you."

"I know. But you've nothing to lose by hearing what I have to say. I'll pick you up in my car. Tell me when and where."

Roper still sensed trouble, but curiosity already had him hooked. "Main gate, this ranch. Twenty minutes?"

"I can be there in ten." She ended the call.

The main gate was a half mile from the house. Roper had long since outgrown the practice of checking in with his parents, but as he crossed the living room to the front door, he called over his shoulder, "Going out," and heard a muttered acknowledgment from the kitchen.

As he strode down the driveway, his boots stirring whorls of dust, Roper remembered the loaded pistol he kept under the driver's seat of his truck. It might be smart to go back and get it. But it was too late for caution. Looking down the road he could see low-slung headlights, distant, but approaching fast.

By the time he stepped through the gate, the white Porsche was waiting a few yards down the road, its headlights reflecting off clouds of night-flying moths.

Lila sat in the driver's seat with the top down. A click from inside the car opened the passenger door. "Get in," she said.

Roper climbed into the kind of car he would never be rich enough to own. The buttery leather seemed to flow around his hips. "Where are we going?" he asked. "You're driving—unless, of course, you'd rather give me a turn at the wheel."

"Dream on." She eased the car back onto the road. She was dressed in the same silk blouse he'd noticed that morning, with a scarf knotted at her throat. "Don't worry, we're not going far," she said. "I'm just taking you to a quiet place where we can talk."

A tap on the gas pedal sent the sleek white roadster roaring into the night. Roper leaned back, savoring the feel of the luxury car gliding beneath him. A side-glance at Lila showed her looking serene and confident—not at all like a woman who'd just been widowed. He'd give a lot to know what was going on inside that elegant head.

A few miles past the ranch, she swung the car onto a side lane and pulled onto a stream bank overhung with willows. The water in the hollow below was down to a trickle, but it made a relaxing sound. If she'd been his date instead of his ex-boss's widow, he might have taken her in his arms and put business on hold in favor of pleasure. But Lila Culhane clearly had something else in mind.

He angled his body to face her. "All right, Lila," he said. "You didn't bring me out here to share the moonlight. Let's talk."

She gave him a knowing smile, as if to tell him he could trust her to keep his secrets. He remembered how Jasmine had described the woman as a floozy who'd charmed Frank away from his first wife. Was she trying to seduce him, too?

But that didn't make sense. Roper wasn't wealthy enough to stir her ambition. The best he could offer her was an unprofitable roll in the hay. Whatever she was after, it didn't appear to be sex. Did she need a spy? Or maybe someone to blame for Frank's death?

After a tense moment, she locked her gaze with his and spoke.

"How would you like to work for me, Roper?"

"Doing what? All I know is horses."

Roper had underestimated her. She was smart, determined, unpredictable, and already moving her plan ahead. He needed to catch up—fast. And for that, he needed to know what she wanted.

"Lay your cards on the table. Then ask me again," he said. "Keep in mind that if I don't like your offer, I won't have to say yes."

"Understood. But I'm betting you'll be interested."

"I'll be the judge of that. Just talk."

"All right. Feel free to ask questions." She paused, gazing at the stars through the swaying willows that etched a pattern across the dusty windshield. Her fingers wore no rings—not even a wedding band. Had she been wearing one that morning when he'd brought her the news about Frank? But why should it matter?

"You just offered me a job," he said. "Tell me more."

She took a deep breath. Her tongue moistened her lower lip before she spoke. "After what happened this morning, you can imagine that the Culhane Ranch has become a war zone. It's me versus Frank's kids. And his ex, Madeleine, will soon be showing up to fight for her babies."

"That's no surprise. But I don't see how I could be much help to you."

"Let me explain. You and Frank must've spent a lot of time together, working with the horses. Did he ever mention that his divorce settlement gave Madeleine fifty percent interest in the ranch?"

Roper hid his surprise. He had never met Madeleine Culhane or even seen her photograph. He'd assumed that she might have lost out to Lila in the youth and glamour department; but at least, she'd been smart enough to hire a good lawyer. "Frank never talked to me about his personal life," he said. "It was always the horses, the competition, the scores, the breeding, the stud fees. He didn't seem to care about much else."

"You've got that right," she said. "Their settlement

gave him the ranch's physical assets, including the land, the house and outbuildings, and the horses. Madeleine took her share in cash, oil stocks, and income from the beef cattle—set up under separate management, to be run by Darrin. In the event of her death, her estate would go directly to her children—not to Frank."

"What about Frank's share—and yours?"

"He had the papers drawn up before our wedding. Frank's fifty percent was to go to me, and then to any children we might have. But now there's only me—" Her jaw tightened. "I was so naïve—to assume that I could trust the bastard to keep his word."

"Go on." Roper was still scrambling to put the pieces together. He'd also begun to wonder why she was telling him the story.

The sound that stirred in her throat was something between an ironic chuckle and a sob. "I'd always wanted children. Frank knew that, and he'd said it wouldn't be a problem. When, after a couple years, nothing happened, I began to worry. Frank had already fathered two children. And I—" It was as if she'd started to say something else but changed her mind. "What if the problem was with me? What if I couldn't give my husband more children?

"Jasmine and Darrin insist that since we had no children, it would be wrong to let the ranch pass out of the Culhane family bloodline," she said. "But Frank and I were legally married for eleven years. As his widow, I should be entitled to his share of the estate. They're already trying to force me out of our house. But as John Paul Jones famously said, 'I have not yet begun to fight.' "

"If you're gearing up to fight, it's not my help you need," Roper said. "It's a good lawyer—or at least a better lawyer than Darrin."

"Godzilla would be a better lawyer than Darrin. Don't worry, I'm already making calls."

"You strike me as a lady who can fight her own battles," Roper said. "It's the horses I'm concerned about. Who's taking care of them?"

"The grooms and assistant trainers—the ones who haven't quit—are feeding and watering them. But nobody's taking charge. Darrin doesn't care about them except for the money they could bring at auction. Even Jasmine—she talks a big line about preserving her dad's legacy. But now that he's gone, she doesn't want to ruin her manicure mucking out that stable."

"And you? What's your stake in this—apart from the house and the money?"

Roper's question was meant to catch her off guard, maybe trip her into betraying her real intent. But her answer came readily, almost as if she'd rehearsed it.

"Now that Frank's gone, I'm probably the only family member who cares about giving those horses the program they deserve. If they aren't fit to compete, they'll be worthless in the arena. We'll lose our investment, our reputation, and our clientele."

A passionate note had crept into her voice. She sounded sincere. But that didn't mean she was on the level. It didn't mean she wasn't out to use him.

"You surprise me, Lila," he said. "I didn't know you were a horsewoman."

"I'm not a great rider. But I love everything about those horses—watching them grow and learn, praising them when they give their all, cheering them when they win. For me, it's more about the thrill than the money."

Roper raised a cynical eyebrow. "Now, that's news to me. Most trainers and owners I've known were all about the money, including Frank."

"Stop patronizing me. I kept Frank's accounts after we were married. I know as well as you do how much it costs to run a high-class horse business and what happens if the money doesn't come in. Why do you think I offered you a job tonight?"

"I was hoping you were about to tell me."

"Frank and I always shared, even in the rocky times. Frank would be heartbroken if he knew the horses weren't going to thrive and continue to win. But I can't do the job myself. I don't have the skill or the time." Pausing, she took a breath. "That's why I'm asking you to come back and manage them—for me."

Roper's heart lurched. This could be everything he'd wanted from the beginning. But he knew better than to appear too eager.

"That's a pretty tall order," he hedged. "So what's in it for me?"

She studied him, as if gauging the effect of her next words. "Twice what Frank was paying you, plus you'd be free to compete under the name of the ranch—and keep your share of any prize money you win."

Roper gave the offer time to settle in. Frank had paid him a decent wage along with a bonus whenever one of the horses Roper had trained scored in the money. Doubling that amount over time would pay off the debts on the McKenna Ranch with enough left over to remodel the family home and build a new covered arena. Lila's offer was almost too generous to be trusted. But this wasn't about money. It was about hunger—hunger for the chance to show the Culhane horses in the big reining events—like the Cactus Classic, the derbies for four- and five-year-olds, and even the Run for a Million.

He imagined the pulse-pounding thrill of galloping an

exquisitely trained horse around the arena, sliding to a stop in a cloud of grit, finishing with a neat rollback, then riding out of the gate to the cheers of the crowd, knowing that he and the horse had given their all for that one perfect moment in time.

He wanted to win—wanted it so much that even the thought triggered a burst of adrenaline in his gut.

Roper could think of uncounted ways this adventure could turn out badly. If he were to take her offer, he might be selling his soul to the devil. But winning had its price—and that price was risk. Embrace that risk, and he could end up with everything he'd ever wanted. Play it safe, and he could miss his last chance.

But Lila wasn't out to do him any favors. Her kind of woman, as Rachel might have put it, would use him until he'd served his purpose, then discard him and leave him in the dust, unless he could manage to outsmart her. In this game, only one thing was certain: if he decided to play, he couldn't afford to let her win.

She stroked her hair back from her face, the gesture tightening her silk blouse against her breast. In the moonlight, Roper glimpsed the outline of her lacy bra through the sheer fabric. He tore his gaze away. This wasn't about lust. It was about power—a duel of wits.

"What do you say? I'm not going to ask you a second time." Her eyes were like a cat's, focusing on small prey in the dark.

"Your offer's tempting." He weighed every word. "But how do I know I can trust you?"

"Because I need you."

"Go on."

"These are perilous times. The house or the stables could burn down tomorrow. And if this drought lasts much longer, the bottom will drop out of the beef market.

"Real estate can be rebuilt. Livestock can be replaced and sold when the market recovers. But the horses—they're the heart and soul of the Culhane Ranch—the treasure and spirit, raised on Culhane grass and wearing the Culhane brand. They're irreplaceable—the bloodlines, the breeding, the drive to win, the instincts that can't be taught. Look at One in a Million. Once he's gone, there'll never be another horse like him. Darrin doesn't understand that. Neither does Jasmine. But Frank did. And I think you do, too."

"So you want me to do my old job—but you'll be my new boss."

"No, there's more," she said. "I've watched you ride. You're better than Frank ever was—and Frank knew it. That was why he wouldn't allow you to compete as a condition of your work. He wanted the golden spotlight all on him. The thing he feared was that you would beat him in the arena with thousands of people watching and a million-dollar prize on the line.

"Now that he's gone, there'll be an open vacancy in the lineup for the Run for a Million. According to the rules, a family member could take Frank's place. But no one else in this family can ride well enough. You'd have to win on your own. There's one big event left, the open shootout in Scottsdale next month. It was scheduled as a derby. But with Frank's passing, it's been opened up to horses of any breed and age. Win there, take Frank's spot, and you'll be in line for the biggest prize in reining."

Roper did some mental math. The odds didn't look good, not even on a great horse.

"Whoa, you're forgetting something," he said. "When

word about that vacancy gets out, the best riders in the world—the ones who didn't make the final sixteen—will be fighting for that spot. If you think that I can just—"

"I'm not a fool." Her coppery eyes blazed with determination. "I'm not expecting miracles from you. Just show up. Raise the banner of Culhane Stables. Be seen. Be noticed. And for God's sake, if you can, win something. If you're about to turn me down, then you're not the man I thought you were—maybe not even half the man."

The challenge was too much. Mentally crossing his fingers, Roper made his decision.

"Then I have just one question."

"Ask." Tension seemed to radiate from her body, charging the molecules of the air around them.

"Just this," he said. "When do we start, Boss?"

Amusement tightened her lush mouth. "As early as you can show up in the morning. Be ready for anything, especially if it looks, sounds, and smells like Darrin. If he gets in your way, I'll back you. Pack some essentials in case you have to stay over. I'll draw up a contract and have it ready to sign after you get there. Oh—you might need this." She took an object from the cupholder mounted on the dash and thrust it toward him. It was a remote control device, like the one he'd tossed over the gate when he'd left the ranch earlier.

"How much trouble should I expect from your stepson?" Roper asked, recalling that morning's encounter with Darrin. "After this morning, something tells me I won't be welcomed back into the fold."

"I could tell you that Darrin's bark is worse than his bite," Lila said. "Mostly that would be true. But you challenged his manhood this morning. Expect anything."

She extended her hand. Her handshake was brusque,

her palm lightly calloused. Roper didn't recall having seen her in the saddle. But there could be reasons for that. Maybe Frank didn't like his cowboys eyeballing his glamorous wife. Roper couldn't blame him for being jealous. Lila Culhane was a highly desirable woman.

"We can talk in the morning," she said. "Right now, I need to get home before something else goes wrong."

"Are you expecting company?"

She shook her head. "Just a feeling I have. . . ."

As she reached down to start the car, her cell phone jangled. With a murmured curse, she pulled it out of the bracket mounted on the dash and took the call. Roper averted his gaze, but he couldn't help hearing Lila's end of the conversation.

"Keeping tabs on me, Darrin?" The acid-edged question was followed by dead silence. "What are you doing in the house? So help me, if you've touched any of my things, or your father's . . . What? When?" More silence. "Don't leave. I'll be right there."

She ended the call and dropped the phone into her lap. With tires spitting gravel, the Porsche fishtailed onto the road and roared back toward the McKenna Ranch. Glimpsed against a cloud of dust and moonlit, her profile was rigid, her jaw set in stubborn silence. Was she angry? Maybe scared?

Or was he being set up by clever people who were only pretending to be enemies?

How well did he know this woman? She appeared beautiful, tough, and passionate. But he had yet to see her cry a single tear over her late husband—the husband who'd given her everything Roper could imagine a woman ever wanting.

But maybe not this woman.

As the sleek white Porsche flew through the night, a distant freight train rattled over a metal bridge. He heard the sound of cold steel laid over oiled timber. The clatter of wheels. The hungry wail of the whistle, fading into darkness.

Nearing the ranch, Lila slowed the car, angled off the road, and stopped a few yards from the ranch gate where she'd picked him up. At the click of a button, the latch on the passenger door popped open again.

"Here's your stop," she said. "Get a good night's rest. If a fight breaks out tomorrow, a weapon might come in handy."

For a moment Roper almost believed her. But then he glimpsed the teasing look on her face.

"You're joking," Roper said.

"Me? I never joke."

"In that case, I think you'd better tell me about that phone call you took. The expression on your face didn't look much like a joke to me."

"Didn't your mother teach you not to eavesdrop?"

"Eavesdrop? Lady, I almost needed earplugs to protect my hearing." Sensing her resistance, Roper took his stand.

"Lila, I know you need help. But I won't give it to you, not even for money, if you don't play straight. I want to hear what that phone call was about and what the hell is going on back at the ranch. If I'm not satisfied that you're telling the truth, I'll get out of this car, walk away, and never give you another chance. You've got fifteen seconds to start talking. The countdown starts now."

Lila sank against the seat back and closed her eyes, her moonlit face pale and strained. Roper counted the seconds, half-afraid she would call his bluff, kick him out of the car, and drive away. But at the last possible moment, she met his gaze and began to speak.

"All right, Roper, you wanted the truth. But once you've heard it, don't say I didn't warn you."

"I'm listening. You can start with the phone call."

"Fine." She took a deep breath, her fingers worrying the polished texture of the rosewood steering wheel.

"As you might've guessed, the caller was His Majesty, Prince Darrin. He was passing on a message from the cop who came to the ranch this morning. Things have changed back at headquarters. There's been a probable FBI investigator assigned to the case. He's flying from Chicago to Abilene tomorrow and should be here the following morning. We're all to be back at the ranch, at first light, for more questioning."

Lila's narrative had slowed. She sounded less confident, almost nervous. "I got the feeling that Darrin was impressed by what he heard. He told me the man who's been recommended has been with the FBI Bureau for eleven years. He's old school—likes to build his cases from the ground up, taking down every detail of the crime scene and questioning anybody within a half mile."

Roper had been listening intently. But even so, he almost missed the words that slammed into him like buckshot. *Investigator. Case. FBI bureau. Crime scene . . .*

"What are you hiding?" he demanded. "What's got you so scared that you're afraid to tell me about it?"

She didn't speak. He could almost feel her quivering.

"We had a deal," he reminded her. "You trust me. I trust you. We work together. Otherwise, we don't work at all. What's it to be?"

Her words spilled out in a long sigh. "There was more to Darrin's message. Frank's preliminary autopsy was put on STAT and the results called in. The tox screen showed a high level of drugs, probably fentanyl, in his bloodstream. It's a new case now."

"Are you saying what I think you're saying?"

Her nod was barely perceptible. "Frank's death wasn't an accident, Roper. It wasn't a medical emergency. My husband was murdered."

Chapter Four

In the overgrown lot behind the Blue Rose Motel, the muddy creek flowed as thick as Texas barbecue sauce. Mosquitos hovered above the murk, the hum of their wings blending in a high-pitched whine. Bats and night-flying birds darted among clouds of insects, catching prey in their gaping mouths.

The night was hellishly warm, the AC boxes on the old motel rusted out and hanging loose on their hinges. Not that the Blue Rose was a place where any self-respecting traveler would choose to stay; but according to the AAA guidebook, it was the only lodging within forty miles of the Culhane Ranch, where Agent Samuel Rafferty had orders to show up at first light.

In his thirteen years with the FBI, Sam had put in a lot of road miles. He didn't usually have trouble sleeping, even in dumps like this one. Too exhausted to drive another mile without rest, and not wanting to arrive at the ranch before morning, he'd checked into his room, fallen into bed, and was drifting off when a new set of neighbors arrived next door, ready for an old-fashioned good time.

Sam already knew what to expect. He tried to ignore the amorous pair, but nothing could muffle the moans of pleasure, drunken giggles, and creaking box springs that filtered through the wall next to his head. He could pound on the wall or the door, but starting fights with intoxicated strangers wasn't in his job description. If he couldn't sleep, he might as well get dressed and leave—even though, if he pulled off the road and tried to sleep in a small car that was too short for his long legs, he couldn't expect to get much rest.

He slid his feet to the floor, shuffled his way to the bathroom, and shooed a swarm of mosquitos out of the shower before closing the plastic curtain around himself. The rusty water was barely lukewarm, but it felt good to sluice away the dust and sweat of the long drive. Before undressing for bed, he'd laid clean clothes over the back of a chair and taken his Glock out of his checked bag. Looking professional was part of a federal agent's public image. And with miles of open country between here and the ranch, he'd be lucky to find anyplace else to clean up and change. Just one more rule for a newly arrived Yankee cop to relearn and remember.

He toweled himself off in the bathroom before opening the door. As he stepped into the room, the mosquitos closed around him like a blood-starved pack.

But something had changed. And it wasn't the mosquitos.

Sam strained to hear through layers of sound—the insects, the gurgle of aging pipes, the rustle of dry willow branches blown against the metal roof. What was missing?

As the answer dawned, Sam exhaled and shook his head. The moans of human lust that had kept him awake had gone dead quiet.

Irony tugged Sam's mouth into a twisted smile. Wouldn't you know? Just when you give up, what happens? The noisy lovers decide to take a break.

Maybe he should crawl back into bed and steal an extra hour of sleep. Lord knew he could use it. The transfer from Chicago—the memories, the losses, the shock of the divorce, and the recent death of his young partner had left him physically and emotionally drained.

But what was he thinking? Sam gave himself a mental kick. What he really needed was to hit the road and arrive at the Culhane Ranch on time and ready to do his job. Anything else could wait.

Minutes later, wearing fresh jeans and a long-sleeved chambray shirt with a light denim jacket, Sam picked up his travel bag and made a last-minute visual sweep of the room. Outside, the wind had risen. Sam could imagine it clawing like an animal on the front door.

As he tossed the room key on the bed and turned to leave, a powerful wind gust wrenched the doorknob out of his hand and slammed it inward against the wall. Sam lunged for the door and yanked it back. As the latch clicked, he saw that the same wind had blown open the door of the next room. With nothing to stop it, the door could rip loose and strike the neighbors, who were probably passed out drunk on the bed.

Sam called a warning. No one answered. Peering past the flapping curtains, he could see the empty, unmade bed next to the wall. There was no car in the lot except Sam's rented Subaru. The mysterious lovers had gone as if they'd never existed.

Sam's undersized compact Subaru stood alone on the far side of the parking lot, dwarfed by the huge willow tree that hung directly over it. One heavy branch swayed in the wind, threatening to fall and crush the car. Even now, Sam could hear the limb begin to splinter.

Instinct took over. His legs propelled him across the yard and into the car. As the gears slammed into reverse, he hit the gas full throttle. The limb barely scraped the car, but the Subaru became a swaying, tilting carnival ride that spun across the parking lot in reverse and came to rest in the bar ditch with Sam slumped against the door.

Time blurred . . .

Sam's thoughts flew backward into the swirl of lights and sounds of the previous day; the flashing directional signs, the tread of a thousand feet on the worn tiles of the airport floor. The announcer's echoing voice over the P.A. The food concessions, smelling of pizza, fries, and greasy sandwiches. The whiny voices of children begging for snacks.

The flight from Chicago's enormous O'Hare International Airport to the pocket-sized Abilene Regional had involved three transfers—all of them either delayed or canceled. By the time Sam trudged down the last concourse, the weight of his wheeled carry-on dragging behind him and another, bigger suitcase waiting in Baggage Claim, he felt ready to drop.

At last Sam recognized a gray-haired senior, walking toward him with the shuffle of an old man who'd stayed up past his bedtime. Nick Bellingham, Sam's boss in the old Chicago years, who had left for a promotion in Texas. Now he was months from retirement, and he looked it. Over time, the two men had kept in touch by phone and email, but face-to-face meetings had been rare. Now Nick had recommended Sam as his replacement and invited him to come to Abilene for an interview. For Sam, the timing couldn't have been better. But he still needed to show his old boss that he could handle the job.

"Sam! You son of a gun!" Nick strode forward to greet the young rookie agent he'd mentored so long ago. "It's a pleasure to see you. I swear that boyish face hasn't aged a day."

"Neither has your bullshit, old friend." Sam chuckled.

"But the face should improve after a few hours of shut-eye. Just point me to the nearest bunk and bring me some coffee when it's time to wake up."

"I'll buy you coffee on the way out of here. But sleep will have to wait. We've got a big case to wrap up before any of us can expect to get a wink—and that includes you, my friend."

"Wait." Sam stared at him. "You said I'd be coming for a job interview. What's this about a case?"

"Oh, the interview's for real, all right." Nick appeared to be playing hide-and-seek. "Truth be told, it's more than an interview. It's an emergency."

Sam could feel the irritation crawling along his nerves. He was impatient. He was tired. All he wanted to do was lie down, close his eyes, and drift off. But that wasn't to be.

"Tell me everything," he said, pulling himself together. "I can't help unless I know what's going on."

Nick stepped into a nearby Starbucks, motioned Sam to a booth, and ordered two coffees. "Have you watched the Texas news?" he asked.

Sam shook his head. "CNN was on in the airports. But it was all I could do to get here. Tell me what we're dealing with."

Nick took the order. Sam sipped his coffee, feeling the caffeine flow into his body while he listened.

"Frank Culhane. Big-time horse breeder. Not like the Four Sixes, but rich enough. You don't read the Texas papers? You don't know about Frank Culhane? He had some of the best stock in the state, including One in a Million, one of the biggest moneymakers in the history of reining."

"Never heard of Frank or the horse."

"You will. Land, cattle, cars, fancy performance horses, you name it, he's got it—or at least he *had* it all, until two days ago when his daughter found him dead in the stall of his favorite quarter horse, One in a Million, a great stallion, retired to stud."

"Sounds like it could be suicide or attempted robbery," Sam observed. "Was the horse all right?"

"Spooked, I assume. But otherwise unharmed. Looked like natural causes at first. But he was injected with fentanyl. Somebody who knew what they were doing wanted him gone."

"His family?"

"I'll give you a copy of the file. I get the impression they're a bunch of jackals and vultures squabbling over the remains. Knives out—and it's already in the morning tabloids. There's his widow, who's his legal heir will be fighting for control. His first wife, who owns half interest is bound to show up. She'll be battling for her son and daughter's inheritance. The son's a lawyer, the daughter an actress. It's going to be war."

"So why do you need me? Can't your office handle this?"

"The county answered the first call, and the FBI took it from there." Nick finished his coffee. "Come on. I'll tell you the rest on the way to the car. Sorry about the vehicle. It was the last one available at the rental agency."

By the time they'd picked up Sam's suitcase and reached the tiny Subaru, Sam had heard the story. Earlier the night before, two local agents had been hospitalized after their vehicle collided with an empty stock trailer. The accident, serious but not fatal, had left the small Abilene squad badly understaffed and their spare car unusable. A senior agent was needed to investigate the sudden death of a wealthy rancher—a death that, after the autopsy, had been ruled a homicide.

Sam knew better than to grumble. Red eyes, aching feet, and gallons of coffee were part of his job.

"I know you've had a long flight, and you'll be looking at a long drive to the Culhane Ranch," Nick said. "But we need somebody at the crime scene first thing in the morning, to interview people while memories and evidence are fresh. You know the drill. And of course you'll be staying around for the funeral, whenever it's planned, and whatever follow-up is needed. That's when the gloves will really come off. Originally, I scheduled you here for a job interview. That's still going to happen, but it's not just up to me. Handle this and I'd say you've got a good chance at my job when I retire this fall. At least, for now, we're planning to hire you on if you want to stay."

"I'll keep that in mind." Sam took the file and climbed into the ridiculously small car, shoving the seat all the way back to accommodate his long legs. He would save the file for daylight, when he was rested and could think. Right now, all he could do was drive. "You said something about follow-up. So how long do you expect me to stay at the ranch?"

"As long as it takes, even if it means being there for weeks," Nick said. "This murder is making tabloids all over the country. Leaving it unsolved would be a black eye for the bureau here in Abilene, just when we need to look good. There's already talk of shutting us down. This case could make all the difference."

In the motel parking lot, the wind was still blowing when Sam righted himself in the seat, buckled himself in, and started the Subaru. The engine coughed and caught on the first try—he'd feared being stranded out here. But when he turned out of the motel parking lot, a suspicious creak under the chassis set his senses on alert.

The broken limb lay a stone's throw away from the car. At least the Subaru hadn't been crushed. But his escape might have damaged something. After a quick check under the car revealed nothing visible, he climbed back in and headed down the road, hoping for the best.

The wind was dying, the sky beginning to fade, revealing the morning shadows of a rolling landscape dotted with scrub and, where springs remained despite the drought, clumps of willow and cottonwood. Cattle dotted the pastures—mostly black Angus, but now and then a pasture with white-faced Herefords, and even one with a half-dozen Texas longhorns, their racks wider than the span of his outstretched arms. A vast cloud of blackbirds rose from the grass and circled the pastures in a stunning murmuration against the opal sunrise.

This was pretty country—peaceful looking, though Sam knew better. It would be a pleasant change from Chicago if he could make the grade. If he failed this case, Nick's small bureau could be shut down, and Sam would likely end up back in Chicago with the drugs, the gangs, the guns, and the memory of his young partner, a family man, dying in his arms.

But there was more. The challenge of Frank Culhane's murder was his, and the mystery was already calling to him—the people, the motives, means, and opportunities. He was good at his job. He was champing at the bit to get started.

But as if fate were conspiring against him, he felt the sudden drop in the car's right rear tire and the too-familiar thumping sound that signaled a flat.

He pulled the car off the road, popped the trunk latch, climbed out, and rummaged through the trunk's odd mechanical contents. The rental agency must've fetched this one off the back of the lot. He checked his cell phone. No service out here. He had the ranch number, but he couldn't call them. *Damn.*

In the trunk there was an undersized spare and a lug

wrench, but no jack. After years of messing with old cars as a teen and college student, Sam was no stranger to improvisation. With a sigh, he turned away from the car and began scanning the road's shoulder for something to shore up the car while he changed the tire.

When the promised FBI agent failed to appear that morning, Jasmine volunteered to drive down the road to look for him. "Maybe he got lost," she told her brother, who'd shown up early. "Maybe he had car trouble, or maybe he took a wrong turn and wandered onto that awful game-hunting farm. What if he got shot by mistake or attacked by one of those poor old toothless tigers?"

"You're an adult, Jasmine. Stop fantasizing. Anyway, we've nothing to fear from the FBI. We didn't hurt Dad, and we never would. My money's on Lila. She had everything to gain by this."

"Let's hope. Who else would it be? I can't wait to see her out of the ranch and behind bars. She would do it, Darrin. She's spent enough time around the stables to be able to give the shot, and she's so cold. She's not even crying over Dad. Not even pretending to grieve."

"Wait till Mom shows up," Darrin said. "She'll kick butt."

"I can imagine." Madeleine Carlyle Culhane was a force of nature. With her on their side, Lila would be up against the three of them.

"Well, the sooner that FBI agent gets here, the sooner it's going to happen. So get in your car and get looking."

Jasmine had always hated being bossed by her brother, who was four years older. But this time he was right. Somebody needed to find the FBI agent. She climbed into the sleek red Corvette her dad had bought her for her birthday and roared off down the road toward Willow Bend.

Would the agent be attractive and single? But that didn't matter. He had a job to do—put Lila Smith Culhane behind bars for life.

Anyway, after last night, Jasmine had sworn off men, especially cowboys. Fighting to keep the reality of her father's death at bay, she'd met Quirt Holdaway in a Willow Bend bar. He was a rising rodeo star, hotter than blazes, and a rendezvous in that run-down motel had sounded funky. They'd drunk a little, bumped around, and had some laughs. But he'd turned out to be a jerk. When he'd demanded to get kinky and threatened to slap her if she didn't cooperate, Jasmine had stalked out to her car and left. Unless he'd passed out drunk and spent the night, she was guessing he must have left soon after.

Now, as she drove, the memory couldn't be ignored— her all-powerful father lying facedown at the feet of his stallion, hands raised like a sleeping baby's. She steeled herself against a surge of tears. It was too soon to cry.

She had adored Frank Culhane. But there'd been times when he'd hurt her, put her down, withheld his approval. He'd wanted another son, a strong boy to follow him with the horses as a trainer, breeder, and rider—something in which Darrin had no interest. He'd regarded her acting ambitions as fluff and her as a useless toy, to be patted and indulged.

But that had been no excuse to drown her emotions with a strange man—especially a jackass like Quirt.

Thinking back, she burned with shame. No more bad decisions, she swore. She'd made her last mistake with a man.

Gleaming through dust motes, she could see something a half mile down the road. It looked like a small car, with a lanky figure standing nearby, as if watching her approach. Maybe he was the agent, but she couldn't be certain. He could be anybody. He might even be dangerous. But as she drove closer, she could see the tilt of the car on the roadside. The man, whoever he was, appeared to need help.

Jasmine kept a Ruger Max .380 pistol locked in her glove compartment. Slowing the car, she lifted it out, dropped it into the center console, where she could reach it, and started up again.

The man had stepped into the road, clearly meaning to flag her down. Jasmine could see him clearly now. Tall— about six-foot-one. Neatly dressed in well-fitting jeans and a denim jacket.

As she pulled to a stop, she saw that he already had his credentials out. And her sharp eyes didn't miss the holstered service pistol clipped to his belt. He had to be their lost FBI agent.

He walked up to the car, flashed his badge, and stood looking down at her—lines of weariness framing his striking cobalt eyes. He was older than the wild cowboys she was usually attracted to—yet Jasmine did find him attractive. He looked a little vulnerable, a lock of dark brown hair hanging down his forehead in a way that made her itch to reach up and smooth it back.

She checked the urge firmly. This guy was all business. Flirting with an FBI agent would only rouse his suspicion. And hadn't she just sworn off men?

He cleared his throat and spoke in a gravelly voice. "Excuse me, Miss, but does your car have a jack I could borrow to change this flat tire? I'll try not to delay you long."

The woman in the open-topped red Corvette was no longer a girl. But there was a fawnlike delicacy about her that Sam found pleasing to look at. The fine-drawn features with a sprinkle of freckles across the nose. The cloud of curly auburn hair. The sleekly proportioned body, clad in tight jeans and a white linen shirt worn with a dazzling native turquoise ring that would probably cost him a week's salary. But he wasn't here to ogle a woman. For all he knew, he was looking at Frank Culhane's killer.

She frowned up at him, her sharp, husky voice breaking the fragile spell that had spun between them.

"There's no time for the tire," she said, popping the passenger door. "Get in. The folks at the ranch are waiting for you to show up and get started with your interviews. We'll send somebody out to bring your car in." She offered her right hand as he collected his bags and slid onto the leather seat. Her palm was satiny, the nails manicured and painted a bright, electric blue. "Jasmine Culhane," she said. "You'll meet the rest of us down the road. All except for my mother. She'll be coming later, before the funeral."

Sam introduced himself. "You're Frank Culhane's daughter?"

She nodded and started the Corvette.

Probably the actress Nick had mentioned. "I'm sorry for your loss, Miss Culhane. I never met your father, but I've been told some impressive things about him."

She made a sharp U-turn and gunned the Corvette back in the direction she'd come. She was a confident driver, her hair fluttering behind her as the vermilion car flew down the road like a comet, leaving a faint trail of dust behind.

"Daddy was a monument of a man," she said. "He was everything to this ranch, this family, to the performance horse sport, and to me. I adored my father. In case you're wondering, I would never have harmed a hair on his head."

Sam knew better than to take her at her word, despite

the barely perceptible choke of tears in her voice. His first interview was already here, beside him.

"I understand you were the one to find your father," he said.

"That's right. It was morning. I had something to ask him. I saw One in a Million's stall door partway open. I stepped to the door and there was Daddy, lying facedown in the straw, almost at the stallion's feet, not a mark on him." The low sob in her throat sounded genuine. But she was an actress, Sam reminded himself.

"Did you see anybody? Anything out of place?"

She braked the car to avoid a family of feral pigs trotting across the road. Sam had seen features about them online. They were dangerous pests, their numbers increasing.

In the distance, Sam could see several tall windmills and the gleam of morning sunlight on a cluster of light-colored buildings. The two-story house, with its wide balconies, rose above them like Tara in *Gone with the Wind*. Cattle and horses made dark clusters in the spreading pastures. The horse arena, with its sheltering roof, lay on the far side of the house.

"I should have taken time to look," she said. "But it was my father lying there. I dropped down beside him in the stall. When I realized he wasn't breathing, I screamed. People came running. Sorry, things are blurred after that. I just remember being helped away, the county police coming, and my brother showing up and throwing his weight around. Darrin is family, but he can be an ass sometimes."

"How did he get along with your father?"

"He worshipped Dad and would have done anything to please him. But he was cowed by the big man. Nothing Darrin did was ever good enough for Frank Culhane. I've felt sorry for my brother sometimes." An ironic smile tugged at her lips. "But only sometimes. With me, Daddy had no expectations. I was his baby. I'm still working past that."

"Do you think your brother could be capable of murder?"

A bitter but musical laugh rippled through her body. "Darrin? He might have motive, but he hasn't got the balls."

"So who might?"

There was a silent pause as the ranch came into full view.

"Lila, the widow," she said. "She was a showgirl in Vegas who stole Dad from Mom for his money. Just ruthless. She didn't care at all about the family she was breaking up."

"How long were they married?" Sam asked.

"Eleven years. She never even gave him babies. But she's ruled the house like an empress. She barely tolerates the rest of the family coming to Friday-night dinners or even just going in and out."

"Who's your father's heir?" Sam could have tried taking notes on his phone, but he wanted her to keep talking.

"*She* is! But it was with the understanding that their children would continue the Culhane line. Since she didn't have any, my mother's lawyers are working on that angle to get her out of our family home. Darrin and I are heirs to our mother's share of the estate—mostly investments and the cattle. She's got plenty of money. But the heart of our legacy, our family tradition, is the house and the horses. And Lila is hanging onto those like a rabid badger."

"So why might she do away with your father? Might not his death weaken her grip on his estate? What was their relationship like?"

"Smooth on the surface. I never heard them fight. But I know my dad, and I sensed something. I think there was somebody else, maybe younger, and he was planning to move Lila aside. They have a prenup. She wouldn't get much if they were to divorce. But with his death . . ."

Her voice trailed off as the house came into full view. Even grander than it had looked from a distance. Old South style with touches of Texas, like the immense rack from a longhorn mounted above the front door.

No one was in sight. Sam assumed that because of his late arrival, the people who'd waited were going about their business. Tracking them down would be up to him. Nick had included a list of family and associates in the material he'd handed over. But Sam didn't need the list to know whom he wanted to find first.

CHAPTER FIVE

Sam studied Lila Smith Culhane from across the patio table, the pool behind her reflecting a halo of morning light. Jasmine had ushered him onto the walkway that led behind the house and disappeared inside. He already knew that the two women were enemies. How would Lila's take on the relationship differ from Jasmine's?

Fortified by the stout, black coffee her cook had delivered with a slab of thick, sourdough toast and blackberry jam, Sam could feel his instincts surging—a raw hunger to get into this case and rip it apart—judiciously—with his bare hands. This drive was part of what made him good at his work, and he ran with it—the tabloid-fodder situation, the clashing personalities, the interactions and motives, all the nuances and details of a challenging crime, perhaps the most challenging of his career. Somebody had murdered a powerful man in cold blood. It was up to him to discover the truth. New job and promotion aside, that was what really mattered.

In Chicago he'd worked as part of a team. The tragic shooting of his young partner there and the accident that had taken out two vital agents in Abilene had left him on his own. He would find a way to make that work for him.

But he couldn't play the traditional good-cop, bad-cop game with his partner playing the gentleman. He would have to walk the line between.

"There's no hotel out here, so I've arranged for you to stay in one of our guest cottages, Mr. Rafferty," Lila Culhane said. "You may take your meals in the kitchen—just walk in and ask the cook. Mariah's her name. And you may call me Lila. I, however, will call you Agent Rafferty. I know you're not here as a friend."

She was a stunner, her voice low and velvety, and she had a lead showgirl's tall, commanding presence. A few years older than Sam, she had the look of a woman who'd taken excellent care of herself. Botox? Sam could usually tell by the slight rigidity. But Lila's flawless golden skin showed no signs of the treatment.

Her hair was tied back with a coppery scarf that matched her striking eyes. Dressed in a silk blouse, khakis, and a fitted leather belt, she wore no jewelry, not even a wedding band. Whether out of habit or in deference to her husband's death, Sam had yet to learn.

She appeared strong and in charge. But something in him sensed her vulnerability. Was she afraid of him? Was he looking across the table at Frank Culhane's murderer?

"How long are you planning to be here, Agent Rafferty?" she asked.

"For now, as long as it takes—and I'm grateful for your hospitality. How soon will you be having the funeral?"

"The mortuary in Abilene has the body. Once we get it back, we'll be laying him in the family plot on that hill behind the arena, with just the ranch family in attendance—you're welcome to join us as an observer, at a respectful distance, of course. Then, in a few days, as soon as we can plan it, we'll be hosting a memorial service with a big Texas barbecue. The governor will be invited, neighbors and friends, officials from the National Reined Cow Horse Association, and more. There'll be a big crowd. You'll be welcome to circulate and meet people. But I would appreciate your discretion in not discussing Frank's manner of death or whom you suspect."

"That shouldn't be a worry. I'm not allowed to discuss an ongoing case." Though if they happened to know who he was, somebody might volunteer information, Sam thought. "You're planning all this now, by yourself?"

"There's a catering service in Abilene that handles big affairs like this one—the food, the seating, the setup, and the cleanup. They'll do the work. I've already chosen the menu and the location. But the family has to plan the program, and for that we need to get together around the table tonight. I'm expecting some fireworks."

Sam knew he couldn't miss this—anything could come out of those fireworks. But inviting himself now could get him turned down. He would find a way. "I'm sure you've got a busy day ahead, Lila," he said. "Let's get this first interview over with. As I learn more, there may be others."

"You'll have to catch up with me first. I didn't kill Frank, Mr. Rafferty. There've been times when I wanted to. But evidently, somebody else wanted to do it even more—and in case you ask, I've no idea who it might have been. Frank had enemies. Any powerful man does. But I don't know anybody who would take the risk of murdering him."

"I'll keep that in mind." He took his laptop out of his briefcase and set it up on the table. Glancing toward the open-sided arena beyond the patio, Sam saw a tall, dark man exercising a splendid roan. A stallion, Sam assumed, though he wasn't close enough to tell. But even knowing next to nothing about horses, he couldn't help admiring the grace of horse and rider, moving as one in a pattern of turns, circles, gallops, and sliding stops. He'd glimpsed reining events on TV and dismissed them as boring. He'd never been much of a horse fan. But he was struck by the skill of this live display.

"Who's that?" he asked Lila.

"Roper McKenna. He was Frank's head trainer. He quit when Frank died but I've rehired him as my horse manager."

"So was he loyal to your husband?"

"As far as I know. He's loyal to me, too, but mostly because I pay the man well and will be letting him compete on our horses, something Frank didn't allow him to do."

"I see." Sam made a mental note to move Roper McKenna near the top of his list. Ambition could be a strong motive for murder. And if the man had designs on Frank Culhane's glamorous and wealthy wife, that would double the motivation.

"Let's get started." He brought up the interview form and started with the basics, as was his custom. "State your name, birthdate, and birthplace."

She did. No surprises there, except that she'd started out as an Idaho farm girl. That she'd moved up through the ranks of beauty contests was less surprising. She would've had the looks, the presence, and the ambition—or maybe a pushy mother.

"Family?"

"I was an only child. My parents died in a farm truck accident when I was nine. My widowed grandma finished raising me. I wanted to be a nurse. But after a semester at Riggs Junior College . . ." She trailed off, paused.

"If you do your job, you'll likely discover this. I'll save you the work. In my freshman year, I got pregnant by a campus lothario who refused to take responsibility. I kept my daughter, with my grandma's help, and got the job in

Vegas to support my little girl. By the time Grandma passed away, I was making half-decent money. I took her in with a nanny. Her name is Jemma. Jemma Smith. She's a nursing student at Texas Christian University in Fort Worth. Frank knew about her. She even spent time here when she was younger. I pay her school expenses, but these days she has nothing to do with this family. She was nowhere near this place when Frank was killed. Promise me you won't involve her in any way."

"You know I can't make that promise. But for now . . ." He shrugged and made a note on his laptop.

"You'll tell me if you're going to contact her?"

"You know better than to ask."

Sam watched the antagonism flit across her chiseled features. She was very protective of her daughter. He couldn't rule that out as a motive for some kind of action.

"Tell me how you met Frank Culhane," he said.

"Not much to tell. It was twelve years ago, at the finals of the National Reined Cow Horse Association. A girl in the show wanted to see her new boyfriend ride, and she talked me into going to watch an event with her. Frank was there with three beautiful horses. I think I fell in love with the horses even before their owner walked around the corner of the stall, and I saw him."

"I take it you're familiar with horses."

"Sure. I'm from Idaho. But I'd never seen champion quarter horses before. I was blown away. And I think Frank could tell that. It was like an instant bond between us."

"Aside from the fact that he was attractive, wealthy, and older?" Sam asked, hoping for a fresh reaction. So far, she'd seemed too cool, too detached.

She drew back, appearing genuinely shocked. "We fell in love, Mr. Rafferty. And the horses were woven into the attraction. That's what I'm fighting for now, to preserve the horses that were Frank's legacy."

Her words sounded a little too noble, Sam thought. "What about his wife and family? I talked to Jasmine. She said you didn't care at all about them."

"Jasmine is a useless, conniving little twit who needs to find herself a life. Frank's kids were lost in their own worlds. I tried to make friends with them, but they weren't open to it.

"His ex-wife, Madeleine, is a dragon. She was a world-class rider, probably better than Frank, and he couldn't stand that. They were on the circuit together, constantly battling for domination. I was the one who gave him peace."

And a pretty good piece. Sam blotted the inappropriate thought from his mind.

"Where's your stepson?" he asked.

"Darrin has a house, a wife, and a law practice in Willow Bend. He was here this morning, but when you didn't show up on time, he left. He said he had appointments."

"What about the wife?"

"Pregnant. Probably throwing up at home. If you want to talk to them in town, we have a few spare vehicles. I'll have one brought around for your use."

"Thanks. If it's not too much bother." Sam was in no position to refuse. He needed a way to get around.

"Nothing's a bother if it leads to justice for Frank's murder. I need this situation resolved. We all do, so we can move forward."

"One final question for now," Sam said. "I know what you said. But do you have any suspicion, even an inkling, of who might have killed your husband?"

"At the moment, Mr. Rafferty, I do not. And now I have a long list of other things to do. I'll make a call for the Jeep. It will be around front shortly." She rose from her seat at the table, turned, and walked back into the house, leaving him alone on the patio.

I need this situation resolved. We all do, so we can move forward.

Were those the words of a grieving widow? Jasmine had mentioned that Lila was cold. Maybe her control was only a front, put up as a show of strength. But something was off about the woman. Unless proven innocent, she would remain near the top of his list of suspects.

Slipping his laptop and the printed file Nick had given him back into the briefcase, he took the path back around the house to the front porch. He'd planned to return to the arena and talk to Roper. But the man appeared to be focused on his job for now. And since a Jeep would be showing up soon, that interview might be better put off until he'd talked to Lila's stepson in town—and the wife as well. A couple carrying the next generation of Culhanes would have a motive to continue the family legacy on the ranch—especially if they suspected their father was about to trade in the legally vulnerable Lila for a younger, and perhaps more fertile, woman.

The sun was already getting hot. Sam stood in the shade of the grand house's overhanging balcony, watching the morning light spill across the scrub flat that stretched beyond the boundary of the ranch. Something could be waiting for him out there, maybe the answer to everything. Now that he had wheels again, he would spend some time exploring and meeting the neighbors—any one of whom could open up new insights into this crime.

Now he could hear the Jeep coming along the access road from behind the stables. A moment later it swung around the front corner of the house, a newer white Jeep Wrangler.

At the wheel was Jasmine.

*   *   *

Roper swung his weight off the prize five-year-old mare, gave her a pat, and turned her over to the grooms to be unsaddled and bathed. One in a Million's daughter, Million Dollar Baby, was already registered, with himself as rider, for the derby in Scottsdale next month. Now that the event had become a shootout, to fill the vacancy left by Frank's death, the competition would be tougher. But she was still a horse that could win it all.

The white-faced roan was big and powerful for a mare, and as precise in her moves as a ballerina. Frank had won a big futurity event with her at the age of three. In full competition she'd scored high, although she'd ultimately lost to more experienced horses. Roper had long known she had the heart of a champion. Now that she was a little older, with more of Roper's training behind her, would she be good enough to take him to the Run for a Million? Would *he* be good enough for her?

The next horse, a client's bay gelding, was ready and waiting to be worked. Roper was about to beckon the groom to bring it in when Lila stepped out of the shadows, motioning the groom back with a wave of her hand.

"How was Baby this morning?" she asked Roper.

"Good as ever," Roper said.

"She'll need to be better than ever. Do you think she'll be ready for the shootout?"

"She'll have to be. She's a lot of horse. I think she can do this."

When Lila didn't say more, he prodded her. "Is there something you need, Boss?" He used the name he'd chosen to call her.

"Just a few words." Her coppery eyes seemed to glow in the dim light around her. A lock of ash blond hair had fallen in front of her ear, half framing her classic face.

Roper liked looking at her. But this was business. He knew better than to treat her like a woman he wanted.

She glanced back at the two teenaged grooms hovering around the bay gelding, within hearing. "Walk with me," she said.

Brushing the small of her back with his fingertips, he ushered her around the arena to the far side. She glanced back toward the stables before she spoke. "Just a heads-up. Our FBI agent finally showed up. He'll be hunting you down for an interview."

"Let him. I've nothing to hide. Frank and I got along, and the only thing I did in that stall was come running when Jasmine screamed—that, and quiet the stallion. What's the man like?"

"He seems quiet, low-key, the kind who'll trip you up in a heartbeat if you lower your guard."

"I told you, I have nothing to hide."

But do you, Boss? Roper found himself wondering. *Are you afraid I might say too much about you—even though you've never told me anything private about your marriage? I know Frank could be an unfeeling jerk. Did you come to hate him for it? Did you hate him enough to kill him?*

He'd signed the paperwork and collaborated with her on her plans for the horses almost since the day of Frank's murder. But he'd never felt he knew her well, let alone understood her. Her refusal to show grief, her drive to preserve her late husband's horse legacy and to keep her hold on his home, was burning her alive. And soon the enemy that was Frank's first family would be closing in on her. He could see the raw fire in her striking eyes, the deepening of the shadows around them.

He had not one shred of evidence that she'd killed Frank, Roper reminded himself. She was innocent until proven guilty. And she was giving him what he wanted most—the right to compete on the Culhane horses. Until something changed, he was Lila's hired man. He had signed away his loyalty, and he would walk any line that might get him into that million-dollar arena.

"Cooperate with him. Show him the operation and anything else he might want to see. But watch what you say to that FBI man," she said, turning away to leave. "Something tells me he's more than he appears to be."

"Got it, Boss."

"Good. We'll talk later."

He watched her stride back to the house before he called for the next horse.

Jasmine had turned the Jeep's steering wheel over to Sam. But she'd insisted on coming with him to navigate.

"You know I don't need a babysitter, Miss Culhane," he said. "I have the address of your brother's house with his home office."

"You're a city boy. You don't know your way around these parts. Besides, I offered to babysit you—for nothing." She'd changed from jeans to denim shorts. Her flawless model's legs were a golden display on the passenger seat next to him. Sam forced himself to avert his eyes. He was not immune to the charms of beautiful women. But he was on duty now. And the last beautiful woman in his life had done a number on him that had left him emotionally bloodied.

It's your work you're married to, not me, Sam. I need a man who cares enough to give me his time—and now, I've found one. I plan to keep him. Thank God you and I didn't have children. At least we can make a clean break.

Those words, and the tone of Cynthia's voice, would never leave him. But he'd learned to stuff them into a figurative black box in his mind, close the lid, and lock it. That was what he did now.

"So you've already given me the third degree, Agent Rafferty." Jasmine twirled a lock of auburn hair around her finger. "I think I deserve to know a little about you."

Self-revelation wasn't a great idea in Sam's line of work, let alone part of his job description. But shutting this woman down wouldn't be in the best interest of the case.

"Not much to tell," he said. "I spent eleven years with the Bureau in Chicago. An old friend told me about a position here. I was due for a change, so I agreed to an interview. They rushed me here because of an emergency in Abilene—two agents are in the hospital, and they needed somebody fast on this case."

"So how are you liking Texas so far?"

"I feel like I just landed on an alien planet. As long as you're here, Ms. Culhane, maybe you can help me get my bearings—tell me a little about the life here."

"Sure. But only as long as you call me Jasmine. We don't hold much with formality around here."

"Fine. Jasmine it is."

"And you?" Her wide, green eyes regarded him expectantly.

"Agent."

"Whatever." She turned away and gazed at the road ahead like a rejected teenager. There was a quality about her that reminded Sam of a younger girl, open and seeking, hungry for approval and acceptance. Frank, for all his indulgence of his daughter, might not have been much of a father. Most likely gifts instead of support. He would keep that in mind.

They were approaching the spot where Sam's rented car had broken down. The little Subaru was gone. "It's been hauled back to the vehicle shed at the ranch," Jasmine said, breaking the silence. "It's the rental agency's problem now. Since we don't have a tire that will fit, they can pick it up."

"It's an old car. They might not want to bother with it." Sam took a moment to steer around a road-killed jack-rabbit. A feeding raven flapped off the carcass and settled back as they passed. "So tell me about Roper McKenna," he said. "How well do you know him?"

A thoughtful pause passed. "He's been here for a year or more—not sure, I was gone when he hired on. He worked as Dad's head trainer until . . . Dad's death. Now Roper belongs to Lila. Bought and paid for . . . the arrogant bastard."

Sam took a mental note. "How did he get along with Frank?" he asked her.

"Fine, as far as I know. They might not've been friends, but I sensed that they respected each other. Right after Dad was killed, my brother announced that he was in charge of the horse operation, and Roper would answer to him. Roper resigned and walked out."

"Then what?"

"Darrin realized that for now the horse operation was more than he could handle. He stepped back and didn't fight it when Lila rehired Roper on her own terms. We need Roper for the horses—even Darrin knows that. But those two men despise each other. That's never going to change, no matter who wins this war."

"And it is a war?"

Jasmine sighed. "You can't imagine! And just wait until Mamá gets here. That's when the big guns will come out. If it weren't for Dad's service, I'd pack up and go back to California today."

"You can't leave while this investigation is ongoing, Jasmine."

"*Ha!*" Her chuckle held defiance. But to run would suggest guilt. She was smarter than that.

Willow Bend, a sleepy community of 2,811, featured a main street with a grocery store, a bank, a saloon, a ranch supply business, a respectable-looking restaurant, and a church. Houses, most of them small, some well-tended, some with junk-cluttered yards, old cars, or kiddie swings, some vacant with boarded windows, lined the side streets. The town had clearly known better days.

"Darrin's place is at the far end of the street," Jasmine said. "It belonged to the cattleman who started the town a hundred years ago. Darrin rented it after Dad married Lila. It's served him as a town office, but he wants to get rid of her and move back to the ranch house. He wants to be the next Frank Culhane." Her tone made it clear that Darrin would never replace her father.

"I get the picture." Sam could see the oversized bungalow with its broad, covered porch at the end of the street. It was probably the most imposing home in Willow Bend, but a poor comparison to the mansion on the Culhane Ranch. He could sense Darrin's ambition as he pulled up to the curb. Jasmine had opened the passenger side door and was climbing out of the Jeep.

"Are you coming along to introduce me?"

"No, you're on your own." She led him up the front steps. "I'll wait on the porch. It'll get hot in the Jeep."

She sank into an Adirondack chair, crossing her lovely, suntanned legs as if fully aware that she had his attention. "Good luck with my brother and his wife. I never know what to expect when I step through their door. That's why I'm not going with you."

"Thanks for the warning." Sam crossed the porch and stepped to the door. He was reaching for the bell when he heard, from somewhere inside, the shrill, almost hysterically angry sound of a woman's voice.

"You promised me that house, Darrin! You vowed you'd fight for it as a home to raise our children and continue your family line. But you're not fighting for that or anything. You're caving in to your stepmother at every turn."

"Simone, I can't just throw her out." The responding voice was male, with a nasal undertone. "This has got to be done legally, based on her failure to provide any descendants to continue the Culhane line. Lila will have lawyers, too. It's going to be a battle. I'm preparing to fight for you and our children, but it's got to be done in court."

"But that could take months, even longer! And this baby will be here in December, Darrin, I'm not bringing our child home to raise in this hovel you've put us in! I'll leave you and go home to my family first!"

CHAPTER SIX

Sam hesitated, but only for an instant. He'd known persons in a state of emotional stress to reveal vital pieces of information. But he needed to follow procedure.

With Jasmine watching him like a cat at a mouse hole, he pushed the doorbell button. The sound of the chime reverberated through the house. He spoke. "Mr. Culhane, FBI. I need to talk with you and your wife."

From the far side of the heavy wooden door came a scrambling sound. The door opened far enough to reveal a slender, russet-haired man in his thirties, dressed in shirtsleeves and a loosened navy-blue tie. A long, brown coffee stain, still wet, dripped down the front of his shirt. He eyed Sam up and down, his gaze lingering on the faint bulge of the Glock 19M service revolver at Sam's hip.

"Oh, hell, talk about timing," he muttered as Sam presented his credentials. "Come on in. We might as well get this over with." He glanced down at the stain. "Sorry about the situation. My wife's in a family way, and she's having an emotional morning. You know women."

Actually, he didn't, or he might have kept the woman he'd had, Sam reflected. But it was a passing thought. He refocused his attention on the job at hand. The entry and living room were cluttered with cast-off odds and ends—a slipper, a knitted throw, a wispy piece of underwear, a pizza box, a magazine, and a couple of recent tabloid papers on the floor next to the sofa. A fifty-inch TV was mounted above the fireplace. The room was clean enough—Darrin's wife would surely have help. But Sam had seen enough in his work to recognize the domain of a woman who felt trapped, scared, frustrated, and physically miserable.

He saw her now, down a hallway to a dining alcove off the kitchen. She was slumped at the table, dressed in a light robe, visibly embarrassed.

"Have a seat." Darrin closed the door and motioned Sam to the sofa. His wife had vanished from the alcove. "I waited for you this morning, Agent Rafferty. When you didn't show, I had to leave."

"Sorry. Trouble with my rental car. Your sister rescued me. She's become my self-appointed guide for today."

"Yes. Jasmine." He glanced toward the door, frowning. "If she's out there, she's probably got her ear pressed to the door right now, trying to listen to us. Don't trust her, Agent. She may look like an angel, and she comes at you sweet as strawberry pie with whipped cream. But don't be fooled. My sister can be a grasping, lying little weasel. And if you happen to get soft on her, she'll suck you dry. I've seen it happen to a couple of our cowboys. They left good jobs here after the thrill faded and she dumped them."

"So noted." Sam opened his laptop and switched it on.

"Jasmine has designs on the ranch, too," Darrin continued. "She can be ruthless when she chooses to be. And she despises Lila. It wouldn't even surprise me if she'd killed Dad with the idea of blame falling on his widow."

Sam had heard different versions of that story. He would

reserve judgment. "Let's get started," he said. "Your full name?"

Darrin gave him the basic information.

"If you've seen the autopsy report, you know your father died between two and three in the morning. Where were you then?"

"Right here in this house, in bed with my wife. Nobody saw us at that hour, but we can vouch for each other."

"Fine." Sam typed his notes. "If you can think of some way to verify that—a TV show, something happening outside, like hearing a police siren, for instance, that would help."

"This is Willow Bend. They roll up the streets at night. And we were fast asleep, not watching TV."

"How was your relationship with your father?"

Darrin dabbed at the coffee stain on his shirt. "The same as a lot of sons. He was the big man, with big expectations of his firstborn. Nothing I did was ever good enough for him. But I was growing into his shoes, and I sure as hell wasn't ready to lose him."

Sam was weighing the wisdom of revealing what he'd overheard before ringing the bell, deciding against it when another presence entered the room—a slender woman in a yellow sundress. Her strawberry blond hair was brushed to a sheen, her pretty, elfin face dabbed with touches of makeup.

Sam had to blink before he realized it was Simone. He stood and introduced himself. She extended a manicured hand, the fake nails a soft pink.

"Welcome to our home, Agent Rafferty," she said. "Please excuse the mess. I haven't been at my best lately. Morning sickness, you understand. I think I must have what Kate Middleton had. I heard about it on *The View*. What can I do for you?"

"You can talk to me while I ask you a few questions. It won't take long. Then, for now, I'll be out of your way."

"I'm at your disposal, Agent." She settled onto an ottoman facing the sofa, smoothing her skirt over her knees. "May I have my husband here while you question me?"

Sam would have preferred to question her alone, but he would make a point of that later. For now, he would play the good cop.

"All right for now," he said. "But this probably won't be our last interview."

"Fire away." She gave him a charming smile. "I'm sure Darrin has already told you that we were here, sleeping, the night his father was murdered. We didn't know anything until the next morning."

"Yes, he did," Sam said. "I'd like to ask you about your relationship with the family. What about Frank?"

"My father-in-law saw me as a baby machine, to usher the next generation of Culhanes into the world. He knew I was expecting, and he was happy about it. But he insisted, on no uncertain terms, that if it wasn't a boy, I was to turn right around and start on number two."

"That's a lot of pressure on a woman."

"Yes. Like something out of *The Tudors*. Did you see that TV show?"

"I missed that one," Sam said. "What about the women in the family?"

"They've tolerated me, as if I were somebody's pet. But now that Frank's gone, things are about to change. Darrin is Frank's firstborn, his only son. He, not Lila, is entitled to that ranch. When she's gone, we'll be *the* Culhanes."

"What about the horses?" Sam asked.

"Those horses cost as much in work and expense as they earn," Darrin put in. "We could sell them for enough to double, even triple our cattle herd. But we're going to have to get Lila out first, and we're going to have to do it legally," he insisted. "That's the only way to make sure she's gone."

"Unless there's a quicker way," Simone said. "Like finding proof that she was already sleeping with Roper McKenna while your dad was still alive."

"Was she? Is she?" Sam was instantly intrigued.

Simone shrugged. "I don't have proof. But the two of them are hand in glove, always giving each other looks and talking with their heads together. That doesn't happen overnight. We could make a case for it."

"As far as you know, was Frank faithful to Lila?" Sam asked. "I've heard rumors to the contrary."

"Dad liked flirting with younger women. I'm not aware that he took it any farther. He liked things stable on the home front, and Lila was always there. She kept his records, handled clients, did a lot for the business. He always came home."

"But that doesn't entitle her to the ranch." Simone's restraint broke. "We've got to get her out of that house, Darrin, any way we can. And you've got to be a man about it—for me, for our baby, and for our future family. Lila is sleeping with that man. I just know she is."

The conversation had come full circle. Sam shut down the laptop, stowed it in his briefcase, and laid two of his cards on the table. "This is enough for now. I'll be talking with you again. Keep yourselves available. If you think of anything you haven't told me, my cell number is on my card. Call me anytime."

"How long do you plan to be around?"

"Hopefully as long as it takes to find out who killed your father. But that remains to be seen." And it did. The trail could go cold, or he could wear out his welcome with the Culhanes. Either outcome would reflect on his job performance, but it would be the failure to find Frank Culhane's killer that would leave the deepest mark on him and on the bureau in Abilene. "I'll show myself out, thanks," he said.

Leaving them together, he stepped out onto the porch, closing the door behind him. Jasmine uncrossed her delicious legs and stood. "Out through the rabbit hole?" she asked with an impish grin.

"No comment. Let's go."

Back in the Jeep, with Sam at the wheel, they drove back through town and took the road to the ranch. "My brother and that little wife of his are a piece of work," Jasmine said. "They remind me of why I never got married a second time. Her family's from old money, going back to the first oil discoveries. Simone was the youngest of a big family. They sent her to finishing school, catered to her every whim, and now she thinks she can get whatever she wants by pouting and stamping her little foot. I already feel sorry for their baby. And you heard how she's pushing Darrin to be a man and get Lila out of that house by force, blackmail, or whatever means necessary."

"You heard?"

"Most of it. I'm a shameless eavesdropper."

"What do you think of her claim that Roper's sleeping with Lila?"

"If he is, it's driven by his own ambition. Roper's good at his job. He was loyal to Dad and he's loyal to Lila— probably because of what he's getting paid. But he's one of the coldest men I've ever met. I sense that he'll do anything to get ahead, even sleep with the boss."

"And Lila?"

"I can't believe she'd be that dumb. It's not like her. But she's only human. Dad could be an insensitive jerk, and Roper's a hottie."

"You sound sympathetic. I thought you disliked her."

"I can't stand her. But that doesn't keep me from wanting to be like her sometimes. She's one of the sharpest, strongest women I know, and I've worked in Hollywood. Maybe by the time I'm her age, I'll have it all together. So far, I can't say much for my track record." She shrugged, gazing ahead at the road.

"Tell me what you know about Roper McKenna. Where's his family from?"

"They live on the little ranch south of here—a rundown old place they bought when they moved from Colorado. Our cook, Mariah, calls them hillbillies and says they're not our kind of people. But they're rodeo folks. Roper doesn't compete—I get the impression he may have done so years ago. But his four younger half siblings—three brothers and a sister—are rodeo superstars."

"Oh—wait." Something clicked for Sam. He remembered the magazine cover he'd seen on an airport newsstand and a glimpse of TV coverage from a recent Texas rodeo. Those four eager young faces—smiling, healthy, and handsome—were hard to forget. The girl was a dark-eyed, ebony-haired beauty. "They're the McKennas, the ones on the news?"

"The same. They're celebrities, at least here in Texas."

"Will the family be coming to your father's memorial? I wouldn't mind meeting them."

"Roper will be there because he worked for Dad and now Lila. But the family isn't invited and probably wouldn't come if they were. The father's a disabled former bull rider, the mother one of those stalwart salt-of-the-earth women who probably home-delivered her babies, does her own housework, goes to church every Sunday, and never gets her nails done. I try not to judge, but like Mariah says, they're good people, just not our kind."

"Was there any conflict between your father and the McKennas? Land issues? Water rights? Animals?"

"Not that I'm aware of, but that would be a question for Roper. If he's around, I'll introduce you when we get back to the ranch."

"Roper was the first one to get there after you found your father, right?"

"Right. He heard my scream, and he handled things. But that in itself means nothing."

"So you think Roper could have killed Frank?"

"He had the strength, the know-how, the ambition, and as much reason as anybody. Dad was holding him back, not letting him compete while he was under contract."

"And your neighbor on the far side?"

They passed the sign that marked the west border of the Culhane Ranch. The sun had climbed higher now, blasting heat through the open top of the Jeep. Sam, still at the wheel, was glancing around for a handle or lever that would free the canvas cover when a brown and white animal, the size of a leggy dog, streaked over the fence and into the road directly in front of the Jeep. Sam's foot slammed the brake, but it was too late. Jasmine screamed as the vehicle struck the graceful creature with a jarring thud. It lay in the road in front of them, alive but with its slender neck bent at an ugly angle.

"No! No!" Jasmine flew out of the passenger seat and raced around the front of the Jeep to drop at the injured animal's side. Climbing out, Sam could see it clearly for the first time. At the first flashing glimpse he'd thought it might be a whitetail deer. But it had taken the eight-foot fence as if it had wings. And it was no deer. Instead of antlers, its long, sharp, black horns jutted straight up. It had a black stripe along its body and an elegant little head which Jasmine cradled between her knees as she tried to comfort it.

Sam's jaw dropped as he recognized it. It was a Thomson's gazelle, an antelope native to the grassy savannahs of East Africa.

"Can't we do something for it?" Jasmine's eyes implored him.

"Its neck's broken. We can't save it, Jasmine," Sam said. "But it's somebody's property. Let's wait a few minutes and hope the owner shows—"

The rest of his words were lost in the roar of a battered-looking four-wheeler, bounding across the pasture toward them. As it came closer, he could see the man at the wheel.

He was middle-aged and blocky of build, dressed in khakis and a pith helmet such as a safari guide might wear in the bush. Behind the stylish aviator glasses, his unshaven face was fat and angry. Sam had long since schooled himself to withhold judgment, but here was a man who seemed to exude malice. Jasmine's posture stiffened as he came closer. It appeared that she knew him.

Next to the fence, the four-wheeler pulled up and swung to the right, giving Sam a view of the logo on the armored side.

CHARLIE GRISHMAN
BIG GAME SAFARIS
123-456-7899
GET YOUR TROPHY TODAY!

Sam fought back a wave of revulsion. He'd read about operations like Grishman's—people with land who bought old, sick, and otherwise unwanted animals from homes, parks, and private zoos and used them for clients to hunt, for a price that was high, but much cheaper than an outfitted foreign trip. He'd been dismayed by online photos of proud hunters posing with their kills. But right now it wasn't in his job description to judge.

Charlie Grishman stood up in the front of his vehicle. The position lent him height, an advantage since he didn't appear to be very tall. A bluster of fury roared out of him.

"You owe me five hundred dollars for that antelope!" he bellowed through the wire fence. "I had a thirteen-year-old kid paid up and ready to make his first kill before it got away. Now I'll have to refund the money, and that gazelle will only be good for lion food."

It was Jasmine who answered, raising a fierce face with the gazelle cradled in her arms. "This antelope was on our property, Charlie. The poor, scared thing ran right in front of our Jeep. The next time one of your animals gets loose on our ranch, we're taking you to court! You need to get out of this awful business! But I know you won't. The money's good, and you love playing great white hunter!"

Charlie sneered. "Spoken like the bleeding heart you are. I'm doing a service. Every animal killed on my ranch saves the life of one in the wild."

"I've heard that one before. It's bullshit."

Sam had moved to stand next to her. This was no time to step in and introduce himself. The situation was too volatile. He would visit Charlie Grishman at his place later. For now, he needed to watch this interaction play out.

"That's not all," Charlie said. "The animals hunted on my ranch get a chance to die a noble death, wild and free, fighting for survival, not being put down like pets or livestock."

"But they don't survive. They die terrified, bewildered, and suffering—even the dangerous ones. You're not getting a cent from us. Go home, Charlie. I'm sick of the sight of you."

Charlie had spotted a narrow gate along the fence line. He swung the four-wheeler around and headed in that direction, pausing long enough to say, "All right for now. But this isn't over. Just let me collect my antelope and get it home. The cats will like the fresh kill."

"This one's not dead. It has a broken neck. At least put it down first."

"The cats can do the job. And this one is wild, their natural food, not like the goats they usually get. Revs up their instincts." He idled the small vehicle while he opened the gate to drive through.

What happened next occurred in a flash. Jasmine's hand, with surprising strength and speed, seized Sam's revolver and wrenched it out of its holster. Bracing herself against the recoil, she fired a single shot into the region of the animal's heart. The gazelle didn't even shudder as the hefty bullet blasted home.

Blood-spattered, Jasmine righted herself. "Now you can have your antelope, Charlie," she said. "And keep your animals off our ranch!"

"Damn you to hell, woman—you'll hear from me." Charlie pulled up beside the dead gazelle. Worried that a second shot might be aimed at the man, Sam reached down and gently lifted the gun from Jasmine's hand. She gave it up without resistance, letting it slide through her limp fingers. Charlie slung the carcass over the back of his vehicle and roared back through the gate toward his own place.

"I did that move in a *Criminal Minds* episode," she said in a flat voice. "It took practice to get it exactly right."

Sam holstered the gun and reached down to pull her to her feet. She was trembling. There was blood sprayed on her clothes and her bare legs. "Blast it, Jasmine, you could be arrested and charged for what you just did." He took his clean handkerchief and began wiping the fine blood spatters from her golden skin. "Seizing an agent's weapon, willful property destruction. You could be in big trouble."

"But I won't be, will I?" The fight had gone out of her, but she was still sharp. "You're not going to let your bosses know I got the jump on you."

"Smart girl." Sam caved, not wanting to create a bad situation for her. "This stays between us. But that doesn't make it all right."

She drew herself up. Sam sensed she was on the edge of breaking. "So punish me! I couldn't let that poor helpless animal be torn apart alive! And you would have let that awful man take it away. The *property* owner! You and your damned rules!" Her fist struck a glancing blow to his chest. "I could hate you for that, Mr. Agent Sam Rafferty!"

Small, hiccupping gasps rose against her resistance to become racking sobs. Tears flowed as her fists flailed at Sam's chest. "I've never . . . killed anything . . . before. It was so beautiful . . . so innocent . . . ."

Sam gathered her close, holding her tightly to control her shaking. For the first moments she fought him, pushing away with her arms. Then she folded, curling against him like a brokenhearted child. His arms gentled, cradling her. She was soft, warm, fragrant, and needing. Holding her triggered a current of warmth in the depths of his body, the first real emotion he'd felt in weeks. It felt good. Too good.

"I'm sorry, Jasmine." His arms released her, easing her away from him. "If you'd said something, I might've shot that poor gazelle myself. But you moved so fast. I never expected that from you."

"I'm not the little fluff everyone seems to think I am.

I'm full of surprises." She wiped her running nose on her shirtsleeve. "Let's go."

In the Jeep once again, they headed back to the ranch. Jasmine had raised the canvas shade against the hot sun. She sat silent at first, her hands clasped in her lap.

"Tell me about Charlie Grishman," Sam said. "How well do you know him?"

"I know him very well." She gave a raw chuckle. "Charlie was my high school algebra teacher. Odd duck, even back then. Never married—probably for the best. Nine years ago, his grandmother left him that land on the far side of our property. Not a huge spread. No livestock. No crops, just wild prairie with big patches of mesquite. The old woman hadn't done anything with it in years. But Charlie had a plan. Now you've seen it. He gets a lot of clients. I'm sure the monster is making piles of money off that godawful business."

"How about your father? Did he and Charlie get along?"

"You mean could Charlie have killed him? Dad hated Charlie. The whole family hates Charlie. So do most of the neighbors. Charlie probably hates us, too, especially today. But he's doing too well to risk his evil empire by committing a capital crime. As long as he maintained his fences and kept his animals on his property, Dad left him alone."

"Have you been to his place?"

"No. But I know people who have. It's about what you'd expect—ramshackle cages, substandard conditions, sick and aging animals who don't get treated because they're just going to be herded out and shot. Charlie's no vet. He can't take care of them. I don't think he even wants to."

"Aren't there regulations in place for the keeping of the animals?"

"Maybe." Jasmine shrugged. "But who's going to enforce them? What government agency has enough staff to come out here and check on Charlie's sleazy operation?" She exhaled. "What he's doing is evil. He needs to be shut down and those animals treated humanely."

Something in her voice, a deeper note of passion, put Sam on alert. There was more going on here. "You're not just spouting words, are you, Jasmine?" he asked.

She gave him a narrow-eyed glance. "This has nothing to do with your murder case."

"Maybe not. But believe it or not, I'm on your side. And I'm concerned."

She sighed. "All right. If you'll keep this to yourself."

"Fine for now."

"I met these people—young, mostly college students, a few of them older—at the bar in Willow Bend a few weeks ago. We've been in touch by text. They're from an Abilene group called ERFA, Equal Rights for Animals. They're planning a demonstration against Charlie—a protest to draw attention. I don't know when, but I said I could help by giving them access to his property."

Sam's heart dropped. He'd seen the outcome of similar demonstrations. "Listen to me, Jasmine," he said. "This isn't a good idea. People like these have the best intentions. But when they go into action, things tend to get out of hand—property damage, arrests, even deaths. They could get themselves and you in a heap of trouble, especially here, where there are dangerous animals involved. Charlie mentioned big cats. Who knows what else he's got out there."

"They're only going to demonstrate," Jasmine said. "Light

some torches, wave some signs, send some photos and videos to the press—you know, call attention to the mess. The only law they'd break would be trespassing. Once the story gets out, there are plenty of animal lovers who'll join the crusade to shut Charlie down. Does that sound sensible enough to you?"

"What sounds sensible is finding a legitimate complaint and taking it to court. Walk away from this group, Jasmine. Anything could go wrong."

"I'm not a child. I'll make my own decision about that." They were approaching the house. Sam swung into the employee parking lot. "Pull around in back, please," she said. "I don't want to go in the front way looking like this. There, outside the kitchen door. Mariah's seen everything. She won't tell on me." As he stopped, she opened the Jeep door, then turned back to him. "We'll be planning Dad's memorial tonight over dinner. I'll try to get you an invite, but no promises."

"Thanks, whatever you can do. And thanks for being my guide this morning. You were helpful. I'll be around the stables in case anybody needs me."

"Going to hunt down the mysterious Roper McKenna, are you?" She gave him an impish grin. "Good luck with that. He'll talk to you, but only on his own terms—or on Lila's."

Bounding out of the Jeep, she strode toward the house. Sam watched her go, admiring her verve and energy. Jasmine Culhane was far more than a pretty, high-spirited woman. But there were things about her that he needed to file in the back of his mind. One was the way she'd wrenched away his revolver before shooting the gazelle. Was she strong and fast enough to overcome a powerful man like Frank and inject him with the fatal drug? Maybe, if he'd trusted her and lowered his guard, though she didn't strike him as capable of murder.

The other thing he'd learned about Jasmine needed to be buried even deeper, to the point of forgetting.

It was the way he'd felt holding her in his arms.

CHAPTER SEVEN

Sam had been assigned one of three guest bungalows on the opposite end of the house from the stables. The smallest of the trio, it was well built and furnished with authentic pieces that appeared to be from the early 1900s, evoking a sense of long-gone people who might have stayed here in past years.

When he returned to clean up after letting Jasmine off, he found a Post-it note on the fridge. Inside was a hearty beef sandwich, a covered plate of homemade cookies, and a variety of cold sodas. Somebody was looking after him. He reminded himself to thank the kitchen staff. He would also need to interview them, especially Mariah, the cook. But that could wait. Right now, the name at the top of his list was Roper McKenna's.

After lunch, resisting the urge to nap, he took the path through the backyard to the arena and stables complex. By now the midday heat was as stifling as a thick, wet woolen blanket. Sam saw no one outside, but there was activity in the shelter of the stable. Most of the grunt workers, boys and girls, shoveling stalls, unloading supplies, and wiping down horses, looked like high school kids, willing to trade a summer of grinding work and low wages for time in the world of their dreams. Their young faces and bodies dripped perspiration in the heat. A college-aged boy appeared to be in charge, but the arena was empty. Sam couldn't see Roper anywhere.

"Roper's taking a lunch break," the older boy told Sam when asked. "He should be in the office, down that hall-way and to your right. Good luck. He likes his private time."

Undaunted, Sam walked down the hall. Private time or not, he'd interviewed mobsters, politicians, and billion-aires. He wasn't about to step back from a surly ranch manager.

The office door was closed. When he knocked, it opened with a whoosh of cool air from the portable AC mounted in the window.

Presenting his credentials, Sam surveyed the man in the doorway. At six-foot-one, his athletic body trained for his job, Sam was a big man. Roper was a good inch taller and twenty or thirty pounds heavier, all muscle.

His darkly handsome face wore a scowl, but as he greeted his visitor, his expression relaxed into what might pass as a neutral smile. This was the man who had worked closely with Frank Culhane. This was the man who, ac-cording to Frank's children, was now paid and owned by Lila, maybe even sleeping with her. This was a man who had his reasons to want Frank dead.

"Come on in and cool off, Agent Rafferty," he said. "I was told you'd be showing up. Your timing's as good as any. I was just updating some performance records. I do that every day. Our clients want to know how much progress their horses are making. With this, I can show them. It helps with our own horses, too."

The large monitor screen of his desktop computer dis-played graphs and tables. "I appreciate your time, Mr.

McKenna," Sam said, taking out his notes. "For now, I'll try not to take too much of it. But as things develop, I'll probably need to talk to you again."

What things? his expression seemed to say. But he spoke cordially. "I've blocked out fifteen minutes for you. After that I have to get back to the arena, but you're welcome to stay and watch me train."

"Thanks. I'd be interested in that. I'm fresh from Chicago, I know next to nothing about the sport, and I've got a lot to learn. Let's get started." Sam took the side chair he was offered. Roper resumed his place behind the large desk. The office was cluttered but orderly.

"I'll get to the big question first," Sam said. "Roper McKenna, did you kill Frank Culhane?"

If Roper was shocked by his abruptness, he didn't show it. "No," he said. "I was at home all night with my parents on the ranch south of here. They can vouch for that. I'm assuming you'll check."

"Of course. You can tell them to expect me. I was told you were the first person to respond to Jasmine after she found him. Tell me your first impression when you entered the stall."

"Frank was lying facedown with his arms up. No trace of blood. Jasmine was kneeling next to him, screaming. The stallion had backed away a few steps, but I knew I had to get him out of the stall before he panicked. By then there were more people on their way."

"The family knows that fentanyl caused his death, so it couldn't have been the horse. Could Jasmine have killed her father earlier, then gone back and pretended to find him? I know she's an actress."

Roper was silent for a moment, then shook his head. "I've thought about it. I don't think Jasmine has it in her to kill. And she didn't have much motive. Frank spoiled her, but she let him. Her conflict is with Lila. It's her brother and his wife who want the house. I'd look at them—but maybe it wasn't family at all. Maybe that idea is off base."

"At this point, nothing is off base. How was your relationship with Frank?" Sam had heard, but he wanted a direct answer.

"It was fine. We weren't personally close, but we respected each other and shared the same goals for the horses."

"But you wanted to compete, and he wouldn't allow it. At least that's what I heard."

"True. I was hoping to change that—but not by killing Frank."

"Do you know of anybody else who might have wanted him out of the way?"

"He had rivals, of course—other trainers and breeders who wanted their horses to win. But that's competition, not murder."

"Any real enemies? Any involvement with organized crime? That could explain a lot."

"If Frank was playing footsies with the mob, he kept it from me."

"I met Charlie Grishman this morning."

"Charlie's no candidate for neighbor of the month, but he's sitting fat and happy with the income from those poor animals. He and Frank clashed over his animals crossing boundaries, but as far as I know, he had no reason to kill the man."

Sam shifted in the chair, cleared his throat, and moved on to a more sensitive topic. "What about your relationship with Lila Culhane?"

Roper didn't blink. "Mrs. Culhane is my employer. We have a professional relationship."

"I understand you quit when her stepson tried to take over the horse operation."

"Darrin's an idiot. He didn't have a clue how to manage the horses. Mrs. Culhane hired me back for more than Frank was paying me. More important, she's allowing me to compete on the Culhane horses—something I'm preparing for at the big shootout in Scottsdale. Think what you will, but what she gives me is enough to buy my loyalty."

Sam could sense the anticipation in the man—how much he must have wanted to ride in competition. Could Frank's restriction have been a motive for murder? That seemed excessive. But there was more.

"I've heard the rumor that you were sleeping with her—before and now after Frank's death."

Again, Roper didn't flinch. "I've heard the rumor, and I know where it's coming from. But there's nothing to it. Mrs. Culhane is a beautiful woman. We share the same goals for the program, and we work well enough together. But I'm not that stupid. Neither is she. Everything between us is kept strictly professional—and wide open in case you want to check."

"And the other rumor, that Frank was scheming to replace her with a younger woman?"

Roper shrugged. "Frank never discussed his personal life with me. But he'd have been a fool to replace her. Lila gave her all to the ranch and the horses for eleven years, and she means to continue. She deserves everything he's left her."

Roper had used Lila's first name. Sam made a mental note. "So," he said, closing his notes, "is there anything more you remember about the morning Frank was found? Anything you saw or heard?"

"Nothing that I didn't tell the police. It should all be in their report." He rose, signaling that the interview was about to end. "The evidence shows that Frank died where he fell, in the straw at the feet of his prize stallion."

"With no witnesses." Sam finished the thought.

"There was one witness who would have seen everything, but he isn't talking," Roper said. "Follow me. If you've got a few more minutes, I'll introduce you."

"I've got all the time you have to give me." In approaching Roper McKenna for an interview, Sam had expected some resistance. But the man appeared to be a complete professional, as cordial as he was competent.

They stepped out into the heat of the stable. The box stall where Frank had died was still crisscrossed with yellow crime scene tape. There were other gated stalls farther down, some with horses looking out. But Roper stopped before a locked door and opened the dead bolt with his key. "You'll want a look at this."

The door opened into a small room lined with counters and shelves. Veterinary instruments, hoses, and clippers hung from a wall rack next to a sterilizer. Bottles and small cartons filled the shelves. "Our vet supply room. Li—Mrs. Culhane wants to build a full facility with an on-site vet, but that's going to take time and money."

"Any fentanyl in here?"

"No. It had to have been brought in."

"Who has keys?"

"Me. Mrs. Culhane. The vet who comes in. There may be a few others around, lent out and never returned. There are some powerful drugs that we keep locked up. We'd be smart to change the locks. But no, we don't stock the drug that killed Frank. Seen enough?"

At Sam's nod, they left the room. After locking the door behind them, Roper ushered Sam down the row of stalls to the widest one and slid the stall gate open far enough for the two men to step inside.

A bay roan stallion raised its majestic head and swung around to face them—not aggressively, but the horse was clearly nervous, showing the whites of its large, expressive eyes.

"This is One in a Million," Roper said. "Some people think a horse is just a big, dumb block of bones and muscle. But horses are highly intelligent and as sensitive as humans. They can feel fear, tenderness, anger, loyalty, even grief. Frank raised this big boy, trained him, and was the only one who rode him in competition. There was a lifetime bond there. Seeing his owner attacked and killed had to be traumatic for him. As you might guess, he's still in shock. We're trying to ease him through it, but it's taking time."

Sam studied the stallion. He knew next to nothing about horses, but even he could recognize a superb animal. "That's a beautiful horse," he said.

"He's the perfect American quarter horse," Roper said. "They're bred for working cattle—sturdy limbs and body, strong neck, angled to keep the head down and focused on their job. And talk about smart—One in a Million may be pretty, but he's a champion because of his intelligence and what they call cow sense. He's been a winner in both reining and cow cutting. I came here too late to see him compete, but I was told that even without a rider, he could work cattle the way a Border collie works sheep."

"So he doesn't compete anymore?"

"I still put him through his paces every day, but he's retired to the breeding shed. His sons and daughters have racked up millions in winnings for their owners."

"The breeding shed. I understand that's pretty much gone high-tech these days." Sam had seen the *Yellowstone* episode with cowboy Jimmy collecting semen on the 6666 Ranch.

"That's right. Breeding these performances horses is mostly done in the lab now. Frank would still do a natural breeding for a price. But when I heard that the 6666 Ranch had gone entirely to artificial insemination and IVF, I decided it was time to make the same change. When you're dealing with powerful, half-million-dollar horses, the natural way is too dangerous. There's too much risk that an injury could end an animal's valuable breeding career."

"So, like so many things these days, the bottom line is money."

"Sadly . . ." Roper had moved to the stallion's head. He stroked the satiny neck, calming the horse for the moment as he whispered comforting phrases. "But it's not just about money. This is more than a sport. This is passion to the point of obsession. There's a whole lifestyle built around these horses. So no, money is just the fuel that keeps the show running. It matters, but so do other things." Abruptly, he turned toward the stall gate. "Time to get back to training. Come and watch if you want. Just stay out of the way and don't interrupt me."

As they left the stall, Roper latching the gate behind them, Sam was struck by a new thought. One in a Million had been witness to a brutal murder. He couldn't speak. But what if the stallion could recognize and react to the person who had killed his owner? It wouldn't provide legal proof of anything. But at least, Sam speculated, it might point him in the right direction.

By the time Roper left work in his truck, the sky was streaked with ribbons of sunset. He was bone weary, but the day had been all right. The extra training session with Million Dollar Baby had been nearly perfect. And the interview with the FBI agent had gone as well as expected. He agreed with Lila's assessment of Sam Rafferty. There was more to the low-key federal man than met the eye. He appeared to be a keen observer who played his cards close to his vest.

As he used the remote to pass through the ranch gate, he glanced back toward the house. The lights were on in the dining room where, over dinner, Lila would be planning Frank's memorial with her family, probably fighting off their attacks on her right to her late husband's ranch—the ranch whose reputation she'd helped to build.

If he'd been included, he would have stood by her, defending her from their jabs. But he knew better. This was family, and Lila would be on her own. She was a strong woman, stronger than her weak stepchildren. But she was outnumbered. And when their mother showed up, the real battle for the Culhane Ranch would begin. Roper had never met Madeleine Carlyle Culhane, but he'd been given to understand that she was a formidable woman with an army of lawyers at her command.

And right now, all he could do for Lila was take care of her horses.

As he neared the home ranch in the deepening twilight, he could see the familiar vehicles clustered in the yard— the motor home, the long horse trailer, the pickup, and two four-wheelers that went on the circuit with the entourage of young McKennas. His brothers and sister were home from the rodeo in Fort Worth.

Roper parked to one side and climbed out of his truck. The aroma of his mother's chicken and dumplings teased his hunger. Rachel always made an effort to have a good meal ready when her children came home.

The boys were lounging on the porch, Stetson and Rowdy on the swing and Chance draped over a chair, with the dog at his feet. Their grins told Roper, without asking, that the rodeo had gone well for them. Cocky little devils.

But Roper was genuinely fond of them and celebrated their victories. The trailer was empty, the horses put away. There was no sign of Cheyenne. She was probably inside.

"We heard about that old bastard, Frank, on TV." Stetson, dark, wiry, and agile, was in line for the PRCA bull riding championship. "So somebody hated him enough to murder him. At least it wasn't us."

How did Cheyenne take the news? Roper held back the question he knew better than to ask his brothers. "Frank was a good boss. He was always fair with me. I'm genuinely sorry he's gone. What did you have against him?"

"Just the way he'd come by here and look down on us, treat us like we were dirt." Rowdy rode saddle broncs. He and Chance, who was barely out of high school, were national leaders in team roping. Chance was also a young wizard with a rope.

"And he was always sniffing around Cheyenne," Chance said. "He even sent her flowers. It was creepy. He was old enough to be her father—hell, almost old enough to be her grandpa."

"Did anything ever come of that?" Roper couldn't resist asking.

"He wanted to take her under his wing and train her for reining and cutting competitions," Stetson said. "He told her that with her talent, he could make her one of the greatest horsewomen in the country and a big money winner. Cheyenne turned him down cold. She wanted to do rodeo with us."

"And when was this?"

"While you were selling our Colorado ranch. By the time you got here, Frank had given up, and Cheyenne was on the circuit with us. End of story. Especially now that Frank's dead."

Chance's grin widened. "And now Mom says you're working for his widow—the *oo-la-la* Lila Culhane. How's that going?"

"Fine. I've got a job to do, and I'm getting paid for it."

Roper went on inside to wash up. He found his sister in the dining room with their parents. She was setting the table. His mother was tending the stove. His father, seated at the table's head, was dribbling Jack Daniel's into his coffee cup.

Cheyenne's sun-browned hands arranged the napkins and silverware on the sides of the plates. She was small in stature, but her fined-boned body was tough and sinewy. A cloud of dark hair, almost black, framed a face with a full, impetuous mouth and Elizabeth Taylor eyes that were dark instead of violet.

Dressed simply in fitted jeans and a faded denim shirt, with no makeup or jewelry, she was a young woman whose beauty and intensity drew eyes to the arena whenever she competed in barrel racing, breakaway roping, or other women's events. Even now, that intensity seemed to burn in her, almost shimmering in the room. Would it last? Roper found himself wondering. Or sometime in the future, would she burn out and drop like a falling star?

"Your sister got an offer from *Vogue* magazine to pose for a fashion shoot," Rachel said. "I told her she should accept. The money would be good, and the magazine issue could open up doors for her."

"Too late." Cheyenne folded the last paper napkin. "I already turned them down. High fashion—the makeup, the jewelry, and those silly costumes—it just isn't me."

"Look around you." Rachel's gaze took in her disabled husband at the table. "Rodeo doesn't last forever. An injury, or even a run of bad luck, could end your career tomorrow. You need to back up your options."

"I'll think about that later. For now, I'm right where I want to be."

"How did the rodeo go for you, Sis?" Roper changed the subject.

"All right." She gave him a smile. "Jezebel and I came close to a record in the barrel racing—thirteen point nine seconds." Jezebel was the beloved palomino mare she'd raised and trained for the sport. "But I missed a throw and came in second in breakaway. I need to work on that. Chance is going to coach me."

"Dinner's ready," Rachel said. "Go and get your brothers, Cheyenne."

Minutes later, the family was holding hands around the table, sharing the grace that Rowdy had been asked to say. As they helped themselves to chicken and dumplings, homemade rolls, and a fresh salad from Rachel's protected garden, Roper reminded himself of how his family kept him grounded. This was a world apart from the craziness and constant pressure of working for the Culhanes. Sometimes, like tonight, it was what he needed.

As for Roper's worries about Cheyenne and her possible involvement with Frank, he would put them to rest for now. Stetson's story made sense. Frank had wanted to take her from her family and make her his protégée. He could imagine that her parents would resent him for that. But Cheyenne had turned him down. End of story. And with so much in limbo at his workplace, Roper had more urgent concerns.

Sam had spent the rest of the afternoon watching Roper train horses and interviewing the stable workers. He was enjoying the evening coolness on the porch of the bungalow when Jasmine showed up with his dinner on a covered tray. Her washed hair was loose, her blood-spattered clothes replaced with plain gray sweats, her face bare of makeup. The effect was wholesomely sexy. Sam struggled to ignore the pleasantly warm stirrings in the depths of his body. This woman was a suspect in his murder case, and today she'd demonstrated the strength and reflexes to kill.

"Mariah's lasagna. It's the best." She placed the tray on the small outdoor table and sank into the empty chair next to Sam. "Sorry, I tried to get you a dinner invitation, but Lila put her foot down, said it was family and none of your business. I think the pressure is getting to her." Reaching out, she lifted the cover off the tray and set it aside. "Enjoy it while it's hot. I've long since eaten."

"Thanks." Sam was hungry; and the lasagna, served with green salad and garlic bread, was superb. "My compliments to Mariah," he said.

"She's the one you should talk to." Jasmine leaned back in the chair, stretching like a cat. "Mariah's been with the family since the early days of my parents' marriage. She knows the history of this place and the people in it. But getting it out of her won't be easy. She's nothing if not discreet."

"I get that," Sam said. "So far, she's barely given me the time of day. I get the feeling she doesn't like having a nosy stranger here, stirring things up."

"I imagine you're right. But for what it's worth, *I* welcome you here. I want justice for my father. You're my best chance of getting it."

"Thanks for the endorsement. I'm beginning to wonder if this investigation is getting anywhere. I know I'm not supposed to discuss the case, but so far, no one seems to be the right fit."

"Everything will come together, Sam. I have faith in you." He caught her use of his first name and let it go. After their time together, it felt all right.

"How did the family dinner go?"

"Testy, but no blood spilled. Darrin and Simone tried to back Lila into a corner over the memorial plans, who is to speak, and what can or can't be said. She held her own in favor of an open invitation for anyone to come forward. As I've told you, I despise what the woman did to our family. But I can't help wishing I had her strength. Lila is one tough cookie. But she can't hold out forever. Wait till our mother gets here."

"I'll be looking forward to meeting her," Sam said.

By the time he finished his meal, Jasmine had made no move to leave. Sam found himself hoping she would stay longer.

"Tell me a little more about yourself, Jasmine," he said, popping open the can of iced Michelob that had come with the meal. There was an extra. He extended it to her. She took it. "It must've been interesting, making those movies and TV shows, meeting those stars."

"It was a job, and they were just people—most of them nice, a few of them assholes. I married one of the latter. We lasted through a miscarriage before we agreed to part ways. Probably for the best. I don't know what kind of mom I would have been. For a while, I stayed in Hollywood hoping to revive my so-called career. All I could get were a few TV commercials. So I'd come home on and off to lick my wounds before trying again. You probably see me as a spoiled brat. And there is that side to me. Dad always gave me whatever I asked for. But this isn't the real me—not the me I want to be."

"After spending time with you, I'm aware of that, Jasmine. You're smart and strong. You'll make it through this."

"Thanks for that endorsement." She laid a hand on his

sleeve. Her touch was light, barely a butterfly's. But it sent a sensual jolt along his nerves that rippled through his body. The memory of holding her this afternoon flashed in his mind.

"Just don't get into trouble," he added, trying to dampen his reaction to her. "Getting mixed up with those animal rights people could set you way back."

"I understand." Her noncommittal reply told Sam she was still weighing her choices. From beyond the ranch's far border, toward Charlie Grishman's ranch, came the faint sound of rifle fire. She shuddered but didn't speak of it.

"You owe me, Sam," she said after a silent pause. "I spilled a private piece of myself to you. I don't care if you are an untouchable FBI agent; you'd be a jerk not to reciprocate."

Sam sighed.

"Do you have a wife back in Chicago? Any children? That's something I deserve to know."

"I have an ex-wife in Chicago—no children. Great woman, but she wanted more of me than I had time to give her. She was tired of competing with my work. It's been five months, and she's already remarried."

"That had to hurt," Jasmine said. "Do you still love her?"

"In a way, I always will. But not like I did. I just want her to be happy. I'm moving on. But some things take time."

"I'm impressed that you don't hate her."

"Don't be. There was nothing to hate. She was unhappy and she changed her life the way she saw fit."

"Are you still friends?"

"She wanted a clean break. Looking back, I can see the wisdom in that."

"So we're both walking wounded—you more than I, I

think." The hand rested on his arm, then withdrew. "What brought you here to Texas? A fresh start?"

"Just a chance for a transfer. It was time." Sam watched the golden rim of the moon rise above the eastern hills. Here he was, alone with a seductive woman whose presence suggested that she might be willing to engage in more than small talk. But no, it was too soon for him. And Jasmine Culhane was a prime suspect in his murder case. To lay as much as a finger on her would be professional suicide.

The urge to open up—to pour out the anguish of his young partner's recent death—welled in him. For a moment Sam was tempted to tell her the story. But no, it was still too raw, too intimate to share with a woman he'd only known for a day. Some things, like deep grief and scathing guilt, were better kept to himself.

But Jasmine was getting to him in more ways than one. It was time to send her back to the house before he gave in to temptation. He stretched and yawned. "The last time I slept was on an airplane," he said. "If you'll excuse me, Jasmine, I need to go to bed before I fall off this chair. Thanks for dinner and your company."

"Of course." She rose, replaced the cover, and picked up the tray. For a long moment she stood in silence as if weighing a confession. Then she spoke.

"I know you didn't get much rest in that old horror of a motel, with the wind outside and that infernal racket from the next room."

Sam's jaw dropped.

"I saw your car," she said. "I was with this sleazy cowboy I picked up in Willow Bend, both of us drinking. When things started to get out of hand, I left. I guess he did, too. I never plan to see him again. I'm not proud of myself, but I'll be damned if I'm going to apologize."

Sam found his voice. "No apology needed, Jasmine. I imagine you were working out your grief any way you could. And what you did was none of my . . ."

The words trailed off as he realized she'd vanished into the night.

What was I thinking?
She hadn't been thinking. That was the trouble.

Jasmine returned the tray to the kitchen, walked out to the patio, and sank into a chair by the pool. The shimmering water reflected the image of the moon like a gold coin dropped into its depths.

That very morning, she'd sworn off involvements with men. She should have reminded herself of that tonight when she'd brought Sam his dinner and stayed to talk. After the parade of jocks, cowboys, and Hollywood types who'd drawn her in and battered her pride over the years, Sam Rafferty was like few men she'd ever known—strong and steady, masculine, intelligent, and gentle. If she let him, he could wreck her heart.

But the man was untouchable. Even if she could heal the pain of his recent divorce—and she wasn't bad at such things—Sam was here for one reason. It wasn't romance or even mindless, no-strings-attached sex. He was here to solve a murder, a job that demanded laserlike focus. She wouldn't be doing him any favors by trying to distract him—especially when she herself could be a suspect.

As the daughter of Frank Culhane, Jasmine had grown up getting whatever she asked for, even when it came to men. But this time the answer was no.

CHAPTER EIGHT

The next morning, after coffee and sourdough toast in the Culhane kitchen, Sam took the Jeep and left for the McKenna Ranch. He'd hoped for the chance to speak with Mariah, but the crusty, middle-aged cook had been busy and brusque, ignoring his efforts to get her attention. Something told Sam that catching her at a good time was never going to happen. For now, he would let it ride and look elsewhere.

As he drove past the house, Sam could see no sign of Jasmine. Maybe she was rethinking last night's confession. Maybe that confession had been her version of goodbye.

Not that it mattered. This was the twenty-first century. It wasn't uncommon for a woman to pick up a strange man in a bar for sex. As he'd said to her, maybe it had been her way of grieving.

He had no claim on the free-spirited Jasmine. Still, what he viewed as a self-destructive act grated on him, almost making him wish he could unhear her story.

Whatever her reasons, she'd been good company yesterday. Alone, Sam found himself missing her sunny, passionate presence. But right now, he had a job to do.

If the Culhane place, with its grand house, reminded

Sam of *Gone with the Wind,* the McKenna spread looked more like his idea of an actual ranch. There was no well-watered lawn, shrubbery, or flowers. The sprawling frame house wanted paint. But the new stable and fences were built to last, with good quality materials and workmanship. The towering windmill turned soundlessly in the light morning breeze.

The dusty yard was cluttered with vehicles—the expensive horse trailer pulled by a heavy-duty pickup, a motor home, a pair of four-wheelers, a specially equipped van with wheelchair plates, and a well-used Ford Escort. Roper wouldn't be here. Sam had already seen him at the Culhanes'. But his younger siblings were in evidence around the yard, doing chores and exercising their horses. One young man was practicing with a rope, twirling, looping it, and tossing the lasso over the fence posts. These weren't regular ranch kids, Sam reminded himself. They were celebrities, rodeo royalty. He was looking forward to meeting the parents who had raised them.

In the paddock, a petite, dark-haired brunette was putting her palomino mare through a series of dashes and turns. Sam recognized her at once. In person, she was even more striking than in her photos.

As he approached the fence, she pulled up her horse. "I take it you're Agent Rafferty," she said. "Roper mentioned you might be paying us a visit. Our parents are in the house. Just ring the doorbell. They'll be expecting you."

Sam thanked her and crossed the yard to the porch. He was curious about these talented young people. But he needed to remember that he was here to investigate a crime.

An aging mongrel dog thumped its tail as he crossed the porch. Sam bent down and scratched its ears before ringing the bell.

The woman who opened the door was dressed in faded jeans and a worn, plaid cotton shirt. Her classic features suggested that, like her daughter, she might have been a beauty once. But it appeared that hard work, childbearing, and frugal living had leached the joy out of her. Tall and lean, like her sons, she exuded an aura of self-sacrifice. This woman, Sam surmised, had given everything to her family. The rewards were outside in the yard and on the wall of rodeo trophies he glimpsed through the opening into the next room. Surely the young McKennas were bringing in plenty of cash in prizes and endorsement offers, but he saw no evidence of it here.

Her features softened but remained guarded as she opened the door wider and welcomed Sam into a home that was sparsely furnished but immaculately clean. As Sam presented his credentials, she gave him a smile and extended her hand. Her grip was as strong as he'd expected. "Rachel McKenna, the mother of this outfit," she said.

"Have a seat at our kitchen table." She pulled out an unmatched chair. "You can talk with my husband, Kirby— he's the head of the family. And you look like you could use a hunk of chocolate cake with some fresh coffee."

"I wouldn't turn that down, ma'am." Sam took the seat she'd offered and greeted the man who sat across from him.

Sam had learned to recognize a chronic alcoholic when he saw one. Kirby McKenna had all the earmarks—the bloodshot eyes, the florid nose, the glazed expression as he dribbled whiskey into his coffee cup. Jasmine had mentioned that he was a disabled bull rider. He appeared to be in some pain.

Sam sensed that he'd been an impressive man. Small and wiry, like most bull riders, his dark coloring suggested mixed ancestry—maybe Spanish or Native American. He had clearly passed his looks to his children, especially his daughter. Sam was aware that Roper, older, taller, and huskier than his agile siblings, was a stepson.

Kirby spoke to Sam without preamble. "We're sorry Frank is dead, but we sure as hell didn't have anything to do with killing him. Cheyenne and the boys were on the road. And Roper was here all night. We know because the dog was barking at a skunk outside, and Roper got up to chase it off before the dumb mutt could get sprayed. Besides, Roper always said Frank was a decent boss. They got along fine."

A generous slab of chocolate cake had appeared in front of Sam like magic. The first bite melted in his mouth. "What about your family's relationship with Frank?" he asked. "Your boys told me he tried to get Cheyenne to train with him."

"She said no. We wouldn't have let her if she'd said yes. She was too young for that decision."

"We're protective of our children," Rachel said. "We've raised them by the Good Book. It takes a lot of trust to send them out to those rodeos, but it's what they want. They look out for each other, and when they come home, they give us a full accounting."

"We don't give a damn about the Culhanes and their fancy lifestyle," Kirby said. "The big house, the cars, those million-dollar test tube-bred horses. They look down their snooty noses at our family, but we've got something they'll never have."

"Look at Frank's kids," Rachel said. "A washed-up actress and a small-time lawyer who'll probably spend his life working for the family. Our children were raised with goals. They're champions. More important, they're decent, respectable people."

Sam made more small talk while he'd finished the deca-
dent cake. Something told him he wasn't going to get any
more out of the McKennas. Either he'd hit a stone wall, or
they were simply telling him the truth.

He put away his notes, stood, and thanked them for
their hospitality. "Best chocolate cake I ever had. My compliments," he said. "Before I go, do either of you have a
final word to say about Frank's murder? Do you have any
idea who might have killed him?"

Kirby took a sip from his stained coffee mug. "All I can
say is, aside from being Roper's boss, Frank was nothing
to us. Just a rich neighbor who barely gave us the time of
day. I don't give a rat's ass that he's dead. It doesn't change
anything for our family."

"You asked who might have killed him," Rachel said.
"My money's on the widow. That ex-showgirl may have
been hot stuff once, but she's no spring chicken anymore.
Frank was probably getting tired of her, looking around
for a sexy young thing to replace her. She had to do something before he put her out to pasture. At least that's my
two cents' worth."

"I'll take that under consideration." Sam left them and
went out to the Jeep. As he drove away, he glimpsed two
of the young McKennas in his side mirror. They were still
practicing their rodeo skills.

Lila stood in the late-day shadows at the edge of the
arena, watching Roper give the mare her extra practice
session. Million Dollar Baby was their best hope—maybe
their only hope—of winning the upcoming shootout and
qualifying Roper for Frank's place in the Run for a Million. The ranch was depending on her. Her reining performance would have to be flawless, as well as fast. Roper
would be allowed to bring two backup horses to the com-

petition. The horses were experienced performers. But they lacked the flash and dazzle that made Baby a star in the arena.

She was a beautiful mare. A daughter of One in a Million, she had her sire's glistening roan body with an all-white face—a marking known as bald—from her mother's line of champions. She was pure aristocrat, and smart like her famous father—maybe smarter, with the extra lick of common sense given to females.

Watching Baby perform her graceful turns, dashes, and heart-stopping slides was a pleasure. But Lila's gaze was drawn to the man—his erect posture in the saddle, the set of his head, the breadth of his shoulders, the hand, leg, and heel movements that were barely visible as he directed the mare with subtle cues.

Roper's focus was total. If he was aware of Lila watching him, he gave no sign of it. She remained quiet. A young groom waited at the stable entrance to take the mare after the workout. Million Dollar Baby would be the final horse out at the end of a long day. Once she was rubbed down and put away, the last hired worker would leave. The stable would fall into stillness until dawn.

At the end of the routine, Roper walked the mare to cool her down, checked her limbs and hooves for soundness, and turned her over to the groom, who would lead her back to her stall and put her away. Roper remained in the arena, standing in a slanting light ray as if waiting. He'd probably been aware of her presence all along, Lila reasoned as she stepped into sight and walked toward him.

He met her partway. His face was beaded with perspiration, his gray cotton shirt plastered to his torso after a day of working in the heat. The scent of horses and masculine sweat clung to his body, teasing her senses.

"Hello, Boss." His voice was weary, with an undertone

of what could almost be taken as tenderness. But Lila knew better. Theirs was a business relationship, advantageous to them both as long as they maintained strict boundaries.

"Baby's looking good," she said.

"Baby will have to be perfect, and lucky, to have any chance of winning the shootout. Every top rider who hasn't qualified for the Million Run will be competing for Frank's spot. On any given night there's bound to be somebody who's better than we are. I've been drilling the backup horses, Topper and Sly, too." He used the short nicknames for the two geldings. "But this will be Baby's prize to win."

Lila glanced back to make sure the groom had taken the mare and gone. "Walk with me," she said.

He followed her across the arena, his fingertips just brushing the small of her back. They rarely touched, but Lila felt the light contact shimmer through her. She stopped at the rail on the arena's open west side. A fiery sunset lit the sky with slashes of crimson, gold, and violet.

"Our FBI man cornered me on the patio today," she said. "This time it was gloves off. He went after every detail of my relationship with Frank and where I was when he was killed."

"What did you tell him?"

"As little as possible. But I know he believes I murdered my husband to get control of the ranch."

"You should be safe. There's been no evidence to place you at the scene."

"You believe it, too, don't you?" She swung to face him. "You believe I murdered Frank, but as long as you deny it, you can go ahead and work toward your dream. I'm not a fool, Roper. As long as it serves you, you'll turn a blind eye to anything."

"Damn it, Lila—" Frustration darkened his handsome features. "What is it you want from me?"

"A little faith and trust would be nice. But I'm not feeling that from you."

He exhaled wearily. "All right. Tell me you didn't kill Frank. I'll defend you to my last breath, and I'll never question it again."

"You don't understand." She backed away a step. "That's not enough. It's not what I'm asking."

"Lila, what—" His hand closed on her arm, pulling her back toward him. His eyes burned into hers.

"Mr. McKenna." The voice of the groom came from the far side of the arena. "Million Dollar Baby's in her stall with food and water. I'm leaving now."

"That's fine, Megan. Thanks. You can go."

By the time Roper finished his reply, Lila had pulled away and stalked off.

Lila knew she was the most obvious suspect, and there was no one to verify that she hadn't left the house, met her husband in the stable, and carried out a plan that might get her sentenced to life in prison.

Despite her resolve to remain strong, Lila was scared.

Sam Rafferty was anxious to wrap up the case. He had zeroed in on her as his prime suspect. With Frank's family and friends closing in for the funeral and memorial, this was the last kind of trouble she needed.

As she neared the wrought-iron gate to the patio, she felt her phone vibrate in her pocket. Taking it out, she checked the display.

The caller was Jemma, her daughter.

She let the call go to voice mail. She would call back from the security of her bedroom upstairs.

Jemma was a nursing student at Texas Christian University in Fort Worth. Lila had done her best to distance her twenty-year-old daughter from the messy situation brought on by Frank's death. But Jemma watched the news. She would be concerned.

In her room, Lila closed the door, sank onto the edge of the bed, and returned the call.

"Mom?" Jemma's fresh young voice was like a sip of water in the desert. "Are you all right? I haven't heard from you since right after Frank died. I was getting worried."

"I'm soldiering on as always, darling. Sorry I haven't called. Just a lot to deal with, funeral arrangements and all. I didn't want to disturb your studies."

"Studies, schmudies. I'm your only blood family. I heard about the memorial service, and I'll be coming to support you. Somebody has to."

"No—please just stay away," Lila protested. "That memorial will be a mob scene. And Madeleine will surely be coming. Things could get ugly. I don't need the extra worry that you might get caught up in the mess."

"Stop arguing, Mom. I'm not a little girl anymore. I'm coming, and I will be there for you." The faint sound of background voices filtered over the phone. "Gotta go. I'll call you later."

The call ended. Slipping the phone back into her pocket, Lila rose and walked out through the French doors onto the balcony that overlooked the patio. She'd truly hoped to keep Jemma at school, away from the conflict and the vicious comments that the girl was bound to hear. But her daughter was stubborn. She would be here, and her presence would be just one more worry.

The moon was rising over the eastern hills, flooding the parched landscape with ghostly light. From the direction of Charlie Grishman's game farm came the sound of rifle fire. Lila hated the thought of those poor, cruelly used animals, many of them overgrown pets, dying in terror and pain. Given her way, she would wipe Charlie and his kind from the earth and sentence them to their own special hell where animals with guns drove them through thickets of thorny mesquite and cholla.

But tonight, she only felt a sense of helplessness. It would be all she could do to save herself.

The tiger had been old and toothless, with half of a rear paw missing from a youthful encounter with a trap. Now it was dead, and Charlie's client, a fifty-year-old female hedge fund manager from Austin, was over the moon.

"I got him!" she warbled to the girlfriend who'd come to watch the hunt. "That hide is going on my bed!"

Charlie stood back, mentally counting the small mountain of cash she'd given him. He could only be grateful that he'd managed to sell a hunt with that tiger before it passed on its own.

Before the hunt, the tiger had been prodded into a cage and hauled to a brushy, isolated area of the ranch surrounded by barbed wire. With the cage camouflaged by brush, local boys dressed as old-time African bearers accompanied the woman to the shooting site, where they made enough noise to scare the miserable creature out of the cage; it promptly fled and hid in a clump of mesquite. More shouts and the throwing of sticks and rocks chased the tiger back into the open where the woman was poised with Charlie's .270 Winchester, waiting to shoot it.

Unfortunately, she had neither a cool head nor a good aim.

She'd fired twice, hitting the tiger once in the shoulder and once in the flank. The animal had gone down, badly injured but still alive. With the fake bearers covering them, Charlie had guided her closer, pointed the muzzle toward the animal's head, and ordered her to pull the trigger. The last shot had done its work.

After that had come the celebratory whoops of jubilation and plenty of photos, which she would no doubt post on the Internet. After the traditional whiskey in the reception area, the woman and her friend had been escorted to their vehicle. The tiger's carcass had been loaded behind a four-wheeler and hauled to the refrigerated shed, where the taxidermist would come by in the morning to skin it and collect the hide for tanning. The woman, whose name Charlie had already forgotten, would be notified when her bed rug was ready.

All in a night's work.

Before turning in, Charlie performed his nightly ritual of walking the animal compounds, making sure the pens were locked and the animals secure. He had close to thirty of them, mostly African and Asian species, but all of them purchased or collected here in the U.S. from owners who needed the money or no longer wanted the creatures because they'd grown too big, too old, too expensive to keep, or too aggressive.

There were three giraffes in a pen—popular because they were easy to hunt and made spectacular trophies. There were zebras and a variety of antelopes. One pen held two chimpanzees, another a male gorilla, nearly full-grown and almost certainly illegal, but a prospective hunter had already put a claim on it. There was even a two-humped camel, though who might want to kill it was something Charlie could only imagine.

The stench of animal waste and spoiling meat rose from the pens in the carnivore compound. There were mostly cats here, Charlie's stock in trade. They were easy to buy and always in demand. He had three more tigers, although none of them were as big as the one the woman had just shot. There were lions, too. Hunters would pay more for a maned male. A lioness was cheaper but still thrilling to hunt. Leopards and cheetahs were more expensive because they were harder to find. A separate compound held the goats, chickens, and rabbits he raised to feed the meat eaters. And he wasn't above hauling home an occasional roadkill if it was fresh enough.

The really big animals—rhino, elephant, hippo, and Cape buffalo—couldn't be contained here. But Charlie was negotiating for an elephant, used for rides in a road-side zoo. Somebody would pay good money to shoot one, even an Indian elephant.

As Charlie passed one heavily fortified pen, the animal inside lunged at him, crashing against the heavy wooden posts, snarling and slavering. It was a hyena—hulking, vicious, and as ugly as sin. Who in their right mind would want such a hideous trophy?

Charlie's employees were afraid of it. He'd considered killing the hyena himself, just to get rid of the troublesome beast. But there were people out there, maybe fantasy geeks, who would get into hunting and killing a real live monster. He just needed to get their attention. Maybe tomorrow he would post online notices on a few of their sites and see who might take the bait.

After locking the compound gates, he mounted the veranda of the frame building that served as his business headquarters and his home. Pouring himself a generous three fingers of whiskey, he stood at the rail, sipping as he gazed across the rolling open land toward the distant lights of the Culhane place.

Earlier today he'd had a visit from that FBI fellow, Rafferty. Not that he'd had much to tell the man. He and Frank had shared no love, he'd said, and he wasn't sorry the arrogant bastard was dead. But Charlie had sworn that he hadn't killed Frank. He was too busy making money.

Rafferty had looked down at Charlie as if he were something he'd found stuck to his shoe, thanked him for his time, and left. With luck, he wouldn't be back. He'd clearly been repelled by everything he saw.

Charlie finished the whiskey in a single gulp, feeling the mellow burn all the way down his throat. He was putting more money into investments every week. But he wouldn't be in this bloody business forever. It was only his path to a bigger dream.

Like a street kid gazing into a store window, Charlie fixed his gaze on the distant lights. He wanted what the Culhanes had—not their vast wealth, which he would never have, but a fine home, tailored clothes, enviable cars, influential friends, and respect. Most of all, respect.

He wanted respect even more than he wanted *her*.

What was she doing now? Was she sleeping, her glorious hair spread on the pillow? Was she with that FBI bastard, Rafferty? He could tell that she liked him, but he would be gone soon.

Was she thinking about their encounter on the road when she'd shot the gazelle? He'd been furious at the time, but her spunk and courage had impressed him deeply. And the sight of that fine blood spray on her bare legs had almost driven him mad with lust.

He had wanted Jasmine Culhane since her high school days, when she'd sat in the front row of his algebra class, her skirt hiked up a little to show him those arousal-triggering legs. She'd done it on purpose, the little flirt. But when he'd tried to get friendly outside of class, she'd barely given him the time of day.

Charlie's visitors and workers had given him second-hand reports on the Culhanes and their situation. He was aware that now Jasmine would be vulnerable—her father gone, the rest of her family grappling for control. She was figuratively alone, with no one to support her. Now would be the time to let her know that she had his sympathy, and maybe more. The gesture would at least crack open the closed door between them. Maybe it would even rev up the simmering attraction he'd always felt from her.

He wouldn't be welcome at Frank's memorial. But there would be a mob of people there. He'd been a teacher. He knew how to socialize. He could blend in and try to get to her.

If ever there had been a chance to make her his, it was coming.

CHAPTER NINE

The next afternoon, Frank Culhane's mortal remains were laid to rest next to his parents in the hilltop graveyard that Elias Culhane had chosen, leveled on top, and fenced for his progeny. Elias had clearly expected to have a tribe of descendants, like biblical Abraham. There was abundant space for more graves, most of it empty.

Wearing a veiled hat and the black dress suit she'd bought years ago when her mother-in-law passed away, Lila stood beside the open grave. The hot sun beat down on her like a hammer. Dust swirled around her, covering the low-heeled black pumps she'd worn for the walk up the steep, winding trail.

The casket had arrived earlier than expected, in a mortuary van with a single driver. The funeral directors had probably expected her to wait for them tomorrow, but Lila had made the decision to bury him that afternoon. Frank had never stood on ceremony. He'd always said he didn't want to be left lying around for people to gawk at. And he hadn't wanted his casket sealed in a concrete vault. But she was already wondering if she'd been too hasty. There would be criticism from his friends, his children, and from Madeleine, who had yet to arrive at the ranch.

Was that why she'd been in such a hurry to bury Frank? To get it done before Madeleine could barge in, call a halt, and take over? Or had she just wanted to get a painful step out of the way and move on to the memorial—bury the body, preserve the memory?

The van driver had brought the floral arrangement—red roses—for the casket. At least there would be pretty color on the grave. The compact-size backhoe, used to bury horses, had been called into service for the digging. Darrin and Roper had put aside their feud to act as pallbearers. Even Sam Rafferty had been called to help at the last minute. The other men needed to carry the casket up the hill had been recruited from among the stable hands.

Now the stable hands had been dismissed. Roper and Sam had stepped outside the wrought-iron fence to observe from a respectful distance. Mariah had been invited but had chosen to stay in the kitchen and prepare a late luncheon of sandwiches and salad.

The Culhane family stood at the graveside—Lila in the middle, Jasmine on her left, Darrin, with Simone clasping his arm, on her right. Both of them had argued against Frank's prompt burial but the legal choice had been Lila's.

She could almost feel the hostility radiating from both sides. For someone flanked by family members, she felt very much alone.

Frank hadn't been a religious man. There was no minister or clergyman present. Lila and his children had agreed that each of them would say a few words of farewell. At least they'd agreed on something.

Darrin spoke first, his voice charged with emotion that might or might not be real. Lila had seen no sign of grief in him, only the drive to claim what had been his father's. But then, everyone grieved in their own way.

"Goodbye, Dad," he said. "You were always bigger

than life to me. All I ever wanted was to live up to your expectations. Now that you're gone, it will be up to me to carry on your legacy as head of the Culhane family. I promise to see your murderer brought to justice. I promise to see this ranch restored to our family, with everything as it should be. I promise . . ." He trailed off. "Rest in peace, Dad. We've got this."

Lila exhaled the breath she'd been holding. She'd hoped that hostilities could be put aside until after the memorial, but the proverbial line in the sand had been drawn. War had been declared, and the first shot had been fired right over Frank's casket.

Jasmine was wrapped in an immense black cashmere shawl that covered whatever she was wearing underneath. It hid her like a burqa. That was clearly what she wanted, to hide. Lila understood. But the shawl had to be stifling in this infernal heat.

"Goodbye, Dad." She sounded as if she might have been weeping, but then, she was an actress. "After all the things you did for me, I never got the chance to thank you. You were my hero, and I was your baby girl. But I've been a baby too long. Now that you're gone, it's grow-up time. I promise to find a path and make something of my life— not just to succeed but to contribute. I promise justice for your death. And I promise to put things back as they should be in your house. If you can hear me, Dad, I will make you proud of me. You'll see."

Another shot fired, this one more subtle but definitely aimed at her, Lila thought. Did Frank's children believe that she'd killed their father? Probably, since it would serve their purpose—unless one of them had done it.

Now it was her turn. But she wasn't going to rise to the bait. This was no place for a battle. Lila stepped closer to the edge of the grave and cleared her throat.

"You were always your own man, Frank. I loved you, and in your own way, I know you loved me. But there was a part of you that was unreadable and unreachable. We weren't perfect, but we had enough love going to hold us together. Thank you for the good times. Thank you for teaching me to love your beautiful horses. If there's one promise I swear to keep, it's that I will fight to protect those horses and continue your legacy of beauty, sportsmanship, and dedication." She drew a sharp breath, trying not to think of Frank's betrayal. Denial was a powerful drug.

"Goodbye, Frank," she said. "Rest easy. Be at peace."

Had she said the right things? Roper stood a stone's toss behind her, outside the fence. The look on his face would answer her question. But she couldn't depend on Roper for validation or anything else except where the horses were concerned. That was his domain. She would have to make sure it was his only domain. This was no time to depend on a man.

Sam had remained silent and inscrutable through the ritual, empty-handed but surely taking mental notes about what had been said, who had shown emotion, and who, like Lila, had kept grief veiled by cool composure. If she'd broken down and wept, would that have changed his mind? Would he still believe, as he appeared to, that she had murdered her husband?

Turning away from the grave, Lila pulled off the veiled hat and passed through the gate. The party trooped after her along the trail that wound its way down the hill. Behind them, the miniature backhoe was already starting its engine to fill in the grave.

As they neared the bottom of the hill, the sound of an engine overhead riveted their gazes to the sky. Darrin groaned. "Oh, hell, it's the news chopper. The mortuary probably alerted them for a little free promo. At least they didn't get here in time to cover the burial!"

Hearing him, Lila felt a spark of satisfaction. If nothing else, she'd made one right decision today.

The TV news helicopter had landed in the pasture beyond the house. The three-person broadcast team—a cameraman, a sound man, and a chatty female reporter in a spotless white pantsuit, descended on the Culhanes where they'd gathered on the patio to await their delayed lunch. Roper had already returned to work in the arena.

Sam, who hadn't been invited to join them, stood well back from the fray, watching and listening. Not surprisingly, the antagonists had put up a united front for the press. What did surprise him was that the one stepping forward to speak for the family was Simone.

Dressed in a fitted black sheath, she'd removed her flattering, broad-brimmed hat and donned a wistful look that fell just short of smiling through tears. Sam couldn't help wondering if she'd practiced the sound bite in front of a mirror.

"Frank Culhane, my father-in-law, was a legend who represented the true spirit of our great state of Texas. It was his longtime wish to be buried without delay, next to his dear departed parents. In the days ahead, the people who knew him, loved him, and felt his influence will honor him with a memorial service—by invitation only, of course—at the Culhane Ranch. Then his family and friends will move on. But Frank's memory will remain always in our hearts. Thank you."

Maybe it was Simone who'd leaked news of the burial to the press. Darrin's wife was full of surprises. At least she appeared to have learned something in that finishing school.

Then there was Lila, stepping forward to dismiss the reporter and her crew. After allowing them a single long-distance shot of the grave with the rose arrangement laid atop the mound of fresh earth, she ordered them off the property.

"You've got enough for a spot on the late news. Now leave our family in peace to rest and mourn. No—no questions allowed at this time. And no interviews." Sam knew that she was talking about the murder. However the news crew might interpret her words, her fierce defense of her home had been unmistakable. Ten minutes later the chopper was in the air.

With a collective sigh of relief, the family sat down at the patio table, under the shade of the umbrella, while Mariah brought out their lunch. Jasmine had shed her enveloping wrap. Underneath she wore ripped jeans and a black tank top. That she hadn't bothered to dress for her father's burial could be interpreted as some kind of statement. But from what little Sam knew of the elusive Jasmine, it could mean anything, or nothing.

Sam had been taking his dinners at the bungalow and his other meals at the kitchen table. Now he stepped into the kitchen, where a place had been cleared and set for him at one corner.

Right now the kitchen was empty. But Mariah would be returning once the sandwiches, salad, and sodas were served. With emotions running high, this could be his best chance to catch her for an interview—if only she would cooperate. Over the past days, he'd done his best to win her trust. But even if he could, he respected the woman too much to try to trick her into talking.

A few minutes later, she came back into the kitchen. There were two sandwiches on the tray she carried. "It's leftovers for you and me, Mr. FBI man." She gave him a rare, tired smile. "Beef or chicken. Your choice."

"I'll take the beef." He left her the chicken.

Passing him a chilled Diet Coke, she sank into the chair across from him. "I know you need to talk to me as part of your investigation. Shall we get it over with now?"

Sam could have kissed her. He didn't have his laptop or his notes. He could only ask, listen, and hope to remember.

She sat across from him, a slightly plump woman in middle age, her silver-streaked hair pulled back in a bun from a face that was bare of makeup. After a lifetime of hard work, she looked strong and healthy. In her eyes and face, Sam glimpsed the pretty young girl she must have been years ago. In her own way, she was still beautiful. But if he were to say so, she might see it as manipulation.

"What are you looking at?" she asked.

"A woman who has lived a long story. A woman with secrets."

"A woman with secrets she'll never tell anyone. So don't even ask me. But if you promise to listen without judging and not interrupt too much, I'll give you a little family history and my part in it. Then we're done. Agreed?"

"Agreed. And I've learned not to judge—either in my work or in my life. Agreed." But if Mariah had hidden knowledge about Frank's murder, he would have to follow the law. He finished the sandwich and sipped the Diet Coke while he listened.

"I came to work here after Frank married Madeleine. It was actually my husband, Jackson, who was hired as head wrangler—they called it that back then. As his wife, I needed a job, too, so I was taken on as kitchen help. Juan Jose Estrada, the fine man who ran the kitchen, taught me everything he knew about cooking for the Culhanes before he retired and went home to his family in Chihuahua. Then his job became mine, as it has been ever since.

"Frank was already the head of the family. His father had passed on early, and his mother was an invalid who rarely left her room. I learned to make her tray—the tea just so, the poached egg and half slice of buttered toast—and take it to her every morning. Toward the end, she had a private nurse. Such a disagreeable woman!"

Questions swarmed in Sam's mind. He forced himself to hold them back. He had promised to listen; and he didn't want to interrupt her flow of thoughts and words, even when they meandered.

"After my husband was killed by a rogue stallion, I lost the baby I was carrying. Frank and Madeleine were so generous to me. They paid for Jackson's burial as well as my hospital bill and gave me time off to recover. Their kindness bought my loyalty—for good, in case you're wondering."

Sam willed himself not to react. But Mariah had just given him something vital. In the coming clash between Frank's two wives, her allegiance, if any, would be to the formidable Madeleine. Lila could expect no support, not even from the kitchen.

"What can you tell me about Madeleine?" Sam hadn't wanted to interrupt, but with Madeleine due to arrive at any time, he needed to know more about her before Mariah's narrative rambled in another direction. "How did she and Frank meet?"

"At an open riding competition in Scottsdale. She'd been a non-pro champion, going for the big time. When her scores beat his, Frank was furious, but she was so striking and so spirited that he couldn't resist asking her out. They were married five months later."

"So they competed together?"

"Not quite. They traveled together, usually taking the children along. But their real competition was against each other. More often than not, it was Madeleine who won, and Frank couldn't stand it. They fell to fighting. That was what opened the marriage up to an opportunist like Lila."

"I take it you don't like your employer."

"I didn't say that. Lila's fine. She treats me well, and we get along. Frank was miserable back then. If it hadn't been Lila who broke up the marriage, it would have been somebody else."

As she spoke, Mariah's gaze shifted slightly. Was she telling the truth about her acceptance of Lila?

"Back to Madeleine," he said. "Does she still ride in competition?"

"She doesn't ride at all. After the divorce and Frank's remarriage, there was a terrible accident in the arena. A horse fell with her and shattered her pelvis. She recovered enough to get around, but she'll never ride again."

"That must've been devastating. Are you still in touch with her?"

"Barely. But she still sends me a nice little bonus at Christmastime and always remembers my birthday."

Still buying her cook's loyalty eleven years after leaving. Clever woman. How much loyalty had these gestures bought Madeleine? Sam wondered. How deep did that loyalty go?

Mariah stirred and rose, as if suddenly uncomfortable. "They'll be needing me outside. If we're finished—"

"For now," Sam said. "Just one more question. You were invited to attend Frank's burial with the family. Why did you choose not to join them?"

She hesitated a moment. "Three reasons, I suppose. First, I'm aware that I'm not really family. I was only invited out of courtesy. Second, I have a job to do, and I chose to do it. Third—" She paused. Sam saw her throat move, as if she were gulping back some hidden emotion. "Third, I didn't want my last memory of Frank to be the sight of his casket in the ground. And that, Mr. FBI man, is all I have to say."

In the next instant she was gone, leaving Sam alone in the kitchen. After carrying his plate to the counter, he left the house and walked back to the bungalow to type up a full report for Nick.

His interview with Mariah had filled in some pieces of the puzzle. But it had left him with more questions than answers. How much influence did Madeleine have over her former cook, and did she plan to use it? And what about Mariah's cryptic parting words to him? Had Frank been more than an employer to her?

But as she'd told him, she was through talking. Unless he found evidence to justify more questions, their interview was over.

As he came around the house, he saw signs of activity in the bungalow next to his—the largest one, grander than its two neighbors. A white van, bearing the logo of a cleaning service, was parked outside. Workers swarmed in and out, carrying vacuums, floor scrubbers, and other cleaning equipment. A landscaper with a noisy chain saw was trimming dead wood from the shrubbery that grew below the porch.

Sam stood back, watching. Clearly, he was due to get an important neighbor. Would it be Madeleine or some dignitary? Either way, things were moving toward the gathering for Frank's memorial. He could only hope the time ahead would bring him some answers.

Roper had given One in a Million some time off after the trauma of witnessing Frank's death. He'd visited the horse several times a day, stroking and calming him, but the stallion was still nervous, jumpy, and suspicious. When put out in the paddock with other horses, he refused to let them get close. Maybe what he needed now was to get back into his usual routine.

At the end of the training day, with most of the staff gone and the other horses put away, Roper led him out of the stall and cross-tied him before wrapping his lower legs to support and protect them.

The horse laid back his ears as Roper slipped on the bridle and eased the light snaffle bit into his mouth. "It's all right, big boy," he murmured. "You're safe. You'll be fine."

One in a Million snorted and tossed his head as Roper saddled him. What had those big, dark eyes witnessed in that stall? Had there been a struggle? Had Frank gone down easy, or had he fought? Had his attacker been a stranger or someone the stallion had known, even trusted?

A shudder passed through the massive body as Roper swung into the saddle and settled his weight. The stallion exhaled with a long sigh as his rider nudged him to a walk. This routine was familiar. So was the man on his back. He began to behave as if he felt safe again.

Roper took him around the arena at an easy lope, then began the patterns that had long since become second nature—the intricate spin, the circles, stops, and direction changes that demanded so much of an animal's mind and body. The sequence would be determined by the judges, but the patterns and moves were always the same. The big circle, the forward gallop at full speed, ending in a sliding stop that raised a cloud of sand and sawdust around horse and rider—then the deft rollback and the exit. All perfectly done—not at the speed demanded for competition, but the stallion's memory was perfect.

"Good boy. You've still got it." Roper gave him praise and pats, took him through his paces again, cooled him down, and gave him a warm shower. He could feel the stallion relaxing into the familiar routine. Given time—time he still needed—he would hopefully be his calm, easygoing self again.

But his deep horse mind would hold the memory. One in a Million had been devoted to Frank. Roper knew that a part of him would never forget the night that had changed everything.

By suppertime, work on the large bungalow had ended. The van had gone. The place sat silent and waiting, one light burning over the front porch, another from somewhere inside.

When Jasmine appeared with his covered tray, Sam couldn't hold back a surge of pleasure. Until now, he hadn't realized how much he'd missed her.

"It's just a salad," she said, placing the tray on the patio table. "After that late lunch, nobody was hungry."

"It's fine. Sit down, Jasmine."

"That sounds like an order."

"Take it any way you want. Sit down."

She sank onto the nearby extra chair. "Was there something you wanted, Sam?"

"Just company."

"You'll have plenty of company soon. *Mamá*—" She spoke the word with a mocking accent on the second syllable. "*Mamá* will be settling in for the duration of the memorial, at least. Maybe longer, until Dad's estate is settled. She owns that bungalow, you know, along with guaranteed access. She can come and go as she likes. Nobody else is allowed to stay there. That was a condition of the divorce."

"When was she last here?"

"Why are you asking?"

"No reason. Just curious. I'm looking forward to meeting her."

"As far as I know, it's been years since she paid a visit. But don't look forward too much. My mother can be charming, but she can be a barracuda. That's why Darrin and I need her here."

"Then I look forward even more." He was tempted to probe deeper with Jasmine, but he didn't want to drive her away.

"You might be wondering why I chose to live with Dad instead of my mother when they divorced," she said. "It wasn't him I chose. It was the ranch where I'd grown up. Even with Lila in Dad's bed, it was more comfortable than Mom's condo in Austin. Also, I was planning to leave and go to Hollywood. I knew Dad would let me go. Mom would try to stop me, probably stick me in some dusty old college. I might have been better off—fat, dumb and happy. But I wouldn't have the things I've earned the hard way."

"Such as?"

"Self-reliance, pride, toughness, humility . . . plenty of that where I've been."

"So, when is your mother planning to arrive?"

Jasmine shrugged. "Whenever she arrives. She'll be driving from the airport in Abilene, so it could be anytime. Believe me, you'll know she's around. So will I."

Jasmine fell silent as the moon began to rise, casting long shadows from the distant hills across the land. Tonight, there were no rifle shots from Charlie's ranch, no sounds except the whine of night-flying insects, the faraway wail of a coyote and, from the paddock, the nickering of brood mares to their colts.

A gentle breeze stirred Jasmine's hair and cooled Sam's sweat-dampened face.

Her profile was almost childlike in its softness, vulnerable but defiant in the set of her lips and the thrust of her small, perfect chin. She sat very near him, within easy reach of his arms. The urge to pull her close and hold her was a cry from the core of his own need.

Sam forced himself to speak.

"Are you all right, Jasmine?"

"I'm fine. Why? Does something make you think I'm not?"

"My eyes have been on you since I got here. I've had enough experience with stressful situations to know when someone's barely holding themself together. Maybe it's time to let go and breathe."

She turned and looked straight at him. "Is this your idea of a proposition, Sam?"

Heat flooded Sam's face. For a moment, he was speechless. Had she misinterpreted his words? Or had he given away too much? He wanted her—that much was beyond doubt. But the situation was impossible.

"I may be stressed, but you can fix that in bed. Is that what you're saying?" she demanded.

Sam collected his thoughts and spoke carefully, weighing every word.

"Jasmine, you're a beautiful, desirable woman. Any red-blooded man would want you, and I'm only human. If things were different, I would ask you out on a date and take things from there. But I'm here on assignment to find your father's killer. I have a job to do and a code of ethics to follow. The kind of involvement you're talking about would compromise the investigation—and my entire career. If my concern gave you the wrong impression, I'm sorry."

Jasmine had risen to her feet. She stood gazing down at him, a sardonic little half smile on her face. "So, you weren't really propositioning me, Sam?"

"Of course not. I apologize if I gave you that impression."

"That's too bad," she said. "Because I would've said yes."

With that, she turned away and vanished into the night.

CHAPTER TEN

S am rolled out of bed at dawn after a restless night. He'd spent most of it either tangling and untangling the sheets or lost in a feverish dream of making love to Jasmine, her sweet, pliant body taking him in, giving him the heaven of release. After waking, damp and spent, he'd turned back the bedding and walked outside to a sky full of stars—a sky such as he'd never seen, growing up in an urban state where artificial light drowned the glory overhead.

He'd cursed his own weakness for wanting a forbidden woman. He might have cursed Jasmine, too, but he couldn't fault her devastating honesty. The bomb she'd dropped at his feet had set off buried longings. But it had been like her to say what she'd said. Vicious tongues might call her shameless and worse. But she answered to herself and no one else. Even if he wasn't allowed to touch her, Sam had to respect her for that.

But never mind last night. He needed to be alert to anything that could happen today. Mulling over realities he couldn't change would only break his focus.

After a stinging cold shower, he shaved, dressed, and rounded the back of the house to the kitchen entrance to prepare his own simple breakfast of coffee and toast. He walked into a beehive of activity—extra help working at the counters, chopping, measuring, and mixing, with Mariah giving orders like a field commander. Slipping among them, Sam got what he needed and carried it back to the bungalow. There, perched on his porch steps, sipping coffee, was Jasmine.

"Hi, Sam." She greeted him as if last night had never happened. "Mamá texted me this morning. She's on her way and should be arriving shortly. I thought you might like me on hand to make introductions."

"Thank you." Sam's gratitude was genuine. He'd been braced for the awkwardness of meeting Madeleine on his own. Jasmine's presence could deflect some of that awkwardness—perhaps for herself, as well. Sam had sensed the estrangement between mother and daughter. This reunion couldn't be easy for her.

Balancing his mug and plate, he sat down on the step beside her. The morning was still cool, the sun pleasantly warm. Their spot gave them a view of the main road from Abilene, still empty except for a white dot, which turned out to be a floral delivery van that parked in front of the main house long enough for the driver to carry in several lavish bouquets.

"So what do you think will happen when your mother gets here?" Sam asked Jasmine.

"Oh, it'll be all kissy-kissy with Lila and everyone else until the memorial service is over. Then the gloves will come off. Mark my words, there's going to be war. And it's going to be bloody."

"I've never asked you where you stand in this fight," Sam said. "I heard what you said at the burial about putting things right. And I know firsthand that Darrin and

Simone want the house for their family. But I can't imagine your wanting to live in it with them."

"You're right about that last part," Jasmine said, finishing her coffee. "I'd rather be tortured than play live-in auntie to the little spoiled brats they're going to have. But I stand with my family. I believe that the person living in the house and running the ranch should be a Culhane by blood. Lila doesn't belong here, and I'll be in the fight until she's out. After that, I'll be free." Her gaze scanned the still-empty road. "Free to go wherever I choose."

Lila stepped out onto the front balcony, shading her eyes as she gazed to the west. A muttered curse escaped her lips. Still no sign of Madeleine. The woman was probably waiting around some hidden bend to make a grand entrance. That would be like her, always the drama queen, letting the tension build before the rising of the curtain.

Lila had prepared as best she could for the battle to come. Her own team of lawyers had examined Frank's will, making sure it was authentic, witnessed, and filed under unquestionable conditions. They had scoured every line of text for double meanings and interpretations. They had found one gray area.

Frank had made the new will a few months into the marriage when he was still youthful, in love, and expecting to sire more children. The language stated that except in the case of a divorce, under which the conditions of the prenup would apply, the ranch was to pass to Lila *and* any offspring the marriage might produce.

And was the critical word. Did it exclude her from the will without the children Frank had assumed they would have?

Heaven knows she'd tried—in fact, she'd never stopped

trying. Lila remembered the fertility treatments, the hopes, the bitter disappointment each month when her period came. Their frustrated efforts had put a strain on the marriage. Maybe, she thought, looking back, that was when Frank's interest had begun to stray.

She'd given birth to Jemma at eighteen. Frank had had children, too. But between them, nothing had worked. Lately she'd begun to wonder if he'd had a secret vasectomy to support his philandering—or even to cast doubt on her right to inherit the ranch. But there'd been nothing on the autopsy report, and now she would never know.

Her lawyers had also checked the title to the property. Only Frank was named as the title holder. No woman—not either of his wives, his mother, or his grandmother, back to Elias Culhane, had ever been an owner of the ranch. Elias's wishes might have had something to do with that. From what she'd heard about him, the old man had never held a high opinion of women.

Madeleine's lawyers would attack Frank's will any way they could. The only other support for Lila's case would be her flawless performance as a faithful wife and steward of her husband's property. Would it be enough?

Looking to the right, she could see Madeleine's bungalow, which had been prepared for her stay, however long that might be. Next door, she spotted Jasmine sitting on the steps with Sam. In the stress of the past few days, she'd almost forgotten the quiet presence of the FBI agent. Now he and Jasmine seemed to have taken a fancy to each other. That was none of Lila's concern, unless the little sneak was poisoning him against her—which would come as no surprise.

But Lila couldn't let that worry her now. In the distance, coming along the road, was a large, black vehicle that took shape as a high-end SUV, most likely a Mercedes. The battle for the Culhane Ranch was about to begin.

Lila had already decided that she wouldn't be downstairs to welcome her rival. Unless Madeleine came knocking on the door, the two women could meet at lunchtime.

She stood watching as the SUV rolled through the ranch gate, which had been left open, pulled up to the bungalow, and parked in the driveway. Sam and Jasmine were on their feet, walking next door to greet the newcomer.

The driver's door opened. The figure that stepped to the ground was as tall and rangy as Lila remembered, her broad-shouldered body more of an athlete's than a model's. She moved with visible effort, whether from arthritis in her injured hips or just stiffness from the long drive remained to be seen. By now, Madeleine would be in her mid-fifties, old enough for gray hair. But her thick, unruly mane had been skillfully dyed to a shade closely matching her daughter's. She was dressed in khaki pants, a white shirt, and functional boots—plain but almost certainly expensive.

Evidently, she'd brought no servants, although Lila knew that she had them at home. The ranch household staff was probably expected to supply hired help as she needed it—and Mariah, of course, would be at her former mistress's beck and call.

Looking down from a distance as she was, Lila couldn't see the woman's face. But as she watched the way Sam hurried to open the SUV's rear door, lift out her luggage, and carry it into the house, Lila felt her stomach contract. She would be up against a force of nature, a master at winning others to her side.

To show any sign of weakness would be to lose.

*   *   *

By midday, the burning sun was hot enough to melt sticky spots of asphalt on the driveway. In the pastures, cattle and horses crowded the water tanks or clustered in meager patches of shade. The metal roofs of the arena and other outbuildings glowed with reflected heat. The days leading up to this one had been hot enough. Today was worse.

A buffet luncheon had been set up in the dining room, the table complete with the good family china and silver on an heirloom linen cloth with matching napkins. Jasmine knew that the formal setting had been Mariah's idea—as was the buffet, perfect from the exquisite little canapés and fresh salads to the flaky crusts of berry and lemon tarts. The cook had never lost her affection for Madeleine—and this was her way of showing it.

The message was clearly not lost on Lila. Now that the family had filled their plates and taken their seats, she sat at the head of the table, a smile frozen on her face as she made polite small talk with her unwanted guest.

From where Jasmine sat below the salt—as she was fond of putting it—she could sense the tension between them. It was palpable, an invisible but real presence in the room.

She glanced across the table at her brother and his wife. Simone, wearing a ruffled sundress, was making a show of listening raptly to the conversation, which was mostly about the drive from Abilene, the weather, and the upcoming memorial service. Her wide-eyed expression shifted with every nuance of the exchange between her mother-in-law and her husband's stepmother.

Darrin sat like a stone monument, probably trying, as the only male, to look like the head of the family and failing in the presence of these powerful women. If he was set on stepping into his father's shoes, he had a lot of growing to do.

But most of Jasmine's attention was fixed on her mother, whom she hadn't seen since Darrin and Simone's wedding outside Dallas. Madeleine Carlyle Culhane had never been a beauty. Her aquiline features and athletic, almost mannish frame radiated strength, confidence, and power. Comparing her to the elegant Lila would be like comparing an eagle to a swan.

The nearest Jasmine had come to describing her mother was that she was like the Ripley character played by Sigourney Weaver in the *Alien* movies. But even that comparison didn't come close. The woman was simply larger than life.

The mother-daughter reunion had been awkward—a stiff embrace with kisses mostly finding air. Jasmine had introduced Sam, who'd offered to unload her mother's luggage and carry it to her room. After that, Madeleine had declared that she was exhausted from the long drive and would be napping until lunchtime, after which she wanted to climb the hill with her children to visit Frank's grave.

"Jasmine, dear." Her throaty voice cut into Jasmine's musings. "Where's that boyfriend of yours? I thought surely he'd be invited to eat with us."

"Sam isn't my boyfriend, Mamá. He's an FBI agent on assignment here to find and arrest the person who killed Dad."

"Oh. That's too bad. I was thinking you'd finally found a good man," she said. "Has he had any luck?"

"He isn't saying. He's not supposed to discuss the case, but that's hard when we're all around him. Until we know otherwise, we have to assume we're all suspects."

"Including me, I suppose."

"I suppose. Although since you weren't here, that should put you above suspicion."

Madeleine shrugged. "Well, you never know. Tell him he's welcome to come and talk to me. I'd enjoy hearing what the man has to say. And now"—she rose, sliding back her chair—"if you'll all excuse me, I really must find Mariah and thank her for this wonderful meal. After that, I'll be ready for a visit to Frank's resting place—Simone, you needn't go, dear. But I want my children with me."

"Mother." Darrin spoke up. "The cemetery is at the top of the hill. And the sun's like a blast furnace out there. We could all get heatstroke climbing up that trail. Can't our visit wait until the sun goes down?"

"I'd rather not wait," Madeleine said. "There are certain things that—"

"I could have a four-wheeler brought around with a driver," Lila said. "We've got a newer Kubota with a shade over the top. It's a double-seater that can hold a driver and three passengers. Would that work for you?"

"That would be lovely," Madeleine said. "But there'll be no need for the driver. I drove those vehicles all the time when I lived here. I'm sure I can remember how. Just have it brought around and left out front with the key."

"You're sure? The driver would be no trouble." Lila was doing her best to take the initiative and to be gracious. Jasmine couldn't fault her stepmother for that.

"Quite sure, thank you," Madeleine said. "Now if you'll excuse me—" She turned and strode through the swinging doors into the kitchen.

The trail up the hillside was just wide enough for the undersized four-wheeled vehicle. On the day of the burial,

Jasmine had made the climb behind her father's coffin, her sandaled feet dragging in the dust. Today she was grateful for the ride.

She sat on the back seat with her brother, while their mother drove, gunning the engine hard on the steep curves. She seemed almost too eager to get to the hilltop cemetery. But maybe that was only Jasmine's imagination. In the time they'd been apart, she'd almost forgotten about the invisible forces that appeared to drive Madeleine Culhane.

They came up onto the leveled hilltop. Madeleine swung the vehicle around in a cloud of dust and parked outside the wrought-iron fence that surrounded the graveyard. Her children followed her lead as they stepped to the ground and entered through the gate.

Frank's grave was a mound of dirt, the unsettled earth piled knee-high. In time, it would sink and weather to look like the nearby graves of his parents. The empty space next to it, Jasmine knew, was reserved for his wife. Which wife—his present widow or the mother of his children—remained to be seen. Maybe it would depend on who died first—a dark thought that she dismissed as the small family stood beside the grave of the man who connected them all.

The red roses that had blanketed the casket had long since dried in the heat. The last shriveled petals, caught in the light breeze, fluttered over the grave and swirled skyward.

"What about the headstone?" Madeleine demanded. "A man like Frank deserves a monument to show who he was—maybe a horse and rider in high relief on the stone, or even a statue."

"Lila already ordered the headstone, Mamá," Jasmine said. "Darrin and I approved the design. It's about this big." She indicated the modest size with her hands. "Natural, rough granite with a polished area to show his name, dates, and the names of his children."

"The little cheapskate probably found it on eBay! Your father deserves more recognition than that. Cancel the order. I have an artist friend who'll give me some designs and a bid. I'll contact him as soon as we get back."

Jasmine had been fine with the original headstone design. It was rugged and simple, like something her father might have chosen for himself. He would have hated a statue. But she wasn't about to jump into the fray against her mother. Madeleine and Lila could fight this one out.

Madeleine stood gazing down at the grave as if she could see and speak to the man who was buried there. "I've come home, Frank," she said. "I'm here for you, and I'm not leaving until your ranch is back in the hands of our family, where it belongs—with that lying bitch, Lila, burning in hell for what she did to you. I swear this oath on your grave that I will use whatever means necessary to see justice done. And your children will swear the same."

Whatever means necessary.

The words sent chills along Jasmine's spine. As for the oath, true, she and Darrin had made promises at the burial. But an oath was something different, something dark and binding. If Madeleine had whipped out a knife and demanded that they make cuts and mix their blood, she wouldn't have been surprised. But so far, there was no sign that would happen—at least not yet.

She glanced at her brother. He stood a few paces behind his mother, rigid and pale. Darrin had argued for settling the ranch dispute in a court of law. But despite the weaknesses in Lila's case, she had Frank's legal will and was in full possession of the property. There was always the chance she would win. Madeleine was clearly unwilling to take that chance.

Did she really believe that Lila had murdered Frank? What if she was right? Would that justify using any means to avenge his death?

"Come, both of you, on either side of me. Take my hands."

Madeleine stood like a pagan priestess, facing the grave with her arms outstretched to the side. She was capable of disinheriting a child who disobeyed her wishes—she'd made the threat before, more than once, and almost carried it out. Jasmine and her brother knew better than to resist her in her present frame of mind. They stepped forward and took her hands. Her palms were almost hot, the grip of her fingers like iron as she spoke.

"Repeat after me. I swear this oath on my father's grave . . . to seek vengeance for his murder . . . and to recover his stolen property by any and all means possible."

Her children uttered the words after her. Jasmine was shaking as they finished. Madeleine released their hands and turned away from the grave. "What this means," she said, "is that if I give you an order, you're to follow it without question. Do you understand?"

Brother and sister exchanged glances. They'd grown up with their mother and her ways. But never before had she pushed them this far. Dreading the consequences of resisting, they nodded their consent.

When Jasmine offered to drive the four-wheeler back down the hill, her mother acquiesced. She sat slumped in the front passenger seat, looking drained. But Jasmine knew she was summoning her energy, and that by the time they reached the house, Madeleine would be wearing the sparkling, charismatic face she presented to the world.

*   *   *

Sam hid a pang of disappointment when his dinner was delivered by the kitchen help instead of by Jasmine. But Jasmine had other priorities, he reminded himself, especially now that her mother was here. He could hardly expect her to wait on him every night.

The tasty Greek moussaka was a nice surprise. Mariah was clearly making an effort to please her former employer. He finished the last bite, as well as the accompanying salad and garlic bread, before covering the tray and setting it aside. If this kept up, he would need to start watching his weight.

Feeling pleasantly logy, he settled himself on the front porch bench to watch the stars come out. The worst of the heat had faded with the setting sun. A light breeze cooled his face.

After lunch, he'd spent most of the afternoon around the stables, talking to the staff and learning about horses—their intelligence, their strength, their fragility, and the vital roles they played in the life of the ranch. He'd watched Roper train several client horses, watched how they were wrapped and prepared for their workouts and cooled down afterward. He'd even witnessed a semen collection from a stallion in the breeding shed and visited the lab where it would be prepared for insemination at a handsome stud fee.

No one he'd talked with had added anything to the account of Frank's death. But if his death had anything to do with what went on in the intricately structured world of the Culhane Stables, Sam needed to understand that milieu.

If he was to stay in Texas, his understanding could prove helpful in future cases. But what if he failed to find

Frank Culhane's killer? He could end up back on the streets of Chicago, any chance of a promotion gone. And so far, all he had were scattered pieces of a puzzle that refused to come together.

"May I join you, Agent Rafferty?" The throaty voice broke into his reverie. Madeleine was smiling down at him. Without being invited, she took her seat on the bench. "My daughter mentioned you'd be wanting to interview me. I thought I'd make it easy for you. Is this a good time?"

"It's fine." His laptop and notes were inside the bungalow. He would leave them for now. He just wanted to get her talking.

"When Jasmine introduced us, I thought you were her boyfriend," Madeleine said. "You strike me as just the kind of man she needs—strong, stable, and decent to the core."

"Sorry to disappoint you," Sam said. "Jasmine's a lovely woman, but I'm here in an official capacity with one job to do—arrest the person who murdered your ex-husband."

"That's what Jasmine told me, and I understand the rules. But what if I were to help you find Frank's killer? You know, like we could be secret allies, and I could report to you. I already know who must've killed him. But we'll need evidence. I can help you get that evidence."

Sam had little doubt whom Madeleine had in mind. "I'm reserving judgment until I know more," he said. "But if you've got new information, and it's reliable, I'm all ears."

Madeleine leaned back on the bench and crossed her long legs. "Allow me to share a story with you," she said. "Mind you, this is just between the two of us. All right?"

"All right for now—unless I hear something that bears investigating."

"I understand." She fished a pack of Marlboros and a monogrammed silver lighter out of her shirt pocket. "Mind if I smoke?"

"It's fine."

She lit a cigarette, inhaled, and sighed with relief. "Thanks. I officially quit six months ago, but sometimes a lady needs a little pick-me-up. Only one, mind you. If I reach for another one, stop me."

"Your story," he reminded her.

"Oh, yes." Her laugh was charming. "Don't worry, I haven't forgotten." She took a deep drag on her cigarette, watching the smoke curl upward before she began.

"Frank and I didn't have a perfect marriage. But it was good enough to keep us together. We had our children. We had the ranch. We had the horses and our shared goals. And we truly loved each other. Of course there were fights. We were two competitive, passionate people who liked to win. But we always settled things between us and moved on."

To Sam, it was what she hadn't said that was most telling. She'd mentioned love and shared goals. But not sex. He suspected that, as in many long-term marriages, the sizzle had faded.

"I was led to believe that you were a better rider than Frank," he said.

"I was—on any given night and on any given horse. My scores and rankings tell the story. Frank hated it. But what was I to do, tone back my performance like a good little wife? That would have been a betrayal of everything I'd worked so hard for. How could I do that, even for the sake of my marriage?"

When Sam didn't answer her question, she continued. "Finally it came to the biggest fight we'd ever had, hours before a big competition in Vegas. I said too much—accused him of putting his anger into jealousy instead of being a man and using it to fire his performance. I knew I'd wounded his male pride, but it was too late to take back what I'd said.

"When we got to the arena to prepare our horses, we were still barely on speaking terms. And there she was—this glamorous young showgirl in skintight jeans and a skimpy tank that left nothing to the imagination. She saw Frank's pain, saw her chance, and she made her move, sidling up to him, asking questions, flattering him, touching him in subtle ways, and looking at him like he was God Almighty."

Madeleine shook her head. "Frank put in his worst performance of the season that night. When he didn't come back to the hotel afterward, I knew where he was. I was prepared to let it pass—he always came back with his tail between his legs, and I always forgave him. It's what you do when you're a family and there are children to think of."

Sam didn't necessarily go along with her view of things. He'd been faithful to Cynthia and had expected the same from her, until the ending proved him to be a naïve fool. So what did he know?

"This time, he didn't come back," she said. "A bellhop came to our room, collected his things, and took them away. At least our children weren't there to witness it.

"Two days later, I spotted the woman at the arena, watching Frank work his horse. I backed her into a corner and let her have it. Frank was a married man with a family. She was destroying that family. If she had any decency at all, she would walk away now. I can still hear her reply. 'This isn't about your family,' she said. 'It's about Frank and me. I plan to be here for him until he tells me to go—

but he won't do that because I'm giving him what he needs. So get used to it.' "

Madeleine's gaze locked with Sam's, intense, burning, and hypnotic in its power.

"I'll never forget the look that little slut gave me. That was when I glimpsed the real Lila Smith—frigid, ruthless, and absolutely capable of murdering Frank in cold blood."

CHAPTER ELEVEN

Everything was bigger in Texas. If Sam hadn't believed it before, he believed it now. Wearing a straw Stetson against the sun, he waited at the rear of the barbecue line, a good vantage point from which to study the crowd of several hundred who'd gathered for Frank's memorial.

Some people he recognized. The governor had arrived by helicopter to give a brief tribute at the opening ceremony. He'd praised Frank as a true Texan whose work with performance horses had made great contributions to the sport. The head of the National Reining Cow Horse Association had also given a tribute, followed by Frank's two children—all on their best public behavior. Thanks to the caterer who'd arranged the seating, the open-sided tent for shade, and the mouthwatering traditional pit barbecue served from a long plank table with bread, beans, and potato salad, everything had gone like clockwork.

Scanning the crowd, Sam picked out a number of celebrities—movie and country music stars, pro athletes, and glad-handing politicians. Frank must've had a lot of friends—or at least contacts who had something to gain by showing up. The press, filming shots for the ten o'clock news, would have no shortage of faces and sound bites to choose from.

But he wasn't here to rubberneck, Sam reminded himself. The person responsible for Frank's murder could be here, mingling with the crowd, in plain sight. Sam's job was to piece together what he knew and to be alert for any signs of guilt.

Lila, chic and immaculate in black, stood under the shade of the front porch, greeting a long line of sympathizers and well-wishers. Her feet, in four-inch stilettos, had to be killing her, but nothing dimmed her gracious smile as she hugged and chatted. This was her show, and she was playing her role to the hilt.

A fresh-faced young woman stood a few feet behind her, hovering almost protectively. Sam had been briefly introduced to Lila's daughter, Jemma Smith, who looked like a pale, youthful imitation of her mother. Dressed in a beige summer suit, with the barest touch of makeup, she seemed to fade into the background next to the vivacious Lila—which may have been her intent.

Someone else was keeping an eye on Lila. Roper stood a stone's throw away, his six-foot-two-inch frame, topped by a weathered straw Resistol hat, jutting above the crowd. Beneath the brim, his gaze was fiercely intense, as if he were on the lookout for trouble and would be swift to respond to any threat against his boss. That look told Sam something else. Regardless of what he'd said earlier, Lila was more than an employer to this man. He cared about her.

As Jasmine had predicted, no other McKennas were here. After meeting the family, Sam couldn't imagine them mingling with this pseudo-sophisticated, glittering crowd.

Madeleine, in a white blouse and flowing black silk skirt worn with high leather boots, was holding court under a corner of the shade tent. Sam had expected her to step forward and speak at the ceremony. She'd clearly de-

cided against it but was making her own time in the spotlight now.

Seated in a comfortable chair that had been brought out
from her bungalow, she appeared to be holding her listen-
ers in thrall with whatever she was saying, smiling, laughing, and gesturing with her long, expressive hands. Sam's
best guess was that she might be telling entertaining stories
about Frank. She was too far away for him to hear, but his
gaze roamed the throng of people she'd collected, until
they fixed on one man—a man he remembered from
Chicago.

With the aid of a sharp defense team, Louis Divino had
narrowly escaped charges of money laundering and racke-
teering before vanishing from the Chicago scene. Now
here he was in Texas, appearing prosperous and respectable enough to have pulled his chair up next to Madeleine's.

But a skunk never changes its stripes. The swarthy,
handsome man might have left Chicago, but he would
never have severed his mob connections. Madeleine could
have used those connections to get rid of Frank and make
her move on the ranch.

Sam's theory involved an unproven leap of logic, but it
was worth a follow-up. He would ask Nick to run a check
on Madeleine's phone records and on Louis' to see if the
two had been in touch before Frank's death. Her bank account records would also be worth checking for any indi-
cation of a payoff.

Scanning the crowd again, Sam spotted Darrin seated at
a table not far from his mother. He watched her as if
awaiting some kind of signal that had yet to come. Simone, wearing a severe black dress that made her look
frail, stirred restlessly beside him, probably wanting to leave.
Neither of them looked happy.

And Jasmine? It took Sam several minutes to find her because she appeared to be in constant motion. Like a butterfly, she flitted between groups, pausing for brief chats, then moving on. With her vivid coloring, she looked ravishing in her lacy black dress, which was cut to show off her creamy shoulders and tiny waist. The engraved silver cuff adorning her left wrist caught the light, casting rainbows. For Sam, watching her was a guilty pleasure.

But Jasmine wasn't alone.

Following her footsteps at a distance of a few paces was a stocky man in a navy blue suit. At first, he appeared to be a stranger. Only when he changed direction, showing his face, did Sam recognize him.

It was Charlie Grishman.

His first impulse was to rush in and rescue her. But that wasn't his place, not unless she was in danger or signaled him for help. He held himself back, watching.

Jasmine knew that she was being stalked. She could feel the creepy presence behind her, like the stroke of an icy hand down her back. Even without turning around, she knew it was Charlie. He'd been a thorn in her side since high school, when he'd sometimes called the ranch if he knew she was home. Twice he'd even sent flowers on her birthday. Fearful of making the situation worse, she'd avoided telling her father or reporting him to the police. Instead, she'd done her best to ignore his overtures. But evidently that hadn't been enough. Here he was, making his most brazen move ever—showing up in person at her father's memorial.

She'd done her best to honor her father today—even wearing the silver bracelet he'd given her for her sixteenth birthday—hand crafted in Taos with a design of jasmine flowers and her name engraved on the inside. She hadn't liked it that much. But she'd worn it today in his memory. And she was doing her best to be polite and friendly to the guests who'd come. Now here was Charlie, his presence threatening to spoil everything.

She'd never given the repulsive little toad a shred of encouragement. But he never seemed to give up.

Her father, when he was alive, would have run Charlie off the ranch with a shotgun. But Frank's absence had emboldened the interloper. Now it was her responsibility to make sure he left before things got ugly.

She could summon Security and have him escorted off the property. But the two security guards provided by the catering company had abandoned their posts and were sitting at a table, gorging on barbecue. And this was a memorial to honor her late father. The last thing she wanted to do was create a distracting scene. Charlie needed to leave as discreetly as possible.

Bracing herself, she turned around to face him.

"Charlie Grishman! What a surprise!" She forced a smile. "I didn't see your name on the guest list."

He gave her a sheepish grin. He reeked of cologne, which he'd probably poured on to hide the animal smell that had worked its way into his skin. "I'm here as a friend and neighbor, Jasmine. I just wanted to give you my condolences on the loss of your father—and tell you that if you need a strong shoulder to cry on, or just someone to talk to, I'm here."

"I'm fine, Charlie," she said. "I understand that your intentions are good, but you should know by now that I'm not interested in a relationship."

"Are you still mad about that gazelle?" he demanded. "You were right to put the poor thing out of its misery. I apologize for what I said."

"Apology accepted. Now, since you weren't invited

here, you need to leave while you can do it quietly. Don't force me to call Security. Let me walk you to the gate."

"Not yet." He stood as if anchored to the ground. "I'm not leaving until you promise to go out with me—to dinner. This week. And wear that dress. It's stunning on you."

Jasmine knew better than to agree. Even if she said yes to get rid of him now, then changed her mind, it would only open the door to more harassment. "I'm not going on a date with you, Charlie," she said in a low voice. "Let me walk you out of here before you embarrass us both."

"So you can be with your FBI agent!" His raised voice was turning heads. "Don't be a fool, Jasmine! A man like him—" He gestured toward Sam, who was watching from his place in the line. "He'll be gone tomorrow. Right here you've got a steady man who'll always be nearby for you—a man who'll work his hands to the bone to provide for your every need."

Everyone seemed to be looking in their direction now. Madeleine had stopped talking, her sharp eyes fixed in an angry glare. Jasmine would have given anything to shrink into the ground and disappear. "Just go, Charlie," she muttered. "Go before I have you arrested for trespassing!"

"You'd like that, wouldn't you?" He seized her arm, his grip strong enough to hurt. "You'd open your legs for any cowboy who feeds you a line, but you won't give the time of day to a respectable man who's standing right in front of you with his heart in his hand! You've been leading me on since high school, but you never delivered. Not to me. I guess I'm just not good enough for you."

They were the center of attention now. His grip tightened, twisting painfully. "I'll go, all right. But only if you come with me."

"That's enough, Grishman. Let her go." The voice was

Sam's, his hands breaking Charlie's grip, wrenching him away from her, setting her free.

Burning with humiliation, Jasmine couldn't look at Sam, not even to thank him. Right now, she couldn't look at anybody. Wheeling away, she plunged toward the house.

Crossing the porch, she fled past a startled Lila, burst through the front door, and raced up the stairs to her room. There she literally ripped off her lace dress, flung away her heels and hose, and pulled on ragged jeans, a faded tee, and boots. Then she was flying down the back stairs and out through the kitchen door to the shed where her red Corvette was stored.

As she settled behind the wheel and pulled out of the parking lot, her tears caught up with her. They dried to salty streaks in the wind that blasted her face as she drove, not knowing or caring where she was going. She had been on her best behavior at the memorial. But that hadn't mattered. With Charlie's help, she'd managed to humiliate herself and create a public scandal that would stay with her, like a disfiguring disease, for as long as she remained in Texas.

Sam had collared Charlie Grishman and was marching him across the crowded parking lot to his truck. When Jasmine rocketed past him in her red convertible and swung onto the main road, he knew she was headed for Willow Bend and the saloon.

For the space of a breath, he was tempted to go after her, to talk some sense into the woman, and bring her back to the ranch. But Jasmine was an adult. It wasn't in his job description to babysit her. Even if he were to try, she'd be in no mood to listen to him. He could only hope she wouldn't drink too much and pick up another sweet-talking cowboy.

And right now he had a different priority. Charlie, whom he'd all but dismissed as a suspect, had just presented him with a motive for killing Frank. That motive was Jasmine. And he showed signs of being in the mood to talk.

After he'd waded into the crowd to rescue Jasmine, it had taken all of Sam's self-control to keep from smashing Charlie's face with his fist. But he would have to answer for that kind of violence. Now he was glad he'd given the man some slack. For now, he would continue to play the good cop role and gain Charlie's confidence.

"That little bitch has been waggin' her butt at me since high school," Charlie grumbled. "But she never would let me get close. I thought maybe it was because of her old man."

"You mean Frank? He didn't approve of your courting his daughter?"

"Didn't approve? Hell, he threatened to kill me if I came within a mile of her."

"So what did you do about that?"

"I didn't murder him, if that's what you're thinking. But I didn't give up. I'd call her every once in a while, send her little notes through the mail. I even had flowers delivered a couple of times, when I knew she was home. I figured now that Frank was gone, I might have a chance with her."

"Maybe it's time you set your sights on a different woman, Charlie." They'd reached his vehicle in the parking lot. "For the record, where were you the night Frank was killed?"

"Home in bed. I'd had a hunt earlier that evening, and it wore me out. Slept like a log. But since I live alone, I can't prove it."

"So you could've made the trip, lured Frank or found him with his horse, killed him, and returned home without anyone knowing."

"I could, but I didn't. I swear to God."

"Would you be willing to put your word to a short test?"

"Do I have a choice?"

"Let's just say that if you're telling the truth, it might cast you in a better light. And it would help me test a theory I have. Come on."

Sam guided the nervous Charlie back through the parking lot to the stable. Roper wouldn't like what he was about to do, but he would take that chance.

The dimly lit stable was quiet except for the soft chuffing and blowing of horses as Sam led Charlie to the stall where, as he remembered, One in a Million had been moved. Taking care, he slid the gate open far enough to step inside.

The stallion was there, raising his majestic head as Sam entered first. So far, the great horse appeared calm. How would he react if Charlie had been the one to kill his owner?

"It's all right, big boy," Sam murmured. "You're fine."

Behind him, Charlie whimpered. "Get me out of here. I don't like horses. They don't like me."

"Shut up, Charlie. It's just for a minute." Sam pulled his companion into the stall.

One in a Million snorted, but softly. His nostrils flared and twitched as he took in the unfamiliar smells that probably clung to Charlie's body. Then his head lowered again. He took a bite of hay from his feeder, munching while he eyed the newcomer.

Nothing.

"Let's go." Sam backed Charlie, who needed no urging, out of the stall and slid the gate shut behind them. Either Charlie was innocent or Sam's idea about the horse recognizing Frank's killer was so much bull. Maybe both.

"Did I pass?" Charlie asked as they left the stable and headed back to the parking lot.

"For now. You can leave, but you're to go straight home and stay there. If I hear that you've contacted Jasmine again, in any way, I promise to make your life sheer living hell. Got it?"

"Got it." They had reached Charlie's truck. "I take it you've staked your claim on her for the time you plan to be here."

Sam shook his head. "Nobody can stake a claim on Jasmine. Not you and sure as hell not me. That lady is a hundred percent her own woman. Now get going."

As the red taillights vanished in the direction of the game ranch, Sam's thoughts were drawn back to Jasmine. Once more, he battled the urge to climb into the Jeep and go after her. He forced himself to resist. No matter how much he might worry about her, what she did was none of his business. And the last thing he wanted was to walk into that small-town dive and see her with another man.

Even the thought triggered a curse. But all he could do was hope that she had the common sense to stay out of trouble.

Huddled in a shadowy booth at the Willow Bend saloon, Jasmine nursed her third Michelob of the night. The beer, which she drank from the can, had gone warm and flat. But why should she care, when all she had to look forward to was going home to face her mother. And Sam. She would have to face him, too—after all those awful things, mostly true, that Charlie had said about her.

At first, she'd both hoped and feared that Sam might come after her. She should have known better. Sam would let her go. He would let her make her mistakes because it wasn't in his damned job description to care what happened to her.

She wasn't drunk—not really. And she'd waved away several interested cowboys. At least she wasn't going to make that mistake again. Right now, she just wanted to be alone.

She'd lost track of how much time had passed when a lanky shadow fell across her table. She heard a vaguely familiar voice.

"Jasmine?"

Her gaze traveled up a skinny frame in a black tee to a narrow face with a sandy beard. It was Kevin, one of the leaders in the animal rights group she'd met earlier. ERFA— that was what they were called. Equal Rights For Animals. "Oh, hi," she said. "Sorry, I was preoccupied."

"Hi, yourself." He gave her a grin. "Thanks for showing up. Since we hadn't heard, we didn't know whether or not you were going to be here."

"Be here for what?" Jasmine blinked herself to alertness. "What's going on, Kevin?"

"The demonstration against the game ranch! It's on for tonight! We've got signs, torches, a video camera, everything we need. It's all outside in the truck."

"How . . ." Her tongue felt thick. "How many of you are there?"

"We've got a good group. Twenty-one, twenty-two counting you. We were told that the main gate to the game ranch is locked. Are you still willing to guide us in the back way, through your property? Don't worry, we promise not to damage anything."

For a moment Jasmine hesitated, her memory hearing Sam's voice, cautioning her that these well-meaning people could put her in danger. But she swiftly dismissed the warning. After her humiliation at home, this demonstra-

tion was just what she needed—to strike a blow for those poor, defenseless animals, and against men like Charlie Grishman. Maybe, if all went well, she could even make a difference in this brutal world.

"So what's it to be?" Kevin asked. "Can we count on you?"

"On one condition," Jasmine said. "I don't just want to be your guide. I want to be part of the demonstration. Give me a sign or a torch and let me march with you."

"Happy to have you." Kevin extended a hand to help her out of the booth. "Come on outside and meet the people you don't already know. We'll be heading out as soon as the moon is up."

The demonstrators, both men and women, were spread among several vehicles. They parked along the road near the spot where Jasmine had shot the gazelle and gathered in a group while someone passed around a jar of black goo that people were smearing on their faces. Assuming it would make them harder to identify in photos or videos, Jasmine followed their example. As she raised her hand to her face, she realized that she was still wearing the silver bracelet. She should have taken it off and left it in her car—or better yet, left it at home. But it was too late for that now.

There was a gate in the fence—the same gate Charlie had used to get to the road. The gate wasn't locked, but the latch had been secured with a length of twisted barbed wire. Wearing borrowed work gloves, Jasmine was about to untangle the wire when a young man stepped forward with a heavy-duty wire cutter. "Out of the way. I've got this." He nudged Jasmine aside. With a single snip, the wire dangled loose, and the gate swung open.

This should have been Jasmine's first clue that the situation wasn't under her control. But she chose to dismiss the vague uneasiness she felt. So the demonstrators had a few tools she hadn't known about. What could it hurt?

After closing the gate with the simple latch, she hurried to catch up with her new friends.

The distance across the pastures, from the road to the heart of Charlie's ranch, was a little less than two miles, with several stout wire fences to cross. Once more, the wire cutters—now more than one—came out, leaving the low fences open and the eight-foot fences with a crawl-through space at the bottom. There were cattle in some of the pastures. They lowed, scattered, and stood watching a stone's throw away.

People in the group were making no effort to be quiet. Someone started singing "We Shall Overcome." Other voices joined in, as if this were more of a party than a protest.

Glancing back over the moonlit landscape, Jasmine could just make out the Culhane Ranch with the security lights on the stable. Faint but unmistakable, another light came on, this one in the house, off the kitchen where Mariah's apartment was. Would Mariah raise the alarm?

"Somebody knows we're here!" she called to the leaders.

No one paid her any attention. Short of leaving—and being suspected of a possible betrayal—all she could do was grip her rolled sign and be swept along with the crowd.

They had cut through the last fence. Now, Jasmine could see the moonlit outline of Charlie's game ranch complex. The group leaders signaled a halt while the tiki torches were lit and the signs unrolled before marching on.

If she knew Charlie, he'd most likely be passed out after drinking off her rejection. The protestors, whom she no longer trusted, could have free run of the animal com-pounds.

Her fear became a chilling certainty when she saw one of the huskier men take a hefty tool out of the pack he wore.

It was a bolt cutter.

Before retiring to the bungalow, Sam had checked the shed and grounds for Jasmine's red Corvette. When he failed to find it, he could only surmise that she'd found herself another cowboy. Struggling to ignore the bitterness he had no right to feel, he forced himself to go to bed.

He was exhausted, but he knew he wouldn't sleep. He would be waiting and listening, hoping to hear the sound of her car pulling up to the house—and despising himself the whole time for caring about her so much.

He was still lying awake, staring up into the dark, when he heard a frantic pounding on the door. He sprang out of bed and flung the door open to find a breathless Mariah, in her robe and slippers, on his doorstep.

"You'd better get dressed and get out here," she said. "I heard people crossing the pastures—they were singing, making plenty of noise. The last time I was in town, I heard rumors of a demonstration with hippie types com-ing in. If that's what it is, they might be headed for Char-lie's place."

Jasmine! Until now he'd forgotten his warning to her. He had no doubt where she would be now. "I'll be right there," he said, grabbing his clothes.

"I already called the county troopers," Mariah said. "They're on their way, bringing a fire crew in case those fools set fire to the grass."

"Good." Fully dressed and wearing his pistol, Sam joined her on the porch. "Is anybody else awake?"

"Just you and me. I didn't want to rouse the family without a good reason."

"Fine. Stay around the house in case anybody else needs to know what's going on." Sam checked his pistol before sprinting to the parking lot where the Jeep was parked.

As he started the vehicle, he heard the distant wail of sirens coming closer, moving fast. Flooring the gas pedal, he gunned the Jeep out of the gate. He had to get to Jasmine before she got hurt or ended up under arrest.

What had begun as an organized protest had become chaos. The door to the compound that housed goats, chickens, and rabbits for the carnivores had been broken open. Animals and birds were fleeing for their lives, bounding and fluttering across the moonlit pastures.

There was no sign of Charlie. Was he in the house, passed out drunk, or had he been arrested and taken to jail? Jasmine had long since lost the sign she'd been given. She pushed against the melee, struggling to get to the inner compound where the house was. Even if she found Charlie unconscious or absent, there would be guns inside. She could fire one into the air and maybe shock the rioters to their senses. But to wade into the thick of the crowd would be to risk getting knocked, shoved, perhaps trampled. And even if she could get a gun, someone stronger could take it away from her and do Lord knows what in the heat of the moment.

Torches flared in the darkness. Any one of them could start a blaze that would kill animals and maybe humans. Jasmine gasped as a giraffe loped past her. People were scrambling to get out of its way. Someone had cut the bolt on another gate and freed the giraffe from its pen. Poor, frightened thing. Lost and confused, it disappeared into the night, followed by a pair of zebras.

Now only one gate remained. Secured by a heavy-duty padlock with a chain was the high-walled compound that enclosed the big carnivores—the lions, tigers, and other cats, maybe a bear or a big wolf as well. Locked up under miserable conditions, probably hating their captors, they would be even more dangerous than in the wild. Surely her new so-called friends would understand the need to stay clear. But no—they were swarming the gate, pushing her back, ignoring her cries of warning. It was as if she was drowning in bodies and noise.

The crowd parted to let the big man with the bolt cutter through. Pulling a whiskey flask from his hip pocket, he raised it to his mouth and took a deep swig. He was probably too drunk to realize what he was doing.

This was a nightmare. And it was about to become worse.

"No!" she screamed as the chain fell away. "Stop!" But she might as well have been shouting alone in the middle of the desert. The heavy padlock parted. The gate swung open, exposing the pens and cages with their wretched captives inside. The shouting mob halted momentarily, stunned by the foul odor that swept out of the compound. Then they surged forward.

That was when a dreaded sound reached their ears—the sound of oncoming sirens.

"It's the cops!" somebody shouted. "Run! If they catch you, you don't know anything!"

Flashing lights and sirens were already pushing in through the main entrance, past the gate they'd broken through. The so-called demonstrators were running back across the pastures toward their cars. The relief that buckled Jasmine's knees was short-lived. She was as guilty as the others. Worse, if anybody were to talk—which was bound to happen—she could be named as the one who'd guided the group across the pastures.

Someone had dropped a torch. Where it had fallen, the dry grass began to blaze. Summoning what remained of her strength, Jasmine joined her former friends, running hard as the troopers, some driving four-wheelers, closed in behind them.

CHAPTER TWELVE

Driven by panic, Jasmine stumbled over the uneven ground. One of her boots had lost its heel, and she was nursing a painful stitch in her side. But to stop, even long enough to catch her breath, would raise the odds of her being caught, charged, and sent to prison. She hadn't just been dragged into this mess. She'd been the guide—a key player who could be named and identified.

Behind her, the fire, started by the fallen torch, was blazing six feet high as it burned its way toward the animal pens. Someone had called the fire crew. They were moving in with hoses and shovels.

The four-wheelers, which would have been trailered to the site, were roaring across the bumpy landscape, their headlights bobbing in the dark. Other troopers had joined the chase on foot. Jasmine glimpsed one runner being cut off and forced to his knees. There would be others, any one of whom could identify her by name.

A rabbit—white, one of Charlie's—streaked across her path. An animal like that one, its color standing out against the landscape, wouldn't last long out here before being caught by an eagle or coyote. Jasmine felt the same about her own chances. It was only a matter of time.

Thirty yards ahead and to her right, a dense thicket of mesquite made a dark smudge against the pale ground. If she could reach it, she could belly crawl under and hide in its deep shadow. There could be snakes in there, and the thorns would rip her skin and clothes, but she would have to take her chances. Anything would be better than going to prison.

Turning toward it, she twisted her ankle. The pain brought tears to her eyes with every step, but she forced herself to keep moving. The headlights were gaining on her. Had she already been spotted?

She had nearly reached the mesquite thicket when a tall figure came at her from out of nowhere, pinioning her arms to her sides. She fought and thrashed, but his grip was too strong for her.

"It's all right, Jasmine. I've got you."

Her legs went limp as she recognized the deep voice that spoke in her ear. It was Sam—here to save her. But he was making no effort to hide or run. What was going on?

"Act like you've been caught," he muttered. "That's the only way we're getting you out of here."

Jasmine understood. She thrashed and cursed as he pulled her hands behind her back, clapped the cuffs around her wrists, and turned her roughly around in the opposite direction. "Now march. The Jeep's outside the main gate. We've got a score to settle, you and me, lady!"

Was he putting on a show, or did he mean what he'd said? Sam had warned her about getting involved with these people. She'd ignored his advice. If he was furious with her, she could hardly blame him.

Biting back a whimper with every step, she let Sam propel her back up the slope. Now she could see the damage to the game complex. The fire, thank heavens, had been brought under control, the gate to the cat compound closed again. But the ground outside was littered with castoff signs, torches, broken fencing, broken glass, and other debris.

A trooper had come out of the house, onto Charlie's veranda. "Nobody home in there," he said, eyeing Jasmine. "Looks like you caught one of the bastards, Agent. If you need help, I can take her off your hands. We've got a van loaded and headed for lockup in the next few minutes."

"Thanks for the offer, but I've been looking for this one a long time," Sam said. "She's got a stack of warrants and a record as long as your arm. I'll be turning her in myself. Meanwhile, I'm not letting her out of my sight."

"Suit yourself." The trooper waved them on.

Limping and handcuffed, Jasmine allowed Sam to prod her down the driveway to where the Jeep waited outside the open gate. She understood that they were probably being watched. What she didn't know was how much of Sam's anger was for show and how much was real.

Leaving the cuffs on her wrists, he boosted her into the Jeep. She avoided meeting his gaze as he reached around her to fasten her seat belt. The grim set of his mouth told her that he wasn't just play-acting. He was furious with her.

He started the Jeep, backed out of the driveway, and turned around. "Where's your car?" he asked.

"Down on the roadside with the others. I was planning to drive straight home after the . . . demonstration."

"We'll need to get it out of there. You'd better hope it hasn't already been towed to impound. Once we're out of sight, you can wipe that black off your face." He passed her a clean handkerchief. His voice was cold as he gunned the engine. The Jeep shot down the graveled lane that provided access from the main road to the game ranch.

Jasmine began rubbing the black off her face. "Sam, I'm sorry—"

"Don't say a word. We'll talk when you're safe."

Tires spitting gravel, they rounded the corner onto the main road. Jasmine could see the line of parked vehicles. Her Corvette was where she'd left it.

"Lean forward." Sam reached behind her and unlocked the handcuffs. "I'll take your car in case there are any questions. You drive the Jeep home—now. Don't wait for me. Keys?"

Jasmine found the keys in the pocket of her jeans. Thankful they hadn't fallen out, she handed them over without a word and climbed down from the passenger side.

With the engine running, he waited for her to come around the vehicle and helped her into the driver's seat. "Go," he said. "They'll be here any minute. If they catch you, we'll both be in trouble."

Jasmine doused the headlights, gunned the engine, and shot down the road toward home. The road was familiar, and the moon lit her way. But only now did it strike her how much risk Sam had taken in coming to her rescue. Not only had he violated his own—or more likely the FBI's—code of ethics, but if caught helping her, he could be arrested himself. Sam, who'd refused to get involved, Sam, who'd barely touched her, had put his job, his freedom, even his life on the line to save her.

Glancing back toward the game ranch, Sam could see headlights coming down the lane. By now, the lawmen would have learned where the demonstrators had parked their vehicles. Soon the place would be swarming with troopers, breaking into the cars, trucks, and sport vehicles, getting vital information about the owners while they waited for the tow truck. He'd made it here just in time.

The Corvette started on the first try, the engine purring to life, then roaring as he pulled out of the parking spot and opened it up. Even without lights, he could see well enough to fly down the road. But there were animals on the loose, both escapees from the game ranch and cows that might have wandered through the broken fences. Caution compelled him to slow down to a reasonable speed.

The Jeep's taillights had already vanished down the road toward the Culhane Ranch. He should have warned Jasmine about stray animals. Knowing her impulsive streak, she might not have thought of the danger. He could only hope she was all right and that he would arrive at the ranch to see the Jeep safe in its parking spot. Only then would he allow himself to think about what he'd just done and the possible consequences.

He was nearing the ranch now. A glance in the rearview mirror reassured him that he wasn't being tailed. But that didn't mean everything was all right. Would the police already know who Jasmine was and where she lived? Had they bought his story about her being a wanted fugitive? Or would they come to the ranch, looking for her—and for him? Worry tightened its grip as he realized her troubles—and his—were far from over.

He opened the main gate using the remote that was clipped to the visor. To his relief, the Jeep was parked in its usual spot. Jasmine had made it home safely.

The house was dark. There was no light in the window that he knew to be hers. But she might have left the room dark on purpose.

He drove the Corvette to the vehicle shed and left it, taking the keys. He could return them to Jasmine in the morning.

Worry and exhaustion overtook him as he followed the path around the back of the house. His body needed rest, but he knew he wouldn't sleep. After tonight, he might not sleep soundly for nights to come.

He could see the porch light burning on Madeleine's bungalow. His own smaller quarters were dark. As he mounted the porch, a slender figure stepped out of the shadows. It was Jasmine.

"What are you doing here?" He spoke in a whisper.

The keys to the Jeep dangled from her hand. "We need to trade," she said, keeping her voice low. "And I might not be safe going back into the house. Those troopers could still come looking for me. Mariah's up. She said that if they showed up, she'd cover for me—and she wouldn't tell my mother or Lila."

Mariah could be trusted to protect the daughter of her beloved former employer. That much, at least, made sense. But it could also mean that Jasmine would be spending the night here, with him.

He unlocked the door and opened it, leaving the room dark. The porch light next door, shining through the blinds, lent a ghostly light. "Come on in," he said. "I'll be a gentleman and take the couch."

"Nonsense!" She closed the door behind her. "We should at least flip a coin. Have you got a quarter?"

Sam had no coins in his pockets. But he forgot about that as she stood looking up at him with those striking eyes of hers. Her hair was wind-tousled, her cheek smudged with the black makeup she'd missed wiping off. Her tank top hung off one shoulder, exposing the strap of a skimpy flesh-hued bra. He could feel himself weakening. He fought the weakness with anger.

"Damn it, what got into your head, Jasmine?" It was all he could do not to seize her shoulders and shake her. "I told you those people were trouble. You could be in jail right now. Or worse, you could've been hurt, even killed. Why in hell's name didn't you listen to me?"

Her look was defiant. "I did listen. But maybe I wanted

trouble. Maybe I wanted to punish myself—or to punish Charlie. I don't know why I did it. I just did." Unshed tears glimmered in her eyes. "And now I have a question for you. You didn't have to come after me. You didn't have to lie to keep me from being arrested. You could have left me to get what I deserved. Why would you risk so much for this spoiled little brat? Tell me the truth, Sam. Why did you do it? *Why did you save me?*"

Her voice broke on the last words. She was shaking, fighting tears.

What had driven him to save her? Sam could find no words to answer that question. All he could do was wrap her in his arms and pull her to him.

She came to him without resistance, the curves and hollows of her body fitting his. As she clung to him, trembling like a broken child, Sam could feel her need—the need to be close, to be comforted, to be loved. It echoed his own. Until now he hadn't realized how alone he'd been, or how deeply he'd yearned to hold her in his arms again.

He buried his face in the soft cloud of her hair, inhaling the aromas of smoke, shampoo, and sweet, sensual woman. With a whimper, she raised her face for his kiss. Her full lips were swollen silk, soft and yielding, tasting of salty tears.

He had broken rules to save her. He was breaking more rules now. Down the road, there could be hell to pay. But right now nothing mattered except her need—and his.

Where their bodies pressed, he could feel her heat going through him like wildfire. His body thrust hot and hard against the fabric of his jeans. Her hips pressed against him, moving slightly, deepening the sensations. A moan escaped his lips.

Under the skimpy tank top she wore, her skin was like satin to the touch. As Sam's fingers worked the catch of her bra and found her breasts, it occurred to him that he should say something noble like, *We shouldn't be doing this.* Or, *Stop me if you don't want to go on.* But they'd already passed that point, and the words went unspoken.

Their kisses grew hungry, then desperate. Her fingers tugged at his belt, loosening the buckle. He unclipped the pistol he was wearing and put it aside. Then swept her up in his arms and carried her into the bedroom.

Their clothes and boots littered the floor as they made it to the bed, naked in each other's arms and wild with need. On her back, she pulled him down to her and opened the way. He slipped inside her like a hand into a silken glove, their bodies fitting, melding into one.

He began to move, gliding on her wetness, then thrusting hard, and harder. His world became Jasmine . . . Jasmine in his arms, Jasmine cradling him inside her, moving with him, gasping as the dizzying sensations mounted, her fingers digging into his buttocks, pulling him deeper as they climaxed together.

I love you, Jasmine. The words were in his mind, but he knew better than to speak them out loud. That could ruin everything.

As he rolled onto the pillow, she snuggled against his side, in the cradling curve of his arm. He'd been braced for her leaving. But she was making it clear that for now, at least, she meant to stay.

"Will you be all right?" he asked. "I should have—"

"No need. Don't worry, I'll be fine."

Jasmine would be on birth control, of course. He was far from the first man in her life. And much as he might want to be the last, that wasn't likely to happen. Somehow, that reality didn't matter as much as he'd expected it might. All that truly mattered was now.

"Talk to me, Sam." Her fingers traced a pattern in the

dark hair on his chest. "Tell me about your life. I want to know where you came from and who you really are."

And so, to keep her beside him, he talked. He told her about growing up in an Indiana suburb, with his parents and older brother, Mike, who'd passed away at seventeen in a car accident.

"He died coming home from a party, with his friend driving. I still miss him."

Mike's death had broken the family apart, with Sam being passed back and forth between his divorced parents until he was old enough to go away to college.

"I never wanted to be anything but an FBI agent," he said. "I applied, was accepted, and never looked back. My wife claimed I loved the bureau more than I loved her. At first that was a joke. Then, as time passed, she began to believe it. I was ambitious, working all hours, trying to get ahead. I didn't have a clue until she left me for a man she'd met at her church."

He fell into silence, his arm drawing Jasmine closer. He could feel his body stirring. If she was ready to make love again, he would do it right this time, slow and sensual. "Heard enough?" he asked.

"Maybe . . ." She paused. "But you haven't told me everything."

"What's to tell?" At the evasion, Sam felt a clenching sensation in the pit of his stomach. He'd never shared Jim's death with anyone outside the bureau—except for Jim's wife, when he'd brought her the news that she'd become a widow. That had been the hardest thing of all.

"You left Chicago in pain," Jasmine said. "I can see it in your face when you mention your old life there—and it wasn't just because of your divorce. Do you want to talk about it, or should I go back to the house?"

"You drive a hard bargain, lady."

"Your choice." Turning in the bed, she rested her head against his chest. "If you choose to tell me, I'm listening."

Sam exhaled. "My partner, Jim Ramirez, was the finest young man you could meet. I'd mentored him since his first days with the bureau. We'd been working as a team for two years. He'd become like a kid brother to me—it's always a mistake to get that close when you're doing dangerous work. I had to learn that the hard way."

"So he died?" Jasmine asked softly.

"He was married, with a toddler boy and a new baby girl." Sam continued as if she hadn't spoken. "He and his wife, Maria, had invited me to supper a few times during my separation from Cynthia. At the time, I'd appreciated the support and the company.

"The day it all went bad was the day my divorce became final—I wasn't in the best frame of mind. That's part of the reason I blame myself. If I'd kept him out of the way—" The words broke off.

"No blame. Just tell me what happened," Jasmine said.

"We got a call from an informant that a known human trafficker we were after had been spotted helping a teenage girl into his van. The tracking signal we'd put on the van earlier led us to an abandoned warehouse. This was our chance to arrest him and to rescue the girl and any other victims he might be holding.

"We put on our Kevlar vests and helmets and checked the perimeter of the building. There were no vehicles outside, and the only tire tracks leading in were from the van. Since our kidnapper wasn't known to be violent, and had at least one victim needing rescue, we decided not to wait for backup—my call. We drew our pistols and went in through a side door.

"Jim went first. No sooner had we stepped inside than somebody out of sight started shooting at us with a high-powered rifle. We had our protective gear on, but Jim was hit lower down, in the thigh. From the way he was losing blood, I could tell the bullet had struck a major artery, probably the femoral. I dragged him back through the door, put pressure on the wound, and called for an ambulance. But nothing I could do was enough. He bled out and died in my arms."

The kidnapper and his sharpshooting companion were later apprehended, the girl rescued. But in the light of his partner's death, Sam had scarcely paid any heed to the news.

Sam took a ragged breath. "Here's where the blame comes. If I'd called for backup and waited, Jim would still be alive. If I'd gone in ahead of him . . . If somebody had to get shot, better me than him. But that's not how it played. The worst part was telling his wife. Now she'll have to raise those kids without their dad. They're so young, they won't even remember him. And don't tell me that it wasn't at least partly my fault."

"Oh, Sam." Her arms cradled him close. "You didn't kidnap that girl. You didn't fire the rifle. Bad things happen. Awful things. And after they happen, there's nothing you can do."

"I did set up a trust fund for the kids at work. Everybody contributed. But compared to the loss of their father, that was nothing. And Maria won't accept any direct help from the man who let her husband die. She said as much when I offered."

"Then listen to me." Jasmine's arms tightened around him. "Beating yourself up won't help anybody. It'll only hold you back from the good things you could do in your life—the good things you owe to your partner and to yourself."

"Pretty words, Jasmine. I've said as much to myself. But

words don't make much difference when your bad decision has ended one life and ruined others."

"Then give it time. I've always believed there's a fine line between self-blame and self-pity. I do my best not to cross it. If I did, I'd be an even bigger mess than I already am. The men, the risk-taking, the aimless waiting for a career break that never comes . . . I teeter on the brink of self-destruction every day. But it doesn't stop me from living. And it doesn't stop me from trying to do better."

Her lips left a trail of little nibbling kisses down his ribs and across his belly to his navel. "Now, before I have to go back to the house, what do you say we stop talking and make love again?"

"Only if we do it right."

"Any way we do it is right."

Sam made it last, kissing her long and deep, stroking her breasts and suckling the intimate parts of her until she gasped and came again, then again. All but bursting, he thrust into her, filling her hot, moist length. She gave a little cry as they climaxed together, then lay still, both of them blissfully spent.

When he woke before first light, Jasmine was gone, as he'd expected she would be. Making love to her hadn't worked any miracles. It hadn't healed his pain. But it had stirred desires he'd feared were buried forever. He felt more human than he had since the divorce and Jim's death.

But as he lay in the darkness, recapturing the memory of their loving, the reality of the situation began to creep in. Jasmine was a suspect, a person of interest in his murder case. He hadn't just crossed the line, he'd broken it beyond repair. If his superiors in the FBI got wind of what he'd done, his career would be over.

Should he confess to Nick? Or should he keep his

mouth shut and hope it would never come to light? Surely, he wouldn't be the first agent to slip off the straight and narrow path and keep his transgression a secret.

And what about Jasmine? What would she expect from him after their night together?

Sam had long prided himself on his integrity. Now that his integrity had crumbled in the heat of desire, he saw his so-called pride for what it was—nothing but vanity. And he was left to face the consequences.

What would he do if Jasmine turned out to be guilty of killing her father?

Charlie woke in his bedroom, wedged between the bed and the wall. His throbbing head felt twice its normal size. The last thing he remembered was coming home after Jasmine's rejection and pouring himself a drink.

Trapped in the narrow space, he struggled to sit up. He must've fallen on the bed and rolled off the side. Too drunk to free himself, he'd lain there for the rest of the night.

Gripping the metal bed frame, he pulled himself back onto the mattress. The empty bottles lying around the room told him how much he must have drunk. Now he was paying the price with an elephant-sized hangover.

And Jasmine would pay, too, he vowed silently. He would make her sorry for the public humiliation she'd dealt him. Before he was through, she would beg him, on her knees, to forgive her and let her be his.

The morning sunlight, slanting through the shutters, stabbed into his eyes. He cursed. It was late, past time he was outside, checking on the animals, making sure the hired help had fed them. Shielding his face from the light, he pushed off the bed and stumbled to the coffeemaker.

The caffeine jolt helped to wake him, but he was still

hurting like hell as he donned his sunglasses and stepped out through the front door, onto the veranda—only to be met with a scene of utter devastation.

His stomach churned as he surveyed the front yard, the patches of burnt grass littered with broken tiki torches and ripped signs displaying slogans like FREE THE ANIMALS and DOWN WITH HUNTING.

Sickened, he was about to turn away when his gaze fell on something lying amid the debris—something that caught the morning light and scattered it into rainbows. Making his way through the litter, he picked it up. It was a silver cuff-style bracelet, familiar somehow. But only as he saw the name engraved on the inside did he remember where he'd seen it. And only then did he realize what it meant.

She had been here. She had been with the hooligans who'd invaded his property and done damage that would take weeks to repair and cost him thousands of dollars.

He could forgive Jasmine for humiliating him at Frank's memorial. He had brought that on himself. But this was something else. As he stared at the bracelet in his hands, Charlie felt years of love freeze and turn to hate. He would bring her down. Now he had the means.

But first things first. He needed to see to his animals. He stuffed the bracelet in his pocket.

Two goats, the door to their empty compound hanging by one hinge, stood at a distance, watching him. The goats and other animals he raised for meat were probably scattered from hell to breakfast. The giraffe, already scheduled for a hunt, was missing, too. Several other grazers, including the two zebras, were gone, although the rest were still in their pens. If the fences had been breached, he might need to ask his neighbors, including the Culhanes, for help rounding up the escapees.

At least the gate to the carnivore compound was closed. But the chain had been cut, the padlock severed with a bolt cutter and hung back in place to secure the hasp. Charlie jogged back to the house to fetch the Winchester before venturing to unlock the gate. There was no sign of his hired men. They could've been scared off by the mob that had paid him a visit in the night, while he was passed out drunk in the house.

With the rifle loaded, cocked, and ready, he trekked back to the locked compound, lifted away the padlock, and opened the door far enough to step inside.

A sigh of relief escaped him as he saw that the big cats—the lions, the tigers, and the leopard, were all securely locked in their cages. Except for being restless and hungry, they were fine. But he would need to find something to feed them. Maybe he could bring down one of those goats that had hung around. Or maybe there was something edible in the refrigerator shed.

He was about to leave when a blood-chilling sight riveted his attention. The door to the fortified cage at the far end of the row was hanging open as if it had been forced.

The cage was empty.

The hyena was gone.

CHAPTER THIRTEEN

Jasmine breaststroked the length of the pool, feeling the chilly water glide over her skin. At this early hour, with the rising sun still low in the sky, the cold was a shock to her system. But it awakened the full alertness she would need to face the day ahead.

She'd spoken with Mariah earlier. A trooper had come by late last night, wanting to question her. Mariah had managed to convince him that Miss Jasmine had gone with friends to an overnight party in Abilene. The names of her friends and the location of the party? Mariah had no idea, she'd told him. She was only the cook.

With luck, he wouldn't follow through. The Culhanes were a powerful family. The local lawmen knew better than to bother them without good cause, especially now, in their time of mourning.

At the pool's far end, she dove underwater and swam back the other way holding her breath. As her muscles warmed, the water began to feel good. Lungs bursting, she kicked her strong legs, propelling herself upward until she broke the surface with a gasp.

There, standing next to the pool, was her mother. She held an open beach towel between her outstretched hands.

"Come on out, dear," she said. "I thought this might be a good time to talk."

Whatever Madeleine wanted to discuss, Jasmine sensed that it wouldn't be pleasant. "Just a few more laps," she said, stalling for time. "I'm barely getting warmed up. And the water feels so good this morning."

"Now, Jasmine." The sweetness had gone from her voice. "While we have a few minutes to ourselves. Come on."

Knowing better than to argue, Jasmine pulled her dripping body up the ladder to be enfolded in the towel. The light morning breeze raised goose bumps on her exposed skin. "I'm all yours, Mother."

"Let's sit over here." Madeleine led her to a bench that was out of view from the upstairs windows. Jasmine huddled in the towel, waiting.

"Now that the memorial is over, the real battle for your father's ranch is about to start," Madeleine said. "I want you to think about the promise you made on Frank's grave—that you would obey me without question."

"The oath, you mean?"

"Call it what you will, as long as you keep it. Here's the first thing I want you to do."

"I'm all ears."

"Enough of your sarcasm, Missy. That FBI agent—I can tell he's taken with you. I want you to encourage him. Get him on our side any way you can. Seduce him. Sleep with him if that's what it takes."

"I understand." Jasmine's voice betrayed nothing.

"I happen to know," Madeleine said, "that in most law enforcement agencies, like the FBI, getting romantically involved with someone who's part of your case, especially a possible suspect, is grounds for dismissal, or at least demotion. If Agent Rafferty becomes compromised, we can force him to work with us against Lila."

"That's called extortion, Mother. Or blackmail, to use a simpler word. By any name, it's illegal."

"It is what it is. You took an oath, remember?"

"I remember." Her mother had always been controlling, which was one reason Jasmine had chosen not to live with her after the divorce. But now it was as if she'd crossed an invisible line. Was something wrong with her? Jasmine wondered. Should she share her concern with her brother?

"I have a question for you," she said. "If Lila is guilty of murder—"

"We both know she is, don't we, dear?"

"Let me finish. If she's guilty, why not just let her get caught? Why should we have to break the law and threaten a man's career to prove it?"

Madeleine snorted, flashing her daughter a contemptuous look. "Don't be a fool. Our family's future on this ranch is at stake. We can't afford any slipups. We have to make sure she's arrested and charged on solid evidence. If that means we help things along, so be it."

"What if somebody else murdered Dad, and Lila is innocent?"

Madeleine shrugged. "She would still be guilty of breaking up a solid marriage and destroying our family. If your father hadn't married her, he might still be alive. I'd say she deserves whatever punishment she gets, including prison. So, what's it to be? I need to know I can depend on you to keep your promise."

Huddled in the towel, Jasmine gazed across the sun-dappled surface of the pool. Last night with Sam, she'd felt something good and real—something she hadn't known in a long, long time. The last thing she wanted was to share their lovemaking with her mother, let alone use it as a threat. For now she would keep their secret, locked inside like a treasure. But she couldn't allow herself near Sam again. She'd already damaged him enough.

"Well, what's it to be?" Her mother's voice was sharp, like the call of a crow on a frigid morning. "Betray me, and you know I can cut you off without a cent."

Jasmine sighed. "I know, Mother. And don't worry. You can count on me." The last words were lies, but what else could she say?

Disgusted with herself, she threw off the towel, walked to the deep end of the pool, and took an angled dive into the water. Down and down she swam until her lungs could no longer hold air.

When she surfaced, gasping for breath, her mother was gone.

By midmorning, some of the loose animals from the game farm had been discovered on Culhane property. The cowboys who tended the Culhane cattle were pressed into service to chase them back to Charlie's ranch and mend the fences behind them. The giraffe and the zebras went first, then the goats, which were rounded up and driven in a herd. The chickens and rabbits would remain free until they were caught and eaten by predators.

Sam volunteered for the fence crew, checking each cleared pasture for strays before helping string and crimp the wire to mend the broken fences. Not only was the work a welcome diversion, but it gave him a chance to listen to cowboy gossip. It also gave him a rare opportunity to talk with Darrin, who was in charge of the Culhane cattle operation.

"Charlie's going to get one hell of a bill for this." Darrin stood back, keeping a supervisory eye on the work. "As I told him, somebody needs to pay my crew to clear his animals off my property or repair the damage those damned bleeding hearts did to my fences."

My property. The words were not lost on Sam. "So, you talked to Charlie this morning?" he asked Darrin.

"I did, before I put my men to work. He claimed he slept through the whole thing, police sirens and all. But I don't buy that. He looked like hell this morning. I think he was passed out drunk all night."

Sam kept his mouth shut. Darrin didn't know that Jasmine had been with the mob who'd cut the fences, started a fire, and turned most of the animals loose. And he didn't know about how she'd been rescued. If Sam had his way, that would remain a secret.

"At first he balked at paying," Darrin said. "But when I threatened to call the press, that brought him up fast. Any animal care regulators who saw that place of his would shut it down on the spot. It would serve the sonofabitch right after the way he crashed my dad's memorial and embarrassed my sister. We should've had him arrested for trespassing and assault. You saw how he grabbed her arm."

"I did. But that would have detracted even more from your father's memorial. With all that's happened to him, I'd say Charlie has suffered enough. But I have to ask— given his obsession with your sister, do you think Charlie could be your father's killer? He works with animals and would probably have connections to buy the drug. That gives him the means and opportunity. What's missing is a motive."

"I know there was bad blood between them. Charlie's an easy man to hate, and my dad wasn't exactly lovable. But I can't think of anything Charlie might have to gain by becoming a murderer—and the killer was careful not to leave evidence. Charlie's a slob. If he wanted to kill somebody, he'd be more likely to use a gun. My money's still on

Lila. Have you searched her room and her car for evidence?"

"Should I?" Sam had thought about a search earlier and decided to wait until he had cause to ask for a warrant, which Nick could get and send him—a safer plan than asking a local judge who might or might not be in league with the powerful Culhanes.

To justify a warrant, he would need something solid that would point directly to whomever he suspected. So far, he had nothing but hearsay and hunches. Lila might be at the top of the list, but the murderer could be almost anyone, including the man standing in front of him—or the woman who'd spent much of last night in his bed.

And once he got that warrant and used it, he would become the bad cop. People who'd felt comfortable enough to confide in him would shut down. And the welcome mat at the Culhanes' would be jerked out from under him. Whatever decision he made next would need to be thought out carefully.

"Hey, I could use an extra hand here!" The shout came from the cowboy who was mending a section of fence where the wire mesh had been snipped and pulled apart from top to bottom.

"That's my cue." Sam excused himself from Darrin and hurried to hold the fence in place while the cowboy wired the cut together.

"Think about what I said." Darrin turned away to walk back to the four-wheeler he'd driven out to the pastures.

"I will." Sam knelt in the dust, pulling the cut fence together with his gloved hands. That was when he noticed something unexpected. On the far side of the fence, where the feet of the demonstrators had trampled the dust, he could make out a set of fresh animal tracks.

He pointed them out to the cowboy he was helping. "What do you make of those?" he asked.

The cowboy studied the tracks, then shrugged. "They're too big to be coyote tracks. And there haven't been any wolves around here in years. Most likely just a dog. A big dog, I'd say, going by the size of those tracks."

"Does anybody around here have a dog like that?"

"Frank didn't like dogs. Never had one that I recall."

"And Charlie?"

"Who knows what Charlie's got in that place. But I work cows out this way, and I never heard a dog bark from over there. Maybe the dog was with those yahoos that cut the fences and let the animals out. Does that make sense?"

"I suppose it does," Sam said. But the tracks were fresh. Unless the dog had been left by the demonstrators, there had to be another explanation—maybe even some kind of missed connection. Had the crime scene investigators found any evidence of a dog in the stable? The McKennas had a dog, but it was medium sized and had looked too old to wander this far from home. But what if the killer had had a dog with him—or even dog hair on his—or her—clothes? The connection was unlikely, but he'd be remiss if he didn't follow through.

He would check the crime scene report later. Right now, he had more important things to worry about. Time was passing, and the pressure to close this case had begun to weigh on him. What he needed was a breakthrough.

By midday, Charlie and his hired men, driving four-wheelers, had rounded up most of the escaped animals, including the ones that had been herded back from the Culhane pastures. Some of them, like the goats, had been hungry enough to come back into the compound on their own.

Charlie was still in a foul mood. The bright sun was killing his eyes, his head was throbbing, and the thought of what he'd have to pay the Culhanes to keep him out of court only made him feel worse. To add to his worries, the damned hyena was still AWOL.

He'd known better than to mention the missing animal to Darrin Culhane that morning. If the hyena were to do some serious—and costly—damage, he would disavow all knowledge of the beast, claiming he'd never owned it, or even seen it. Except for his own workers, who could prove otherwise?

When Charlie had acquired the hyena six months ago, there'd been no papers signed, no money exchanged. The owner of the small roadside zoo had been happy to get rid of the creature that had been cute as a cub but had out-grown its tiny cage and become ferocious enough to scare away visitors. Looking back, Charlie wished he'd just told the man to shoot the god-cursed thing.

At some point, he had used Google to learn more about his captive—a spotted hyena, native to many parts of Africa. A hyena was neither cat nor dog, but classified in a group of its own. Charlie had assumed his hyena to be male. But after reading that females were larger and more aggressive than males, and actually had something that looked like male sex organs, he'd decided that his hyena must be female.

A large female hyena would weigh about a hundred and fifty pounds. But rare specimens had been known to reach two hundred pounds, which was what he'd estimated for this one. A hyena could run more than forty miles an hour with higher bursts of speed, but its most formidable weapon was its powerful jaws, which were strong enough to crush the leg bone of a giraffe. Hyenas were also known to be extremely cunning.

The research did nothing to ease Charlie's worries. His missing hyena was a savage animal, intelligent, and raised with no fear of humans. And now it was running loose.

It was early afternoon. Lila had spent most of the morning in the ranch office, updating the accounts. That done, she'd ordered Mariah to deliver her lunch on the patio by the pool. Her visibility would serve as an invitation for Madeleine to join her—or not—as she chose. Sooner or later their one-on-one confrontation would have to happen. If controlling the time and place could give her the slightest edge, Lila would take it.

Seated in her usual spot, at the table in the shade of the umbrella, she forced herself to lean back and take a few deep breaths. Lila would never have described herself as easily intimidated. But today she was up against a charismatic, iron-willed woman bent on taking back what she believed to be rightfully hers—a woman who, if she had her way, would strip away all Lila had worked for and leave her with nothing.

Lila's thoughts drifted back to their last confrontation eleven years ago in Las Vegas, when she'd told Madeleine that she didn't care about Frank's family. It hadn't been her proudest moment. But her words had been born of desperation. As a single mother, she would have done anything to save her daughter.

Jemma, at nine, had been diagnosed with a congenital heart defect. The medical name for her condition was atrial septa defect, ASD for short. In layman's terms, she had a hole inside her heart. Her doctors had recommended surgery as her only chance for a normal life span.

For a single mother with no health insurance, Lila's dilemma was a nightmare. She'd appealed to several charities, but her applications had been turned down, most likely because her salary as a dancer just barely cleared the poverty line.

Only one person had offered a helping hand. Art Royston, who'd held Lila's contract and owned the casino where she worked, had offered to pay for Jemma's operation and recovery—but only on condition that Lila marry him. Otherwise, no deal.

She had almost said yes. Art, who was in his fifties, was nice enough looking. His employees seemed to like him, and he had plenty of money. She didn't love him, but what was love compared to her daughter's life?

Then two of the hotel maids had come to her with their stories. Both of them had seen girls—young girls, not even into their teens—being escorted into Art's suite. That was when she'd realized why Art really wanted to marry her, and why she needed to get Jemma as far away from him as possible.

That had been her situation when she'd gone to the horse competition, met Frank, and agreed to go out with him. That she'd hung onto him and even stood up to his wife was nothing to be proud of. But as a desperate mother, she would have done anything. Given the choice, she would do it again.

Jemma had received her life-giving surgery and made a full recovery. As an unexpected bonus, Lila had come to love her new husband. A happy ending—but not ever after. Once, she'd told herself that she'd already paid the piper. But she'd been wrong. Now the piper was demanding more.

"Hello, Lila. Do you mind if I join you?" The throaty voice was unmistakable. Lila raised her head to see Madeleine standing directly in front of her. She was wearing a chic khaki jumpsuit that made her look as if she'd stepped out of the African bush after shooting a lion.

"You're welcome to join me, Madeleine," Lila said. "I'll ring for Mariah and ask her to bring your lunch out here."

"No need. I already asked her. Do you mind if I smoke?" She already had a pack of Marlboros in her hand and was tapping out a cigarette.

"It's fine," Lila said, although she hated the smell, and she was sitting downwind of the wretched woman. Score one for Madeleine.

"I was hoping to get more time with your lovely daughter," Madeleine said. "Has she already gone?"

"She left early this morning. I was hoping she'd stay longer, but school keeps her so busy."

"Nursing school, isn't it? Such a noble calling, and so in demand these days. A good nurse can work anywhere she wants and write her own ticket in terms of pay. I wish to God my daughter had chosen something like that instead of wanting to become an *actress*." The inflection she put on the last word suggested that it was barely a step above prostitution.

"Jasmine's still young," Lila said. "We don't talk a lot, but I get the impression she's still charting her course."

"She needs to chart a course to a good man—like that adorable FBI agent. I can tell they like each other." Madeleine blew a stream of acrid smoke into the breeze.

Lila's eyes felt the sting. "I don't think Sam is allowed to like a woman who's involved in his case," she said. "Especially if she could be a suspect."

"Jasmine a suspect? But that's ridiculous. She loved her father."

"As far as Sam's concerned, we're all suspects," Lila said. "Maybe even you."

"Ridiculous!" Madeleine might have said more, but at that moment Mariah arrived with their lunches—artfully arranged plates of sandwiches and salad—on a tray.

"Oh, my, this looks too pretty to eat, Mariah!" Madeleine was all smiles and charm as the cook set the plates, utensils, and glasses of iced tea on the table. "You're not just a cook, you're an artist. You belong in a five-star restaurant, not on some ranch where nobody appreciates you."

"You know I wouldn't be happy in a fancy restaurant, Ms. Madeleine," Mariah responded. "The ranch is my home. And now, I'll leave you ladies to enjoy your lunch." She walked away and disappeared into the house.

So far, Lila had made an effort to be polite. But Madeleine had crossed the line. "What makes you say we don't appreciate Mariah?" she demanded. "How would you know?"

A smile teased Madeleine's lips as she picked up a daintily cut sandwich. "Maybe she told me."

"I'm not sure I believe you," Lila said. "As for appreciation, I might not gush all over her like you just did. But she's paid very well. Anything she wants, all she has to do is ask. That includes time off when she needs a break—and paid health insurance, which she didn't have when she worked for you. Things have been unsettled since Frank's passing, but I'm sure Mariah knows that she's valued."

"My, did I touch a sore spot?" Madeleine's expression was all innocence. "I certainly didn't mean to. I only wanted to say something nice to Mariah. What do you say we forget about it and enjoy our lunch?" She took a nibble of her sandwich. "Now this is tasty. I'd steal Mariah from you in a minute if I thought she'd ever leave the ranch. But maybe, given time, that won't be necessary."

Another shot fired—subtle but unmistakable. Madeleine was making her intentions clear. That was no surprise. Lila's only question was whether she should return fire now or hold back and keep her enemy guessing.

Whatever happened, she vowed, she would remain cool and under control. If she let Madeleine play with her emotions, she would lose.

Madeleine sipped her tea. For a lifelong Texan, as she was, it would most likely be sweet tea. Lila had never learned to like it that way. When she tasted her own tea, she discovered that it was unsweetened, the way she preferred. At least she and Madeleine could agree on one thing. Mariah was irreplaceable.

"What a shame your daughter had to leave so soon." Madeleine speared a sprig of watercress from her salad. "You must miss her terribly. I know what that's like. It broke my heart when Jasmine chose to live with Frank after the divorce. He spoiled her, of course. Frank spoiled all his women—except me.

"You were wise not to compete with him," she continued. "I was too smart, too capable, and too honest to pretend I was the kind of woman he wanted—a woman who would sit at his feet and make him feel like a king."

"If you think that's what I did, then you don't know me," Lila said. "When I married Frank, the business side of the ranch was a mess—overdue bills, clients who hadn't paid in months, workers waiting for their paychecks. Frank didn't even know how much money he had in the bank. All he cared about was riding and winning.

"If you're so smart, why didn't you lend a hand—or at least have the good sense to hire a manager? I had to step in and organize everything. It's a full-time job—one I still do, even for the cattle operation."

"I'll keep that in mind." Madeleine's eyes narrowed to catlike slits. "Maybe when we take over the ranch, we should hire you."

"That's a mighty big *maybe*, Madeleine! I've got a signed, witnessed, and notarized will that says otherwise."

"And where are you hiding those baby Culhanes you were supposed to give Frank? The will isn't valid if you didn't live up to its terms. You really should consider that job offer, Lila. When my lawyers get through with you, you're going to need it—unless you plan to go back to Vegas and put on your G-string and pasties. For that, you might want to lose a few pounds and sign up for Botox injections. Or you could just marry your lover and move in with his redneck family."

Lila had made a silent vow to remain calm, no matter what Madeleine might do or say. But her anger was surging out of control. The woman was playing her and enjoying every minute of it.

It was all she could do to keep from snatching up her unfinished lunch and smashing the plate in Madeleine's insolent face.

The temptation was growing when a sudden interruption changed everything. One of the cattle boys came pounding up the walk and burst through the wrought-iron patio gate.

"Where's Mr. Culhane?" He was pale and out of breath. "We need him to come right now."

"Are you talking about my son, Darrin?" Madeleine was all kindness and concern now. "I believe he's at his office in Willow Bend. He said something about having appointments this morning. I could call him, but he won't be happy about having to reschedule his clients."

"What's this about, Smokey?" Lila asked. "You can tell me."

"Dead calf in the east pasture—one of the yearlings. Something killed it. Something awful. It's just—" He took a ragged breath. "Somebody needs to decide what to do."

"I'll go with you and have a look. Did you bring a four-wheeler?"

"It's out front. But a lady like you—you don't want to see this."

"I'll be fine. Will I need a gun?"

"It wouldn't hurt to have it."

"I'll get one of Frank's rifles and meet you outside." She dashed into the house, leaving Madeleine at the table.

CHAPTER FOURTEEN

Sam had just finished lunch when the cowboy, nicknamed Smokey, drove the four-wheeler around the house. Curious, Sam had approached the young man to find out what was happening. By the time Lila joined them, carrying a Weatherby Mark V rifle, he had learned about the dead yearling.

"Could it have been coyotes that killed it?" Sam asked.

"No, sir," Smokey replied. "I've seen coyote kills. It takes a pack of 'em to bring down a healthy animal the size of that yearling. There was just one set of tracks—a lot bigger than coyote tracks. The calf had been drug into the mesquite. And the way the carcass was tore up—" Smokey shook his head. "It was awful, like nothing I ever seen before."

"I'd be interested in seeing it." Sam remembered the tracks he'd spotted earlier. There had to be a connection. Even if the killing of a calf had nothing to do with his case, it would be a good idea to keep abreast of happenings on the ranch—especially if it meant spending more time with the elusive Lila.

"Why don't you come with us, Sam?" Lila took her place in the front passenger seat, leaving the back seat empty. "We can always use another pair of eyes."

"I was hoping I wouldn't have to ask." Sam climbed into the back. With Smokey driving, they flew across the pastures. The engine roared as they jounced over the bumps and hollows.

The mesquite thicket was the size of a city lot, a dense tangle of low-growing trees with thorny branches. One of the few patches that hadn't been chained that spring, it grew near the ranch's far border that separated the Culhane pasture from the game ranch. Sam was the first to notice the distant ravens and vultures flocking above the green mass. He touched Lila's shoulder and pointed to the birds.

"Slow down," she told Smokey as she chambered a shell in the gun. "If the beast that killed the calf is in that thicket, I don't want it scared off before I get a shot."

Sam drew his service pistol as a backup, but as he had expected, when they came up on the mesquite, there was no sign of a predator, only the birds flocking on the carcass, which had been ripped open at the throat and down through the belly. The head was almost severed by a bite to the neck. The kill was fresh. It had probably been done after the early-morning repairs to the fence.

The ground showed signs that the yearling calf had been dragged—the carcass probably weighing close to five hundred pounds. Sam muttered a curse. What kind of monster would have that kind of strength and that kind of bite? A lion or tiger, maybe, or even a bear. But those animals would have left distinctive paw prints.

Looking down from the vehicle, he could see the predator's tracks in the dirt—the same doglike prints he'd seen earlier. But no dog, or even a pack of dogs, could have done this kind of damage.

"What do you think?" Lila asked.

"I think somebody needs to talk to Charlie," Sam said. "The animal that did this probably escaped from his menagerie. I don't know what kind of beast it is, but if you've got a better guess, I'd like to hear it."

"No, I agree with you. Darrin is in charge of the cattle operation. He should be the one to handle this. There's no cell service out here, but I'll call him when I get home. Meanwhile, we'll need to protect the cattle and horses. Smokey, tell the boys they can expect guard duty, with extra pay for extra hours. They'll be issued guns if they don't have their own."

"I'll tell them. Have you seen enough?" Smokey was clearly nervous. "That animal could be anywhere."

"It's probably hiding in the mesquite," Lila said. "With its belly full of meat, we can only hope it'll stay put. Take us back to the bunkhouse, Smokey. I'll leave you there to spread the word that the cattle are to be kept away from this pasture, and that Darrin will be coming to take over. I'll drive home and call him from there."

"I could have a talk with Charlie," Sam said. "If the beast is his, at least he should be able to tell us what it is. Maybe he'll even have a trap or a tranquilizer gun we can use."

"That would be helpful," Lila said. "But don't bother with the tranquilizer gun. I just want that thing dead."

Had she wanted Frank dead, too? The thought crossed Sam's mind as Lila let Smokey off at the bunkhouse and moved into the driver's seat. Today he had seen a new side of Lila—calm and cool, even cold. The confident way she'd handled the big game rifle showed that she knew how to use a deadly weapon. And she hadn't been the least rattled by the sight of the slaughtered calf or the scavenger birds with their bloodied heads.

Was Lila capable of killing her husband? Sam couldn't rule it out. Had she actually done it? That was a question he had yet to answer. The fact that a woman was strong and capable could hardly be held against her.

Lila parked the four-wheeler behind the house and disappeared inside to call her stepson. After a short break, Sam took the Jeep and set out for Charlie's place.

He'd looked for Jasmine but failed to see her. Maybe she was avoiding him. She could be having second thoughts about their night together, just as he was. But she had a way of showing up when he least expected it. Maybe he would come home and find her on his front porch. Against his better judgment, he would welcome her.

For now, all he could do was wait.

Last night, with his mind on saving Jasmine, Sam had been barely aware of the damage to Charlie's property. Only as he parked the Jeep and walked in through the open gate, did he begin to see what the demonstrators had done.

A good-sized hill of debris had been raked up in the front yard. There were broken signs and tiki torches, pieces of fence and shattered glass. The fire had left ugly patches of blackened grass. The compound gates were closed, but Sam knew that the ERFA group had broken in and released many of the captive animals. By now, most of them appeared to have been herded back into their pens. The graceful head and neck of a giraffe rose above one high log fence. From behind another fence came a chorus of bleating goats.

As Sam walked up to the house, Charlie came out onto the veranda. Red-eyed, dirty, and exhausted, he'd probably had a rotten day. And what Sam was about to tell him wouldn't make it any better.

"What the hell do you want?" the man snarled. "Haven't

I had enough harassment without the friggin' FBI showing up on my doorstep?"

Sam stood at the bottom of the steps. "I know it might not be the best time, but this can't wait. One of your animals is still loose on Culhane property. It killed a calf, out by that big mesquite thicket."

Charlie's scowl deepened. "That can't be. None of my carnivores are missing. What did it look like? Did you see it?"

"Only its tracks. It wasn't a cat. But it was strong enough to rip that yearling calf open and drag the carcass under the mesquite. If the animal is yours, the Culhanes will expect you to pay for that calf."

"Like I say, whatever that beast is, it isn't mine, and I'm not paying a cent for that damned calf." Charlie's fury was mounting like an old-fashioned pressure cooker about to explode. "Why don't you go after those vandals that trashed my property? They're the ones that should pay—at least one of them ought to, and I know who she is!"

He reached into his pocket, withdrew a shiny, silver object, and held it out, close enough for Sam to see but not to take from him. "Recognize this, FBI man? It belongs to your girlfriend. It's even got her name inside. I found it in the yard with the rest of the trash. She was here, with the others. And after I take this to the police, your little honey's going to be wearing an orange jumpsuit!"

Sam had recognized Jasmine's bracelet at once. She'd been wearing it at the memorial. But it had been missing when he'd cuffed her wrists to get her past the police.

"You can't prove you found it here, Charlie," he said. "The police might even think you stole it."

"I don't think so." Charlie stuffed the bracelet back into his pocket. "It might not be final proof, but it'll be enough to put the police on the right track. The scumbags she was with should be able to identify her. And once the cops put her in a lineup, it'll be over."

Cold dread congealed in Sam's stomach. If this threat was real, Jasmine could be in serious trouble. "How can you do such a thing, Charlie?" he asked. "I thought you liked her."

"I didn't just like her. I loved her. But what she did last night opened my eyes to who she really is. She and her friends cost me thousands of dollars in repairs and lost business—and I'm betting she doesn't even care. Now I just want the lying little bitch to get what she deserves."

"I hope you'll give this plan some thought before you act on it," Sam said. "I can't imagine that Jasmine meant to hurt you. But she couldn't control the actions of her friends. Maybe you need to hear her side of the story."

"I don't give a damn about her side of the story. I only know what I see. This place is a mess. I'm already getting billed for the fence repairs. And now you show up expecting me to pay for a dead calf. Why don't you tell Jasmine to pay for it? Hell, maybe she should pay for all the damage."

"She can't pay if she's in jail." Sam didn't know if that was true, but at least it might be a bargaining chip. Jasmine had money, or at least her mother did. But this matter would have to be handled very carefully.

"Listen, Charlie," he said. "If you'll hold off on taking that bracelet to the police, I'll talk to Jasmine and see if she's willing to help you out with money. No promises, but can you wait a day or two for an answer?"

"What's this? Are you working for the Culhanes now?" Charlie demanded. "I thought Darrin was the family lawyer."

"I'm only trying to help. Would you rather deal with Darrin or with me?"

Charlie was silent, but watching him, Sam could imagine his mind working. The market price of the calf, at the going rate of $130 per hundredweight, would be about $650, not an exorbitant amount. And the salaries of the cowhands for rounding up Charlie's loose animals and repairing the fences couldn't total more than a couple thousand. To Jasmine, that would be pocket change. But how much would revenge on the woman who'd broken his heart be worth to Charlie?

Charlie wiped the hair back from his sweating forehead. "I'll sleep on the idea. But if you want to change my mind, be back here by this time tomorrow with Jasmine's offer. Then."—his smile glinted with malice—"after I hear what she's willing to pay for her bracelet, I'll make my decision—and don't try taking it away from me. I've taken plenty of photos for proof."

"What about your animal? The one that killed the calf?"

"Whatever that beast is, it isn't mine, and I won't be responsible for any damage it does."

"Then you shouldn't care about the order to shoot it on sight."

"Knock yourself out." Charlie didn't flinch, even though he had to be lying. "If I don't hear from you by this time tomorrow, I'm going to the police. You can pass that on to Miss High and Mighty. Maybe she'd like to come and plead her case in person. I'd enjoy seeing her on her knees—especially with you watching."

Reining back the urge to smash his fist into Charlie's face, Sam forced himself to leave. None of this messy affair was his business, he reminded himself as he drove back to the ranch. But he was wrong. He'd made it his business by rescuing Jasmine, by making love to her, and by stepping in now to protect her. He was in this up to his neck.

He arrived at the ranch to see Darrin's Mercedes parked in front of the house. Frank's son had wasted no time getting here. It would be up to him to organize the cowboys for guard duty and decide what to do about killing the predatory creature before it struck again.

Would Darrin talk to Charlie? Would Charlie tell him about Jasmine's part in the demonstration? Sam had no control over that possibility. All he could do was warn Jasmine and pass on Charlie's ultimatum. The next step would be her decision.

Sam parked the Jeep in the employee lot and walked around the house to find Jasmine on the porch of his bungalow. She was sitting on the bench, her long, tanned legs stretched out in front of her.

She gave him a tentative smile. "We need to talk, Sam," she said.

The words that every man dreaded hearing from a woman.

"I need to talk to you, too," he said. "Why don't you go first? All right?"

She sighed. "All right. I guess somebody has to." She glanced around, as if to make sure no one was listening. When she spoke, her voice scarcely rose above a whisper.

"It's my mother. I know she can be charming, but she can also be manipulative. She's determined to prove that Lila killed my father."

"No surprise there. That proof would get her everything she wants. Do you believe that's true?"

"I don't know. But here's the thing. She knows that your relationship with a possible suspect would compromise your case, and your career. I'm under orders to get you in trouble, so she can threaten to expose you if you don't find a way to arrest Lila."

He gave her a bemused look. "After last night, I should already be in trouble. Does your mother know about that?"

"No. And I don't plan to tell her. Last night was for you and me. I don't want to share it with anybody, especially my mother. But we can't give her reason to believe anything has happened between us, or she'll use it as an excuse to threaten you. Does that make sense?"

"Just barely. But if it means we need to keep some distance between us, I'll understand and follow your lead."

"Now it's your turn," she said. "What was it you were planning to tell me?"

Sam told her the whole story—the slaughtered calf, the visit to Charlie's, the bracelet he'd found, and his threat to go to the police with it. The expressions that flickered across her face ranged from bewilderment to anger to fear.

"What does he want, Sam? Money? I've got that. I'll pay whatever he demands—within reason. But I've known Charlie for a long time. What he craves most is respect—and I humiliated him at the memorial."

"He humiliated himself, Jasmine."

"But he won't see it that way. I think what he really wants is to see me brought down to his level."

"I sensed the same thing," Sam said. "That's why I plan to face him alone tomorrow. I don't want you going anywhere near that place."

"Shouldn't that be my decision?" Defiance sparked like flint in her eyes.

"I just want you safe," he said.

"But this isn't your problem," she said. "The mistake was mine. I should be the one to handle the consequences."

"You didn't see him today. The look in his eyes—he's dangerous, Jasmine. He wants to hurt you." Sam reached into his shirt pocket and pulled out a folded sheet of notepaper and a pen, which he'd found in the glove box of the Jeep.

"Take a look at this. I made a list of the expenses Charlie might want to collect, including what he'll have to pay your family." He handed her the paper. "Take a look, change anything you want, and do the math. If you want to write a check, I'll take it back to him tomorrow."

"And what if he turns it down? What if he wants more? I don't want to go to jail. I've got to be there."

"I can't stop you. But if you insist on going, I'll be right there with you."

"Sam, this isn't your problem."

"I seem to have made it my problem. This is non-negotiable. You're not going to face that man alone."

She hesitated, then sighed. "All right. But I'll do the talking."

"That's fine as long as Charlie behaves. What time tomorrow do you want to leave?"

"We could go now and get it over with," she suggested.

"Darrin's car is here. He could be anywhere on the ranch. Do you really want to risk getting him involved?"

"Not unless I need a lawyer. What if he gets to Charlie first, and Charlie shows him the bracelet?"

"It could happen," Sam said. "But I don't think it will. Charlie has more to gain by bargaining with you than with Darrin."

"And Charlie would relish the satisfaction of seeing me beg. I know him. I know what to expect. I can meet you at eight o'clock in the parking lot."

"That should be fine."

Madeleine had come outside. She stood on the porch, watching them, as if expecting a performance from her daughter.

When Jasmine turned away and headed for the house without so much as blowing Sam a kiss, Madeleine pivoted, strode back into her bungalow, and closed the door behind her with an audible click.

Even before Lila stepped into the arena, Roper had sensed that she was there, watching him from beyond the railing. Or maybe he'd been so hungry for the sight of her and the sound of her voice that he'd imagined her presence. Either way, the woman walking toward him now, silhouetted against the fading light, was real.

He had dismounted after Million Dollar Baby's workout and was waiting for the groom as she crossed the arena, her boots stirring the thick layer of sand, loam, and sawdust that cushioned the floor. As she came closer, he could see the shadows of weariness that framed her eyes. She was no longer young. Today she looked her age.

"Hello, Boss," he said. "Is there something I can do for you?"

"Not really. I just need to see a friendly face. How's Baby doing? Will she be ready to show next weekend?"

"She's ready now. So far, the only challenge will be to keep her at this level until the shootout." He gazed down at Lila, fighting the urge to cup her face in his hands and gaze into her eyes. The last time they'd parted, she'd been angry when he appeared to question her innocence in Frank's death. Now he found himself wondering how he could have doubted her.

"You look like you could use a rest," he said. "Are you taking care of yourself?"

"I'll be fine. But it's been a hellish day."

"I heard about the ruckus over at Charlie's place and the dead calf," Roper said. "I thought it was Darrin's job to take care of the cattle."

"It is. At least it's supposed to be. After we found the calf, I called and turned the whole mess over to him. He did show up, but I can't count on him to follow through. He passed out guns to the cowboys and assigned them to their guard stations, and then he went home. Some excuse about his wife not feeling well."

"So he dumped the responsibility back on you." Roper made no secret of his contempt for Darrin. "Maybe you should give the job to his mother."

"Don't even mention Madeleine to me. I got into it with her over lunch. Maybe I should be relieved that the gloves are off and the pretending is over. But it was brutal. The woman is out for blood. And she won't let up until I'm gone and the ranch is hers again."

The groom, a young man called Cruiser, had come out of the stable to take Million Dollar Baby. One of the prettier girls, looking flushed and rumpled, waited for him inside the stable entrance. Roper could guess why the boy hadn't been right there to take the mare after her workout. He'd warned Cruiser once that these shenanigans wouldn't be tolerated. Should he warn him again or just fire him in the morning?

He would sleep on it, Roper decided. Right now, Lila was here, and he didn't want to break away from her to dress down his employee.

"So, what do I do now?" she asked. "Should I ride out and check on the cowboys myself, or can I trust them to do their jobs? Some of them are just kids—barely eighteen or nineteen. There's a deadly animal out there, and nobody's in charge. Darrin should be out there with them, or at least close enough to be in touch."

"Do you want me to stay?" Roper asked. "It wouldn't be any trouble."

She hesitated, maybe thinking of the rumor her enemies

might start if he were to spend the night at the ranch. "No, it's not your job. Just make sure the stable is secure when you leave. That creature, whatever it is, had plenty to eat this morning. We can only hope it won't need to hunt again soon."

"Have the cowboys got walkie-talkies?"

She nodded. "They were Frank's idea. He insisted that they take them and know how to use them. I'll have one at the house, too, if the signal will reach that far."

"Good idea. If they stay in touch, they should be all right. I'll say this for Frank—he knew how to run a ranch. But then, he had you to help him." Roper added the last thought lest she think he was belittling her own invaluable work. "You and Frank made a good team."

"Yes, in some ways, we did. I need to go."

"You've got my phone number," he said. "If there's trouble, or if you need anything, call me. I can be here in fifteen minutes."

"I'll keep that in mind." She was already on her way out of the arena. Roper watched her go. Then he went back into the stable to check on the horses and to make sure the outside doors, which were never locked in case of fire, were latched. The roar of a motorcycle from the employee lot told him that Cruiser and the girl were leaving. He couldn't count on a couple of hormone-crazed kids to close up. But they'd done it right. All the horses had hay and water, the brood mares and their foals were in their stalls, and the doors were closed as they should be. Maybe he would let the boy off with a lecture this time.

He knew that he was too softhearted. Frank would have fired the young Romeo on the spot. But tonight he was too tired to argue with himself.

As he walked back along the row of stalls, One in a Million thrust his regal head over the gate, nickering for attention. Roper paused long enough to stroke the stallion's neck and talk to him for a moment. "What's this, old boy? Are you feeling neglected? We'll see what we can do about that tomorrow. I promise you a good workout with lots of petting."

Leaving the horse, Roper exited through the arena, closing the stable doors behind him.

From beyond the border of the McKenna Ranch, the wail of a prowling coyote echoed on the night wind. Stirring from sleep on the front porch, the dog barked a warning, then settled back into dreams.

Turning over in bed, Roper raised himself on one elbow to check his bedside clock. It was 3:00 A.M., too early to start the day. But after a night of lying awake, staring into the darkness, and worrying, he'd given up on sleep. Maybe getting dressed and moving around would settle his nerves.

After pulling on sweatpants and a tee, he picked up his cell phone and dropped it into his shirt pocket. It probably wouldn't ring, but he'd promised Lila that he would be there for her if she called. Roper was a man who believed in keeping promises.

Barefoot, he padded across the living room, opened the front door, and stepped out onto the porch. The night breeze was cool on his damp face. He inhaled the fragrances of sage and dust. The dog raised its head and thumped its tail. He reached down and rubbed its ears.

Only then did he notice a dark shape huddled on the top step. Moving closer, he recognized Cheyenne, wrapped in a thin cotton blanket.

"Hey," he murmured, not wanting to startle her. "Are you all right?"

"Fine," she said in a flat voice. "I know I should try to

sleep. We'll be leaving for El Paso tomorrow. The boys will be doing most of the driving, but I'll be the relief driver. I owe it to them to be alert."

Roper understood the concern behind her words. The most common cause of death and injury among rodeo riders wasn't wrecking in the arena. It was highway accidents from the long, exhausting drives between rodeo gigs. At least the McKennas had good equipment and extra drivers to switch off at the wheel. Still, anything could happen, and Roper knew his parents worried.

He settled onto the step beside her. Clouds drifted over the face of the waning moon, casting shadows across the yard. "Is something keeping you awake?" he asked.

"Not really. I'm just wishing I had a longer break."

"Being a superstar is hard work. Isn't that what you wanted?"

"I wanted to be a top competitor in the big rodeos. I never wanted to be interviewed on the *Today Show* or get offers to model for *Vogue* magazine. But for now, I owe it to the boys to go along with them. We're a family."

"Any men in your life? Besides your brothers, I mean?"

"Who's got time?" Cheyenne's laugh sounded forced. "And there are so many phonies and exploiters out there—I'm lucky to have three brothers protecting me."

"Do you ever regret turning down Frank's offer to train you?" Roper's question pushed the limits, but he was curious enough to ask anyway.

Her body stiffened beside him. "Reining is a beautiful sport. But it's all about control. Frank was all about control, too. That's why he was so good at what he did. But he would have insisted on controlling me. So, no. No regrets."

Had Frank insisted on controlling Lila, too? Roper had known nothing about their marriage. But he couldn't imagine the strong-willed woman he'd come to know submitting to her husband's every demand.

"How did you feel when you heard he'd died?" he asked his sister.

She adjusted her blanket, pulling it tighter around herself. "I felt nothing," she said. "Nothing at all."

Roper might have asked her more, but just then his cell phone jangled. He pulled it out of his pocket. The caller was Lila.

"Something's wrong, Roper. Maybe something awful." Lila's words were broken, her voice hoarse with strain. "If you can come—"

"Hang on," he said. "I'll be right there."

CHAPTER FIFTEEN

Lila had chosen to spend the night on the patio to get the strongest possible signal from the walkie-talkies. The cattle had been rounded up and herded into the largest pasture with the cowboys, mounted and armed with flashlights and loaded rifles, guarding the perimeter. Lila had ordered them to keep in touch with each other, and to check in with her anytime they felt the need.

This should have been Darrin's job, not hers. But he'd gone home, leaving her to manage this crisis. Because she was concerned about the young cowhands, she had stepped in. Maybe she could use this incident in court as an example of how he would manage the ranch if it were to go to him. Not that it would matter to a judge.

Sometime after midnight, she'd begun to drift. Then a frantic voice came through the receiver of the walkie-talkie.

"Smokey's horse just showed up with an empty saddle. His rifle's in the scabbard. No answer when we try to call him. Over."

Lila's pulse slammed as possible scenarios flashed through her mind. Maybe the young cowboy had dozed off, slid out of the saddle, and was walking safely back to the herd.

Or maybe . . . But she couldn't allow herself to imagine the worst.

"I'll be there as soon as I can," she'd told the cowboy who called. "If you go to look for him, stay together and make plenty of noise. Nobody goes off alone. Call me if you see anything. Understood? Over."

"Understood. Over and out."

One of the four-wheelers was parked behind the house with the loaded Weatherby, a powerful spotlight, a first-aid kit, and a spare can of gasoline already inside. She could leave this minute. But she'd warned the cowboys not to go out alone. She'd be wise to follow her own advice. If she got into a situation she couldn't handle, with no backup, she'd only be making matters worse.

She could wake Sam. But he didn't work for the ranch. And with a young cowboy missing and death lurking out there in the darkness, there was only one man she wanted at her side.

She made the call to Roper.

Ten minutes later, with no word from the cowboys, she saw his truck swinging into the employee drive, engine roaring, tires churning up gravel. She met him partway in the four-wheeler. He parked and bailed out of the truck, rifle in hand. Minutes later, with Lila at the wheel, they were flying across the pastures toward the place where the boys had been guarding the herd. The roar of the engine, at full throttle, made conversation difficult, but feeling Roper's calm presence beside her, Lila was grateful that she'd waited.

They stopped at the herd. The steers didn't appear to be in danger, but they were stirring and lowing, as if scenting something on the wind. The cowboys were gone. Lila used the walkie-talkie to call them.

"Have you found any sign of Smokey?" she asked. "Over."

"Not yet. Over."

"Come back, then, all of you. Stay close to the herd. We'll continue the search. Over."

"Roger. Over and out."

Heading away from the cattle, they met the cowboys coming in. The young men looked drawn and nervous, all of them probably thinking the same thing.

"We'll find him." Lila raised her voice over the sound of the four-wheeler's idling engine. "We won't stop looking until we do."

They raced into the darkness, Lila driving a wide zigzag pattern and Roper sweeping the landscape with the spotlight. A small cluster of goats, escapees from Charlie's debacle, scattered at their approach. A coyote flattened its body in the grass and slunk away. But there was no sign of Smokey or anything he might have left behind. Lila remembered the polite young man who'd driven her and Sam out to the mesquite thicket earlier. She tried not to think about the worst thing that could have happened, but as the minutes passed, the unthinkable became a possibility, then a worry, then a near certainty.

How much would a lanky young cowboy weigh? Surely no more than a hundred and fifty pounds—a feather to drag, compared to the weight of a yearling calf.

Steeling herself, she turned the four-wheeler in the direction of the mesquite thicket and gunned the engine.

Roper didn't question her action. He would know how and where the calf had been discovered earlier. His fear would be the same as hers.

His breath quickened as the spotlight fell on the brushy outline of the thicket. As they drew closer, he moved his rifle into position with his free hand.

Lila didn't expect to see the predator. If it was close by, the sound of the four-wheeler would either cause it to flee or drive it deeper into the mesquite. All that mattered now was finding the missing cowboy. Maybe he wouldn't be here, she thought. Maybe, minutes from now, they would come upon him, dazed and disoriented, trying to find his way back to the herd. There was still hope.

But that hope died as she neared the mesquite and swung the vehicle in a forty-five degree turn to view the thicket's east side, where the dead calf had been found. Roper swept the edge of the trees with the spotlight, stopped, and sucked in his breath. The light quivered in his hand.

"I'm sorry, Lila," he said. "You can call your cowboys. Tell them the search is over."

Slowing the engine to an idle, Lila could see where he was shining the light. Smokey had died much the same way the calf had been killed. She could only hope that death had come swiftly.

She forced her emotions to freeze. "The call can wait. We can't just leave him out here. There's a tarp under the back seat."

"Drive in closer," Roper said. "I'll wrap the boy in it and load him on the back seat. You'll need to cover me with the rifle. We'll be robbing a dangerous animal of its kill. If it charges, do you think you can shoot it?"

"I'll have to, won't I?" she said. "I've never killed anything, but Frank taught me how to use a gun."

"Then our best bet is to keep the beast at a safe distance. Do anything to make noise. Rev the engine, maybe fire a shot over the thicket to scare it. Sing if you have to. Whatever you do, don't get out of the vehicle."

"I understand." She pulled up within a few feet of the thicket. With the headlights shining on the spot where

Smokey's remains lay, she applied the brake and chambered a shell in the Weatherby—a big game rifle capable of bringing down a rhino. Roper dragged the tarp out from under the seat. The heavy canvas appeared large enough to do what was needed.

Danger senses prickling, he climbed out of the four-wheeler. He could see the doglike pawprints and the flattened, bloodied grass where the body had been dragged. A stone's toss away, the calf's carcass was nothing but bones. The vultures and ravens had picked it clean.

Trying not to think about how the cowboy had died, he spread the tarp on the ground. He could see that the animal had started to feed before their arrival had driven it off. It would be watching him from the mesquite. He could only hope that it wouldn't charge, and that if it did, Lila wouldn't freeze or miss.

Roper clasped the booted feet, dragged the body onto the tarp, and lined it up with the edge. Dropping to a crouch, he checked for any sign of a charge. Seeing nothing and hearing only the roar of the engine, he lifted the tarp's edge and began rolling the body to wrap it. The job took less than a minute, but it seemed longer, knowing the predator could spring out at any second to reclaim its kill.

Standing, he lifted the wrapped body in his arms and began backing away, one step, then another. Once he thought he saw a branch move, but that was all. He reached the vehicle, laid his burden across the back seat, and sprang into the passenger side. Lila handed him the rifle and floored the gas pedal. The vehicle roared away, leaving the thicket behind.

At a safe distance, Lila slowed the engine to an idle. "Did you see anything back there?" she asked.

"No. But I could feel something close by, watching me.

I was glad to get out of there. Have you called your cow-boys?"

"I was about to do that. They'll take it hard. Everybody liked Smokey. I'll need to call nine-one-one, too, when we get back in signal range."

"Did the boy have a family?"

"I don't know. But Darrin hired him. That information should be on file in the office. Blast Darrin, I'll need to call him, too. Maybe if he'd stayed here and done his job, this poor boy would still be alive."

With the four-wheeler briefly stopped, she called the cowboys on the walkie-talkie and exchanged a few words. "I told the boys we were taking the body back to the ranch," she said, shifting the gears. "Seeing their friend would only make things worse for them. Remind me to make sure they get some breakfast in the morning and a chance to rest—I can't count on Darrin to do that." She started off again, taking the vehicle at a slow pace to avoid spilling the wrapped body off the back seat.

"And what about you? You're going to need some food and rest, too," Roper said.

"I can rest after Darrin shows up. But there's no need for you to stay after we get back to the ranch. You'll want to go home, get cleaned up, and change."

Roper glanced down. He'd paid little attention to his blood-splotched hands and clothes. They were nothing compared to the tragedy that had just taken place. "I'll get around to that. But meanwhile, somebody needs to hunt that monster down and destroy it before it kills again."

"Whatever it is, it's got to be one of Charlie's escaped animals," Lila said.

"Then Charlie should be held responsible. He should kill it and pay compensation for the damage it's done." Roper glanced back to check the canvas-wrapped bundle on the back seat. "As if any amount of money could make up for the loss of that boy."

"What about those animal rights people who broke into Charlie's compound and opened pens and cages? Shouldn't they be held responsible, too? And what about Darrin? Those cowboys were working for him. He was in charge, and he left them out there on their own. What about me? Was there something I could've done differently? Where does the blame stop, Roper?"

"Nothing that happened was your fault." He wanted to touch her shoulder, but he remembered his bloodstained hands.

"I have an appointment with my lawyers in Abilene tomorrow," she said. "It concerns a different matter, but I'll ask about liability for Smokey's death and the other damages. Darrin will probably have his own answers, but I suspect they'll be geared toward protecting him and making money."

They were coming up on the ranch house now. Roper could see lights—more lights than had been on earlier when he and Lila had left. Maybe somebody had gotten word of what had happened.

Lila drove in the main gate and up to the house. Three figures were standing on the front porch—Sam, Jasmine, and Madeleine.

Stopping the vehicle, Lila jumped to the ground and strode up the porch steps. "One of our cowboys has been killed by that wild animal," she said. "The body's in the vehicle. Madeleine, call your son and tell him to get here—now. Sam, how soon can you get the police here with an ambulance?"

Sam had his phone in his hand. "What happened? They'll want to know."

"The same thing that happened to that yearling calf. The beast is still out there. So are the rest of the cowboys. They've been guarding the cattle all night. As nearly as we can tell, Smokey was separated from the others. His horse must've spooked and bolted. The rest of what happened, you can imagine."

The aroma of fresh coffee drifted from the kitchen. Mariah must be up, too. Maybe she'd heard the four-wheeler leave earlier and roused the others.

Lila glanced back toward the vehicle where she'd left Roper. He was gone—probably to where he could wash the blood from his hands.

Dressed in a black silk robe, Madeleine was on her phone, gesturing with her free hand as she spoke. Sam was making a call, too. Jasmine, in the ragged leggings and faded Grateful Dead tee she favored for sleeping, stood apart, her face in shadow.

"Are you all right?" Lila asked her.

"Not really. But I suppose I will be. Did you see the animal? Do you know what it is?"

"Not yet. We're pretty sure it was hiding in that big mesquite thicket, but we never saw it. Why? Do you know something about it? Does the animal belong to Charlie?"

"Probably—I mean, who else would it belong to? But no, I don't know what it is or anything else. Are you going to kill it?"

"We'll have to kill it, hopefully before it attacks again. Did you know the cowboy? Smokey, they called him."

"I knew him, but not very well. He was a sweet kid. I'm sorry it had to be him. Nobody deserves to die like that."

She turned away from Lila and walked off, clearly not wanting to say more. Roper had reappeared, his face and hands damp from washing. He took his place by the four-wheeler, as if standing vigil over the young cowboy's body.

Mariah brought out coffee and cups on a tray, which she placed on a low table. Lila poured a cup and took it to Roper before she filled a second cup for herself.

She was just finishing her coffee when the headlights of Darrin's Mercedes emerged from the darkness. Tires screeching, the big sedan swung off the road and headed down the driveway. As Darrin pulled up to the house, Lila set her cup back on the tray and summoned the last of her self-control.

Rumple haired, with his shirt half unbuttoned, he climbed out of the car. "Mother told me what happened," he said. "Where's the body?"

"Right over there." It was Sam who answered, nodding toward the four-wheeler. "The police are sending a van to pick it up and take it to the morgue. You can look, but you'll want to prepare yourself."

Darrin looked vaguely ill. "I'll pass, thanks."

"No!" Lila's frayed nerves snapped. She seized her stepson's arm and dragged him over to the vehicle where the cowboy's body lay wrapped in the tarp. Motioning Roper aside, she yanked open the end flap far enough to reveal a boyish face, dead white, bloodied, and frozen in a rictus of terror.

"Take a good look, Darrin. Do you even know his name?" she demanded. "He was called Smokey, and he was just a boy. If you'd stayed here to manage things, he might still be alive." She folded the canvas to cover the ravaged face again.

Darrin grew pale and turned away. His back heaved as he threw up behind an oleander bush.

Lila waited for him to compose himself. He faced her, still pale, wiping his mouth on his sleeve. "So now what, since you seem to have all the answers?" he asked.

"Now it's time to do your job," Lila said. "The rest of

your cowboys have been out on their horses, guarding the cattle all night. Those boys will be hungry and exhausted—as well as grieving for their friend. They need to come in."

"So if they come in, who'll be watching the cattle?"

"That's your problem, not mine, Darrin. But the most urgent thing is to hunt that beast down before it kills again. Get Charlie to help you—it almost certainly belongs to him."

"If that creature is Charlie's, he can be held responsible for damages," Darrin said.

"The legal question can wait," Lila said. "That animal just killed a young man. It's got to be stopped now. You can take the four-wheeler out—we'll need to move the body to the porch. I can deal with the police when they get here."

"You're expecting me to go out after that thing *alone*?"

"I'll go with you, Darrin." Roper stepped forward. "I've got a score to settle with that monster."

"I'll go with you, too," Sam said. "But I suggest we forget about Charlie. He's denied that the beast is his—probably a lie, but he'll do it again. That aside, going to get him will take time we don't have. We know where the kills were found. We can take our search from there."

Lila caught the furtive glance that passed between Sam and Jasmine. Something, she sensed, was going on between the two. But this was no time to worry about it. Of greater concern was the fact that Roper and Darrin loathed each other. She could be grateful, at least, that Sam would be going out in the four-wheeler with them.

Roper and Sam had their own guns. Darrin hadn't brought one with him. Lila handed him Frank's Weatherby. "Take this," she said. "It's loaded, and I know your father taught you to shoot. Don't forget to put gas in the tank before you leave."

Darrin gave her a contemptuous look and walked away. She'd humiliated him before his family and bossed him as if he were a child. He would not soon forget that.

While Darrin emptied the gas can into the four-wheeler's tank, Sam and Roper lifted the body by the ends of the tarpaulin and laid it carefully on the top step of the porch. Then, with Darrin at the wheel, Sam in the passenger seat, and Roper in the back, the vehicle roared away across the parking lot and onto the trail that led through the pastures.

The three women stood looking after them.

Jasmine sighed. "Men have all the fun."

"Maybe you should have volunteered to go with them," her mother said. "As for me, now that the excitement's over, I'm going back to bed." In her black silk robe, Madeleine looked like an old-time Hollywood star—maybe Gloria Swanson in *Sunset Boulevard*, Lila thought.

"Should you call Simone and tell her where her husband's gone?" she asked Madeleine.

Madeleine tightened her sash, cinching in her small waist. "No, let Simone get her beauty sleep. If she wants to know where he is, she can call me. And, by the way, there's no need to remind me of my motherly duties."

"So noted," Lila said. "Enjoy your rest. I'll be right here waiting up for the police."

After Madeleine had strode back to her bungalow and Jasmine had disappeared into the house, Lila settled on the steps next to the canvas-wrapped body. Such a gentle young man. It was as if she felt the need to keep him company before his journey to the cold police morgue with its sliding trays, gloved hands, and invading scalpel. *I'm sorry,* she wanted to say. *You deserved a life, Smokey. You deserved love and a family, with a wife and children and grandchildren. You deserved to learn and grow and have adventures. Now . . .*

Lila wiped away a tear. Did the boy have parents somewhere, maybe brothers and sisters? She would find out and call them first thing in the morning. She didn't know whether she believed in heaven. But she hoped that Smokey had, and that he was there.

By now, the sky above the eastern hills had begun to lighten. Earlier, Lila had heard the sounds of the returning cowboys putting away their horses and trooping into the bunkhouse for breakfast. At least she knew they were safe. But from the three men who'd gone off to hunt the monster, she'd heard nothing. And the police were taking their time, too.

Standing, she stretched, yawned, and wandered into the kitchen for more coffee and a slice of cinnamon toast. "Are the boys all right?" she asked Mariah.

"They will be, given time. But they weren't talking much over breakfast. Awful, losing a friend that way. First Frank, and now that nice young man. They say that deaths happen in threes. It makes you wonder who'll be next, doesn't it?"

Lila suppressed a shudder. She'd never believed in that old superstition, but something in the tone of Mariah's voice made her blood run cold. Anything could happen to anybody, at any time.

It came as a relief to hear a vehicle stopping in front of the house. It was the police van. Lila hurried outside to sign the paperwork and give the officers the needed information. Not that she knew very much about the young man. She watched as Smokey's wrapped body was eased onto a stretcher and loaded into the back of the van.

The boy deserved better, Lila thought as the vehicle pulled away from the curb and headed down the driveway. She was tired, but with the day already beginning, it didn't make sense to go to bed. Instead, she would spend some time in the ranch office, going through the files. Smokey must've filled out an application when he came to work for Frank—for tax and social security purposes if nothing else. If he had a family somewhere, she would take it upon herself to call them. It would be kinder to get the news from someone who cared than from a gruff police officer doing his job.

It took her about thirty minutes to find the file. The information was scant but it told her what she needed to know. Smokey's real name was Benjamin Pollard. He had aged out of the foster system at eighteen and had no known relatives. His birthdate and social security number were given, as well as his work history, which had consisted of washing dishes in a restaurant before he came to the ranch. A murky photo, attached to the single page, confirmed his identity. That was all.

Lila called the desk at the police station and passed on the information. "Do you want to claim the body?" the officer asked.

The question hadn't occurred to Lila until now, but the answer came to her at once. "Yes," she said. "I'll arrange with the mortuary to pick it up when it's released. We'll bury him here, on the ranch."

The sun had cleared the horizon by the time the three hunters returned to the ranch, tired, irritable, and empty-handed.

"We combed every inch of those pastures," Darrin grumbled as Jasmine met him in the kitchen. "We even threw rocks into that patch of mesquite. But we never caught a glimpse of that damned, murdering beast. All we saw were its tracks. But we did see a goat it had killed. At least it might not be hungry for a while."

"Maybe it's too smart for you," Jasmine said.

"Shut up." Darrin took a seat at the kitchen table and dug into the plate of bacon and scrambled eggs Mariah had set before him. He was the only one eating in the kitchen. Roper had headed for the stables to start his work. Sam had filled a mug of coffee, snatched an oatmeal cookie off a plate, and strode out the door. Guessing that he was headed for his bungalow, Jasmine took a shortcut through the house and was waiting on the porch when he arrived.

"Was it that bad?" she asked, taking stock of his dour expression.

"If you mean, was it a waste of time? Yes. And I can't say much for the company, either." Balancing the cookie atop the mug, he unlocked the door, leaving it open for her to follow him inside.

She closed the door behind her. "I just wanted to thank you for keeping Charlie at bay this morning. He's got a big mouth. If he'd been with you, he could have put me in a lot of trouble."

"This isn't just about trouble anymore, Jasmine." Sam set his makeshift breakfast on the table. "A man has died because of what your so-called friends did. You could be charged as an accessory to wrongful death, negligent homicide, or even manslaughter."

As the words struck home, Jasmine knew what she had to say. "Then I can't involve you anymore, Sam. I've already caused enough problems for you. You need to step back and let me deal with Charlie on my own."

She saw the conflict in Sam's face. If he helped her buy Charlie off and something went wrong, he could be implicated, too. He could lose his career, maybe even his freedom. She could tell he wanted to help her. But she couldn't allow it.

"I can handle Charlie," she said. "He may drive a hard bargain, but he won't hurt me. I've got my checkbook in my purse, and I know how much is in my account. I'm prepared to pay him whatever it takes to get my bracelet back and to buy his silence."

"Jasmine, you don't have to go alone."

"Yes, I do. You saved me once. Now it's my turn to save myself." Before he could argue, she stepped out the door and closed it behind her. She needed to go now, this minute, before she lost her nerve.

With her purse slung over her shoulder, she strode around the house to the vehicle shed, climbed into her red Corvette, and took the road to Charlie's place.

The main gate was open. Jasmine drove through and pulled up to the house. Charlie, freshly washed and shaved, was drinking coffee at a small table on the veranda. Rising, he greeted her with the smile of a man who knows he can't lose.

"Well, now, if it isn't Miss Jasmine Culhane, come to pay a call. Where's your boyfriend?"

"He's not my boyfriend, and this isn't about him," Jasmine said. "This is between you and me. I've got my checkbook in my purse. I'm prepared to negotiate for the bracelet—and your promise that once we've reached an agreement, I was never here that night. Fair enough?"

"Fair enough." He beckoned her up the steps, offered a chair, and took his seat to face her across the table. "All right, Miss Jasmine, make me an offer."

"Five thousand dollars," she said, knowing it wouldn't be enough.

"You're joking. That wouldn't buy me a hot weekend in Vegas."

"All right, ten."

Jasmine had a little over twenty thousand dollars in her account. But without her father's generosity to depend on, she would have to make it last until she could find a job.

Did Charlie know that his escaped animal had killed a

man? If he did, his asking price for the bracelet would soar. She was holding back one ace—but to play it would break her heart.

"Get serious, Jasmine. That bracelet could put you away. What's your freedom worth?" He gave her a playful wink.

Her face went hot. "If you think I'd—"

He roared with laughter. "You put a high price on yourself, lady—especially for soiled goods. But a hundred-dollar whore would give me better loving than I could get from you. You've got to do better than that."

"Fifteen thousand, then. That's my final offer. Take it or leave it."

"And if I choose to leave it?" He was enjoying this.

"Then make me a counteroffer," she said. "I can't go to my father anymore. And even if she'd give it to me, I'd rather eat rocks than go to my mother."

"Try fifty."

"Fifty thousand?" Her jaw dropped. "You know that if I can't pay you, the bracelet is only worth what you can get from a pawnshop."

"Then I'll have to settle for the satisfaction of seeing you in handcuffs and an orange jumpsuit, won't I? That would be worth something."

As he spoke, the suspicion that had crept into Jasmine's awareness became cold certainty. If she'd believed that she could manipulate Charlie, she was wrong. When he'd found her bracelet amid the debris, any love he might have felt for her had turned to hatred. He would show her no mercy.

It was time to play her last card.

Taking a deep breath, she forced herself to speak the words. "Then I have one last offer to make—the most valuable thing I own. It was a gift from my father, so it's paid for. And it's in mint condition, not a scratch . . ."

She paused, holding her breath as she waited for Charlie to reach his own conclusion. His gaze shifted to the sleek red Corvette parked at the foot of the steps. A greedy smile crept over his face.

"I have the title in my purse," Jasmine said. "But before I sign it and hand you the keys, I want to see that bracelet."

Charlie's grin showed his crooked, stained teeth. Lifting the bracelet out of his vest pocket, he laid it in front of her. "Allow me to drive you home in my new car," he said.

CHAPTER SIXTEEN

Lila's appointment with her lawyer was scheduled for 2:00 P.M. in Abilene. She'd planned extra time for lunch in a cozy Italian restaurant that she liked. The food was good, and the quiet time was badly needed after the bedlam the ranch had become.

She'd debated taking along the evidence her investigator had turned up. Now that Frank was gone and divorce was no longer an issue, it seemed beside the point even to keep it.

Still, in case some question about Frank's behavior arose, it wouldn't hurt to have them with her. Decision made, she slipped the envelope into her purse and went downstairs to her white Porsche, which had been freshly washed and brought around to the front of the house for her. She climbed into the car, laid her purse on the passenger seat, and fastened her seat belt. With the powerful engine purring, she had soon left the ranch behind.

The sun was climbing toward midday with no clouds in the sky. The drive home in the afternoon heat would be blistering. But she could always stay longer in town and return at a later hour—maybe go shopping after the appointment, get her hair done, or even take in a movie.

Right now, the thought of sitting by herself, munching buttered popcorn in a dark, air-conditioned theater, had some genuine appeal.

But the thought of a brief escape couldn't stop the worries from creeping in—the unseen monster that could strike at any time, the threat to her ownership of the house and horses, the FBI agent who appeared to be building a murder case against her—and the actual murderer, who could be anyone in her so-called family, even the one man she'd come to depend on—the man she had no choice except to trust.

She was halfway to Willow Bend, where the road branched off toward the freeway, when she spotted something ahead. Brown and white, the size of a small deer, the animal was standing in the middle of the road as if rooted to the spot.

It was a goat, she realized as the car drew closer. Probably one of Charlie's escapees that didn't have the sense to get out of the way. Her fist hit the horn and gave it several loud honks. The goat didn't budge.

Her foot pressed the brake. When nothing happened, she slammed it down hard. The pedal sank to the floor, but the car kept on hurtling forward. She couldn't stop or even slow down. She was going to hit the creature, probably kill it, and wreck her car.

Seized by panic, she swung hard right. The tires went off the shoulder. The Porsche tilted sharply. Lila screamed as the car rolled down the steep embankment, over and over. As it crunched into the bar ditch, Lila's world went dark.

It was Mariah who took the call from the highway patrol. Lila had a possible concussion. She'd been transported to the nearby clinic in Willow Bend for observation. The

Porsche, which had rolled and landed on its side, was badly damaged. If Lila hadn't been buckled in, she could have been killed.

Mariah passed the news on to Sam, who happened to be nearby. Concerned, but welcoming the chance to learn something new, he volunteered to check the condition of the vehicle and retrieve any personal belongings that might have been left behind.

After clearing his identity with the police, who agreed to give him access on condition that an officer meet him at the wreck, he went back to the bungalow to get a few things he needed.

Jasmine had returned earlier, walking in from the front gate without her beloved Corvette. Ignoring Sam, she'd gone up to her room and emerged in a black bikini. The last he'd seen of her, she was in the pool, swimming furious laps.

Guessing what had happened at Charlie's place, Sam had known better than to question her. Jasmine had paid a bitter price for her adventure, and she was dealing with it in her own way. When she felt like talking, she would come to him.

Darrin's Mercedes was parked in front of his mother's bungalow. Sam could only hope that Frank's son was doing his job, protecting the cattle and the cowboys from the danger that prowled the pastures. No one would rest easy until the creature was dead. But right now he had his own job to do.

Leaving Mariah to tell Roper about Lila's accident, Sam collected his evidence kit, climbed into the Jeep, and left the ranch. It didn't make sense that Lila would lose control of the car on the familiar road between the ranch and Willow Bend. There were some places where the shoulder was narrow, and the bank steep. But navigated at a reasonable speed, they couldn't be called dangerous.

Had something gone wrong with Lila's car? The steering, maybe? Or the brakes? But that didn't make sense either. The Porsche was fairly new and had to be in good condition. Maybe the wreck wasn't an accident.

Ahead, he could see the police car pulled off on the left side of the road. The right-hand lane here had only a narrow shoulder that dropped off steeply. That had to be where the car had gone off.

Sam recognized the trooper as the older man he'd interviewed about Frank's death. He was standing at the edge of the road, gazing down into the bar ditch.

"From the looks of that car, I'd say it was totaled," the trooper said. "Damned shame, fine automobile like that. I'll bet it's worth more than I take home in a year. But the Culhanes probably have good insurance."

"Thanks for meeting me," Sam said. "This shouldn't take long. I'm still investigating Frank's murder, and I need to make sure I haven't missed any evidence."

"Knock yourself out," the trooper said. "If you ask me or any cop, they'll tell you that the most likely suspect is the spouse."

After pulling on a pair of latex surgical gloves, Sam made his way down the steep bank. The position of the car, with the underside exposed, made it easy to check the brake lines. They were intact, but fluid was leaking around a loosened seal between the line and the master cylinder. This shouldn't have happened with a well-made and well-maintained vehicle. It appeared that somebody had sabotaged Lila's car—somebody who knew enough to make the brake failure look accidental. He took a closer look, using his penlight. That was when he saw the small, fresh marks of a tool used to loosen the seal.

This threw a whole new light on the case. Sam used his phone to take several photos, then moved forward to inspect the inside of the car.

"Mrs. Culhane's purse went with her in the ambulance," the trooper said. "But it was open and got tossed about in the crash. Some odds and ends were scattered around the car. With the need to get her to a doctor, it wasn't worth taking time to gather them up. Go ahead and look if you want. You'll need to sign for any evidence you take."

Getting into the tilted car was awkward. Sam had to lift the driver's side door and lower himself through the opening. The interior was cramped, with most of the loose objects scattered on the passenger door, which was now on the bottom—a lipstick, a ballpoint pen, an oil change receipt, a packet of tissues . . . That was when he saw the business-sized manila envelope trapped between the door and the side of the passenger seat.

As he grasped the envelope by a corner to lift it, the unsealed flap fell open, and several photographs fluttered out. Gathering them up, Sam stared down at the pictures—the sort that a private investigator might take. They showed a man and a dark-haired woman embracing and kissing in the doorway of a motel.

Frank's image, a closeup that must've been shot with a telephoto lens, was unmistakable. But the woman, a petite brunette with a cloud of dark hair, had been facing Frank with her back to the camera. None of the photos showed her face. Could it be Cheyenne McKenna? There was no proof, but Sam couldn't rule that possibility out.

He checked the date stamp on the back of the pictures. They'd been taken less than a month ago. Sam wasn't surprised that Frank had been cheating. Even more intriguing was that Lila had the photos and seemed prepared to use them. Had she been planning to divorce Frank?

A wealthy man like Frank would've been smart to have a prenup in place before remarrying. If so, that would've given Lila reason to choose murder over divorce.

One thing was certain. Frank hadn't been killed in the heat of the moment. The crime had been carefully and coldly planned by someone who knew his habits—probably someone Frank trusted. That would include his wife.

Slipping the photos back into the envelope, Sam closed the metal clasp and prepared to climb out of the car. He was looking for a secure foothold when something else caught his eye.

Stuck in the apparatus that adjusted the position of the driver's seat was a hypodermic needle, the size that a large animal vet would use. Could this have been the murder weapon?

Sam took a folded evidence bag out of his pocket and used it to enclose the hypodermic. At this point, he couldn't assume anything. Finding the needle in Lila's car was almost too much of a coincidence. If she'd used it to kill Frank, why would she keep it where it could be found? It made more sense that she'd destroy it or throw it away. And what about the leaking brake fluid that had caused her accident?

Was somebody trying to frame her, or even kill her?

Sam had hoped to find answers in the wreckage of the white Porsche. But he'd only found more questions.

Sam returned to the ranch to find Jasmine on his porch. She was barefoot and dressed in faded blue sweats. Sunlight sparkled on the water drops in her hair. She made a feeble effort to smile at him.

After leaving the evidence kit and the envelope inside the door, he joined her on the bench. "Sorry about your car," he said. "Wasn't there any other way?"

"What other way? I didn't have a choice. A young man died, Sam. If I hadn't guided those people to Charlie's, or, better yet, if I'd reported them to the police ahead of time, he'd still be alive. And that bracelet was enough evidence to put me behind bars."

"Smokey's death wasn't your fault," Sam said. "If Darrin had stayed around to supervise those cowboys and make sure nobody went off alone—"

"There'd have been no need for Darrin if I'd made the right decision. I paid with my car. Smokey paid with his life. And Charlie won."

"What have you told your family about the car?"

"They haven't asked, but they will. I'll think of something. Thanks for keeping the real story to yourself." She gazed out toward the road. "Mariah told me about Lila's accident. Is she going to be all right?"

"As far as I know. Otherwise she'd be on her way to the hospital in Abilene, not the clinic in Willow Bend."

"And Mariah said you looked at the car."

"I did. I'm no expert, but I'd say it's totaled." Sam wasn't about to tell her what he'd found. As he saw it, there were three people who would profit from having Lila dead or charged with Frank's murder. One of them was sitting next to him, asking questions.

Jasmine had brought him back to life. She had stirred emotions Sam had believed he would never feel again. But if she was guilty of murder, attempted murder, or even being an accessory, his feelings couldn't be allowed to matter. He had sworn to uphold the law, and he had a job to perform.

"What are you going to do for transportation?" he asked her.

She shrugged. "There are a few spare vehicles in the shed. I'll find one that runs. It'll have to do for now. Of course, I'd like a new car. But I don't have the money, and I'm not desperate enough to go to my mother." She stood, one hand brushing back her damp hair. "Meanwhile, today I'll be spending time on my computer. There are jobs out there that I can do remotely. But I'm going to need a new résumé. That's what I'll be working on."

"Good luck. I've got work to do myself." Sam stood with her.

"I'm up for sharing dinner if you want some company later."

"Let's see how it goes—for both of us." Sam would have enjoyed being with her, but given what he'd found in Lila's car, he needed to back off. Where Jasmine was concerned, he was already in too deep.

After she'd left him, he went back into the bungalow for a closer look at the evidence he'd taken from the wreck. The hypodermic needle was still in the plastic evidence bag. He'd thought about dusting it for prints. But it might be a better idea to take it to the crime lab in Willow Bend. Not only could they check for prints, but they should be able to determine whether the hypodermic had been used to deliver fentanyl.

Another question surfaced. He remembered Darrin urging him to get a search warrant. Had Jasmine's brother been the one to slip the hypodermic into Lila's car, hoping it would be found? Why would he, or anyone, go to the trouble unless it could be proven to be the actual murder weapon?

Leaving the hypodermic untouched in the evidence bag,

he slipped it into his briefcase. If he could get away, he would drive to Willow Bend this afternoon. He needed answers that only the lab could give him.

He took a few minutes to study the photo he'd taken of the leaking brake fluid. The seal had been loosened partway, probably so the fluid would leak slowly and run out later. If Lila had been speeding on the freeway when the brakes failed, the accident would have been worse, possibly fatal. But on that narrow, two-lane road, she wouldn't have been going more than forty or fifty miles an hour. Had something caused her to slam on the brakes early, pumping more fluid out of the line? Or had the person who loosened the seal simply miscalculated the flow? Sam was no mechanic. Maybe someone at the police station would know, or there would be a garage in town.

Whatever the answers to his questions might be, Sam couldn't ignore the new evidence of the photographs. They gave Lila an even stronger motive for murder.

And his list of suspects still included four other people: Madeleine, Darrin, Jasmine, and Roper.

Roper still had a motive for killing Frank, but not for sabotaging Lila's Porsche. Anyone with eyes in their head could see that the man was in love with her. That left the three Culhanes, likely working together, who had every reason to pin Frank's murder on Lila, or to see her dead.

But did that mean Madeleine and her offspring—one or all three—were guilty of killing Frank, or did they honestly believe that Lila had done it?

He studied the photos of Frank and the unknown dark-haired woman. Was there anything to the rumor that Frank had planned to divorce Lila and marry a younger replacement? Could that woman have been Cheyenne McKenna?

Sam had run out of answers. It was time to take a chance with the one person who might be able to tell him more. He needed to talk to Roper.

It was lunchtime for the stable work crew. It stood to reason that Roper would be in his office, probably resting. Sam knew he might not like being disturbed, but it was a challenge to catch him when he wasn't in the arena. Sam tapped on the closed door.

"What is it?" Annoyance edged Roper's voice. Like Sam, he'd been up most of the night hunting for the escaped predator.

"Just doing my job," Sam said. "I need to show you something and ask you a couple of questions."

Roper's sigh was audible through the closed door. "All right, Sam. Come in and sit down. You're probably as tired as I am."

Sam took the chair opposite the desk. "Any more word about Lila?" he asked.

"I just got off the phone with her." Worry shadowed his deep-set eyes. "She's got a slight concussion, but the clinic isn't equipped to keep her overnight, so they're letting her go home. I'll be leaving early to pick her up. After that, she'll need to take it easy for a few days. But you know Lila. Holding her down won't be easy."

"Is she aware—and are you—that the brakes on her car were sabotaged?"

"What?" Surprise flashed across Roper's face. "She said something about a goat, and not being able to stop. But I thought maybe she'd just panicked and swerved." His hand tightened into a fist. "*Damn!* So somebody wanted her dead?"

"It looks that way. The question is who."

"Give me three guesses. I guarantee you that one of them will be right."

"Guessing is easy. But I can't make a move without proof."

"Proof?" Roper's fist crashed onto the desktop. "What kind of proof do you need?"

"The kind of proof that would hold up in court against the priciest lawyers in the state. I'm still working on that."

Sam thought about the hypodermic. He would keep the device a secret until it had been tested in the lab. It could be the vital evidence he needed—or it could be a worthless distraction. But that wasn't why he was here now. He laid the manila envelope on the desk.

"I found this in Lila's car," he said. "Open it and tell me what you see."

Roper picked up the envelope and dumped the three photos on the desk. His jaw tightened as he arranged them in a line. Sam kept silent as the other man studied them, turning one over to check the date stamp.

"Frank never told me anything about his personal life," Roper said. "I assumed that he was faithful to Lila—or at least that it was none of my business. You say you found these in Lila's car?"

"I'm assuming she had them taken to use against Frank in a possible divorce. But of course, all that changed when he was killed."

"Are you implying that Lila might have killed him? I can't believe she'd do that. It's not who she is."

"I'm not saying she did or she didn't. I believe that people are innocent until proven guilty. But that's not why I'm here. I'd like you to look at the woman in these photos and tell me whether she could be your sister."

Shock flashed across Roper's face. He took a few moments to examine the photos, then shook his head. "No. That's not Cheyenne. Even without seeing her face, I'm sure of it."

"How do you know? I've met your sister. The build and hair are similar here. And I've heard the story of how Frank wanted to train her, so there's at least a past connection."

"But Cheyenne turned him down. She didn't even like him. As far as I know, they haven't been in touch since then. Then there's this. Look closely." Roper shoved one of the photos toward Sam. "The woman has her hand on Frank's shoulder. Look at those long, fake nails and those rings. Cheyenne handles horses. She works with her hands. And even when she's not competing, she dresses like a cowgirl. She wouldn't be caught dead in a nail salon—and she'd never wear anything like those fancy, glittery rings. I don't keep track of her schedule, but she was probably out on the circuit when these photos were taken."

"So who's the woman? Do you recognize her?"

Roper shook his head. "I don't recall ever meeting her or even seeing her. If she was at Frank's memorial, I didn't notice—not that she would've been invited."

"Would Lila know her?"

"I have no idea. You'll have to ask her."

Sam gathered the pictures and slipped them back into the envelope. So another piece of the puzzle had presented itself—a mystery woman who might or might not have been involved in Frank's murder.

Back in the bungalow, he used his phone to shoot the clearest picture, front and back to include the date and the name of the photographer. He texted the images to Nick with a brief message. Maybe the detective who took the photos would have some idea who the woman was.

A glance at the clock told him there was enough time left in the day to drive to Willow Bend, drop the hypodermic off at the police lab, and maybe even visit Lila in the clinic before Roper came to drive her home.

Lila wouldn't be glad to see him. And Roper wouldn't appreciate his calling on her when she needed rest. But he wasn't here to make friends—so far that approach had gotten him nowhere. He was here to solve a murder case. It was time he pulled the pieces together, did his job, and got back to Abilene.

As for Jasmine, Sam told himself, he meant no more to her than some cowboy she'd picked up in a bar for a one-night stand. Maybe if he thought of her that way, he'd be able to put that night behind him and do what needed to be done.

Lila supposed she could count herself lucky to be alive. The accident had left her with an aching head and a battered body from being jerked against the seat belt while the car was rolling. But the drugs the doctor had given her had dulled the pain to a tolerable level. Now all she wanted was to get her life back. That was going to take time—time she didn't have.

Now, dressed and checked out, she sat on a couch in the empty waiting room, thumbing through a tattered copy of *People* magazine and trying not to watch the clock. Roper had said he would try to be here early. But things tended to come up at work. She knew better than to expect him anytime soon, and she didn't want to bother him with a phone call.

She glanced up as the outside door opened. A tall figure stood backlit by the late-afternoon sun. For an instant her pulse quickened. But when the man stepped into the waiting room and walked toward her, she saw that it was Sam.

"Don't get up," he said as she started to rise. "I saw Roper earlier. He still plans on driving you home. But I was in town on an errand and needed to show you something. May I join you?"

Feeling a prickle of apprehension, she moved over to make room for him on the couch. The FBI agent was on the side of the law; the warning she'd given Roper still stood. Sam Rafferty was a man who played his cards close to his vest. She could never be sure of his intent.

"I took a look at your car," he said. "You're lucky to be in one piece. How are you feeling?"

"Sore. I'll heal, but I loved that car. As soon as I can arrange things with the dealer and the insurance company, I plan to get another one like it."

"Has anyone told you that the brakes were tampered with?"

She gasped. The details of the events leading up to the accident were still foggy. She forced herself to concentrate. "It does explain why I couldn't stop for that goat. I had to swerve to keep from hitting it. That was when I rolled. I thought maybe I'd panicked and stomped on the gas pedal instead of the brake." She took a sharp breath, feeling the stress on her bruised body. "But you're saying somebody damaged my brakes—that they were trying to kill me?"

"Take a look." He found the picture on his phone and held it for her to see. "From the looks of the loosened seal, I'd guess that somebody wanted you on the freeway before the fluid ran out. If your brakes had failed at eighty miles an hour, you could've been killed and taken others with you. If my theory is right, that fool goat might have saved your life."

He closed his phone. "So my question is, who would have access to your car, and who would hate you enough to want you dead?"

Lila shivered beneath her thin blouse. "Is this a trick question? We both know who you're talking about and why."

"But we don't for certain. And even if we could be sure, we don't know which one."

"Why not all three? They've got to be working together. And they all have reason to see me convicted of Frank's murder or dead—or both."

"That brings me to something else." He drew a manila envelope out of his vest. Lila recognized it at once. "I found this in your car. Is it yours?"

"Yes, it's mine." Lila curbed the impulse to try to snatch it from him. She was too weak to take it. "It must have fallen out of my purse. What's in there is none of your business."

His expression hardened. "What's in here is very much my business, Lila. But if you'll give me a few honest answers, I'll return it to you. That's why I'm here."

"Go ahead and ask. I have nothing to hide."

"You paid to have these taken?"

"Yes. I suspected Frank was cheating on me. It turned out I was right. And thinking back, I have reason to believe he'd been doing it all along. I was faithful to my husband for eleven years. I expected the same thing from him. I should've known better."

"But according to his children, he cheated with you while he was married to Madeleine. That should've been a red flag."

"Yes, I suppose. But I was naïve enough to think I could give him everything he needed. Women can be such fools."

"And the woman in the photo?"

ONE IN A MILLION   251

"One of many, I suspect. Frank liked them young. That was one thing I couldn't change about myself."

"Could the woman have been Cheyenne McKenna?"

"I don't think so. Frank had a schoolboy crush on Cheyenne. He even talked about wanting to train her. But she wasn't interested. And now she's a celebrity. What would she want with an old man like Frank?"

"So, you don't know the woman in the photos?"

"I've no idea who she is. Frank wouldn't have had any trouble getting girls. They flocked around him like buckle bunnies at those reining events."

"And what about the rumor that he was going to leave you for a younger woman?"

"Somebody started it. But Frank had it good with me. And I was too deep in denial to face the reality that he was having fun on the side. Why should he give up what we had for a whole new set of problems?"

"One last question," Sam said. "What were you planning to do about these photos?"

"I hadn't decided. Should I divorce Frank? Expose him? Lock the pictures away in case I needed them later? I was still making up my mind when he was killed."

"So, you could have killed him. Motive, means, and opportunity. You had all three—and nobody to confirm your alibi."

Lila felt as if the bottom had dropped out of her stomach. She'd hoped Sam might change his mind about her guilt. But no, she was still a suspect. Summoning her dignity, she gave him an honest answer.

"Yes, I could have killed him. I didn't hate Frank—in fact, I loved him. But love can hurt. I was angry enough to meet him in the stable and plunge that needle into his neck. But I didn't do it. I had too much to lose. And as

Frank's widow and heir, I would never have gotten away with his murder. Frank's killer was somebody else. Somebody angrier and stronger than I was—and less likely to get caught."

She stood, her signal that the interview was over. "Now, Agent Sam Rafferty," she said, "I suggest you give me back my property and go find the person who hated my husband enough to kill him!"

CHAPTER SEVENTEEN

Roper had left work an hour early. Driving the road that Lila had taken, he passed the spot where her car had veered off the road and rolled down the embankment. A tow truck with a winch was hauling the wreckage out of the bar ditch. *Totaled* was the word for the elegant white Porsche, its chassis crushed like a soda can. Lila was lucky to have survived the crash with minor injuries. Maybe he shouldn't even be driving her home. Maybe he should take her to Abilene and check her into the hospital. At least she'd be safe there.

But knowing Lila, she would have none of that.

The idea that someone had tried to kill her filled him with helpless rage. Frank's ex and her two offspring—or someone in their pay—had to be behind the sabotage on the Porsche. Their plan was as evil as it was obvious. Remove Lila, making her death look like an accident; blame her for Frank's murder, and the ranch would be theirs.

But Sam was right. They might have motive, means, and opportunity, but so far, there was no evidence that would hold up in court.

Right now, all that mattered to Roper was keeping Lila safe.

The clinic parking lot was nearly empty. He pulled his truck close to the building, climbed out, and strode through the main door. Lila was alone in the waiting room, watching the overhead TV. Her face looked pale and strained below the white bandage that circled her head, but she gave him a faint smile.

"Hello, Boss." Tenderness and worry crept into his voice, betraying his emotions. "What do you say we get out of here?"

"Let's go." She stood, clutching her purse.

"Whoa." He strode forward to steady her. "You look like you could blow over in a stiff breeze. How are you doing?"

"Better than my car. Sam showed me the pictures he took of it."

"Sam was here?" Roper felt a surge of annoyance. Was it jealousy? He willed himself to ignore it. "Did Sam tell you that your brakes had been tampered with?"

"Yes. Somebody's not playing by the rules. Three guesses who."

"This isn't a joke. Somebody wanted to kill you. They almost succeeded. I'm worried about you." He held the door for her, supported her to the parking lot, and helped her into the truck.

"I'm worried about me, too. But I'll be damned if I'm going to let them know it." A grimace tightened her face as she reached around to fasten her seat belt. "I've called Mariah and asked her to prepare dinner. Everyone's to be invited, including you and Sam."

"Are you out of your mind?" he demanded. "You're under a doctor's orders to rest. This is the last thing you should be doing."

"Which is exactly why I need to do it. They'll think

they've got me running scared. I need to show them they're wrong."

He started the truck and backed out of the parking slot. "You could overdo it and end up in the hospital. Listen to me. I'm trying to talk sense into you."

"You know better than that, Roper," she said, a teasing note in her voice. "Just be there for me. That's all I ask."

"What if I refuse to be a part of this crazy plan? Would that stop you?"

"No, but please don't refuse. You're the only one I can count on. The others, even Sam and Mariah . . ." Her words trailed off. "I never know what they're thinking." She settled back into the seat as if the conversation had exhausted her.

The sun sank lower in the sky. Distant clouds, drifting above the horizon, deepened from white to rose. Lila stirred and spoke.

"What's being done about that killer animal?"

"Nobody's seen it. But the cowboys will be guarding the steers again tonight. They'll have strict orders to stay together."

"And what about Darrin? Is he going to be with them this time?"

"Now here's where it gets interesting. According to one of the cowboys, Darrin's made a deal with Charlie Grishman to help him hunt down the beast. They plan to stake out a live goat as bait, hide and wait for the creature to show up, then blast it to kingdom come."

"Well, for all our sakes, let's hope it works. But why the deal? That animal belongs to Charlie—it has to. That's the only explanation."

"But Charlie has never admitted it. Maybe that was the deal—in exchange for his help, he'll be held harmless for any damage the thing has done. Darrin's a lawyer. He knows all the angles."

"And what about Simone? I know she hates being alone at night."

"Evidently she's going to stay in the bungalow with her mother-in-law."

"Good. Then she'll be there for dinner."

"You're really going through with this crazy plan?"

"It's that or hide in my room. I can't let them think they've scared me."

"And are you scared?"

"I'm petrified. But they don't have to know that."

Roper sighed. "Fine. I'll be there. But if I notice you fading, you're going straight to your room."

He waited for a snappy retort. When it didn't come, his thoughts began to wander to other concerns. As he'd left the stable early today, there were people still finishing their work. He'd given Cruiser the responsibility of staying to close up, which included checking every stall and making sure the outside doors were latched. But with Cruiser's girlfriend, Janae, around, the kid was running on hormones. If he hadn't done his job, he was asking to be fired.

After he got Lila safely home, Roper would check everything in the stable. Cruiser had been given a second chance. If anything was left undone, there would be no third chance.

After delivering Lila to the house and alerting Mariah that she might need help, Roper went out to check the stable. He found the outside door not only unlatched but ajar. Cruiser's motorcycle was gone. The young Romeo would get his walking papers in the morning.

Roper walked up and down the rows of stalls, checking

each one. Most of the horses were all right, but some still needed hay and water. Roper took care of them and made sure the brood mares and their foals, brought inside while the predator was at large, were safe.

Million Dollar Baby was in her roomy box stall. As Roper paused to check on her, she thrust her elegant head over the gate, nickering for attention. Roper stopped to stroke her white face. "Getting spoiled, are you, Baby?" he murmured. "Just wait till you win the shootout this coming week, and then the Run for a Million. You'll find out what real spoiling is."

As he turned to go, she caught his sleeve with her teeth, as if trying to tell him something. Laughing, he tugged himself free and continued down the row of stalls to One in a Million's new quarters.

Roper had made the decision not to put the stallion back in his old stall. The horse had made progress since witnessing Frank's death. But going back to where the trauma had taken place might reawaken bad memories. Why risk it, as long as One in a Million was comfortable in his new home?

But what was wrong with him now? As Roper entered the stall, the stallion snorted, tossed his head, and stamped restlessly in the straw. Maybe there was a mare in estrus nearby, and he could smell her.

"Easy, big boy." Roper stroked the massive neck, feeling the tightness in the stallion's muscles. Nothing seemed amiss in the stable—in fact, most of the other horses were calm. But One in a Million was unhappy about something. Roper checked his belly for any sign of colic. Nothing. There was a healthy pile of manure in a corner of his stall. He'd eaten some hay, and he had plenty of water. There were no snakes in his bedding straw or his feeder. Everything seemed fine.

Roper left the stable, making sure the outside doors were securely latched. That done, he washed his hands at the tap and went back to the house to join Lila and the others for dinner.

Given short notice, Mariah had made spaghetti with salad and garlic bread. The seven people seated around Elias Culhane's great plank table filled their plates and began to eat—some, like Sam, with gusto. Others, like Madeleine and Simone, toying with their food as if they didn't trust their hostess.

Lila had taken her seat at the head of the table, Frank's traditional place. Her unspoken message was clear. She was the head of the Culhane family, and anybody who wanted to take her place would have a fight on their hands.

She was conscious of Darrin's glare. He was sending a message of his own—that as a man, and a blood Culhane, that place at the table belonged to him.

Had Darrin been the one who'd damaged her brakes? She remembered Frank mentioning that his son had enjoyed tinkering with cars as a teenager. He probably knew enough to have done the damage. But how many other men—and even women—on the ranch had that same level of expertise? How many cowboys and stable hands would have grown up fixing their own cars? How many among them would have sabotaged her Porsche for a generous and discreet offer of cash?

She had taken the bandage off her head. The pain was about the same. She'd also put on a fresh blouse and slacks, brushed the tangles out of her hair, and dabbed makeup over the visible bruises. She looked all right. But barely all right. And she felt worse than she looked. Roper was watching her, his dark gray eyes revealing his worry. She gave him a forced smile, as if to reassure him that she was fine. His answering nod told her that he knew better.

Conversation was awkward. Lila had planned on being a sparkling hostess. She couldn't quite muster the energy, but she had to try.

"Darrin, I hear you've enlisted Charlie to help you catch that awful animal," she said.

"It's about time we did it right," Darrin said. "Charlie's a professional hunter. And even though he won't admit it, we all know that beast must have escaped from his menagerie."

"So, Charlie knows what it is?" Sam asked.

"I'm sure he does. But we made a deal. As long as he helps us kill the thing, he's not to be held responsible."

"Just be careful, Darrin," Simone said. "This baby is going to need a father."

Ignoring her, Darrin turned to his sister. "Speaking of Charlie, Jasmine, what's he doing with your Corvette? He said he made a trade for it. Dad gave you that car. I thought you loved it."

Jasmine, wearing a blue sundress, shrugged. "I did. But I traded it for something I needed more than a car."

"What on earth would that be?" Darrin demanded. "That car's got to be worth close to a hundred thousand dollars."

"That, brother dear, is my own business. I don't owe you, or anybody else here, an explanation."

"Well, I hope you're not expecting me to buy you another car," Madeleine said. "Until you learn to appreciate the value of money, you'll just have to make do. Honestly, Jasmine, when are you going to grow up and become responsible?"

"I'm trying," Jasmine said. "Leave me to make my own way, and I might surprise you."

"What are you going to do for transportation now?" Darrin asked. "You can't just wait for a car to fall out of the sky."

"I've been looking around here," Jasmine said. "There's that old black truck in the shed—it's vintage, kind of cool. I think with a little work—maybe clean the carburetor and put in new spark plugs—I could get it running. At least it might be fun to try."

Sam was quick to hide his surprise. But Lila hadn't missed the expression on his face. For an instant, he'd looked as if he'd been punched by a giant fist.

Lila, too, had been caught off guard. She'd forgotten how Jasmine, as a lonely teen, had taken to hanging out in the garage and machine shed, helping the grandfatherly mechanic who'd since passed on. In the early days of her marriage, Lila had tried to befriend the girl. But she'd never gotten past the wall of anger that Jasmine had built between them. That wall, she knew, was still there.

Had Jasmine's comment about the truck been made in innocence, or had it sent Lila a defiant message? Knowing Jasmine, either could be true.

As for Sam, Lila could sense the conflict in him. He liked Jasmine, maybe even loved her. But she had just become one more suspect in an attempted murder.

Lila's gaze met Madeleine's. The look in the older woman's eyes was so cold that it raised goose flesh on the surface of Lila's skin. Madeleine could easily have ordered the damage to the car and had maybe even orchestrated Frank's murder. She was the mistress of secrets, the puppet master, pulling the strings.

It might be a stretch to call Madeleine evil. But she was clearly a woman who would do anything to get what she wanted. And it wasn't just the ranch she wanted. If Lila hadn't realized it before, she knew it now. It was revenge.

Mariah emerged from the kitchen with bowls of chocolate ice cream, which she passed around the table. Pausing next to Lila, she leaned close and spoke. "I meant to deliver a message earlier. The mortuary called. They have the young man's body prepared for burial. You need to let them know which casket you want and when you'd like it delivered."

Madeleine's eyebrows shot up. "What's going on? It sounds like you're burying somebody on the ranch."

"That's right." Lila had expected objections. "It's the young cowboy who was killed guarding our cattle from that wild animal. He was a foster kid, with no family, so I'm making him part of ours. He'll be buried in the family cemetery on the hill."

"How dare you?" Madeleine was on her feet, her voice raised. "I won't allow it! That land was set aside for the Culhane family, not for some homeless piece of riffraff. Let the state take care of him."

"This isn't your decision, Madeleine." Lila stood, one hand gripping the back of her chair to steady her balance. "This ranch is mine. Frank's will left it to me. That includes the cemetery. I have the right to choose who gets buried there. That young man could've had a good life—an education, a home, a wife and children. He lost his future protecting Culhane property."

The faces around the table were beginning to blur. She forced herself to keep talking. "My decision stands. If you want to fight it, take it to court."

"Bury him anyplace you want, then." Madeleine's lip curled in an angry sneer. "But I promise you this. When we get our ranch back, the first thing I plan to do is dig him up and turn his body over to the state."

"Leave it alone, Mother!" Jasmine sprang to her feet. "I've stood by you and done everything you wanted. But that boy deserves a resting place with our family."

Madeleine turned to confront her daughter across the table. "Have you lost your mind, Jasmine? What's gotten into you?"

"That cowboy is dead because of me, Mother. I was with that mob of activists who broke into Charlie's compound and let the animals out. One of those animals killed Smokey. I could have stopped that riot before things got out of control. I could've warned the police ahead of time. But I didn't. I let it happen. And the least I can do is fight to give that poor young man an honorable grave."

"Be quiet and sit down, Jasmine," Madeleine ordered. "We need to talk in private."

"No, there's more," Jasmine continued, ignoring her mother. "Charlie found evidence that could prove I'd been at his place with those people. He threatened to go to the police. That's why I had to give him my car. It was the only way to keep him quiet. So now you know. And now I need to leave."

Stepping away from the table, she turned and fled from the dining room. Her footsteps rang on the tiles as she raced through the entry hall and out the front door, slamming it behind her.

As stunned silence settled around the table, Sam rose from his place and strode after her.

"Well, that's that." Simone carved out a dainty spoonful of ice cream. "I always said Jasmine was too impulsive for her own good. I certainly don't want her anywhere near our baby."

Madeleine remained standing. "Darrin, don't you need to meet that animal hunter soon? It's getting dark outside."

Darrin glanced at the IPhone on his wrist. "Yes, it's getting to be that time. I'll be meeting him at his place. We'll pick up the goat and set up a blind by that mesquite thicket."

"Please touch base with your cowboys," Lila said. "They'll need to know what's going on."

"They know." Darrin stood. "As long as they stay together and keep an eye on the cattle, they'll be fine. They've been warned that if they lose another calf, it's coming out of their pay."

"Shall we go now, Simone? I can't imagine there's anything left to be said here." Madeleine extended a hand to her daughter-in-law and pulled her to her feet, then turned briefly to Lila. "Please thank Mariah for preparing this wonderful dinner on such short notice. We enjoyed the food."

She stalked out of the house, following her son and sweeping Simone along beside her. Lila and Roper were left alone in the dining room.

"Are you all right, Boss?" He sat at the far end of the table, his face in shadow.

"I'm fine. Just tired. I didn't know the meal would turn out to be so . . . stressful. Is that a good word for it?"

"As good as any. But you held your own."

"I suppose I did. But it was all I could do to keep myself under control."

Roper stood. "Well, you can let yourself go now. You've had your dinner and proven your point. Now it's time you got some rest. Can I help you upstairs to your room?"

Lila almost said yes. But there was the question of appearances. If it reached Madeleine's ears—by way of Mariah—that Roper had escorted her upstairs, the report could be blown up into something it wasn't.

But there was an even deeper reason for caution. If

Roper were to help her to her room, the temptation to invite him in could prove too compelling to resist—especially if he didn't say no.

"I'll be fine." Lila shook her head. Their relationship worked because of the invisible line they'd drawn between them. Crossing that line, even by a step, would create nothing but trouble.

Mariah came out of the kitchen and began gathering up the dishes. She'd probably overheard everything that had been said at the table, but it wasn't her place to mention it.

"Let me make you an offer, Mariah," Roper said. "I'll finish clearing the table if you'll help this lady upstairs and see that she gets to bed. She's had a long, rough day. We don't want her ending up on the floor."

"I can do it. There's no need for you—" Mariah protested.

"No, fair's fair," Roper said. "You've had a long day, too. I'll leave when I've finished." He shot Lila a stern glance. "Get going, Boss. Call me if you need anything. I'll see you in the morning."

Too tired to argue, Lila allowed Mariah to support her up the stairs to her room.

Sam found Jasmine on the patio. She was huddled in a chair, gazing at the reflected moon in the pool.

"Hi." He pulled up another chair and sat down next to her. She didn't reply or even look at him.

"For what it's worth," he said, "I was proud of you in there."

"For what?"

"For telling the truth."

"The truth doesn't buy me a thing," she said. "It just saves me the worry that my family will find out what I did.

That poor, sweet cowboy is still dead. That awful animal is still on the loose, and Charlie will never give my car back. Nothing's changed—except that my mother will probably disinherit me."

"I'm sorry," Sam said.

"Don't be. I've been making bad decisions most of my life. I just added a few more to the string." She pulled her skirt above her knees and stretched her glorious legs in front of her. A sudden kick sent one sandal flying into the water. She kicked the other one after it. They sank out of sight.

"Regret is a wasted emotion, Jasmine," Sam said. "I'm still learning that myself. You can't go back. All you can do is learn from your experience and move forward."

"You sound like one of those self-help articles. That might be true with some things—like my drunken romp with that jerk from the saloon. But when your bad decision has hurt other people, you live with it forever." Her fingers raked her curls back from her face. "You and me—was that a bad decision, Sam? Did I hurt you?"

He took a moment to think about her question. His night with Jasmine had compromised him professionally. But on a deeper level, he wasn't sorry. Given the chance, he wouldn't hesitate to take her to his bed again.

"You didn't hurt me," he said. "It was more like you saved me."

Her laugh was laced with irony. "Saved you? That's a good one. I don't have an unselfish bone in my body. I didn't do it for you. I did it for me—because I needed you."

"Then I guess we both got what we needed."

"I guess we did. I may not be a saint. But I've never lied to you, Sam. And I swear to God I didn't kill my father. If that isn't good enough for you, then I'm out of luck."

And you didn't tamper with the brakes on Lila's car?

That question could wait until he'd checked out other possibilities, Sam told himself. But as long as she was here, he had a different question to ask her.

"Did you know your father was cheating on Lila?"

She gave him a startled look, then nodded. "I caught him stepping out on Mother when I was thirteen. After that, he never tried to hide his affairs from me. It was our dirty little secret. Darrin didn't even know."

"How did you feel about that?"

She shrugged. "I felt bad for Mother—she knew, and she always took him back. But after he was married to Lila, I didn't care. I felt she deserved it."

Sam took his phone out of his pocket and scrolled to the photo he'd copied. "Lila hired a detective to take some pictures. This is one of them. Do you know this woman?"

Jasmine shook her head. "Dad never introduced me to his girlfriends. That was part of our understanding."

"And what about the rumor that your dad was planning to divorce Lila and marry a younger woman?"

"Dad actually mentioned that to me. But I didn't take it seriously. He depended on Lila to manage his world. Maybe the sizzle was gone, but he'd have been lost without her."

"Do you still believe she killed him?"

"More than ever now that I know about the photos. He was fooling around, like always, and she caught him. Men have been killed for less."

"You don't have a very high opinion of men, do you?" Sam said.

She pulled her skirt down and stood. "My dad was a charming, lying rascal, but I loved him. My ex-husband was the same. I loved him, too, but only at first. I don't know if I'm brave enough to try love for a third time—not even with someone like you."

"Jasmine—" He reached for her, but she stepped back.

"Oh, did I say too much? Forgive me, I can't seem to stop telling the truth tonight. Yes, I'm falling in love with you, Sam. And my survival instincts are screaming at me to run for my life."

"Damn it, Jasmine!" He caught her waist and spun her against him, clasping her tight, feeling his body respond. "Don't you know how hard I've been fighting this?"

"Yes, I know." She gazed up at him. "I know because I've been fighting it, too. We're poison for each other. You know that, don't you?"

"So, what are we going to do about it?" His voice was thick and husky with need.

She stretched on tiptoe, bringing her lips close to his. "I have a suggestion," she whispered.

His kiss was hungry, even brutal. She caught fire in his arms, whimpering as his tongue found hers, thrusting deep. Her hips curled inward to mold against his hardness.

If there was a price to be paid, he would pay it. Right now, nothing mattered except making love to her. With a curse, he swept her up in his arms and carried her through the darkness to the bungalow.

After clearing the table and stacking the dishes on the kitchen counter, Roper left the Culhane house and headed for home. He found his three brothers and his sister loading the horse trailer for a rodeo in El Paso. They planned to drive through the night and arrive in the morning to unload the horses at the rodeo grounds, then catch a few hours of sleep in the motor home before the evening show.

Roper pitched in to help load the feed and the tack. In the kitchen, Rachel was packing fresh bread, cookies, sandwich fillers, and a casserole into long-used Tupperware containers. These would go in the motor home's tiny kitchenette, which included a microwave and a miniature fridge.

"You missed supper," she said as Roper walked into the kitchen. "Where were you?"

"I had dinner at the Culhanes'. It was just spaghetti. Not as good as yours, Mom."

"So now you're getting invited up to the big house." Kirby dribbled whiskey into his coffee mug. "Next thing you know, you'll be too uppity to even sit down with us."

"Stop it, Kirby. Roper's just been doing his job. He knows better than to think those highfalutin folks will ever see him as an equal. But it's how God sees us that matters, not a big house and fancy cars." Rachel sealed the lid on a container of potato salad. "Has that FBI fellow figured out who killed Frank?"

"Not yet—unless he's figured it out in his head. He's got a way of keeping things to himself." Roper might have told his parents about Lila's so-called accident and the killer beast that was still at large on the ranch. But they would probably keep him in the kitchen until they'd heard every detail of their wealthy neighbors' misfortunes. Tonight, he didn't have the patience. All he wanted was to get some sleep before an early-morning return to the Culhane Ranch.

Maybe he shouldn't have come home at all. As he walked down the hall to his bedroom, he couldn't shake the feeling that something was wrong. Worries swarmed in his mind. There was Lila, who could still be in danger. There was the way Cruiser had walked out on his responsibilities, and the stallion's odd behavior. There was the coming shootout that would determine Frank's replacement in the Run for a Million. Would Million Dollar Baby be ready to perform? Would he be able to bring out the best in the beautiful mare?

Tired as Roper was, sleep refused to come. As the first light turned the sky pale, he dressed and went outside to his truck. The sense of foreboding he'd felt last night hadn't gone away. If anything, it was stronger than ever—too strong to question.

Driven by an urgency he couldn't explain, he floored the gas pedal all the way to the ranch. Arriving in minutes, he swung the truck through the employee gate, parked in his usual place, and sprang to the ground.

The house and guest bungalows were dark, the stable closed as he'd left it the evening before. As he approached the door, a pair of vultures, perched on the peak of the roof, flapped into the sky. Roper had never been superstitious, but the sight of the grim, black birds sent a chill through his body. As they vanished into the sunrise, he opened the stable door.

First to strike him was the sound of horses, snorting, shrilling, and slamming against the sides of their stalls.

As he raced into the stable, a fetid odor swept into his nostrils. He recognized the blended aromas of blood and death.

Turning the corner, he could see down the line of stalls. One in a Million was snorting, tossing his head and rolling his eyes as he plunged against the five-foot, open-topped gate. The other horses were agitated but appeared safe— except for Million Dollar Baby. There was no sound from the mare's stall, no sign of her head above the gate.

Roper was unarmed, but this was no time to go for a

gun. Sick with dread, he slid the gate open far enough to look into the stall.

Million Dollar Baby was backed into a corner, her head hanging down, blood oozing from a gash in her side.

At her feet lay a trampled carcass, the head broad and ugly with massive jaws, the spotted body crushed into the straw.

Chapter Eighteen

The veterinarian shook his head. "It's your choice, Mrs. Culhane. I can try to save her. But she's got some deep wounds, and there's no telling what kind of bacteria she got from those bites. Even if she survives, she'll never be fit to compete. You might want to consider putting her down."

"No, I want her saved," Lila said. "Million Dollar Baby is a warrior. She's earned the right to live."

"I'll do everything I can," the vet said. "But I can't promise to save her. You need to understand that."

"I don't care what you have to do." Lila's expression was resolute. "I don't care how much it costs. After the fight she put up, we can't just throw away her life."

"All right. If that's your decision, I'll clean and suture her wounds and pump her full of antibiotics. After that, all we can do is wait."

Million Dollar Baby, weak and bleeding, had been transferred to a clean stall for treatment. Roper, wearing gloves and a disposable gown, stood by to support the mare and assist the vet. He'd seen enough injured horses to know that Baby's chances were slim. No bones appeared to be broken, but if infection and fever set in, her fight would be over.

The hyena's battered, lifeless body had been photo-graphed, bagged, and hauled out for burial. Roper had pieced together a rough idea of what had taken place. The creature must have snuck into the stable when Cruiser left the door open. When Roper had returned to check the stalls, it had still been inside, which would explain the stal-lion's nervous behavior.

Roper's departure had trapped the hyena in the stable. Sensing prey, it had chosen a stall at random and either jumped or climbed over the five-foot gate. Dropping to the other side, it had found Million Dollar Baby ready to fight for her life.

The battle in that confined space must have been terri-ble—the hyena with its agile body and slashing jaws, the mare with her superior size and pounding, iron-shod hooves. At last, wounded and bloodied, Baby had struck a disabling blow, probably to the hyena's head. She had fin-ished the fight by stomping her enemy's body into the straw.

As Lila had said, this mare was a warrior. Whatever the odds, she deserved a chance to live.

With Lila hovering outside the stall gate, the procedure began—the cleansing, dressing, and suturing of the wounds, the massive doses of saline and antibiotics delivered by IV. Roper lost track of time as he soothed and steadied the mare, stroking her neck, giving her water, and rigging a sling to keep her on her feet.

At last everything that could be done for the mare had been done. The floor of the stall was cleared of debris from the surgery, and the wait began.

The vet left on another emergency call, promising to check back. By that time most of the stable workers had arrived. They would need to be told what had happened and how it would affect their work today. That would be Roper's job.

"Go on," Lila said. "You've got work to do. I'll stay here with Baby. She shouldn't be left alone."

"You're sure? You must be tired."

"Nothing could make me leave her right now." She spied a low wooden stool, moved it into the stall, and sat down. "I've got my phone. I'll call you if you're needed."

By the time Roper called his work crew together, rumors were flying. He was able to calm them and tell his workers what had happened. "Do your usual jobs," he told them. "Just stay away from the part of the stable where Baby is. We want to keep things quiet so she can rest."

"Will she be all right?" a girl asked.

"It's too soon to know. The big worry is infection. All we can do is wait and hope."

Roper's gaze took in the group. He didn't see Cruiser or his girlfriend, Janae, among them. Maybe they'd decided to quit and save him the trouble of firing them both. "That's all," he said. "Get to work."

As the hirelings dispersed, one of the girls walked up to him and stood waiting. "What is it, Megan?" he asked. "Is something wrong?"

"Just something you need to know. Last night I talked to Janae. She told me that Cruiser took her out for a fancy dinner. A man paid him a lot of money to do a job, so he won't be coming back to work here. Neither will Janae. I think they're going to California. She asked me to pick up their last paychecks."

Fat chance of that. "Did she say what kind of job Cruiser got paid for?" Roper asked.

"Something about fixing a car. He showed Janae the cash. Mostly hundred-dollar bills, she said."

"Who was the man? Did she tell you?"

"No. I don't think Janae saw him."

"Thanks, Megan. You can go now." As the girl hurried off, Roper replayed her words in his mind. His pulse was racing. Had he just found the answer to the question that had been tormenting him since Lila's so-called accident? Had Cruiser been paid to sabotage the brakes on Lila's car?

The pattern fit almost too neatly—like the way Cruiser had dropped everything and left before completing his work. Why should he bother to finish when he had a bundle of cash in his hand?

And if he'd gotten paid at the ranch, who might have been on hand to deliver the money?

Roper reined back a surge of volcanic fury. Assuming his logic was sound, not only had Cruiser sabotaged Lila's car, almost killing her, but his careless exit from the stable had left the door open for a killer animal that had destroyed an irreplaceable mare.

The urge to hunt down the worthless little rat and beat the truth out of him was so powerful it almost drove Roper out the door. But no, he had responsibilities here. The sensible course of action would be to tell Sam. As a federal agent, Sam could arrest Cruiser, haul him to jail, and threaten him within an inch of his life. If Cruiser could be made to give up the person who'd hired him, that might give Sam a solid lead to solving his case.

Taking a deep breath, he walked back down the line of stalls to check on the mare. Lila loved Baby. She would be distraught. For her sake, he needed to be steady and supportive.

He found her where he'd left her, huddled on the stool, her hands holding her phone. "How is she?" he asked, although little could have changed in the short time he'd been gone.

"The same. No worse at least. I've been talking and singing to her, just to let her know somebody's here. But Roper—" She turned to look at him. "What are you going to do about the shootout and the Run for a Million?"

Roper shrugged. "To tell you the truth, I've barely thought about it. With Baby's life hanging by a thread, somehow it doesn't seem as important as it was."

"Listen to me. I've been thinking," she said. "We can't walk away from this chance. Your two backup horses can do the patterns and put on a good show, but we both know they don't have the heart to win. Only one horse in this stable does."

Roper's breath caught. He knew what she was going to say. He had entertained the notion himself and dismissed it as too much of a gamble. But Lila's decision was the one that counted.

"Go on, Boss," he said. "I'm listening."

She hesitated briefly, then spoke. "How do you feel about riding One in a Million in the shootout?"

At 5:00, the vet stopped by to check on Baby. "No change," he told Roper and Lila. "I wish I could say it was an encouraging sign, but it's too soon to tell. We'll know more, one way or the other, in the morning."

Roper stroked the mare, carefully avoiding the stitches across her shoulders. It appeared that at one point the hyena had jumped on her back and tried to sever her spine with its crushing jaws before Baby was able to throw it off.

The stitches, dressings, and supportive sling had to be misery for the mare. It would have been a kindness to put her down. But Lila was right. An animal that had fought as hard as Baby deserved a chance to live.

By this time, the hired help had left for the day. Roper and Lila were alone in the stall with the mare. "Have you given any more thought to my suggestion?" Lila asked him. "You said you need time. But the shootout is next week. Time is running out."

"I'm aware of that," Roper said. "One in a Million is still jumpy from what happened earlier. And hearing the uproar in Baby's stall must have made him even more nervous. I could try him in the arena now. If he does all right, we can talk about it."

One in a Million snorted and rolled his eyes when Roper came to lead him out of his stall. But the well-trained stallion allowed himself to be cross-tied and saddled, his lower legs securely cushioned and wrapped for protection. The strenuous moves in the arena would make heavy demands on those aging legs. That was just one of Roper's worries.

"Let's go, big boy." Roper swung into the saddle, rode into the arena, and warmed the horse up with an easy lope. Then he started the more demanding work.

The patterns, spins, and slides had long since become second nature to the stallion. Once begun, the routine seemed to comfort him. With Lila watching, he executed every move with flowing precision.

"That's perfect!" Lila exclaimed. She clapped as One in a Million slid to a stop and finished with a deft rollback.

"It was perfect for what it is." Roper dismounted and gave the stallion a pat of approval. "But you have to understand that I wasn't pushing him. To win in competition, the moves will have to be done a lot faster. If I can't get him up to speed in the next few days, taking him to the shootout will be a waste of time. Do you still want me to try?"

"Yes—unless the strain becomes too much for him. You'll have to be the judge of that."

"You're the boss. Get some food and some rest. I'm going to put this boy away. Then I'll be staying here to keep an eye on Baby."

"I don't want to leave her. I'll call the house and have some supper sent down."

Roper was already out of hearing. He unsaddled the stallion, removed the leg wraps, brushed and curried his coat, and put him in his stall with oats and water. He was closing the gate when he saw a tall figure walking toward him. It was Sam.

Roper had spoken with the FBI agent earlier and told him about Cruiser. Had he discovered anything new? Roper strode along the row of stalls to meet him.

"Jackpot." Sam was grinning. "I tracked down Cruiser, arrested him, and took him to the police station—he even had the cash on him. Once he'd been cuffed, strip searched, dressed in jail duds, and stood up for a mug shot, the young hooligan was so scared that he would have ratted out his own mother."

"Did he give you a name?"

"He didn't know the name, but he gave us a description of the man who hired and paid him. Red hair, wearing a suit, and driving a Mercedes. Does that ring a bell?"

The question required no answer. "Now what? Are you going to arrest Darrin?" Roper asked.

"Eventually. But I've got bigger fish to catch. From what I've seen of Darrin, I believe he was acting under orders. I need to arrest the person behind those orders, and I can't do that without solid evidence. That's why I'm asking you to give me the time and space to finish my job here, and to do it without asking questions. Are you willing to do that?"

"I'll try to be patient. But he almost killed Lila. That's attempted murder."

"Just a few more days. Maybe less. That's all I'm asking. And you don't talk to anybody about this. Not even Lila. All right?"

"All right." Roper sighed. "I hope you know what you're doing."

"I hope so, too." With a nod, Sam walked away.

Back in the bungalow, Sam placed a call to Nick. It was after hours, and his old mentor would probably be at home in his solitary apartment. But Sam had spent enough time playing with pieces of this bewildering puzzle. Now that they were beginning to fit together, it was time to move.

"This had better be good news, Sam." Nick sounded as if he'd been roused from a nap.

"It might be," Sam said. "I may be getting close to a breakthrough. But I need a response to the request I made after Frank's memorial."

"Refresh my memory."

"I need a record of any and all connections between Madeleine Culhane and Louis Divino. Phone calls, texts, bank records, any communication that can be traced— especially her bank records, any big withdrawals around the time of Frank's death."

"So, you're thinking it was a paid hit."

"It's the only thing that makes sense. But before I can make an arrest, I'll need evidence to back it up."

"I remember now," Nick said. "I passed your request on to our research person. She's sharp, doesn't usually let things fall through the cracks. I'll ask her about it first thing tomorrow and get back to you. Oh—and what about that hypodermic you turned over to the crime lab? Any word on that?"

"It wasn't the murder weapon. No sign that it had ever been used. And no prints on it. I'm guessing it was a plant, and not a very convincing one."

Ending the call, he sat in the fading light examining his thoughts. With the door closed, the air in the room was close. The porch would be cooler. But if he were to go outside, Jasmine might see it as an invitation to join him. And this was no time to be with her—not while he was waiting for the proof he needed to destroy her family.

Last night, their lovemaking had crossed the line between casual sex and real emotion. He loved her. He wanted her—not just in his bed but in his life. And he sensed that she felt the same.

But their situation was impossible. His relationship with her had been a breach of ethics from the beginning. And if he succeeded in putting her brother and mother behind bars, Jasmine would have every reason to hate him.

Was he right about Madeleine? His gut instinct, which he'd always trusted, told him that she'd orchestrated both Frank's murder and the so-called accident with Lila's car.

Cruiser had admitted to tampering with the brakes and described Darrin as the man who'd hired and paid him. But Darrin had always pushed for a legal solution to the dispute over the ranch. And he struck Sam as too spineless to have come up with the plot and carried it out on his own. He would almost certainly have been acting under orders—his mother's orders.

Tying Madeleine to her ex-husband's murder was more of a stretch. The hit had appeared professional, and she was friends with a known mobster. But that was just circumstantial evidence. Hopefully, one way or the other, the information Sam had requested from Nick would give him solid proof.

But even if Sam's instincts proved right, one question remained. How had the killer known Frank would be in the stable? Had Frank been lured there, perhaps by a phone call, or had the hit man simply shadowed him, waiting to catch him alone—or even forced him into the stall at gunpoint? That mystery had yet to be solved.

The lights in the stable were set to come on at dusk. Mounted on the rafters, they were dimmed to a twilight glow, like distant moons in the darkness.

When Lila had refused yet again to leave the mare, Roper had found a clean blanket in his office and spread it on the straw. "Get some sleep," he'd ordered her gruffly. "I'll be right here. I'll wake you if anything changes."

"Now who's the boss?" she'd complained, half teasing. But after fighting sleep for a few minutes, she'd put her head down and drifted into exhausted slumber.

Roper checked the mare for any sign of fever. So far, nothing appeared to have changed, but Roper couldn't be sure. On the Colorado ranch, hours from the nearest vet, he'd become skilled at doctoring horses with common ailments and minor injuries. But he'd never treated a horse in Baby's critical condition. If infection were to set in, the humane solution would be to put her down. Lila would be heartbroken, but she knew the realities of owning horses. For all their size and strength, they were fragile animals, subject to a myriad of life-threatening issues.

As he settled in the straw, his back against the side of the stall, he could hear the mare's breathing, shallow but regular. Lila lay within reach, curled on the blanket, her profile pale in the overhead light. The temptation was there, to lie down beside her and spoon her body against his—not so much in lust as in comfort. But Roper knew better. She was his newly widowed employer. And he had been alone for so long that he'd forgotten how to be tender with a woman.

He was bone weary after the long day. Despite his resolve to stay awake, his eyelids were drooping. Little by little, his resistance ebbed. Lulled by the sound of Baby's breathing, he sank into sleep.

A coyote call, from somewhere beyond the stable, roused him with a jerk. He blinked and sat up. How long had he slept? It couldn't have been long. Lila was still sleeping, curled like a child on the blanket.

But he could no longer hear the mare's breathing.

He scrambled to his feet. Suspended by the sling, she stood with her head hanging down. Her eyes were closed. When he touched her there was no response, no breath, no pulse. In the silent darkness, Baby had slipped away. Her brave fight was over.

Heartsick, he bent over Lila and laid a hand on her shoulder. "Wake up," he whispered.

Her eyes shot open. "Is it Baby? Is she any better?"

"Look at me, Lila." He pulled her up and took her hands. "Baby's gone. She passed away while we were both asleep. Her suffering is over."

"No!" Stifling a sob, she moved to the mare's head and kissed the beautiful white face. "She was the perfect horse, and so brave at the end. Oh, Roper, of all the horses, why did it have to be her?"

"There's no answer to that question." He controlled the urge to take her in his arms and hold her. If it happened, it would have to be Lila's move—a move she didn't make. She was tough and proud. Like his mother.

"I'll call the vet first thing in the morning and tell him what happened," he said. "And I'll get help taking her down and burying her. You can choose the spot and let me know."

"I'll call the vet and make the burial arrangements," she said. "You'll be busy getting One in a Million ready for the shootout. That's going to be a full-time job for the next few days."

She gathered up the blanket she'd slept on, shook out the loose straw, and draped it to cover the mare's body. Her stoic expression told Roper how much emotion she was holding back. "You may as well go home and get a few hours' rest before the day starts," she said.

"I think it's already started." He ushered her out of the stall and closed the gate behind them. "Come on, Boss, I'll walk you back to the house."

Roper hadn't checked the time, but he estimated it was after midnight. The sky glittered with stars, the Milky Way spilling its galaxies across the peak of the heavens. He slowed his steps. They both needed time to settle their nerves.

"Why haven't you ever married, Roper?" The question came out of nowhere. "You're attractive, ambitious, kind. I can't believe some woman hasn't snapped you up."

He shrugged, scrambling for an answer. "For one thing, I feel responsible for my family. With my stepfather disabled and the younger kids out on the circuit, somebody has to take care of the ranch. My mother can't do it all."

"But you could still do that and be married."

"In this day and age, with so many options, I can't imagine a woman choosing the kind of life she'd have with me. Why? Do you have somebody in mind?"

She managed to laugh. "Hardly. Just curious, that's all." Her gaze followed the trail of a falling star. "You said 'for one thing.' Is there something else?"

"It was a figure of speech, that's all."

"No, I can tell when somebody's holding back. There's something you aren't telling me."

"There might be. But I don't talk about it." Only Roper's family knew about his tragic past. He'd never shared the story with anyone else, and he didn't intend to share it now.

"Maybe you should talk about it. Nobody gets to be our age without some kind of track record. Besides, tonight I need a good story."

Roper hesitated. Maybe she did need it. But it wasn't a good story. It was a tragedy that he would carry with him for the rest of his life. "Maybe another time," he said. "But not tonight."

"Then why did you bring it up?"

"I didn't bring it up. You did." They had reached the front porch. "Get some rest, Boss. It's been a long, rough day, and the one coming up won't be any easier."

"Fine. Let me know how One in a Million is doing. I'll take care of Baby's . . . burial." She choked on the words, turned away from him, and stalked up the front steps onto the porch.

Roper watched her go. Had he been too brusque with her? Should he call her back, apologize, and offer her the story she'd asked to hear?

Maybe he should have been more sensitive to her pain. In such a short time, Lila had lost her husband, a young employee, and her prize mare. She'd also discovered Frank had been cheating, dealt with a deadly wild animal, and suffered an accident that could have ended her life.

Through it all, she'd kept an iron grip on her self-control, refusing to give way to emotion. Only in the last moment, as she'd mentioned Baby's burial, had he sensed that she was close to breaking.

He found himself wishing he could call her back and let her know that he understood, and that he was here to support her. But it was too late for that now. The next time he saw her, Roper sensed, the tentative bond that had formed between them would be gone.

Turning away from the house, he walked slowly back toward the stable. Lila had suggested that he go home and get some sleep. But it hardly seemed worth taking the time. He would rest a little in his office, make some coffee, and be ready for work at first light.

Lila had made it clear that she only wanted one thing from him—to prepare One in a Million for his return to the arena. Not only to compete but to win.

But bringing the champion out of retirement had been an idea born of desperation. Lila was depending on the stallion, and on him, to continue the tradition of the Culhane Stables with her as the new owner. But could he, riding One in a Million, give her the victory she needed?

His own future was at stake, as well. With Baby, he'd felt confident that he could win or at least rack up an impressive score. But the stallion, Baby's sire, was past his prime. The years had cost him strength and speed and made him more vulnerable to injury. Roper was concerned for his safety. In a competition that demanded everything of a horse, what if that concern caused him to hold the stallion back?

He could still go to Lila and tell her that One in a Million wasn't fit to compete with the younger horses, and that he should be withdrawn from the event. Roper could still compete with one of the backup horses. Even if he didn't win, he could make a respectable showing. But knowing Lila, she would never accept that decision. And the decision was hers to make.

He entered the stable, the lights dim, the smell of death lingering in the air. Walking down the row of stalls, he stopped at the one where One in a Million was quartered. The stallion came at his low whistle, thrusting his head over the top of the gate and butting his nose against Roper's shirt.

Roper stroked his neck, feeling the muscles ripple beneath the satiny hide. "The boss is counting on you, big boy," he whispered. "It's all up to you now."

CHAPTER NINETEEN

It was midmorning and already getting hot. Sam sat at the kitchen table in his bungalow, drinking iced coffee and updating the report to Nick on his laptop. He hadn't seen Jasmine since yesterday. She'd mentioned something about working on the vintage truck in the shed. That could explain why he hadn't seen much of her. But they were both aware of their circumstances and the need to give each other space. That, or she could just be biding her time, waiting to surprise him.

His phone lay on the table. He glanced at it repeatedly, as if the extra attention could coax a ring out of it. He was hoping for some word on Madeleine's phone calls and bank records. If his hunch about her involvement in Frank's death was wrong, he needed to know. If it was right, he needed to act.

He hated keeping secrets from Jasmine. But telling her that her mother could be arrested for murdering her father would tear at her loyalties, possibly with dangerous results.

Not warning her could spell the end of their relationship. But his sworn duty had to come first. He could only hope she would understand.

From the pasture below the cemetery hill came the sound of the backhoe digging Baby's grave. Sam had learned from Lila that the mare had died after her valiant battle with the escaped hyena. A crushing loss. Million Dollar Baby had been the best hope for the future of the ranch. Now Roper and Lila were going to need another plan.

The jangling phone broke into his thoughts. He snatched it up, his pulse breaking into a gallop. The caller was Nick.

"Good morning, Sam. I've got some news for you," he said. "We found Madeleine Culhane's phone and bank records. You seem to be on the right track. We did find several phone calls between Mrs. Culhane and Louis Divino. And there was a withdrawal of fifty thousand dollars from her account three days before Frank's death. What we don't have is proof that the calls with Divino were about a hit, or that the money went to pay for that hit. But maybe you can find a way to fill in the blanks."

"Text me the photocopies. I'll figure it out."

"If you make an arrest, will you need backup?"

"Having another agent show up would just set off alarms. If my plan works, I shouldn't need backup. But I'll be wearing my Glock. The only thing I need from you is the authority to make a promise." He told Nick what he wanted.

"That's fine," Nick said. "I should be able to arrange it. I don't need to tell you to be careful."

"Don't worry. I know better than to take anything for granted, especially when a woman's involved."

"That's a lesson we've all had to learn." Nick chuckled. "Fine. I'll get those copies to you in the next few minutes. Text or email?"

"Can you do both?"

"No problem. Keep me posted."

The photocopied records arrived as promised a few minutes later. Sam studied the pages on his computer. There had been several calls between Madeleine and Louis Divino in the days preceding Frank's death. But there was no way to prove what the calls were about. The pair could be business partners, even lovers. But it was just as likely they were arranging a hit, especially given the withdrawal of $50,000 from Madeleine's bank account.

Sam was experienced enough to know how a professional hit usually worked. Divino wouldn't make the hit himself. He would make the arrangements, probably with someone whose identity Madeleine would never know. Divino would take his cut of the money off the top and forward a down payment, usually half the agreed-upon fee, to the hit man. When the hit had been made, and the target proven dead, the hit man would collect the balance.

Sam knew of at least a dozen hits in Chicago that Divino had probably set up. But the mobster was smart. He'd made sure that none were traceable to him.

He took time to study the documents that had been sent to him, setting dates and times in his mind, looking for patterns and connections. He could only do this once. He had to do it right.

Roper finished the stallion's third routine of the morning and checked the stopwatch. Perfect execution, but even with urging, no faster than before. One in a Million had done his best. But his best wasn't enough to win.

The great horse was getting tired. His coat was flecked with foam from sweating in the heat. Roper walked him around the arena at an easy pace to cool him down before his shower. Where was the line between improving his performance and putting the horse at risk? The stallion hadn't competed in five years. What if the pressure proved to be too much for him, physically and mentally?

One in a Million was a horse who would give his all for his rider. But he had never competed with anyone but Frank on his back. Would he perform for Roper? What if the stallion were to give his all, to the last ounce of strength, and it broke him in body and spirit?

How badly did they need this competition? Roper asked himself. How badly did Lila need it? Was she out to prove that she could step into Frank's place and continue the winning tradition of the Culhane Stables? Was he so set on breaking into the big time as a trainer and rider that he would push a horse past its limits?

There was no chance of winning the Run for a Million on an aging horse. But there would be other events and other years.

There would be time to choose other promising colts to train for greatness and buy new bloodlines to breed with Culhane mares.

As he turned the stallion over to the waiting groom, Roper could hear the distant sound of the backhoe digging Baby's grave. Was entering the great stallion in an unwinnable contest worth inviting more heartache?

He needed to talk with Lila.

After a word with the staff, he left the stable and set out for the pasture below the cemetery hill. By then, the digging had stopped. The grooms who'd trailered the mare's body to the grave site would use the sling to lower her into the earth. Lila would be mourning. But would she be vulnerable to suggestion or would grief make her more determined than ever?

He reached the graveside as the four-wheeler was pulling away with the empty trailer. Lila stood looking down into the grave. As Roper approached, she tossed a small bouquet of wildflowers into the opening, then turned away.

Her head came up as she saw him. The expression on her face was unreadable.

"I'm sorry," Roper said, "I meant to be here."

"Never mind, it's done." She walked at his side as the backhoe started up behind her. "How is One in a Million doing?"

"The same," Roper said. "Flawless execution, but not up to speed. I don't think he's going to be ready."

"But he's got to be. I've seen you work him. He's beautiful. All he needs is a push."

"He's an old horse, Boss. I can only push him so hard before he injures a leg or, worse, goes down in the arena. I can go with Topper or Sly. They're young, but I can drill them hard over the next few days and go with the one that performs best."

"They won't win. I know what Frank would do. He would gamble with One in a Million. He would go for the win."

Roper could sense an impasse coming up. He didn't like it. "It would be reckless to risk him. He's too valuable as a stud and too much a part of the ranch. We just put one horse in the ground. Why take a chance on another one?"

"Are you saying you won't ride him in the shootout?"

The line had been drawn. He chose to step over it. "That's right. I don't give a damn what Frank would have done. I won't push that stallion past what he can do. I'll quit first. And there's no one else on this ranch with the pro card and the record to qualify for the competition. You'll have to drop out."

She turned to face him, her coppery eyes blazing. "I care about the stallion, too. But I also care about the ranch's reputation for showing the best. It's your choice. We go with One in a Million, and we go for the win, or you're fired."

With the Glock covered by his denim jacket, Sam climbed the steps of the bungalow, crossed the covered porch, and rang the doorbell. From the hall on the other side came the sound of footsteps. Madeleine opened the door.

"Come in, Sam." She was dressed in an aqua silk caftan, her hair hanging loose around her shoulders. Her breath smelled faintly of bourbon. "Won't you have a seat? I can pour you a drink if you like."

"Thanks, but I'll pass on the drink." Sam took a seat on the edge of the sofa. "I'm afraid this isn't a social call."

"Oh, that's too bad." She joined him, the caftan floating around her as she sat. "I was hoping you'd come to ask for my daughter's hand in marriage. I was primed to say yes and welcome you into the family. Do you mind if I smoke?"

"It's fine."

She took her time selecting a Marlboro from the pack on the table, lighting it, and exhaling a column of smoke. "Now, what's your business, FBI man? If it's something you're selling, I'm not buying."

"I'm afraid it's bad news. Are you aware that Lila's car rolled off the road and crashed because the brakes failed?"

"Of course. Would it be too much to say that I'm sorry she survived that accident? After what she did to Frank, she deserved to die. And it would have simplified everything."

"The wreck wasn't an accident. Somebody tampered with the brakes. A seal on the master cylinder had been loosened."

"Well, that certainly wasn't my doing. I wouldn't know the master cylinder from a hole in the ground."

Sam didn't smile. "We already know who was responsible. The young man who did the damage worked here as a stable hand. He's been arrested and jailed—and he identified your son, Darrin, as the man who hired and paid him."

"You're sure? Kids will say anything these days." Her expression hadn't changed, but the hand holding the cigarette shook, spilling ash onto the coffee table.

"He had the cash on him—the bills can be dusted for fingerprints. But he described Darrin perfectly."

Madeleine took a deep drag on her cigarette. "There has to be some mistake."

"No mistake," Sam said. "I'm here to give you a heads-up. Darrin is to be arrested and charged with attempted murder—a felony. For that, he could get as much as ten years in prison, maybe more. Of course, he'd lose his law license. He'd never be able to practice again. And his wife would have to raise their baby without a father. I'm guessing she'd probably remarry. She's—"

"Stop!" Madeleine seized his arm. "Why are you telling me this?"

"Because I know you love your son and want to help him. There's a way—it's called the truth, and we know what it is."

Madeleine stubbed out her cigarette in a porcelain ashtray. "All right, since you've already guessed. Darrin was following orders—my orders. He was only being a good son. He shouldn't be punished for that."

"But he did take part in the crime," Sam said. "If you confess, he can still be charged, but only as an accessory. He'll still lose his license and might have to serve some time. That would depend on your lawyer."

"And his life will still be ruined. All right, Agent Rafferty, I know when a man's come to negotiate. How can I make this go away?"

Sam laid his briefcase on the coffee table. She seemed almost too willing to cooperate. He sensed a possible ambush coming, but he needed to follow this lead.

"I saw you talking with Louis Divino at the memorial," he said. "He's an old acquaintance of mine from Chicago. How well do you know him?"

Madeleine lit a fresh cigarette. "I hardly know him at all. We'd met at a party, and he stopped by to say hello, that's all."

"Then how do you explain this? My colleague in Abilene sent it to me." Sam opened his laptop and brought up Madeleine's phone records. "That's Divino's private number. You made these calls to him in the days before Frank was killed."

"He wanted me to invest in a business he owns. I turned him down."

"But according to these records, you called him several times. Why, if you turned him down? I know the kind of business Divino is in. So far he's never been caught. But his luck won't hold out forever. And when it runs out, he won't be going down alone. What can you tell me about this?" He brought up Madeleine's bank statement, showing the $50,000 withdrawal. "This money was taken out three days before Frank's death."

"That money was personal. It had nothing to do with Divino or Frank."

"I'm not sure I believe you, Madeleine. But there's one thing I know for sure. You're a good mother. You'd do anything to restore this ranch to your children. As long as Frank was in charge, there was no way he would give up control—and he was healthy enough to live for another twenty years. But with him out of the way, Lila would be vulnerable." Sam closed the laptop. "Was there anything to the rumor that Frank wanted to marry a younger woman—maybe this one?" He showed her the photo on his phone.

"I heard that rumor. If there was any truth to it, wouldn't that have been a reason for Lila to kill him?"

"I don't think so. Frank was her protection. Even with a prenup, a divorce would have been a hard step to consider. But his death would leave her wide open to attack—as it did." He slipped the phone into his pocket. "I think you paid a hit man to kill Frank, Madeleine. But you didn't do it for yourself. You did it for a totally unselfish reason. You did it for your children."

A single tear trickled down her cheek. That tear told him more than words.

"So, what now?" she asked. "How do I save my son and his family?"

"And Jasmine?"

She laughed, a raw, humorless sound. "Jasmine will be fine. She hasn't done anything illegal. The only thing my daughter is guilty of is falling in love."

Sam forced himself to ignore the stabbing sensation in the region of his heart. "I think you know how to get the charges dropped against your son," he said.

"Do I?" she asked. "How?"

"Suppose you tell me." Sam took a yellow legal pad and a pen out of his briefcase and laid it on the coffee table.

"So, I confess to having Frank killed, and the case against Darrin goes away?"

"That's right. I've already cleared it with my supervisor."

She picked up the pen and began to write. The written

confession was short, barely half a page, but the important details were there. She added her signature and passed the notebook back to Sam. "Now what?"

"You'll surrender to the authorities, who'll arrange to have you picked up. You'll have access to your lawyers; they'll advise you what to do next. You'll likely be granted bail and time to prepare for a hearing."

"How much time?" Madeleine asked.

"This is a capital case. Sometimes it can take months to schedule and prepare, especially if you elect to plead not guilty. Your lawyers will guide you through the process."

Madeleine laid her cigarette in the ashtray and rose to her feet. "I don't think all that will be necessary."

He stared at her. "I don't understand."

She gave him a mysterious smile. "I'm dying, Agent. I have a brain tumor. The doctors have given me less than two months to live. Now be a good boy and read me my Miranda rights."

Sam sat alone on the bungalow porch, watching the cloud bank move in from the west. Crickets sang in the darkness. The midnight breeze smelled of rain.

By morning, the storm would be here. Not long after that, the police van would be arriving to take Madeleine to Abilene for her arraignment and bail hearing. Sam would be going with them, to his new job. His work here was done.

Would he get a chance to say goodbye to Jasmine? He hadn't seen her all day. She was probably avoiding him. But maybe that was for the best. He had done his duty and arrested her mother for murder. She would never forget that, let alone forgive him. What more was there to say?

Except that he would never forget *her*.

A meteor flashed across the sky and burned into darkness. Sam rose, walked to the edge of the porch, and stood looking out into the night—the dark house and stable, the quiet pastures, the glorious, starry sky. For years to come, his memory would take him back to this place and the woman who had saved him. But tomorrow would be here soon enough. Now it was time to get some rest.

He turned around to go back inside—and stopped. Jasmine was sitting on the bench he'd left, as if she'd appeared by magic.

"Hello, Sam," she said.

"Surprise. I wasn't sure I'd see you again."

"Why? Did you think I'd be angry?" She shook her head. "You did what you had to—in the gentlest way possible. She told me everything. Sit down."

Sam joined her on the bench, relief washing over him. "How is your mother?" he asked.

"She's finally asleep. I've been with her most of the day, helping her prepare for what's ahead—making lists, who to call, what to say. Darrin has yet to be told."

"So, he doesn't know that she confessed in order to save him?"

"We'll tell him in the morning. The whole time my mother has been here, I've sensed that something was wrong with her. I just didn't know it was . . . a tumor. I can barely say the word."

"I'm no lawyer, but I imagine a plea of mental illness will get her acquitted."

"Not that it will make much difference." Jasmine sighed. "But that's not why I'm here. There's something I need to say." She paused, taking a deep breath. "I've been selfish, Sam. I wanted you so much that I didn't care about the rules or the wreckage I left behind—wreckage you'll have to deal with."

"I didn't exactly fight you off. Are you sorry?"

"I wish I could say yes. But no, I'm not sorry. I fell in love with you. And it was so good, so real . . . Even when you go, I won't be sorry. After a lifetime of bad decisions, loving you was the best choice I ever made."

Sam reached out and pulled her into his arms. She trembled, giving way to tears as he held her. "So help me, I'm not sorry either. I'm in love with you, Jasmine. You brought me back to life, and I want to keep what we've found. But—" He paused, searching for the right words.

"I know." She found the words for him. "We need a break. We need time to deal with our separate lives before we pick up where we left off."

"When this murder case is settled, when you're no longer part of it, and when you're ready, we can do that. We can make it happen. Do you believe that?"

"I do." She pressed closer, her arms stealing around him. "For now, just hold me."

EPILOGUE

The Following Week:
Saturday in Scottsdale

Mounted on One in a Million, Roper waited at the entrance to the arena. As the loudspeaker boomed over the crowd, announcing the score for the previous rider, the stallion quivered with anticipation. Clearly, he knew the reason he was here.

After an explosive standoff, Roper and Lila had reached a compromise. One in a Million would take part in the event, but only as a tribute to Frank. He would perform at his own pace and not be pushed to the point of risk.

The stallion's bay roan coat gleamed like polished copper. His black mane and tail had been brushed and braided by Lila into an intricate design. He had never looked more majestic.

Some of the best horses and riders in the country were here today, competing for one last chance at the Run for a Million. The two lead riders were tied with a judges' score of 227.5 points. If no horse scored higher, there would be a runoff at the end of the competition to determine the winner. Now, with only One in a Million left to perform, the runoff would almost certainly take place.

Roper had to hold the horse back as the announcer talked about how Frank Culhane and his magnificent stallion had become a legendary pair in the sport of reining. Now Frank was gone, but his horse had been brought out of retirement to honor the memory of his master.

"Ridden by Roper McKenna of the Culhane Stables, ladies and gentlemen, put your hands together for One in a Million."

As the last words were spoken, Roper leaned forward and whispered in the stallion's ear, "For Frank . . . and for Baby."

The crowd roared as One in a Million galloped into the arena. Roper had memorized the sequence. He cued each move with the pressure of his knees. The stallion did the rest—and he was on fire.

First came the big circle around the arena, then a stop and the spin in place that could be so punishing on a horse's legs; then more circles and direction changes, and finally the long gallop ending in a sliding stop and a perfect rollback. Roper couldn't have held the stallion back if he'd tried. One in a Million was going all out. Roper could only hope they could finish the routine without an injury.

The crowd cheered as horse and rider galloped out of the arena into the waiting area. When the judges announced the score—228.5—the stands went wild. Lila came running to meet them, leaping like a child, hugging and kissing her horse. One in a Million had won the event, a handsome cash prize, and a place for his rider in the Run for a Million.

Tuesday in Abilene

Sam took one last look at the file on the Frank Culhane murder and put it away. Case closed. Now that the killer had been arrested and Sam transferred back to his new job in Abilene, the memory of his time at the ranch had become almost dreamlike. Only Jasmine had been real. She was still part of his life—and hopefully part of his future.

In consideration of her illness, Madeleine had been allowed to return to her condo in Austin under house arrest, wearing an ankle monitor. Jasmine had gone along to care for her mother in the last months of her life.

"I know she had my father killed," Jasmine had told Sam. "But she's my mother. She needs me. I truly believe it was the tumor that compelled her to do the terrible things she did. If she lives to go to trial, that's what her lawyers are going to argue."

"Do what you need to," Sam had told her. "Come back when you're free. I'll be here."

"You'd better be." She'd kissed him and disappeared into the police van.

He was reviewing his new case, a drug bust gone bad, when Nick knocked on the door of his office. In six weeks, Nick would be retiring, and Sam would be stepping into his job. But for now, Nick was working an ongoing case against Louis Divino.

There was a chance that this latest involvement in the Frank Culhane hit would provide enough new evidence to put the mobster behind bars. But something told Sam that wasn't likely. Divino would skate free, as he always did.

Nick stepped through the door and closed it behind him. "I've got some news, Sam."

"Good news?" Sam motioned his old friend to a chair opposite the desk.

"Not necessarily. I can guarantee you're not going to like it. We just interviewed Divino about the hit on Frank. Divino's claiming that the hit was never made."

"What? But Frank was found dead. And the timing fits Madeleine's phone calls and that big cash withdrawal."

Nick shook his head. "Oh, Madeleine meant to have Frank killed, all right. The hit man had even been given his up-front payment. But he never collected the rest. Before he could make it to the ranch to kill Frank, he heard on the news that somebody had beaten him to it. Frank was already dead. Nobody bothered to tell Madeleine. Divino kept the money and let her assume the hit had been carried out."

Sam stared at Nick, his pulse pounding like a sledgehammer. "So you're saying that somebody else murdered Frank?"

"That's right," Nick said. "We're back to square one."

Wednesday at the Culhane Ranch

Lila sat by the pool, sipping a mojito and enjoying the peace and quiet. Madeleine was gone. Sam was gone. Even Jasmine was gone. The silence, broken only by the sounds from the stable and the call of a passing crow, was blissful. But Lila knew better than to believe it would last.

The ownership of the ranch was still in dispute. Madeleine might be gone, but Darrin, spurred by Simone, was still around. He would be working on the legal angles, preparing to take her to court. And she would be working with her own legal team to prove the validity of Frank's will. Lila was not looking forward to the fight, only to having it over.

Then there was Roper. Their argument over the stallion, with him threatening to quit and her threatening to fire him, had driven a wedge between them. And now Roper's victory on One in a Million had drawn the attention of some wealthy horse breeders. They would be clamoring to hire him, offering him big money and the chance to compete on his choice of blooded champion horses.

He had won his place in the Run for a Million as a trainer and rider. He had no obligation to compete on a Culhane horse. He could be gone tomorrow, with a ticket to the big time. Why should he stay with her?

Roper didn't need her anymore. The trouble was, she needed him. She couldn't run her stable or compete for prize money on her own. But how could she keep him? There was just one possibility that came to mind.

Offer him something he couldn't get from any of the big breeders—a partnership.

"Mrs. Culhane." Mariah had appeared in the doorway. "You have a call on the house phone."

"Who is it, Mariah?" Lila put down her drink with a sigh.

"A woman. She didn't give her name, but she said you'd want to talk with her."

"All right. Thanks, Mariah. I'll take it in the office." Lila stood and walked into the house. The way was dark after the glare of the afternoon sun.

The ranch office was just down the hall. Lila walked in and picked up the phone. "This is Mrs. Culhane. What is it you want?"

"My name is Crystal." She sounded young. "Crystal Carter. You don't know me. But you've probably seen my picture. A man you must have hired snapped a photo of me with your husband. I saw the flash and knew we'd been caught."

Lila felt vaguely sick. This was the last thing she needed. "You have no business calling here," she said. "Frank is dead, and I want nothing to do with you. Never call me again."

"Please don't hang up." The young woman sounded as if she were crying. "I've nowhere else to turn."

"What could you possibly need from me?" Lila demanded.

"I need help." The girlish voice quivered. "I'm pregnant, Mrs. Culhane. The baby is Frank's."

Dear Reader,

Here's hoping you enjoyed this book. Our story will continue in Book 2 of the Rivalries series. Watch for LIE FOR A MILLION in late 2024!

Travel to Kentucky with Janet Dailey, in
LONE OAKS CROSSING!

The New Americana Series

In the lush rolling hills of Lone Oaks, KY the good life is measured in sips of aged bourbon and the thrill of the world's most famous horse race: the Kentucky Derby . . .

When news of her grandfather's stroke sends Jo Beth Ellis back to the family farm, she finds it in danger of foreclosure. Lone Oaks Crossing is in rough shape, but Jo has big plans—she'll use her expertise as a Derby-winning horse trainer to reinvent the property as a healing retreat. But renovating the property while trying to keep her independent grandfather in check is a huge job for one woman— and even more challenging when she receives her first client, the unruly fourteen-year-old Cheyenne, who is determined to do anything but cooperate. Jo is at the end of her rope when neighbor Brooks Moore offers her a deal she can't possibly refuse . . .

Jo may have sworn to leave the gambling and vicious competition of horse racing behind her, but training Brooks's gorgeous thoroughbred is a challenge she can't resist, especially when sulky Cheyenne takes a shine to him—and when Brooks is sinking an outrageous amount of money into rehabbing the farm and even rolling up his sleeves to help. With a troubled teen's spirit and her grandfather's faith in her on the line, Jo steps into a tentative partnership with the undeniably attractive Brooks. Against all odds, she dreams of winning a trifecta—a champion horse, a happy family and a forever love.

CHAPTER ONE

Jo Beth Ellis had never been a quitter and she wouldn't start today.

"This morning's events were unfortunate. I'm sorry this happened to you."

Jo, her bottom lip bleeding, stood by a window in the principal's office of Stone Hill High School, ignoring the somber drawl of the man behind her and the silent vibrations of the cell phone ringing in her pocket (one she never had time to answer—even during her planning period) and stared out at the parking lot that bordered the front of the school. A cool September breeze rustled the thorny hedges along the cracked sidewalks, and the Kentucky sun struggled to nourish life, glinting off the metal hoods and rear-view mirrors of parked cars, barely piercing the shadows covering sparse tufts of grass hidden between the brick wings of the school.

For a place that was intended to be a safe, nurturing environment, the landscape lacked warmth or welcome. Inside, the atmosphere was worse: hallways reeked of bleach and floor wax, profanities echoed against cinder blocks behind locked classroom doors, and voices of harried administrators crackled through static-laden two-way radios clipped to the hips of patrolling campus security officers.

The place had become more of a prison than a high school.

Heart pounding, Jo closed her eyes and tried to remember her first day as a teacher six years ago when she'd been an energetic twenty-one-year-old college graduate. The day she'd marched up that sidewalk and into Stone Hill High School, head high and smile wide, eager to make a difference in the lives of students she loved, to help them improve their futures and achieve security.

But the realities of teaching were far different from the ones she'd been led to envision in college, and thoughts of quitting—along with the realization that she'd thrown away what amounted to a decade of her life—were stronger than ever.

Only, there was no way she could walk away and abandon the same student body to whom she'd committed herself faithfully years ago. How many other adults had abandoned these children when they had been needed the most? And hadn't she told her students to stick with it countless times over the years? To keep trying? To not give up? She couldn't let them down—especially not now . . . not when she'd sacrificed her relationship with what was left of her own family for them.

Earl. She thought of her grandfather, whom she'd left behind for her career, mucking stalls, grooming horses, and carrying the full weight of their family horse farm, Lone Oaks Crossing, alone. She thought of him, exhausted, ending each day in an empty house, a shot of bourbon and a view of dark pastures his only comforts.

An ache spread through her, stealing her breath.

"Perhaps," her principal, Dr. McKenzie, continued, "employing a more effective de-escalation technique would have deterred Natasha from striking out at you. Next time—"

"Next time?" Jo winced as the act of speaking split the wound in her bottom lip more deeply. She touched her tongue to it, tasting blood, and faced him. "Twice wasn't enough? Natasha has attacked other students and teachers like this before—all through elementary, middle, and now high school. And what else was I supposed to do? Ask her midswing to have a seat, give her a talking stick, then tell her to share her feelings? And what about the other thirty-two teens in the class, sitting there, with nowhere to go, having to watch that play out?"

She spread her hands, searching for words.

"Our kids are exposed to violence every day in this building," she continued. "Not to mention the amount of quality instruction incidents like this cost their education. The interventions you've dictated to us aren't working. The entire schoolwide behavior plan hasn't been working for years. I have no voice, no autonomy—not even in my own classroom. Our kids—especially Natasha—need more help than we're giving them. As it is—"

"As it is"—McKenzie leaned forward in his seat and rested his elbows on his wide desk—"Natasha's mother is threatening to sue the district and you, personally."

"For what? Natasha attacked a female student half her size from behind—unprovoked—in my classroom." Voice catching at the images the memory conjured, Jo inhaled a shaky breath. "She was slamming the other child's head into a cinder block wall. If I hadn't stepped in, that child might've walked away with more than just a bleeding forehead and bruised eye."

He picked up a pen. Twirled it between his thumb and forefinger. "I instructed you, as well as the entire faculty and staff, at the start of the year not to intervene in fights."

"I pulled Natasha off the student, stepped in front of

her to protect the other child, and Natasha took a swing at me." Oh, dear God, her lip throbbed. "That's what happened, from beginning to end. The other child's blood is still on the wall. Check the classroom camera, it's all there."

He frowned. "We already have, but that's not the point. You're not allowed to restrain students. Stepping in is someone else's job. Our administration is dedicated to ensuring a safe environ—"

"Then where was the safety officer? Where were you? I hit the emergency call button." She shook her head. "If a shooter enters the building, I'm expected to step in front of a bullet to save a child, but if that same child is attacked by a peer, I'm supposed to simply stand there and watch the child be beaten to death? If I fail to act in the first scenario, I'm crucified. In the second scenario, if I do act, I'm in danger of being sued. Do I need to ask for permission before I'm even allowed to protect *myself*?" A mirthless chuckle broke free of her chest. "And when, in the midst of all of this, am I supposed to be able to teach?"

Sighing, he put down the pen. "You're a great teacher, Ms. Ellis. One of our best. Admittedly, today was a bad day. But one bad day shouldn't make or break an entire career."

"But it's not just one bad day," she said softly.

There had been so many, and increasingly more every year. More violence, more anger, more arguments, more blame, more politics, more chaos, more confusion, more criticism . . . but always less time and support, fewer resources. The more she spoke up about the toxic school culture and working conditions and the more she asked for help, the more she paid for voicing her concerns— personally as well as professionally. Every day inside these walls, students' and teachers' safety, well-being, and futures were gambled. And today, a typical Monday at Stone Hill High School, had been no exception.

Something wet plopped onto her collarbone. She looked down and a second drop of blood fell from her lip to join the first, rolled over her skin, then settled against the collar of her blouse. The white cotton absorbed it, the stain spreading.

Oh, dear God. Here she stood, bleeding in her boss's office, as he blamed her for being physically assaulted on the job. This was no way to make a living . . . and certainly no way to live.

"I can't do this anymore," she whispered.

"Then do it for the kids," he said quietly.

McKenzie stood, tugged a tissue from a tissue box on his desk, and handed it to Jo. "As punishment, I've suspended Natasha from school for the rest of the week, but she'd like to speak to you before she leaves today." He crossed the room and opened the closed door of his office. "Natasha, please come in."

There were hushed voices and footsteps outside the door along the corridor of the school's main office, then a tall, blond girl sauntered in and crossed her arms over her chest. Another blonde, who appeared to be in her late thirties, propped her fists on her hips, and stood on the threshold of the room, glaring at Jo.

"Natasha," McKenzie said. "Don't you have something to say to Ms. Ellis?"

The teen narrowed her eyes at Jo and remained silent.

"Natasha," he prompted again.

Natasha's lip curled as she locked eyes with Jo. The sheer hatred in the girl's gaze made Jo shudder. "Sorry you got your lip busted. Next time, stay out of my way."

McKenzie's chest lifted on a sharp inhale. "Natash—"

"She ought to be fired." The blonde in the doorway—

Natasha's mother, Jo presumed—stabbed a finger in the air, aimed toward Jo. "She had no right to put her hands on my child. Had no idea what that other girl said about her. From now on, I expect this woman to report to me every day on Natasha's progress—academically and other-wise. And if Natasha sees fit to take care of gossip again herself, that woman had better not interfere."

"If an incident occurs in Ms. Ellis's classroom, Mrs. Bennett," McKenzie said tightly, "Ms. Ellis has no choice but to address it, just as she did in this instance. And district leadership has also decided to leave it up to Ms. Ellis as to whether charges will be filed against Natasha for striking her in the face." He leveled a look at Jo. "Though I'm sure that's not what Ms. Ellis wants. She, like district leadership, cares deeply for all students, and I don't think she'd want one unpleasant mistake to mar a student's permanent record." He paused, holding Jo's gaze, then asked, "Do you, Ms. Ellis?"

Jo lifted her bloody chin. "Or the school's record?"

He blinked, then stared back at her. "Excuse me?"

"You mean, you don't want to mar the school's record either."

He didn't answer, and he didn't have to. McKenzie had a family to support. Everything he did was in support of his efforts to boost Stone Hill High's public image and ensure he kept his position—a position that paid triple the salary of the average classroom teacher who worked tire-lessly in the trenches.

This was McKenzie's first year serving as a high school principal. Prior to his current position, he'd taught U.S. History and coached football for a few years before being promoted. McKenzie was a good guy, but an inexperienced and ill-prepared leader, which, over the years, had become the rule rather than the exception in public education as more and more experienced educators left the profession.

Jo looked at Natasha again, her eyes searching the younger girl's face as a residual trickle of sympathy moved through her. She'd noticed Natasha on the first day of class seven weeks ago, the girl's stony expression and disdainful gaze having caught her attention, raising the hairs on the back of her neck.

Natasha, like so many other students at Stone Hill High, was hurting—that had been easy to detect. No teenager her age became so hardened, angry, and cynical without external influence of some kind. But despite repeated— and exhaustive—attempts, Jo had failed to reach her. And even now, Jo, lip split and dignity stripped, still found herself wanting to reach out, to strive to make a connection of some kind. To prove to Natasha that someone did, in fact, care.

"Natasha," Jo said. "Hurting someone else won't solve your problems, and the only reason I teach—have ever taught—is to educate, protect, and support students like you in a healthy way. If you need help, I want to help y—"

"I'm not listening to this, bitch." Natasha spun around, pushed past her mother, and stalked out of the office. "Let her press charges. I don't give a damn."

Natasha's mother shot Jo one more hard glare then left, too, following her daughter down the corridor.

Jo stood silently for a few moments, her breaths coming in tandem with the painful throb in her bottom lip. Her mouth had begun to swell and the adrenaline that had shot through her veins for hours had subsided. She felt heavy suddenly, as though her limbs were made of dense concrete.

"I won't file charges." She removed her classroom keys,

which were attached to a lanyard, from her neck, then lifted the lanyard over her head. "And I won't be back."

McKenzie's mouth opened then closed, soundlessly, as she handed him the lanyard and keys as well as the unused tissue he'd given her earlier. He stared down at them then lifted his head, a stern gleam in his eyes. "You signed a contract, Ms. Ellis, and we're not even two months into the current school year. If you leave now rather than honoring your obligations for the full year, I'll be obligated to report you to the Professional Standards Board for neglecting your duties. Your teaching certificate will be suspended or, possibly, revoked. And there's a financial penalty for breach of contract."

Jo shrugged. What did it matter? She'd been broke for ten years. First, she'd struggled to pay her way through four years of college to earn a teaching degree, and for the past six years, her teaching salary had been barely enough to pay for her tiny, one-bedroom apartment and buy groceries, which left her with nothing left over to save. So, what was one less paycheck anyway?

She headed for the door. "I'll mail a check to you to cover my financial obligation for breach of contract. Do whatever you have to do as far as my teaching certificate. I won't need it again anyway."

"Ms. Ellis." His voice changed, the stern bravado fading, a desperate tone taking its place. "You've done an exceptional job in the classroom for six years. You're appreciated and we need you—especially now that we're understaffed. Please don't give up now. We'll sit down and talk. Explore your ideas and find a compromise."

Hmm. If only he'd said that years ago . . . and if only he meant it now.

"Please don't go," he said.

Jo kept walking, shocked by the depth of her apathy. "I'm already gone."

The sun hit her hard when she stepped outside the building, her eyes squinting, her injured mouth tightening painfully against its warm rays. She forced her legs to keep moving until she reached her car, then got in, cranked the engine, and drove away, refusing to allow herself to look back.

She'd sacrificed so much for a thankless job—including precious time she should've spent with Earl, helping to ease his burden at Lone Oaks Crossing—serving gate duty at athletic events, staying hours after school to tutor struggling students and conduct parent conferences, grading lesson plans at night, writing lesson plans on weekends and holidays, holding down a second job and attending professional learning sessions during the summer break. Years of time she could never recover.

Teaching had been a mistake. One she'd rectify, starting now.

Jo drove on, past the apartment complex that housed her meager belongings, through the bustling city limits of Stone Hill and into the rural landscape that lay on the outskirts of the small Kentucky town, her hands and foot sending the car in the familiar direction of her childhood home.

The car ate up the miles toward Lone Oaks Crossing. She hadn't visited in over a year, but the place had been on her mind more often than not recently. She'd have to tell Earl, of course. He'd say he'd told her so, and he'd be disappointed in her—but no more so than she already was with herself.

Soon, emerald hills emerged, rolling peacefully alongside her car, the breeze gracefully bending the lush bluegrass of sprawling fields in an easy rhythm. She rolled the windows down and inhaled, the swift wind cooling her hot cheeks, slowing her pulse.

The loud peal of her cell phone rang through her car's speakers, the computer system connecting the call.

"Hello?" A female voice chimed through the speakers. "I'm trying to reach Ms. Jo Beth Ellis."

Jo licked her dry lips and cleared her throat. "This is Jo. Who is this?"

"This is Sarah Wyndham," the voice said. "I'm a nurse, calling from Lone Oaks Hospital."

Lone Oaks? Home. *Earl.* Jo straightened in her seat. "Does this have something to do with Earl? Is he okay? Has h—"

"Yes, I'm calling about Earl Ellis, but please don't be alarmed. He's resting comfortably now and was very lucky."

"What do you mean? What's happened?"

"I see here"—rustling crossed the line—"that you're listed as Mr. Ellis's granddaughter. Is that correct?"

"Yes."

"I've been trying to reach you all morning. Your grand-father has had a stroke."

Jo's pulse picked up again, her muscles clenching.

"But he's stable now and resting well in room four-o-eight," Sarah continued. "He'll need to stay here for a few days. He'll require an extensive period of rehabilitation, and as you're listed as his emergency cont—"

"I'm already on my way." Jo pressed the pedal harder, the car picking up speed. "But I'm two hours out."

"There's no rush, Ms. Ellis. As I said, your grandfather's resting peacefully now and will be for some time. If any-thing changes prior to your arrival, I'll call you immedi-ately."

Jo nodded, then, remembering she was on the phone, said, "Thank you."

"You're welcome. We'll see you soon."

The call disconnected.

Thoughts racing, Jo drove for an hour then, tank running low, pulled into a gas station—Jimbo's Pit—and fueled up. A man exited the small convenience store and walked by her car on the way to his, an odd expression crossing his face as he eyed her face then chest.

Jo looked down at the blood staining her white blouse. Oh, no. She couldn't show up at Earl's bedside looking like this. She touched her fingertip to the dried blood on her bottom lip and flinched. There were two restrooms outside the convenience store, both with signs that read SEE CLERK FOR KEY.

Tank full, she replaced the pump handle and went inside to pay, grabbing salt, bottled water, and gauze before approaching the checkout counter. The clerk, a young man with blue hair, rang up her purchases, bagged them, and handed the sack to her.

"May I have the restroom key, please?" She kept her eyes down but felt the intensity of his scrutiny on her bloody lip anyway.

His hands left the counter briefly then returned, holding a key out toward her. "Ma'am?"

She took the key, then looked up, meeting his concerned gaze.

"Are you okay?" He glanced out the window then back at her and whispered, "If you need help . . ."

That mirthless laugh returned, bursting from her lips before she could stop it, her eyes burning. "D-do you know I offered someone the very same thing today?"

He tilted his head and his concerned expression changed to confusion.

"No, I—" She backed away, clutching her bag. "No, thank you."

Jo went inside the restroom and locked the door, dumped the salt she'd purchased into the bottle of water, soaked a strip of gauze in the mixture, and dabbed at her bloody mouth. She hissed at the sharp sting, her eyes welling.

She thought of Earl, ill and alone; McKenzie, short-handed and disappointed; Natasha, angry and full of hate; and her students who sat in a classroom without her. She thought of how she'd failed them all and how she'd failed herself.

Then her fingers stilled against her throbbing lip, and an unexpected surge of determination coursed through her as she realized how much Earl would need her in the coming days . . . and how—even though her life was crumbling around her—she wouldn't fail him again.

"What do you mean you're quitting?" Brooks Moore demanded.

He had spent the past decade of his thirty-two years of life adhering to a strategic business plan he'd infused with one primary goal: justice. A hard-fought objective he'd been on the brink of achieving but that now squirmed in his clenched fist, threatening to slide between his fingers and bolt out of his reach.

"I can't believe you're doing this to me now," Brooks said. "We're only nine months away from the Derby." The fall breeze tugged at the resignation letter he held, fluttering the crumpled corners against his knuckles as he eyed the older man who stood in front of him. "Your reputation for loyalty is unblemished. That's the reason I hired you in the first place."

Rhett Thomas, sharp-eyed, thin-lipped, and hard-bitten—a testimony to thirty years spent navigating the corrupt underbelly of horse racing as a trainer—stepped closer on the porch of Brooks's three-story colonial-style home and met him head-on. "Is that the only reason?"

Brooks cut his gaze to the left, past Rhett's stocky physique, to the eight hundred acres of sunlit Kentucky land that housed his custom-built home, state-of-the-art stables, and bourbon distillery buildings. He'd undertaken a risky venture—blending bourbon, thoroughbreds, tourism, and his ultimate life's goal into the thriving business of Original Sin—but his plan had been solid and successful . . . until now.

Gritting his teeth, he faced Rhett again. "I hired you because you were known as the most highly skilled and devoutly loyal trainer in the business. Both of which I witnessed myself throughout your two-year tenure in my stables, training my thoroughbred. And now, at the eleventh hour, you tell me you're walking." An unexpected pang moved through Brooks, cutting deep, twisting his mouth. "I thought we were in this for the long haul. I thought we'd established some level of trust between us."

Rhett nodded. "We have. You've been a great partner, Brooks. I'd even go so far as to say you've been the best partner I've had in my three decades in this sport."

"Then wh—?"

"You're also in this for the worst reasons." Rhett gestured toward the lush bluegrass, massive oaks, and rolling hills extending beyond them. "Look at what you have. Look at how much you've achieved at such a young age. You've got more here, deeded and thriving, than all your ancestors combined. More than most men could accumulate over ten lifetimes." His tone softened. "Forgive me, Brooks. But your father didn't know when to stop . . . and neither do you."

Brooks bristled. The words were a familiar refrain he'd heard often over the years, but he'd discovered that no matter how much time passed, the wound that festered inside his soul was still as fresh as the day it had been inflicted.

His father had never walked the straight and narrow path—no, not Deacon Moore. He'd developed a gambling habit in his twenties that had morphed into an addiction over the years, and beset by vices and tremendous losses, he'd struggled to remain loyal to his wife and son. Deacon had gambled and lost his life savings, but he'd always safeguarded the deed to Moore family land, especially Rose Farm—a gorgeous stretch of Kentucky acreage where healthy thoroughbreds were bred, and which would serve as a financial safety net for his wife and son.

The Moore family business had thrived for generations until seventeen years ago when Deacon's gambling losses had left him vulnerable, and the Harris family—Spencer Harris, in particular—had wielded their wealth and power and connived their way into stealing the only financial asset Deacon had left. Months after losing Rose Farm, Spencer had taken the Moore family home as well. Deacon, devastated and destitute, had succumbed to his demons and taken his own life, leaving Brooks and his mother, Ada, grief-stricken, homeless, and the target of ridicule.

One month after that, Ada had died from heart failure (a broken heart, Brooks recalled a nurse whispering) and he'd been placed in a local foster home, where he'd spent three years nurturing the rage inside him. Anger with a purpose, he'd discovered quickly, made a man stronger than tears.

It'd taken Brooks years to rebuild and surpass his family's wealth—thanks to a blend of luck, risk, and hard work that would've shocked even his own mother . . . if she'd lived to see it. Still, no amount of money could buy a good family name, sincere respect, or entry into the social circles of the local elite. A sphere Brooks had to enter to gain access to Spencer and hit the other man's pride, power, and wealth where it would cause the most damage.

Brooks clenched his jaw as he scanned the expansive grounds of his estate then smiled tightly at Rhett. "I think it's obvious I'm not careless with money."

"I never said gambling was your addiction." Rhett's gaze roved over his face for a moment, and then he sighed. "Look, I'm not doing this on a whim. Fact is, I don't have much choice in the matter."

Brooks narrowed his eyes. "Who didn't give you a choice?"

Rhett looked away, lifted his face into the cool breeze rustling the bluegrass, and closed his eyes. "Brooks—"

"What's he holding?"

Rhett remained silent.

"What's he holding, Rhett?" A rueful smile lifted Brooks's lips. "Or maybe I'm wrong? Maybe our enemy isn't the same after all?"

Rhett ducked his gray head, opened his heavy-lidded eyes, and stared at his worn boots. "I'm not a young man, Brooks," he said softly. "I'm not a rich or influential one either—never have been. I'm two years away from being able to afford to retire and, hopefully, have a long, peaceful stretch of rest in front of me to spend with my wife and grandkids. My time is the second most valuable asset I possess."

"What's he hol—"

"My name." Rhett lifted his head and glared. "Spencer Harris has my reputation in his palm, threatening to crush it if I continue working with you. If it were just my loss, I wouldn't care. But it's my family's. My sons are in this business, and as talented as they are, they're set to climb as high as they aim—but not without a decent rep. In this business, word-of-mouth makes or breaks a man, and my boys—as hard as they've worked for what little they have—don't deserve to have their livelihood stripped from them by that bastard because they share my name."

Brooks held out Rhett's letter of resignation. "All the more reason to see this through with me. You've trained Another Round since his birth—you know what he's capable of, and so do a lot of others betting on this sport—including Spencer. That's the only reason he's doing this. He knows what a Derby win will bring. Spencer won't be able to touch us when we wi—"

"*If* we win." Rhett shook his head. "You of all people know nothing in horse racing is a sure bet. Luck plays its part no matter what we do."

Brooks held Rhett's gaze. "Another Round will win."

"I hope he does," Rhett said. "I truly do. I just can't take that chance with you. I hope you can understand."

The finality in his tone hollowed Brooks's gut, a sensation at odds with the surge of admiration that coursed through him. He shoved the resignation letter in his pocket and spun away, bracing his hands on the porch rail and eyeing his stables in the distance.

"You're a good man," he forced between stiff lips, "and I won't fault you for doing what you think is best for your family. Stop by the main office on your way out. I'll instruct my secretary to have your final check ready at the front desk. It'll include a hefty bonus—enough for you to start that retirement and spend your time with your wife and grandkids now, if you see fit."

"Thank you, Brooks. You've always been a generous man." Rhett's footsteps, heavy and slow, receded then paused several feet away. "I also know you well enough to know that you're not giving up without a fight. Spencer's gonna do everything he can to impede your progress. And even if I'd stayed, I don't know that my help would've been enough. You need a great trainer—one far better than me."

Brooks watched as one of his employees led a small group of tourists along one of the trails leading from the stables to the stillhouses. The sun, which had shone strong throughout the day, was beginning to slide lower in the sky, and the tourists, the fifth tour group today, would've already been given a personal introduction to a few of his thoroughbreds and were now on their way to tour his distilleries and sample his best whiskey.

The unique blend of horses and bourbon on one estate had enabled Brooks's business to thrive. The only element that could substantially enhance Original Sin's value would be the prestige of having a Derby winner born, raised, and trained on the estate. Another Round, Brooks's soon-to-be three-year-old thoroughbred, fit the bill. But now, with the Derby only nine months away and qualifying races already underway, Brooks had no trainer to see him through to the finish line.

"You need a trainer whose horse has won before," Rhett said.

A rueful laugh burst from Brooks's lips. "I've already been down that route. No one at that level will give me the time of day on account of my name—or rather, lack thereof—and the fact that they know of my rivalry with Spencer and want no part in it." He glanced at Rhett and managed to smile. "Not that that's the only reason I hired you. You're an excellent trainer."

"I know the best there is. Someone who's trained a Derby winner. Someone who's beyond Spencer's influence and whose hands are clean. Someone with integrity and honor."

"Who is he?"

Rhett's mouth twisted. "She."

Brooks frowned. "No woman is on record as having trained a Derby winner."

"No. She wouldn't be." Rhett dipped his head. "She's never been officially named as a winning trainer—she's only served as an assistant and only for one Derby race. But everyone on the backside knew she was behind that win. The woman behind the man, so to speak. And lucky for you, you know the man. Her grandfather's your neighbor, Earl Ellis. The guy that owns Lone Oaks Crossing."

Brooks recalled the name of both the man and the property, but he'd only seen him once, from a distance. Five years ago, the day the construction crew had broken ground on Brooks's house, Earl had appeared between the oak trees that divided their properties and watched from afar for over an hour as the crew worked. Eventually, Brooks crossed the field and introduced himself.

Earl, his tan, leathery skin creased with age and a world-weary expression on his face, had given his name, shaken Brooks's hand, and said one thing before he clucked his tongue to the mare he was mounted on and rode back to his home.

What you got right there's a dream. Best keep your eyes open and hold it tight.

"I only met him once," Brooks said. "And I haven't gotten a good look at his land. Just saw the outskirts from a distance when I broke ground here."

"Lone Oaks Crossing used to be a breeding and training farm but it's run-down now," Rhett said. "Earl's best days as a trainer have been behind him for quite a while, I'm afraid. Ever since his granddaughter left, really. Now he just boards horses occasionally to make ends meet." He reached into his back pocket, withdrew a tightly folded paper, and held it out. "Her name's Jo Beth Ellis. She has the touch but left the sport and Lone Oaks some time ago. Hasn't trained a horse in years, from what I've been told. Been teaching at a high school across state instead."

Brooks strode across the porch, took the paper, and unfolded it. Two phone numbers, the name of a local hospital, and a hospital room number were scrawled on the page.

"That first number," Rhett said, "which won't do you any good right now, belongs to Earl, and the second to one of his friends, Frankie Kyle. I gave her a call earlier, trying to track Earl down, and she told me he had a stroke sometime early this morning. She was still at the hospital with him when we spoke."

Brooks frowned. "How's he doing?"

"Good, from what Frankie told me, though she said he'll have a ways to go before he's back on his feet. She also mentioned that Jo's on her way into town to see him." He gestured toward the paper. "Earl's room number is on there in case you decide to give it a go. I expect you'll find Jo there if you go tonight or first thing tomorrow morning."

Brooks grimaced. "A hospital isn't an appropriate place to pitch a business venture."

Rhett nodded. "I agree. But it's an opportunity to introduce yourself, and it may be your only chance to snag a word with Jo. She didn't leave the sport on very good terms and, from what Frankie told me, doesn't make it out this way often. You have a lot of convincing ahead of you."

Brooks looked at his stables again, his hopes sinking. Until now, everything had played into his hands. He was so close to success—*so close!* But without a trainer, his plan was shot. And Spencer, who'd taken advantage of the weaknesses of others, would ruin more lives.

"To beat Spencer, you need Jo," Rhett advised. "You either go all in now or fold."